PENGUIN  CL/

COUSIN PON>

HONORÉ DE BALZAC was born at Tours in 1799, the son of a civil servant. He spent nearly six years as a boarder in a Vendôme school, then went to live in Paris, working as a lawyer's clerk then as a hack-writer. Between 1820 and 1824 he wrote a number of novels under various pseudonyms, many of them in collaboration, after which he unsuccessfully tried his luck at publishing, printing and type-founding. At the age of thirty, heavily in debt, he returned to literature with a dedicated fury and wrote the first novel to appear under his own name, *The Chouans*. During the next twenty years he wrote about ninety novels and shorter stories, among them many masterpieces, to which he gave the comprehensive title *The Human Comedy*. He died in 1850, a few months after his marriage to Evelina Hanska, the Polish countess with whom he had maintained amorous relations for eighteen years.

•

HERBERT J. HUNT was Senior Fellow at Warwick University. Educated at the Lichfield Grammar School and Magdalen College, Oxford, he was a Tutor and Fellow at St Edmund Hall from 1927 to 1944, then until 1966 he was Professor of French Literature and Language at London University. He has published books on literature and thought in nineteeth-century France as well as a biography of Balzac, and a comprehensive study of Balzac's writings: *Balzac's 'Comedie Humaine'* (1959, paperback 1964). Herbert J. Hunt died in 1973.

Honoré de Balzac

COUSIN PONS

PART TWO OF
POOR RELATIONS

TRANSLATED AND INTRODUCED BY
HERBERT J. HUNT

PENGUIN BOOKS

PENGUIN BOOKS

Published by the Penguin Group
Penguin Books Ltd, 27 Wrights Lane, London W8 5TZ, England
Penguin Books USA Inc., 375 Hudson Street, New York, New York 10014, USA
Penguin Books Australia Ltd, Ringwood, Victoria, Australia
Penguin Books Canada Ltd, 10 Alcorn Avenue, Toronto, Ontario, Canada M4V 3B2
Penguin Books (NZ) Ltd, 182–190 Wairau Road, Auckland 10, New Zealand

Penguin Books Ltd, Registered Offices: Harmondsworth, Middlesex, England

This translation first published 1968
9 10 8

Copyright © Herbert J. Hunt, 1968
All rights reserved

Printed in England by Clays Ltd, St Ives plc
Set in Monotype Garamond

Contents

Introduction 7

1 A glorious relic of Imperial times 19

2 Decline and fall of a prize-winner 23

3 The two 'Nutcrackers' 33

4 One of a collector's thousand thrills 43

5 One of the thousand insults a parasite has to swallow 54

6 The Concierge Species – male and female 59

7 'The Two Pigeons': a fable come true 65

8 Prodigal sons from Frankfurt-am-Main don't always end up with the husks of the swine 75

9 Pons brings the Présidente something better than a fan 85

10 A German whimsy 96

11 Pons under a landslide of gravel 107

12 'Why, what a god is gold!' 117

13 A treatise on the occult sciences 128

14 A character from Hoffman's Tales 139

15 Tittle-tattle and tactics – elderly concierge style 150

16 Corruption in conference 161

17 How all careers begin in Paris 171

18 A 'man of law' 182

19 Fraisier makes things clear 192

20   La Cibot at the theatre   201

21   The Fraisier blossoms forth   215

22   A warning to old bachelors   226

23   Schmucke climbs to the mercy-seat of God   237

24   A testator's cunning   248

25   The spurious will   259

26   Re-enter Madame Sauvage   270

27   Death's gloomy portals   281

28   Schmucke's Via Dolorosa   292

29   When wills are opened all doors are sealed   303

30   The Fraisier bears fruit   314

     Conclusion   329

Introduction

'THE great events in my life,' Balzac once wrote, 'are my works.' Yet the life-span of this robust, boisterous, indefatigable genius contains more than the normal ration of events comic, dramatic and pathetic. From his boyhood, much of which was spent at the Oratorian College of Vendôme, through his years as apprentice lawyer, apprentice writer, publisher, printer, through the years when, domiciled mainly at Paris, he was producing the voluminous series of works later to be arranged systematically in what he called his *Human Comedy*, in fact right through to his dying days, he was avid for experience of all sorts. Hence his incursions into the social life of his times, the merry-makings which compensated for his long and arduous sessions at his writing-desk, and his persistent quest for perfect satisfaction in love, which eventually and after long anguish led him to marriage with his Polish countess, Evelina Hanska – about five months before his death, in August 1850, at the age of fifty-one.

But all this was secondary to his real life-purpose: to achieve glory as a Napoleon of letters, as the historian of his own times, as the 'secretary' of French society. Long before he embarked upon the series of 'studies' – Studies of Manners, Philosophical and Analytical Studies – he had written, under various *noms-de-plume*, such a quantity of novels as might well have satisfied any normal man with an itch for scribbling. But he rightly discarded all these 'pot-boilers', written between 1820 and 1824, and in 1829 he launched upon the most ambitious project which a novelist (who claimed also to be a philosopher) had ever yet undertaken. The *Human Comedy* was the result of this. He only found a title for his collected works about 1840, and he only began to edit or re-edit them under this title from 1842. But he had the whole scheme roughed out at least as early as 1834. It was an ever-expanding project. Disease and death caught up with him before it arrived at completion. Yet, as it stands, it comprises about ninety-seven novels, short stories and other 'studies'.

His 'Studies of Manners' are assigned to six compartments: *Scenes of Private Life*, in which the main interest is the exploration of emotional situations within or on the margin of family life; *Scenes of Provincial Life*, in which Balzac gives his attention to the more parochial and sometimes petty struggles taking place in what are, relatively speaking, 'closed' communities; *Scenes of Parisian Life* – Balzac both hated and adored Paris as the hub of the French universe, and the novels in this compartment generally present a terrible picture of human ruthlessness; *Scenes of Political* and *Scenes of Military Life*, categories which are perhaps less important because they were inadequately filled; and finally *Scenes of Country Life*, which establish a curious contrast between the normal animality of the French peasants (according to Balzac's view) and the efforts made by benevolent reformers to improve their lot and thereby convert them into responsible human beings.

Of the 'Philosophical Studies', mainly important because they express more directly Balzac's general outlook, *The Exiles* (1831), *Louis Lambert* (1832–5) and *Séraphita* (1834–5) are noteworthy examples. But in this respect two points should be noted: one is that Balzac's 'philosophy' obtrudes even in the 'Studies of Manners', *Cousin Pons* forming no exception to this rule; the other is that the 'Philosophical Studies' include some of Balzac's finest novels, for instance *The Wild Ass's Skin* (1831) and *The Quest of the Absolute* (1834).

As for the 'Analytical Studies', Balzac never had time to deal adequately with this category, but it contains his amusing, and at the same time penetratingly critical disquisitions on relations between the sexes; *The Physiology of Marriage* (1829) and *The Minor Vexations of Married Life* (1830–46).

All this was a stupendous performance. Does it argue for quantity rather than quality? It might have done so with a lesser genius, and Balzac's feverish method of composition did not allow for meticulous attention to niceties of style and finish. He was usually occupied with several novels at one and the same time, and he felt himself continually obliged to press on,

8

not only thanks to the urgency of ever-mounting debts, but also in order to bring into being that 'world' – modelled upon the real world, but transformed by his particular vision – which was seething in his brain. Balzac has his own peculiar quality. He was, in the first place, a born storyteller. He had remarkable powers of observation and a prodigious memory. But he had something more: an astounding faculty for sympathetic divination, an intuitive vision of men and things which he himself, borrowing the term from Sir Walter Scott, called 'second sight'.

His claim to be the 'secretary' of contemporary society was no vain one. Chronologically speaking, his novels and short stories cover the period of his own life, from 1799 to about 1847. When he came of age, France was emerging from the very troubled period of the Revolution and Empire, and was living through the uneasy years of the 'Restauration' (1814–30), with a whole set of social, religious and economic problems to face and solve. They were not solved, not even when Louis-Philippe, the 'Citizen-King', in 1830 seated himself on the Bourbon throne for eighteen no less uneasy years. The aristocracy, anxious to regain its former wealth and prestige, was being shouldered out of its privileged position by that indeterminate class of people known in France as the *bourgeoisie* – a new land-owning plutocracy, a Napoleonic *noblesse* largely consisting of civil servants and lawyers; functionaries, academics and legal luminaries; industrialists and manufacturers 'on the make'; and even the shop-owning sections of the community. The Industrial Revolution in France, later than its counterpart in England, was just about to get under way, and 'capitalism' with its attendant evils – sweated labour not least among them – was in the offing. These evils, observed or foreseen, led to the formulation of many different pre-Marxist systems of socialist doctrine.

In his religious, political and social views Balzac was a reactionary, but in diagnosing the ills of his own times he laid his finger on two outstanding features: the reign of unbridled individualism – 'Get out and make place for me!' – and the worship of money – 'the only God people believe in today'. So, in ranging through the classes and sub-classes of the early nineteenth century – from the hereditary aristocracy downwards to shopkeepers and tradespeople, in Paris and the provincial towns, and the half-civilized, grasping peasantry of the countryside – he showed generally that idealism, human-kindness and all the traditional virtues were being pounced upon and destroyed by the forces of acquisitiveness and ambition. His allegorical 'Philosophical Study' of 1831, *The Wild Ass's Skin*, gives a remarkable general diagnosis, particularized in such novels as *Gobseck* (1830–35), which shows a usurer sitting like a spider at the centre of his web and asserting his power over the 'socialites' and ne'er-do-wells who come to him for loans; *Eugénie Grandet* (1833), which traces the rise to affluence and domination of a man who had started life, before the Revolution, as an insignificant cooper and vine-grower; *Old Goriot*, which is one of Balzac's first revelations of Paris as a jungle wherein human nature is no less 'red in tooth and claw' than the animal nature from which it derives; the *Rise and Fall of César Birotteau* (1837), which gives the life-story of an honest but stupid manufacturer of cosmetics who, thanks to his social and financial ambitions, becomes a prey to a group of blood-sucking bankers and speculators; and *La Rabouilleuse* (a nickname – 'fisher in troubled waters' – given to the provincial-town trollop who occupies the centre of the story): in this novel, written in 1841–3, is laid before us the struggle for an inheritance undertaken by a Napoleonic veteran soldier whose movements and stratagems afford us a vivid picture of life both in Paris and the stagnating town of Issoudun.

Balzac's conscious purpose as the social historian of his country and times should not of course blind us to the human interest in his tales. He certainly spends a lot of time describing the material background against which the action of his tales is set. Readers of *Cousin Pons* will see for themselves how many pages are devoted to basic atmosphere and initial characterization before we are allowed to witness the opening scene between Pons and the Camusot mother and daughter. They will also notice that he reaches almost half-way before arriving at the essence of his story:

And here begins the drama, or if you prefer, the terrible comedy of the death of a bachelor delivered over by the force of circumstances to the rapacity of covetous people assembled round his bed [page 181].

But though description abounds, there is action in plenty, and action of an intensely dramatic nature. Balzac's long preparations lead up to a sequence of 'scenes' in which we are shown the real stuff of human nature as he saw it: all his invented creatures (many of them modelled on people he knew), good, bad and indifferent, pursuing their various ends – and as a rule the good fare ill in the rough-and-tumble of life.

Balzac's conception of character is an interesting one. Thanks to a peculiar 'philosophy' which he had largely drawn from the writings of Mesmer – his weakness for the less reputable 'sciences' of his age is well illustrated in Chapter 13 of this novel – he believed that all men and women are endowed from birth with a certain measure of 'vital fluid' or energy which they may spend as they will. Some husband it carefully, some expend it recklessly, some direct it exclusively to a chosen end: to the acquisition of wealth and the advantages wealth brings, like Gobseck, Félix Grandet and the bankers Nucingen and Du Tillet; to the (questionable) welfare of their children, like Jean-Joachim Goriot; to personal vengeance, like 'Cousin Bette'; or even to the advancement of science, like Balthazar van Claës in The Quest of the Absolute (1834). Such direction or misdirection of energy accounts for the many 'monomaniacs' to be found in the Human Comedy in general, and in the Poor Relations in particular: 'Cousin Bette' thinks only of destroying the family on whose condescending patronage she has been for so long forced to live; 'Cousin Pons' has made the search for succulent dinners his main purpose in life. As with the 'tableau-mane' Elias Magus – and, to some extent, with Balzac himself in the 1840s – the pursuit of antiques has become a second ruling passion. Though in these cases exceptionally violent, this élan vital is a common feature in Balzac's characters, great or small. As the great French poet, Baudelaire, an ardent admirer of Balzac, wrote: 'All his characters are endowed with the same vital flame which was burning within himself.'

This energy is usually devoted to selfish or malevolent purposes – as it is by the venomous 'Présidente', Madame Camusot, the concierge Madame Cibot, once the demon of greed has

11

seized hold of her, the relentless Fraisier, once he discovers a way of redeeming himself from a shady past, and the poisoner Rémonencq, anxious to set up as a dealer in antiques and to acquire 'the comely oyster-girl' as his consort. Relatively few of Balzac's characters – Dr Benassis in *The Country Doctor*, Judge Popinot in *The Interdiction*, or Véronique Graslin in *The Village Priest* – direct their will to a good end. His rank and file, in so far as they are 'good', are generally the dupes or victims of the 'go-getters', as will be seen in *Cousin Pons* with regard not only to the main characters, the 'delicate-souled' Pons and the 'innocent' Schmucke, but also to Topinard, La Cibot's husband, Dr Poulain and perhaps also the lawyer Villemot.

Cousin Pons, as the Conclusion to the novel (page 331) makes clear, has a sort of 'twinship' with *Cousin Bette*. For long Balzac had thought of including in his scheme a series of novels dealing with 'Poor Relations'. An earlier work, *Pierrette* (one might compare this novel with Dickens's *Oliver Twist*), had told of the tribulations an orphan child met with at the hands of the cruel cousins who adopted her as a household drudge. But he relegated *Pierrette* to another category (*The Celibates*), and only in 1846 and 1847 returned to the 'Poor Relations' idea. The heroine of *Cousin Bette*, of which a translation by Marion Ayton Crawford appeared in 1965 in the Penguin Classics, is the very incarnation of competent vindictiveness. *Cousin Pons* offers a diametrically opposite case – a mild, harmless old man who is treated with spiteful contempt by his well-to-do relations. The latter novel hung fire for a while, and the former one was published first. Balzac turned his attention to *Cousin Pons* in the later months of 1846, and published it first of all as a serial novel in a contemporary periodical, *Le Constitutionnel*, in the spring of 1847. As was usual with him, he expanded it considerably in course of composition; having intended it first of all merely as a study of a man contemned and repudiated by his kinsfolk and their satellites, he decided to enrich it with two new themes – the friendship theme (Pons and Schmucke as a nineteenth-century Orestes and Pylades) and the inheritance theme: the determination of Madame Camusot, once she has discovered that the despised 'cousin' has a rich collection of antiques, to assert family 'rights' and grasp his estate for herself. As usual, Balzac was writing in a hurry. Had he lived long enough, no doubt he would have ironed out the minor inconsistencies that readers will discern in the novel. When he was composing it, his health was failing. He was still making a frantic effort to achieve solvency in order to marry his Polish countess, now a widow. He himself had suffered from hepatitis in earlier years. He was subject to a form of chronic meningitis, and already the cardiac disease which was to carry him off was showing alarming symptoms.

And so, in the lugubrious account of Pons's physical collapse and death, and all the attendant funereal circumstances, there is probably more than a presentiment of the fate which was shortly to overtake him. Therefore the blending of sentimentality with a calm, even ironic acceptance of the world and its evil ways has a notable significance. The composition of this novel is not perfect, but it betrays no falling-off in creative power. In fact, *Cousin Pons* is at once a great contribution to Balzac's sociological studies – he has moved forward in time and is writing of Paris in the 1840s – and also one of the best examples of his rueful contemplation, pessimistic but not despairing, of human nature at an age, and in a *milieu*, when the blackest crimes were blandly committed under a cloak of legality.

As published in *Le Constitutionnel*, *Cousin Pons* consisted of thirty chapters and a Conclusion. In 1848 the editor Pétion published it in book form, with seventy-seven chapters and a Conclusion. In November 1848 it was again published as part of the *Human Comedy*, and now, for reasons of economy, all chapter divisions were suppressed. In fact, since that time, readers of Balzac have had to cope with editions in which no pause or relief is vouchsafed from the beginning to end, though in present-day editions the tendency is to revert to the original chapter divisions. This translation adopts the divisions and titles of the *Le Constitutionnel* version, with asterisks inserted within chapters to indicate where further divisions were made in the Pétion edition.

As nearly always in Balzac's novels, money is an important, if not a paramount consideration. Balzac loved to make financial computations and calculations, and he tended to deal in enormous figures, largely perhaps to compensate himself in imagination for his failure to acquire – by his work, by speculative ventures, and, in the middle 1840s, by the purchase of antiques – the large sums he himself needed to put his affairs in order: so that the value of the Pons collection (the 'heroine' of the story!) is, in the text, reckoned to be not much less than a million francs. If we take the exchange value which remained relatively stable until the First World War, namely twenty-five francs to the pound, a million francs would be equivalent to £40,000 sterling. But, since 1918, currency values have declined at least to one-fifth of what they were. And so the Pons collection would have been worth no less than £200,000 in our present inflated currency!

One of the most intriguing devices in the *Human Comedy* is the system, invented round about 1834, of introducing 're-appearing characters': the same people recur, now in the foreground, now in the background of the various novels and short stories. This was one of the ways by which Balzac sought to create the impression of a closely-knit society in which, as in real life, the reader would be continually coming upon people he had met before. Not of course in chronological sequence – one novel may bring such and such a character on to the stage of the *Human Comedy* when he has reached the peak of his attainment, the next novel in which he figures may show him in his obscure or humble beginnings, while others will enable the reader to fill in the gaps and form for himself a picture of that individual's complete career. This device has inspired two compilations – the *Repertory* of Cerfberr and Christophe in 1887 and the *Dictionary* of Fernand Lotte in 1956 – thanks to which any curious reader may look up the 'biography' of any character in whom he is interested.

Naturally *Cousin Pons* conforms to this practice. Pons, Schwab, Brunner, the Cibots, Madame Sauvage, Poulain, Fraisier and Topinard are all new inventions. But the Camusots, the Popinots, the Berthiers, the Cardots, Crottat, Hannequin, Gaudissart, Bixiou, Madeleine Vivet, Héloïse Brisetout, Madame Fontaine, Magus, Schmucke himself and others are recurrent – some of them even familiar – figures in the *Human Comedy*. 'Madame la Présidente Camusot de Marville' had begun

life as an art student in *The Vendetta* (1830); her astounding ignorance about art in *Cousin Pons* is explained by the fact that
Balzac had, in a later edition of *The Vendetta*, substituted her
name for that of the original character, a practice he often adopted
in working out these life-schemes. Thereafter, in various novels,
he had shown her marrying the rather stupid and incompetent
Camusot and pushing him upwards in a legal career which, as
will be seen in *Cousin Pons*, still does not satisfy her ambitions.
As for Schmucke, only one of his other appearances – in *A
Daughter of Eve* – has much importance. Gaudissart had first
come to life in 1833 (*The Illustrious Gaudissart*) as a jovial, pushing but gullible commercial traveller. In *César Birotteau*
Anselme Popinot, the future politician and count, had given
him a helping hand by employing him as a publicity agent for
the sale of a cosmetic product. In *Cousin Pons*, thanks to the
same man's benevolence, he has become a theatre manager, but
is sighing for new worlds to conquer.

Finally, a word on certain peculiarities of diction in the
present translation. Balzac makes Schmucke talk a curious
brand of Germanized French (he does the same with his Alsatian banker, the Baron de Nucingen). This is purely phonetic,
for Schmucke's French is otherwise normal in grammar,
syntax and idiom. In this translation the same principle is
followed. The utterances of Rémoncncq, a native of Auvergne,
reproduce, but only for a certain number of pages, the *charabia*
of that region: it consists mainly, in Balzac's text, of the substi-
tution of 'sh' for 's'. This translation drops it from the beginning. Madame Cibot has a conversational trick (mostly in her
hypocritically affectionate moments) which consists of inter-
polating 'n's in her sentences – when Balzac remembers to do
it. This also is discarded. Also she and 'La Sauvage' are generally deemed to speak the popular Parisian of the uneducated
classes; it was felt that the attempt to find an equivalent in
popular English would give a very un-French atmosphere.
Moreover, on occasions, Madame Cibot rises to quite sophisticated French.

H. J. H.

COUSIN PONS

1. A glorious relic of Imperial times

ABOUT three o'clock in the afternoon, one day in October 1844, an old man of some sixty years (though anyone who saw him would have thought him older) was walking along the Boulevard des Italiens, with his nose thrust forward and a smug expression on his lips, like a merchant who has just made an excellent deal, or a bachelor emerging from a lady's boudoir, pleased with his prowess – in Paris the expression of male self-satisfaction can go no further. Whenever this old man came into view, habitual idlers sitting about and enjoying the pleasure of sizing up passers-by let their features relax into a typically Parisian smile, indicative of irony, mockery or compassion. But it takes a keen and lively curiosity to light up the face of a Parisian, surfeited as he is with strange spectacles. Perhaps the witticism of an actor named Hyacinthe, famous for his sallies, will help to explain this creature's value as an archaeological specimen and the smile which, on his appearance, flitted from face to face. When Hyacinthe was asked where he had the hats made which sent his audiences into fits of laughter, he replied: 'I don't have them made; I just go on wearing them.' So, among the million actors who play their parts on the great stage of Paris, you will find unwitting copies of Hyacinthe who just go on wearing all the absurd fashions of their time. They seem to be personifications of a whole period. They can arouse you to mirth even when you are wandering about trying to stomach the bitter grief of being betrayed by someone who was once a friend.

By maintaining in certain points of his attire an unconquerable fidelity to the modes of 1806, this passer-by reminded one of Imperial times without going so far as caricature. To an observant eye, there are subtleties which give high price to such remembrances of time past; but only those expert in idle observation can bring to such an accumulation of details the close analytical inspection it deserves; and, for a passer-by to provoke laughter even from afar, he had to stagger his audience with some such extravagance as actors contrive when they want to make sure of an effective entry. And so this thin, dried-up old man wore a nut-brown spencer over a greenish coat with white metal buttons! In 1844, meeting a man in a spencer made it seem as if Napoleon had deigned to come back to life for an hour or two.

Now spencers were invented, as the name implies, by an English lord who was doubtless vain of his elegant figure. Some time before the Peace of Amiens, this Englishman had solved the problem of covering his torso without burying himself in a carrick, that horrible garment which is now ending its days on the shoulders of old-fashioned cabmen. But as slender waists are scarce, the male fashion in spencers was short-lived in France, even though it was an English invention. At the sight of this gentleman's spencer, spectators in their forties and fifties mentally arranged him in top-boots and ribbon-bowed, pistachio-green kerseymere breeches. They saw themselves back in the costume of their youth. Old women started living their love-lives over again. Young people wondered why this venerable Alcibiades had cut off his coat-tails. Everything else about him went so well with this spencer that you would not have hesitated to set this passer-by down as an 'Empire man', just as one speaks of 'Empire furniture'. But he symbolized the Empire only for those who knew something, at least from illustrations, about that superb and impressive era. The Empire is already so distant from us that not everybody can conjure it up in all its Gallo-Grecian reality.

His hat, tilted backward, left his forehead practically bare. This gave him the kind of jauntiness with which, in those times, officials and civilians tried to counter that of the military man. But it was a horrible silk hat, and had cost fourteen francs. On the underside of the brim a pair of tall, broad ears had worn whitish patches which no amount of brushing could remove. The silk, as usual clumsily applied to the cardboard block, was wrinkled here and there, and appeared to be suffering from leprosy, in spite of the grooming it received every morning. Beneath this hat, which was all but falling off, loomed a quaint, comical face – only a Chinese potter could model such a figure –

a vast countenance, pitted like a skimming-ladle, each hole in it casting a shadow, and scooped out like a Roman mask. It gave the lie to all the laws of anatomy. It seemed to have no definite shape. Where a draughtsman would place bone-structure were planes of gelatinous flesh; where ordinary faces sink in, this one rounded out into flabby bulges. This fantastic face, squashed flat at each end like a pumpkin, saddened by two grey eyes arched over by two red lines in guise of eyebrows, was dominated by a Don Quixote nose, just as an incongruous boulder might stand out from a plain. Such a nose, as Cervantes no doubt observed, denotes that inborn capacity for devotion to great causes which easily declines into gullibility. For this ludicrously exaggerated ugliness did not excite derision. The excessive melancholy abounding in this poor man's pale eyes immediately struck anyone who might have mocked, and froze the jest on his lips. In a flash, the thought came that nature had forbidden this man to make tender advances, because they could only awaken laughter or distress in a woman. A Frenchman is speechless when he meets with that misfortune which in his eyes is the cruellest of all misfortunes: the inability to attract.

*

This man so ill-favoured by nature was dressed like poor people of good social standing, whom the merely rich quite often try to copy. Over his shoes he had gaiters of Imperial Guard style, which no doubt allowed him to keep on wearing the same socks for some time. His black cloth trousers had reddish streaks on them, and along the creases ran white or glossy lines which, like their cut, relegated the date of their purchase to three years back. The bagginess of this garment scarcely disguised a leanness which was constitutional rather than the result of a Pythagorean diet, for this worthy man had a sensual mouth and gross lips, and when he smiled he displayed white teeth which a shark might envy. His shawl-waistcoat, also of black cloth, but lined with a white waistcoat under which, as a third line of defence, gleamed the fringe of a red jersey, put one in mind of the five waistcoats of Garat. A huge white muslin cravat, with the showy kind of knot sported by lady-killers to allure the 'alluring women' of 1809, came up so far over his chin that his face seemed as if plunged into an abyss. Across his chest was a silk cord, plaited like strands of hair, which protected his watch against the unlikely prospect of theft. His greenish coat, remarkably clean, was three years senior to the trousers; his black velvet collar and white metal buttons, recently renewed, showed signs of meticulous domestic attention.

His way of securing his hat by pressing it down on the occiput, his triple waistcoat, his voluminous cravat engulfing his chin, the metal buttons on the greenish coat – so many relics of Empire fashion – were in keeping with the old-fashioned perfumes – all the rage with the dandies at the turn of the century – which he exuded; so too was a curious trimness in the folds, and an indefinable dry meticulousness in the total effect, redolent of David's school and Jacob's dainty furniture. What is more, you could see at a glance that he was a well-bred man addicted to some secret vice, or one of those persons with private means whose every disbursement is so strictly limited by the modesty of their income that a broken window-pane, a torn coat, or that plague of our philanthropic age, a charity collection, would cancel out their petty enjoyments for a month. Had you been there, you would have wondered why a smile lit up this grotesque face, for its usual expression must have been sad and cold, like that of all people quietly struggling to meet the trivial needs of existence. But as you noticed the motherly care with which, in his right hand, this strange old man was holding an obviously precious object, tucked under the two left-hand flaps of his double coat to protect it from any possible damage; above all when you saw him fussing along with the self-importance of a man of leisure entrusted with an errand, you would have suspected that he had found something like a Marchioness's stray lap-dog and, with the eager gallantry of an Empire man, was bearing it back in triumph to the fair lady of sixty who was still loath to renounce her admirer's daily call. Paris is the one city in the world where you might meet with such sights: thanks to these, its boulevards provide a non-stop theatre show, performed gratis by Frenchmen for the greater glory of Art.

2. Decline and fall of a prize-winner

JUDGING by the man's bony contours, you would not, despite the challenge of his spencer, have readily assigned him to the conventional world of Paris artists, who, like the Paris street urchins, enjoy the privilege of stirring the middle-class imagination to astonishing hilarity. Yet this passer-by had held the 'Grand Prix'. He had composed the first cantata to win an award at the Institut, just after the Académie de Rome had been set up again. In short he was MONSIEUR SYLVAIN PONS, the author of several well-known ballads that our mothers used to warble; he also had a few unpublished scores to his credit. His ugliness had got him work as a music-teacher in several girls' boarding-schools, and he had no other income but his salary and the fees his lessons brought him. Private lessons at his age! What a host of mysteries were latent in this unromantic situation!

In fact this last of the spencer-wearers not only carried on his person the symbols of the Empire period; he also carried a great warning inscribed on his three waistcoats. He gave you a free view of one of the many victims of that fatal and deplorable system known as *Competitive Examination*, which still holds sway in France after having been unproductively applied for a hundred years. This mode of recruiting talent was invented by Poisson de Marigny, the brother of Madame de Pompadour who, round about 1746, was appointed Director of Fine Arts. Now you can count on the fingers of one hand the men of genius produced in the last century by this system of awards. In the first place, no administrative or scholastic endeavour will ever supersede the miracle of chance which throws up great men. Among all the mysteries surrounding genetics, that is the one which our ambitious modern analysis is least able to probe. In the second place, the ancient Egyptians are supposed to have invented incubating ovens. What would be thought of them if they had given no food to their chickens once hatched? Yet that is how France proceeds by trying to rear artists in the hot-house of the competitive examination system. Once these sculptors, painters, engravers and musicians are thus artificially produced, she worries no more about them than a dandy cares, when evening comes, about the flower he pinned to his button-hole that morning. Men of real talent – Greuze or Watteau, Félicien David or Pagnesi, Géricault or Decamps, Auber or David d'Angers, Eugène Delacroix or Meissonier – give no thought to State Prizes. They are bred in open ground under the rays of that invisible sun which we call Vocation.

Sent to Rome by the State to become a great musician, Sylvain Pons had returned with a taste for antiquities and fine works of art. He was an expert judge of all those masterpieces, wrought by hand and brain, which in recent times have been popularly known as bric-à-brac. And so this nursling of Euterpe came back to Paris, in 1810 or thereabouts, as an avid collector, laden with pictures, statuettes, frames, wood and ivory carvings, enamels, porcelains, etc. While living in Rome on his Academic scholarships, he had used up the greater part of his paternal heritage either in paying for or in transporting his purchases. Likewise he had squandered his mother's estate on a journey he made through Italy after his three statutory years in Rome. He planned a leisurely visit to Venice, Milan, Florence, Bologna and Naples, mooning and musing around each town with the usual heedlessness of an artist who expects to live on his talent as a courtesan lives on her charms. Pons was a happy man while this trip lasted – in so far as happiness was possible for a man of feeling and delicacy, whose ugliness debarred him from 'success with the fair sex', as the phrase went in 1809; and who always found that reality fell short of his own ideal. But he had grown reconciled to the discordance between the music he found in his soul and the jarring notes of real life. A feeling for beauty remained keen and pure in his heart and doubtless inspired those clever, subtle and graceful tunes which gained him some reputation between 1810 and 1814. Any reputation in France founded on vogue, fashion and the crazes which have their day in Paris, brings men like Pons into being. In no other country are great achievements so harshly received and trivial ones welcomed with such disdainful indulgence. His melodies were soon submerged under the flood of German harmony and the operas of Rossini, and if in 1824 he was still accepted as an agreeable composer – thanks to a few recent ballads – imagine what his standing was by 1831! And so, in 1844, when the stage was set for the only drama that occurred in his insignificant life, Sylvain Pons struck but a feeble and antiquated note in the musical world. Publishers were unaware of his existence even though, for a modest reward, he wrote the music for several plays performed in the theatre he worked in and others in the neighbourhood.

And yet this worthy man did justice to the famous masters of our time. A fine rendering of a few choice compositions reduced him to tears, but his devotion to music did not reach the verge of mania, as it did with the Kreislers in the *Tales of Hoffmann*. He made no show of it, but cultivated an inner enjoyment like a hashish-eater or an opium addict. The genius for admiration and understanding, the only faculty by which an ordinary man becomes the brother of a great poet, is so rare in Paris, where ideas tread on one another's heels like travellers filing into a hostelry, that we must accord respect and esteem to Pons. The man's lack of success may seem unreasonable, but he naïvely confessed his weakness as regards harmony. He had neglected the study of counterpoint, and he felt that modern orchestration, which had developed immeasurably, was beyond his grasp, even at the time when renewed studies might have enabled him to keep up with the modern composers and become, not indeed a Rossini, but at any rate a Hérold. To sum up, he found such lively compensation for his failure to reach fame in the pleasures his collecting gave him, that if he had had to choose between the reputation of a Rossini and the possession of his curios – believe it or not – Pons would have preferred his beloved collection. This old musician applied as axiomatic the claim made by Chenavard, that expert collector of priceless engravings: that a work by Ruysdael, Hobbema, Holbein, Raphael, Murillo, Greuze, Sebastian del Piombo, Giorgione or Albrecht Dürer, is only pleasurable to look at when it has not cost more than fifty francs. Pons ruled out all purchases above the sum of a hundred francs. An object had to be worth three thousand francs before he would pay fifty francs for it. The loveliest thing in the world, if it cost three hundred francs, ceased to exist for him. Rarely had he made great bargains, but he possessed the three requisites for success in buying: fleetness of foot, plenty of leisure-time and the patience of an Israelite.

This policy, which he had put into practice for forty years, both in Rome and Paris, had borne fruit. Since his return from Rome, at a cost of about two thousand francs a year, Pons had jealously stored away a collection of all kinds of masterpieces; duly catalogued, they reached the fabulous figure of one thousand nine hundred and seven items. Between 1811 and 1816, while browsing around Paris, he had picked up for ten francs objects which today could only be bought for a thousand or twelve hundred francs. They consisted of pictures sorted out from the forty-five thousand pictures exposed for sale each year in Paris, and Sèvres porcelains in soft paste, bought from the Auvergnat dealers, those satellites of the 'Black Gang' who carted away on their barrows the marvels of Madame de Pompadour's France. In short, he had accumulated the forgotten relics of seventeenth- and eighteenth-century art, giving just recognition to the brilliance and genius of the French School, to those neglected masters Lepautre, Lavallée-Poussin, etc., who created the Louis Quinze and the Louis Seize styles, whose works nowadays provide inspiration for the so-called creations of our artists – those who are for ever poring over the treasures in the Cabinet des Estampes so that they can rise to originality by making clever pastiches. Many of Pons's pieces were acquired by exchange, a method which brings ineffable bliss to collectors! The pleasure of buying *objets d'art* is only second to that of getting them by barter. Pons had been first in the field as a collector of snuff-boxes and miniatures. He was scarcely known among the bric-à-brac confraternity, for he did not frequent auctions, nor did he show his face in the prominent dealers' establishments. And so he was ignorant of the sale value of his treasure.

The late Dusommerard, that prince of the bric-à-brac trade, had tried hard to get in touch with the musician, but he died without ever gaining admission to the Pons museum, which was the only one to be compared with the well-known Sauvageot collection. Pons and Monsieur Sauvageot were not without their similarities. Monsieur Sauvageot, like Pons, was a musician, and had no great fortune. He proceeded in the same way, and followed the same methods; he had the same love of art, and the same hatred for those illustrious rich people who build up collections in slick competition with the dealers. Just like this man – his rival, his emulator and his antagonist in the acquisition of all these prodigies of skill and craftsmanship – Pons was at heart an insatiable miser. He loved them as a man might love a beautiful mistress, and the sale of them under the hammer at auctions in the rue des Jeûneurs seemed to him an act of treason against bric-à-brac. His museum was a thing to be enjoyed at all hours of the day; for those who have it in them to admire great works have the sublime capacity of true lovers for feeling as much bliss today as they did yesterday; they never weary in admiration, and fortunately masterpieces enjoy perpetual youth. And therefore the object which Pons was now carrying with such fatherly care was undoubtedly one of those finds which one bears away, lovingly, as only true amateurs can.

As the first lines of this biographical sketch are traced out, every reader will exclaim: 'But this person, ugly as he may be, is the happiest man in the world!' For in truth, to adopt a mania is like applying a poultice to the soul: it can cure any *taedium vitae*, any spleen. Let all those no longer able to drain what has always been called 'the cup of joy' take to collecting something (even advertisement bills), and in this they will find the solid gold of happiness minted into small coinage. A mania is pleasure transmuted into an idea! But no envy should be felt for the worthy Pons: so impulsive a reaction, like all such, would be born of misunderstanding.

This man of such delicate fibre, whose spiritual self was kept alive by his tireless admiration for the splendour of human handiwork, so magnificently vieing with Nature's own handiwork, was a slave to one of the seven deadly sins, the one which, in all probability, God deals with most leniently. Pons was a gormandizer. His poverty and his craving for bric-à-brac restricted him to a diet so repugnant to his sensitive palate, that, as a bachelor, he had solved the problem from the start by dining out every evening. Now, in Imperial times, much more than in our days, notable people were much sought after, perhaps because they were scarce and had few political ambitions. It was so easy to be a poet, a writer or a musician! People looked on Pons as a potential rival of such men as Nicolo, Paër and Berton, and therefore he had so many invitations that he was obliged, like a barrister, to keep an engagement-book. Moreover he played his part as an artiste; he presented all his hosts with copies of his ballads; he 'played on the ivories' in their drawing-rooms; he brought them tickets for boxes at the Feydeau theatre for which he worked, he organized concerts, and sometimes even improvised dances in the homes of his relatives, with himself as fiddler.

*

In those days it was a common occurrence for the most handsome men of France to exchange sabre-cuts with the most handsome men of the Coalition. Consequently the ugliness of Pons was reckoned as *originality*, in accordance with the great principle set forth by Molière's Eliante:

> They count a blemish as a beauty spot
> And find perfection where we find a blot.

When Pons had rendered a service to some elegant lady, he was occasionally qualified as a *charming man* – not that this compliment was ever followed by a more tangible reward.

This period lasted about six years, from 1810 to 1816, and Pons got into the disastrous habit of dining well, of seeing his hosts sparing no expense, procuring out-of-season delicacies, uncorking their best wines, taking pains over the dessert, the coffee and the liqueurs, regaling him as best they could, as was customary in the Empire period, when many private houses copied the lavishness of the kings, queens and princes then teeming in Paris. It was fashionable then to ape royalty, just as today one apes Parliament by forming all sorts of societies complete with chairmen, vice-chairmen and secretaries: societies of flax-growers, vine-growers, silk-growers; agricultural and industrial societies; and so forth. We have even got to the point of discovering social ills in order to form societies to cure them!

Now when a stomach gets such schooling, the moral person is affected, is corrupted by the high degree of culinary knowledge thus acquired. Sensual pleasure worms its way into every recess of the heart, establishes itself as sovereign, makes inroads into will-power and sense of honour, demands satisfaction at all costs. The exigencies of gluttony have never been depicted; literary critics have to live, and they keep off such themes; but one can hardly imagine how many people have been brought to ruin by the pleasures of the table. In Paris, in this respect, the table competes with the trollop; incidentally, the former represents the credit side, the latter the debit side of the account. When Pons, sinking lower and lower as an artist, degenerated from the position of habitual guest to that of a sponger, he could not bear the thought of quitting these well-served boards for the Spartan gruel of a cheap restaurant. Poor man, he shuddered at the thought that dependence on his own resources would entail such great sacrifices, and he felt capable of the greatest cowardice so long as he could still enjoy good fare, smack his lips over all the season's first-fruits, and mop up (a coarse but expressive verb) exquisite little dishes. He hopped about like a bird, filling his crop, and piped a note or two by way of payment. He also derived some pleasure from living well at the expense of society people who after all asked for nothing but flattery in return. Like all bachelors who hate dining in and love dining out, he was conversant with the meaningless phrases and social grimaces which, in polite society, do duty for genuine feeling, and he dealt round compliments like small change. As for those he received, he was content to read the label without examining the contents.

This fairly tolerable phase lasted ten years more, but they were like a succession of rainy autumns. All this time, Pons enjoyed a free table by making himself useful in the various houses he frequented. He started on the downward path by carrying out numerous errands, on many occasions doing the jobs of porters and household staff. Entrusted with many purchases, he became the honest simpleton sent forth by one family to spy on another; but he earned no gratitude for so many services rendered and so much self-abasement. 'Pons is a bachelor,' they said; 'he has nothing to do with his time and is only too glad to trot about for us ... What else could he do?'

Before long there could be sensed that chilly atmosphere which an old man spreads about him: a cold wind which blows all round and has its effect on the moral temperature, especially when the old man in question is poor and ugly. Old age in triplicate! The winter of life: red nose, hollow cheeks and numbed fingers!

Between 1836 and 1843, Pons was rarely invited out. He was no longer an acquisition, but a hanger-on. Each family put up with him as one puts up with rates and taxes. The families in which he performed his party tricks had no respect for the arts, bowed down only before tangible success, and attached importance only to what they had themselves acquired since 1830 – bank balances and high social position. Now Pons had neither the loftiness of spirit nor of manner to inspire that awe which wit or genius can arouse in the middle classes, and so in the end he had naturally become of no account, though he was not as yet completely despised. He suffered keenly in the society he frequented, but kept his sufferings to himself. Then, by degrees, he had got used to bottling up his feelings and retiring into the sanctuary of his own heart. Many shallow people would put this phenomenon down to egoism. So strong is the resemblance between the solitary man and the egoist that spiteful tongues can always make a case against a sensitive person, particularly in Parisian society, where no one is really observant, where life rushes by like a torrent, where everything is as transient as governments.

That is why Cousin Pons was found guilty – by a retrospective verdict – of self-centredness. When society accuses, it always condemns. Do we realize how overwhelming unmerited disfavour can be to shy people? Who will ever depict the woes they suffer? The predicament of this poor musician became worse every day. It accounts for the sadness we have seen imprinted on his countenance. Abject humiliations became his daily fare. But the acts of self-abasement which every passion demands are like so many bonds. The more of them the satisfaction of a craving imposes, the more one is enslaved. Such a craving converts every act of self-sacrifice into an imaginary treasure – a minus quantity – and this the victim looks on as being infinite wealth. After tolerating the insolently patronizing glance of some starkly stupid self-made man, Pons took his revenge by sipping his glass of port and savouring his *caille au gratin*, telling himself the while: 'It's not too dear at the price!'

For the moral observer, however, there were extenuating circumstances in this mode of life. In truth, a man only lives by the satisfaction he obtains for himself. Your passionless man, your righteous man, is a freak of nature, a burgeoning angel whose wings have not yet sprouted. In Catholic mythology cherubs have a head and nothing more. On earth the righteous man takes the form of a tedious Grandison, in whose eyes even a Venus of the streets would be sexless. Now Pons had never won a woman's favour – except for the few commonplace successes, due no doubt to climatic factors, which he had had with women during his Italian travels. Such is the inevitable destiny of many men. Pons was a freak from birth. His father and mother had come by him in old age, and the stigmata of this untimely conception showed forth in his cadaverous complexion, which seemed to have been acquired in the jar of spirits of wine used by embryologists to preserve certain abnormal foetuses. This artist, so tender, dreamy, delicate of soul, was forced to accept the character which his countenance imposed upon him; he despaired of ever being loved. So he was a bachelor less by choice than by necessity. *Gourmandise*, a sin to which even virtuous monks are addicted, opened its arms to him: he flung himself into them as he had flung himself into the worship of masterpieces and devotion to music. The small change of good food and bric-à-brac stood him in lieu of a woman's affection – for music was merely his profession, and few men are found who love the profession they live by. In the long run, any profession is like the married state: only its drawbacks are perceived.

Brillat-Savarin, in his *Physiologie du Goût*, took it upon himself to justify the tastes of gastronomes. But perhaps he did not sufficiently emphasize the essential pleasure of the table. The digestive process brings all the human forces into play. It is a kind of inner combat which, for those who make a god of their bellies, gives as much enjoyment as sexual intercourse. The vital functions are involved on so wide a scale that the brain abdicates in favour of a second brain seated in the diaphragm, and intoxication ensues through the very inertia of all our faculties. Boa constrictors, when they have gorged down a bull, become so intoxicated that they are easy to kill. What man over forty dares settle down to work after a good dinner? This accounts for the sobriety of all great men. Convalescents who are recovering from a serious illness, and to whom a carefully chosen diet is so sparingly meted out, may often experience a sort of tipsiness caused by the mere consumption of a chicken-wing. Pons was wise in this respect: his every enjoyment was centred upon his gastronomic activities. He was continually in the position of such convalescents: good fare had to provide him with all the sensual pleasure it can give; and so far it had not failed to do so. No one dares to say good-bye to his daily habits. Many intending suicides have halted on the threshold of death at the thought of the café in which they are wont, every evening, to play their game of dominoes.

3. The two 'Nutcrackers'

IN 1835, a lucky chance compensated Pons for the coldness of the fair sex, and gave him something to lean on in his old age. He had been an old man from the cradle, and friendship provided him with a prop: he contracted what was for him the only kind of marriage possible in his situation – wedlock with a man, an elderly man, a musician like himself. But for La Fontaine's wonderful fable, the title of this sketch would have been *The Two Friends*. But would that not have been a literary impropriety, a profanation from which any reputable author would shrink? The fabulist's masterpiece, at once an intimate confession and a revelation of his dreams, must for ever enjoy the privilege of this title. The page on whose pediment he engraved these three words: *The Two Friends*, is his inviolable property, a temple which men of every generation and every country will reverently visit as long as the printed word subsists.

Sylvain's friend was a piano teacher, whose life and manners concorded so well with his that he professed he had known him too late for his happiness – their acquaintanceship, which had begun at a prize-giving in a boarding-school, only dated from 1834. Never, perhaps, in the sea of humanity which, against the Divine will, welled up from the terrestrial paradise, had two souls found themselves so alike. In a short space these two musicians became necessary to one another. Each one of them being sure of the other, in a week they became like twin brothers. In short, Schmucke had no more believed that a Pons could exist than Pons had suspected the existence of a Schmucke. This alone would suffice to depict these two worthy people, but every type of mind cannot appreciate so summary a synthesis. Some measure of illustration is needed for the incredulous.

This pianist, like all pianists, was a German: a German like the great Liszt and the great Mendelssohn, a German like Steibelt, a German like Mozart and Dusseck, a German like

Meyer, a German like Doelher, a German like Thalberg, Dreschok, Hiller, Leopold Mayer, Crammer, Zimmermann, Kalkbrenner, like Herz, Woëtz, Karr, Wolff, Pixis, Clara Wieck, and more specifically, like all Germans. Schmucke was a great composer, but he could be no more than a demonstrator of his art because, by nature, he was so incapable of the boldness needed for a man of genius to manifest his musical quality. The ingenuousness of many Germans does not continue indefinitely: they manage to shed it. If at a certain age any of it has remained in them, it has been piped, as water for a canal is piped, from the springs of youth in them. They use it to fertilize their success in various spheres – science, art, or finance – and to avert mistrust. In France, some wily people affect instead the obtuseness of a Paris grocer. But Schmucke had kept all his childish ingenuousness: in like manner Pons, without realizing it, had retained in his person vestiges of Imperial times. This true and noble German was at once both orchestra and audience: he performed music for his own hearing. He lived in Paris like a nightingale in a forest; unique of his kind, he had been singing there for twenty years before he found an *alter ego* in Pons.

In heart and character both Pons and Schmucke were abundantly given to those childish sentimentalities noticeable in Germans: for instance, a fondness for flowers and nature's artistry which induces them to set up large glass globes in their gardens so that they may recapture in miniature the full-scale landscape they see in front of them; or the predilection for research which sends a gaitered Teutonic botanist on a hundred leagues' journey in order to discover a truth already smiling at him from the margin of his well under the jasmine of his courtyard; or, lastly, the urge to find psychic meaning in material trifles which is responsible for the uninterpretable works of Jean-Paul Richter, the tipsy fantasies which Hoffmann has put into print and the folio volumes which, in Germany, ward off access to the simplest questions and delve down into unfathomable depths, only to reveal a *mens teutonica* at the bottom. Both were Catholics and attended Mass together, discharging their religious duties like children who never have any sins to confess. They firmly believed that music, heaven's own language, bears the same relation to ideas and feelings as ideas and feelings bear to speech, and used it *ad infinitum* as a means of communication, replying to one another in orgies of music in order, like lovers, to persuade themselves of the truth of their convictions. Schmucke was as absent-minded as Pons was sharply alert. While Pons thought of his collection, Schmucke day-dreamed; the latter was attentive to spiritual, Pons to material beauty. Pons could pick out and snap up a china tea-cup while Schmucke was sentimentally blowing his nose over some theme by Rossini, Bellini, Beethoven or Mozart, searching for the source or equivalent of this musical phrase in the realm of feeling. Both Schmucke, whose budget was at the mercy of his absent-mindedness, and Pons, whose mania made him a spendthrift, reached the same result by the end of the year: an empty purse.

Had it not been for this friendship, Pons's disappointments might well have got the better of him; but life became endurable for him once he found a kindred soul to confide in. The first time he poured out his woes into Schmucke's sympathetic ears, the kindly German advised him to live as he himself did, at home, on bread and cheese, instead of dining out at such a cost to his self-respect. Unfortunately Pons dared not admit to Schmucke that his heart and his stomach were at daggers drawn, that while his heart bled, his stomach throve and needed a good dinner to savour no matter the price, just as a gallant needs a mistress to caress. It took Schmucke some time to fathom Pons, being too much of a German to have a Frenchman's quickness of perception; but he only loved poor Pons the better for it. Nothing fortifies friendship more than one of two friends thinking himself superior to the other. An angel would have cast no blame on Schmucke when he saw him rubbing his hands on discovering what intense enjoyment gourmandizing gave to his friend. In fact, the very next day, the kindly German embellished the lunch-table with delicacies he went and bought himself, and he took care to provide new ones each day for his friend – for since their first meeting they had been lunching together every day.

You would have to know nothing of Paris to imagine that the two friends were immune from Parisian mockery, which has never shown respect for anything. Schmucke and Pons, on taking each other for better or for worse, had decided to live together for economy's sake. They paid equal shares for the rent of a flat which was divided in very unequal proportions. It was situated in a quiet house in a quiet street – the rue de Normandie, in the Marais district. Since they often went out together, strolling side by side along the same boulevards, idlers in those quarters had nicknamed them 'the two Nutcrackers'. This soubriquet makes a description of Schmucke superfluous at this point: he was to Pons what Niobe's nurse, the famous statue in the Vatican, is to the Venus of the Tribuna.

Madame Cibot, the concierge, was the pivot on which the two 'Nutcrackers'' ménage turned, but she plays so important a part in the drama which broke up this dual existence that it is better to postpone her description until she is about to walk on to our stage.

What remains to be told about the spiritual plight of these two people is just what ninety-nine per cent of readers in this forty-seventh year of the nineteenth century will find it most difficult to comprehend, probably thanks to the prodigious development of finance caused by the founding of the railways. There is little, and yet much, to say. In fact, we have to give some idea of these two persons' excessive sensitivity. Let us borrow a metaphor from the railways, even if only to recoup ourselves for the sums they have borrowed from us. The trains of today, as they speed along the rails, grind up imperceptible grains of sand. Introduce one of these grains, invisible to a traveller's eye, into his kidney, and he will feel the tortures of that fearful and sometimes mortal disease known as the gravel. Now the equivalent of this invisible grain of sand, unheeded by the world of today as it hurtles along its steel track with the speed of a locomotive, this grain which at all times and occasions was being forced into the very substance of these two souls, was like a sort of gravel lodged in the heart. Each of them had an excessively tender compassion for other people's griefs and wept at his impotence to cure them. As for the sensations they themselves experienced, they were like those of a *mimosa pudica*, so acute as to amount to a disease. Nothing –

neither old age itself nor the continuous spectacle which life on the stage of Paris affords – had hardened the pure, unspoilt, child-like souls of these two. The farther they went, the keener their inner sufferings became. Such, alas, is the lot of those unsullied natures, those peaceful thinkers, those true poets who have never fallen into any excess.

Ever since these two old men had come together, they had pursued their almost similar daily tasks as fraternally as a pair of Paris cab-horses trotting along together. They got up at seven, winter and summer, breakfasted and set forth for their lessons in their respective schools, and at need took one another's place. About noon Pons went off to his theatre when a rehearsal was on, and he spent every minute of freedom roaming the streets. Then in the evening the two friends met again at the theatre in which Pons had also found work for Schmucke.

*

This is how it came about. When Pons first met Schmucke, he had just obtained – without asking for it – his conductor's baton: as good as a field-marshal's baton for an obscure composer! Monsieur le Comte Popinot, that bourgeois hero of the 1830 Revolution, then a minister, had earmarked this post for the poor musician at the same time as he obtained a theatre licence for one of his friends, the kind of friend who makes a parvenu blush when, crossing Paris in his carriage, he espies an old comrade of his youth, down-at-heel, with frayed trouser-bottoms, in an incredibly discoloured frock-coat, but still on the look-out for business deals which are too adventurous to attract that elusive thing, capital. This friend, whose name was Gaudissart, formerly a commercial traveller, had in his time contributed much to the success of the great Popinot firm. Popinot was now a count and had been made a Peer of France after occupying two ministerial posts: he did not disown THE ILLUSTRIOUS GAUDISSART. Far from it: he decided to put the traveller in the way of renewing his wardrobe and replenishing his purse; for neither politics, nor any snobbishness acquired at the Citizen-King's court, had corrupted the heart of this erstwhile manufacturer of cosmetics. Gaudissart, still hot on the trail of women, asked to be given the licence of a bankrupt theatre, and the minister, when he handed it over, took the precaution of sending along a few old roués who were rich enough to found a strongly financed company whose shareholders were partial to what a pair of tights conceals. Pons, as a hanger-on in the Popinot mansion, was thrown in as part of the bargain.

In any case the Gaudissart Company prospered, and in 1834 decided to carry out the great idea of providing an opera-house for the masses, on the Boulevard. Ballet-music and fairy-plays demanded a tolerably good orchestra conductor who could do a bit of composing. The management which the Gaudissart Company replaced had for a long time been short of a copyist of parts, and so Pons got Schmucke into the theatre to take charge of copying – a subordinate occupation, but one requiring a sound knowledge of music. At the advice of Pons, Schmucke came to an arrangement with the director of this service at the Opéra-Comique, and thus saved himself the donkey work involved. The partnership of Pons and Schmucke produced wonderful results. Like all Germans, Schmucke was a master of harmony, and he looked after the orchestration of scores for which Pons furnished the singing parts. When certain attractive compositions, written expressly for two or three important theatrical successes, won the admiration of connoisseurs, the latter did not bother about the composers, but explained them in terms of *progress*. Pons and Schmucke suffered eclipse in this flood of glory, just like certain people who get drowned in their baths. In Paris, especially since 1830, no one gets to the fore without thrusting aside, vigorously and *quibuscumque viis*, a formidable throng of rivals: one needs excessively sturdy loins for this, and the two friends were suffering from that gravel in the heart which impedes all activity prompted by ambition.

As a rule, Pons betook himself to the orchestra-pit of his theatre about eight in the evening. That is the time when the curtain rises on popular productions, whose overtures and incidental music call for the tyrannical sweep of the baton. Most minor theatres make shift with this unpunctuality, and it suited Pons so much the more because he was quite indifferent about his relations with the management. Besides, when Pons was not there on time, Schmucke took his place. As the years went by, Schmucke's position in the orchestra had become well-established. The illustrious Gaudissart, without saying a word, had taken note of both the value and the serviceableness of Pons's collaborator. As in the bigger theatres, it had become necessary to bring a piano into the orchestra. This piano, which Schmucke played without extra payment, was installed close to the conductor's stand, where the willing supernumerary took up his post. Once this good, unambitious and unassuming German became known, all the musicians took to him. The management put Schmucke – at a modest salary – in charge of those instruments which have no regular place in the orchestras of the Boulevard theatres, but which are often needed – such as the piano, the *viol d'amore*, the *cor anglais*, the harp, the cachucha castanets, the bells and the inventions of Sax, etc. Germans may not be able to perform on the great instruments of National Freedom, but they are at home with all instruments of music.

The two old artists were exceedingly popular with all the theatre staff, and took life there philosophically. They had cultivated a blind spot for the ills endemic in a theatrical company consisting of a *corps de ballet* mingled with actors and actresses – one of the most frightful medleys which the needs of the box-office have created for the torment of managers, authors and musicians. The great respect he showed to others and his self-respect had gained general esteem for the good and modest Pons. Anyway, in any sphere of life, transparent integrity and unimpeachable honesty command a kind of admiration even in the most ill-natured people. In Paris real goodness makes as much stir as a monster diamond or a rare curio. Not one actor, author or dancing-girl (however impudent she might be) would have risked the lightest sally or practical joke at the expense of Pons or his friend. Pons sometimes made an appearance in the foyer, but Schmucke kept to the underground passage leading from the street to the orchestra pit. Between the acts of the performances he attended, the kindly old German ventured to glance round the auditorium, and he sometimes questioned the first flute – a young man born in Strasbourg of a German family from Kehl – about the eccentric characters who almost always grace the front stalls. This flautist undertook his social education, and Schmucke's infantile imagination gradually came round to admitting the existence of such fabulous creatures as *lorettes*, the possibility of marriages contracted in the thirteenth arrondissement,* the prodigality of leading ballet-girls and the shady transactions of theatre-attendants. To this worthy man the lightheartedness of vice seemed the last word in Babylonian depravity, and he gazed at it benignly as if he were contemplating Chinese arabesques. Men of the world must realize that Pons and Schmucke were exploited, to use a word in vogue; but what they lost in money was made up in consideration and friendly services.

After a successful ballet had set the Gaudissart Company on the way to rapid prosperity, the directors sent Pons a group in silver attributed to Benvenuto Cellini: the exorbitant price asked for it had been talked about in the foyer – a matter of twelve hundred francs! The poor good man tried to give the present back, and Gaudissart was hard put to it to make him accept it. 'Oh,' he said to his partner, 'if we could find actors cut to the same pattern!' These two lives thus linked, apparently so tranquil, had only one disturbing feature – Pons's besetting sin, his fierce craving for dining out. And so whenever Schmucke was at home while Pons was dressing for dinner, the kindly German lamented over this baneful habit. 'If only it mate him fat!' he often exclaimed. And Schmucke pondered over some means of curing his friend of this degrading vice, for true friends have a moral perception as keen as a dog's scent: they sniff out their friends' vexations, divine the causes of them, and worry about them.

Pons, who always wore a diamond ring on the little finger of his right hand – a fashion which was tolerated in Empire times, but which is laughed at today – was too much the wandering minstrel, too much the Frenchman for his physiognomy to reflect that divine serenity which tempered Schmucke's appalling ugliness. The German had discerned in his friend's melancholy cast of countenance the mounting difficulties which rendered his occupation as a parasite more and more painful. Indeed, by October 1844, the number of houses in which Pons

* i.e. illicit unions. There were then only twelve arrondissements (administrative districts) in Paris.

dined had naturally dwindled considerably. The unfortunate conductor, finding his rounds reduced to his family circle, had, as we shall see, inordinately extended the meaning of the word 'family'.

Our one-time laureate was first cousin to the first wife of Monsieur Camusot, the rich silk-mercer established in the rue des Bourdonnais: she had been Mademoiselle Pons, sole heiress of one of the famous brothers Pons, embroiderers by Royal Appointment. The musician's parents had been sleeping partners in this firm which they had founded before the Revolution of 1789. It had been bought in 1815 by a Monsieur Rivet from the first Madame Camusot's father. In 1844, this Camusot, who ten years before had retired from business, was a member of the General Council of Manufacturers, the Chamber of Deputies, etc. The worthy Pons, having been on friendly terms with the Camusot clan, reckoned himself to be a cousin of the silk-mercer's children by his second wife, although they were not even relations by marriage.

And since the second Madame Camusot was a former Mademoiselle Cardot, Pons wormed his way as a kinsman of the Camusots into the extensive Cardot family. These formed a second middle-class clan which through intermarriage constituted a whole society no less influential than that of the Camusots. Cardot the notary, a brother of the second Madame Camusot, had married a Mademoiselle Chiffreville. The celebrated family of the Chiffrevilles, the foremost manufacturers of chemical products, was linked with the big pharmaceutical concern for a long time lorded over by Monsieur Anselme Popinot whom, as we know, the July Revolution had flung into the centre of entirely dynastic politics. Pons lined up behind the Camusots and the Cardots and gained access to the Chiffreville's, and thence to the Popinots – still as a cousin of other cousins.

This simple glance at the old musician's more recent connexions show how he was still able to receive family hospitality in 1844; first, from Monsieur le Comte Popinot, Peer of France, former Minister of Agriculture and Commerce; secondly, from Monsieur Cardot, once a notary, now Mayor and Deputy of a Paris electoral district; thirdly, from Monsieur

41

Cardot senior, a member of the Chamber of Deputies, the Paris Municipal Council and the General Council of Manufacturers, and moving towards a peerage; fourthly, Monsieur Camusot de Marville, Pons's only real cousin, since he was born of his father's first marriage; but he was only a second cousin. This latter Camusot, in order to avoid being confused with his father and his half brother, had lengthened his name by adding to it that of his Marville estate. In 1844 he became a president of the Royal Court of Justice in Paris.

The retired notary, Cardot, had married his daughter to his successor, one Berthier, and Pons, as if he were handed over with the practice, secured the right to dine – legally attested, as he put it – with the Berthiers.

Such was the middle-class firmament which Pons claimed as his family and in which he had so laboriously conserved the privilege of plying knife and fork.

Of these ten households, the one on whose hospitality the artist had the strongest claim, the household of Président Camusot, caused him the greatest concern. Unfortunately, the Président's wife, daughter of the late Messire Thirion, Cabinet Usher during the reigns of Louis XVIII and Charles X, had never been kind to her husband's second cousin. Pons had wasted his time trying to soften this terrible kinswoman, for although he gave free lessons to Mademoiselle Camusot, he had found it impossible to make a musician of this carroty-haired girl. And now, on this particular afternoon, clutching the precious object we have mentioned, he was making his way to the house of his cousin the Président, and he felt, as he crossed the threshold, as if he were entering the Tuileries Palace, so gravely was he impressed by the imposing green draperies, the Carmelite-brown tapestries, the moquette carpets and the sober furniture so redolent of magistracy in all its austerity. Strangely enough, he felt at ease in the Popinot mansion in the rue Basse-du-Rempart, no doubt because of the art treasures it contained; for the erstwhile minister, since his entry into politics, had contracted the mania for collecting things of beauty, no doubt as a reaction against the political mentality which produces a secret collection of ugly deeds.

4. One of a collector's thousand thrills

PRÉSIDENT DE MARVILLE lived in the rue de Hanovre, in a house bought ten years ago by his wife, after the death of her parents, the worthy Thirions, who left her their savings – about a hundred and fifty thousand francs. This house faces north, and looks out rather gloomily on to the street, but its inner court enjoys a southerly aspect, and beyond it lies a quite attractive garden. The first floor is entirely occupied by the magistrate – under Louis XV it had lodged one of the most important financiers of the time. The second floor being let to a wealthy old lady, this dwelling has a tranquil and respectable appearance, as befits a magistrate's abode. What remains of the magnificent property of Marville, which the magistrate had paid for with twenty years' savings and the money his mother left him, consists of a *château*, one of those splendid piles still to be found in Normandy, and good farmland bringing in twelve thousand francs a year. Round the *château* is a park of about two hundred and fifty acres. This flourish of wealth, princely by present-day standards, costs the Président three thousand francs a year, so that the estate scarcely yields more than nine thousand francs net. At that time these nine thousand francs, together with his salary, provided the Président with a fortune of about twenty thousand francs a year: adequate enough, one would say, particularly in view of his expectations – half of his father's inheritance, since he was the sole child of the first marriage. But life in Paris and the need to keep up appearances had forced Monsieur and Madame de Marville to spend almost the whole of their income. Up to 1834 they had been in straitened circumstances.

This inventory explains why Mademoiselle de Marville, a girl of twenty-three, was still unmarried in spite of her dowry of a hundred thousand francs and her expectations, skilfully and frequently, but vainly, offered as a bait. For five years Cousin Pons had been listening to the wailings of the Président's wife, who watched all the deputy-attorneys getting married and the newly appointed court judges becoming fathers – and this after fruitlessly parading Mademoiselle de Marville's expectations before the undazzled eyes of the young Vicomte Popinot, eldest son of the pharmaceutical giant, for whose benefit, at least as much as for that of the younger branch of the Bourbons – so said the envious tongues of the Lombard quarter – the July Revolution had been carried through.

Pons arrived at the rue de Choiseul, and, as he was turning in to the rue de Hanovre, there came upon him that unaccountable emotion which racks clear consciences and inflicts on them the tortures undergone by the most hardened criminals at the sight of a police officer. Its sole cause was his uncertainty about the sort of reception he would get from the Président's wife. The grain of sand which lacerated his heart-strings had never worn smooth; its angles had become more and more acute, and the inhabitants of the house were constantly sharpening its edges. In fact, the little store which the Camusots set on their Cousin Pons, his devaluation in the bosom of the family, had its effect on the domestic staff: they were not rude to him, but they looked on him as a variety of the pauper species.

Pons's chief enemy was a certain Mademoiselle Vivet, a thin, desiccated spinster, chambermaid to Madame Camusot de Marville and her daughter. This Madeleine, despite her blotchy complexion – perhaps because of it and the fact that she was as long as an adder – had set her mind on becoming Madame Pons. In vain did she dangle before the old bachelor's eyes the twenty thousand francs she had put by; Pons had declined this far too blotchy bliss. And so this Dido-in-waiting, who wanted to claim cousinship with her employers, played the wickedest tricks on the poor musician. When she heard the poor man mounting the stairs, Madeleine called out lustily enough for him to hear: 'Ah! here comes the meal-cadger!' If she was serving at table in the manservant's absence, she poured little wine and much water into her victim's glass, giving him the difficult task of lifting an over-filled glass to his mouth without spilling it. She forgot to serve the poor fellow, and the Président's wife had to remind her to do so – in such tones as brought a blush to her cousin's cheeks. Or else she spilt gravy on his clothes. In short it was a war waged by an underling sure of impunity upon a helpless superior.

*

Being both housekeeper and maid, Madeleine had stayed with Monsieur and Madame Camusot since their wedding-day. She had witnessed the penury of her master and mistress in their beginnings, in the provinces, when the master was a simple Alençon magistrate. She had helped them to make ends meet when Monsieur Camusot, after presiding over the judicial bench at Mantes, came to Paris in 1828 to take up a post as examining magistrate. She was therefore too much a member of the family not to have motives for rancour against them. No doubt, under this desire to score off the Président's proud and ambitious wife by becoming her master's cousin, seethed an inarticulate hatred born of some slight – one of those pebbles which pile up into landslides.

'Madame, here is your Monsieur Pons – still wearing his spencer!' Madeleine came and told the Présidente. 'He really might tell me how he has managed to keep it going for twenty-five years!'

Hearing a man's step in the ante-room which separated her spacious drawing-room from her bedroom, Madame Camusot threw a glance at her daughter and shrugged her shoulders.

'You're always so clever at giving me warning, Madeleine,' said the Présidente, 'that I never have time to decide what to do.'

'Madame, Jean is out, I was alone, Monsieur Pons rang, I opened the door to him and as he almost belongs to the place, I couldn't stop him from following me; he's in there taking off his spencer.'

'My poor pet,' said the Présidente to her daughter, 'we are trapped. Now we shall have to dine at home.' Then she added as she caught the woebegone expression on her poor pet's face: 'Look, hadn't we better get rid of him once and for all?'

'Oh, the poor man!' replied Mademoiselle Camusot. 'Do him out of a dinner?'

A simulated cough resounded in the ante-room – that of a man trying to intimate that he was within earshot.

'Oh well, let him come in!' said Madame Camusot de Marville with a shrug.

'You have come so early, cousin,' said Cécile Camusot, putting on a winsome air, 'that you have caught us just when my mother was about to dress.'

Cousin Pons had not failed to notice the Présidente's shrug, and it struck home so cruelly that he was at a loss to find a compliment, and could only utter this profound remark:

'Little cousin, you are as charming as ever!'

Then he turned to the mother and making his bow went on:

'Dear cousin, you can't be cross with me for coming a bit earlier than usual. I've got something for you which to my great pleasure you asked me to find . . .'

And poor Pons, who made the Président, the Présidente and Cécile writhe every time he called them *cousin*, drew from his pocket a delightful little oblong case made of Mahaleb cherry-wood, exquisitely carved.

'Why, I had forgotten all about it!' was the Présidente's curt response: an atrociously cruel rejoinder, since it robbed her kinsman, whose sole crime consisted in being a poor relation, of all merit for the pains he had taken.

'But,' she continued, 'it is very kind of you, cousin. Do I owe you much for this absurd little article?'

At this question, his heart missed a beat, for he had reckoned that the gift of this gem of craftsmanship would pay for all his dinners.

'I thought you were allowing me to make you a present of it,' he said in a moved tone of voice.

'Really, really!' replied the Présidente. 'But let us not stand on ceremony, please. We know one another well enough to have things out sensibly. I know you are not rich enough to go off campaigning at your own expense. Haven't you already done a lot, bothering to waste your time rummaging in the dealers' shops?'

The poor man was deeply offended at this, and he retorted:

'My dear cousin, you certainly wouldn't want this fan if you had to buy it for what it's worth. It's a masterpiece by Watteau,

46

with his paintings on both sides. But don't worry, cousin, didn't pay a hundredth part of its value as a work of art.'

To tell a wealthy person, 'You can't afford it!' is like Gil Blas telling the Archbishop of Granada that his homilies are no good. Madame la Présidente was much too proud of her husband's position, of owning the Marville estate and being invited to Court balls, not to be hurt to the quick by such a remark, particularly when it came from a wretched bandmaster whose lady bountiful she professed to be.

'What fools they must be then, the people who sell you such things,' was the Présidente's sharp reply.

'You won't find any fools among Paris dealers,' replied Pons in almost cutting tones.

'In that case, you must be pretty smart,' said Cécile, in an attempt to soothe his feelings.

'Dear little cousin, I'm smart enough to recognize a Lancret, a Pater, a Watteau or a Greuze; but all I wanted was to give pleasure to your dear Mamma.'

Being ignorant and vain, Madame de Marville was loath to appear to be under the slightest obligation to her parasite, and her ignorance served her admirably, for she did not even know who Watteau was. Now if anything could demonstrate how far collectors' self-esteem can go – certainly there is nothing more touchy, not even an author's self-esteem – it was the audacity which Pons had just shown in standing up to his cousin for the first time in twenty years. Aghast at his own boldness, he recovered his mild demeanour by detailing to Cécile all the fine points of the delicate carving on the ribs of this marvellous fan. But, if the reader is to enter fully into the secret of the good man's flurried state of mind, we must briefly sketch the Présidente's lineaments.

Madame de Marville had formerly been a dainty little blonde, plump and fresh. At forty-six she was still *petite*, but had lost her curves. The arch of her forehead and the grim set of her mouth, once graced with the delicate tints of youth, had by then imparted sourness to her naturally disdainful appearance. The absolute domination which she had habitually exercised at home had given her a hard and disagreeable expression. The passage of time had darkened her fair hair to a crude brown.

She had always had a keen and caustic eye: now it conveyed magisterial arrogance and a full measure of incessant envy. The truth is that the Présidente was conscious of virtual poverty in the milieu in which she moved – that of the middle-class parvenus at whose tables Pons was accustomed to dine. She could not forgive the affluent pharmaceutical wholesaler, the former President of the Chamber of Commerce, for becoming successively a Deputy, a Minister, and then a Count and Peer of France. She could not forgive her father-in-law for having over-stepped his eldest son in getting himself elected as member for his constituency at the time when Popinot was promoted to the peerage. After her husband's eighteen years of service in Paris, she was still hoping he would become a Councillor in the Court of Appeal – his incompetence, well-known to the legal confraternity, barred him from this. The man who was Minister of Justice in 1844 looked back with regret to Camusot's appointment to a presidency in 1834; but he had been assigned to the Chamber of Indictment, and there, thanks to his routine experience as examining magistrate, he proved of service by virtue of the indictments he drafted.

*

All these disappointments told heavily on the Présidente de Marville, and since she cherished no illusions about her husband's worth, turned her into a fury. Her character, already imperious, became embittered. She was not old, but ageing; she made herself as rough and harsh as a scrubbing-brush in order to obtain by intimidation everything that society was inclined to refuse her. She had too caustic a tongue to have many friends. But she was a person to reckon with, for she had gathered around her a few pious old crones of her own stamp who stood by her so long as she stood by them. And so poor Pons's relations with this demon in petticoats were those of a schoolboy with a master who rules by the cane. Consequently the Présidente was at a loss to explain her cousin's sudden audacity, for she had no idea of the value of his gift.

'But where did you get it?' asked Cécile, as she studied the fan.

'In the rue de Lappe, from a dealer who had just brought it in from a *château* near Dreux which was being dismantled, a *château* where Madame de Pompadour sometimes resided before building Ménars. The most splendid panelling known has been salvaged from there, so lovely that Liénard, our celebrated wood-carver, has kept two of its oval frames for patterns and as a *ne plus ultra* in craftsmanship. This *château* was full of treasures. The dealer in question discovered this fan in an inlaid cabinet. I would have bought it myself if I collected such work. But the price is prohibitive – a piece of Riesener furniture is worth between three and four thousand francs! People in Paris are beginning to realize that the famous German and French inlay-workers of the sixteenth, seventeenth and eighteenth centuries used wood as a medium for real painting. It's up to a collector to be ahead of fashion. Why, in five years' time Frankenthal porcelain, which I have been collecting for twenty years, will fetch twice as much as Sèvres soft paste.'

'What is Frankenthal?' asked Cécile.

'The name of the Elector Palatine's china factory; it is older than our Sèvres factory, just as the famous Heidelberg gardens, destroyed by Turenne, were so unlucky as to exist before the gardens of Versailles. Sèvres copied Frankenthal a great deal ... one must do the Germans the justice of admitting that, well before us, they produced admirable ware in Saxony and the Palatinate.'

Mother and daughter exchanged glances as if Pons had been talking double Dutch, for Parisians are inconceivably ignorant and narrow-minded; all they know is what they have been taught when they have wanted to be taught.

'And how do you recognize a piece of Frankenthal?'

'By the signature, of course!' was Pons's heated reply. 'All these ravishing masterpieces are signed. Frankenthal bears an intertwined C and T (Charles-Theodore) beneath a prince's coronet. Dresden ware has two swords and a serial number in gold. Vincennes has a hunting-horn for its trademark. Vienna has a closed V with a bar across it. Berlin has two bars. Maintz has a wheel. Sèvres has a double L, and the Queen's ware has A for Antoinette, surmounted by the royal crown. In the eighteenth century all European sovereigns vied with one another in the manufacture of porcelain. There was ruthless competition between them to get craftsmen. Watteau designed china services for the Dresden factory, and his works have risen to exorbitant prices (you need an expert's eye, for today they make replicas and copies of them in Dresden). They manufactured wonderful things in those days, such as will never be produced again.'

'That's hard to believe.'

'It's a fact, cousin. Certain kinds of marquetry and porcelain will never be produced again, any more than a painting by Raphael, Titian, Rembrandt or Cranach. For instance, the Chinese are very clever, very skilled. Well, nowadays they are making nothing but replicas of "Great Mandarin" porcelain... Now a pair of antique Great Mandarin vases, of the largest size, fetches six, eight or ten thousand francs, whereas you can buy a modern copy of them for two hundred francs.'

'You're just joking!'

'Cousin, you may be surprised at such prices, but that's nothing. A complete twelve-place dinner service in Sèvres soft paste – which is not porcelain – costs a hundred thousand francs, but that is only the scheduled price. In 1750 you paid fifty thousand francs for a service in Sèvres like that. I have seen the original invoices.'

'But tell us about this fan,' said Cécile, who thought that the curio was too old-fashioned.

'You can guess that I started looking round as soon as your dear Mamma did me the honour of asking for a fan,' Pons continued. 'I visited all the old curiosity shops in Paris without finding anything worthwhile – naturally I wanted our dear Présidente to have a masterpiece, and I thought of giving her Marie-Antoinette's fan, the finest among all the well-known fans. But yesterday I was dazzled by this heavenly masterpiece, undoubtedly made to order by Louis XV. You may ask why I went to the rue de Lappe to find a fan: to an Auvergnat dealer, a vendor of copperware, scrap-iron and gilt furniture? Because I believe that *objets d'art* are not without intelligence. They recognize real connoisseurs. They beckon to them! They make eyes at them!'

The Présidente threw a glance at her daughter and shrugged her shoulders, but this dumb-show was too rapid for Pons to notice it.

'You can't tell me anything about those sharks: "Anything new, Papa Monistrol? Anything in carved lintels?" I asked this dealer – he lets me take a look at his acquisitions before the big dealers see them. Thereupon Monistrol tells me how Liénard, while he was doing some lovely carvings in the chapel at Dreux on a state commission, had attended the Aulnay auction and snapped up the carved panelling before the Paris dealers, who were interested only in porcelain and inlaid furniture, could lay their hands on it. "I didn't get much," he said, "but here is an article which will pay for my travelling expenses." And he showed me the escritoire, a positive marvel! Designs by Boucher done in marquetry with consummate art – enough to make you get down on your knees! "Look, sir," he said to me, "I have just discovered this fan in a little locked drawer without a key which I had to force open. You might well find me a customer for it." And out came this little case, carved in Mahaleb cherry-wood. "Have a look: it's the kind of Pompadour style you would take for ornate Gothic." "H'm," I replied, "the case is pretty. I could do with that. As for the fan, I have no Madame Pons to whom I could give this old trinket. Besides, one can get new ones, very pretty ones. Nowadays such designs on vellum are marvellously painted and don't cost much. Don't you know that there are two thousand painters in Paris?" And I nonchalantly opened out the fan, hiding my admiration, and cast a cold glance at these two tiny paintings, ravishingly unconstrained in conception and execution. I had Madame de Pompadour's very own fan in my hands! Watteau had put all he knew into it. "What are you asking for the case?" "Let's say a thousand francs – I've already been offered that much." I offered him a price for the fan which would cover his supposed travelling expenses. We then looked each other straight in the face, and I could see he was ready to clinch. I immediately put the fan back in the case, to prevent the Auvergnat from making a closer scrutiny of it, and I went into ecstasies over the carvings on the case – they were certainly exquisite. "If I buy it," I said to Monistrol, "that's the reason, you see; it's the case that tempts me. As for the cabinet, you'll get more than a thousand francs for that. Just look at the copper chasing on it. What a pattern for copying! There's money in that. There were no replicas made of it; everything done for Madame de Pompadour had to be unique." And the fellow was so busy ogling the cabinet that he forgot the fan, and I got it for a song in return for enlightening him about the beauty of the Riesener piece. So there we are! But one needs a great deal of practice to bring off such bargains. It's a close contest between two pairs of eyes – and there's nothing wrong with the eyes of a Jew or an Auvergnat!'

The old artist's vivid mimicry, the zest with which he told how smart he had been in getting the better of the dealer's ignorance, made him an ideal model for a painter of the Dutch school. But all this was lost on the Présidente and her daughter. The cold, disdainful glances they exchanged said quite plainly: 'What a character!'

'So you find that an amusing occupation?' asked the Présidente.

Pons was so chilled by this question that he felt like giving the Présidente a good slap.

'But of course, my dear Présidente,' he went on, 'it's like a day in the hunting field – stalking great works of art. You are up against adversaries who are warding you off the game you are hunting. It's a case of Greek meeting Greek. Between you and the masterpiece you are after, there's a Norman, a Jew or an Auvergnat. Why, it's just like a fairy-story: a princess in the power of a sorcerer!'

'And how do you pick out a Watt ... ? – What did you say his name was?'

'Watteau, cousin, was one of the greatest eighteenth-century painters. Come now, can't you see it's as good as signed?' he said, pointing out to her one of those pastoral scenes showing make-believe shepherdesses and great lords disguised as swains dancing a reel together. 'What fire! What verve! What colouring! And it's just thrown off like a calligrapher's flourish; it seems quite effortless. And on the other side, look, a ball in a salon: winter one side, summer the other. What ornamentation, and how fresh it has kept! See, the ferrule is in gold, and finished off on each side with a tiny ruby which I have cleaned up!'

'If that's the case, cousin, I couldn't take anything so valuable

as that from you. You ought to sell it and invest the money.'
None the less the Présidente asked nothing better than to keep
this splendid fan.

'It's high time that the plaything of Vice should become an
adornment for Virtue,' said the old fellow, recovering a little
of his self possession; 'and it will have taken a hundred years to
accomplish the miracle! Be assured that no princess at Court
will have anything comparable to this masterpiece, for unfortunately it is typical of human nature to do more for a Pompadour than for a virtuous queen!'

'Very well, I accept it,' said the Présidente with a laugh.
'Cécile, my angel, go and arrange with Madeleine for the
dinner to be worthy of our cousin.'

The Présidente merely wanted to even things up with Pons.
This instruction, given audibly against all the canons of good
taste, was so like settling an account that he blushed like a girl
caught in some unseemly behaviour. It was rather too large a
piece of gravel and it rolled over in his heart for quite a time.
Her red-headed daughter, who bore herself with some prig-
gishness, aped her father's grave magisterial manner, and had
more than a touch of her mother's asperity, disappeared and
left poor Pons to the tender mercies of the awe-inspiring
Présidente.

5. One of the thousand insults a parasite has to swallow

'SHE's a darling child, my little Lili,' said the Présidente, still using the pet name given to Cécile in her childhood.

'Charming,' replied the old musician, twiddling his thumbs.

'I just can't understand the times we live in,' the Présidente went on. 'What's the good of having a father who is a President at the Royal Court of Justice in Paris and a Commander of the Legion of Honour, as well as a millionaire grandfather, at present a Deputy, and soon to become a Peer of France – the richest wholesale silk-mercer in France?'

The Président's attachment to the new dynasty had recently earned him a Commander's ribbon, and some jealous spirits put this favour down to his friendship with Popinot. This Minister, despite his modesty, had, as we have seen, consented to be made a Count – 'for my son's sake', as he explained to his many friends.

'Only money matters today,' answered Cousin Pons. 'Only the wealthy get any consideration, and . . .'

'Where should we be then,' exclaimed the Présidente, 'if my poor little Charles had been spared!'

'Oh, you would certainly be poor if you had two children,' Cousin Pons continued. 'That's what comes of the equal partition of property. But don't worry, dear cousin, Cécile will make a good match in the end . . . I don't know any other girl with such accomplishments.'

And that shows to what low mental level Pons had sunk in the houses of his amphitryons. He served up their ideas, and made platitudinous comments on them, like the chorus in a Greek play. He did not dare to give vent to the originality which brings artists into the limelight. In his youth it had inspired him with many a subtle shaft, but his habit of self-effacement had by now almost suppressed it; and even when it reappeared, as it had done just then, it met with a snub.

'But I got married with a dowry of no more than twenty thousand francs . . .'

'Yes, cousin, in 1819,' Pons broke in. 'And look what you were – a capable girl, a *protégée* of Louis XVIII!'

'Well, after all, my daughter is an angel of perfection, extremely intelligent, a girl of genuine feeling, with a marriage-portion of a hundred thousand francs – and great expectations into the bargain. And she's still on our hands!'

Madame de Marville went on talking for twenty minutes about her self and her daughter, indulging in the lamentations peculiar to mothers who have daughters to marry off. For twenty years Pons had been dining at the house of Camusot, his only real cousin, and the poor man was still waiting for a kindly inquiry about his own affairs, his life and health. What is more, he was treated as a sort of drain down which domestic confidences were flushed. Complete reliance could be placed on his discretion, which was well-tried and indeed necessary, for one rash word would have barred him from ten households. And so he had not only to listen, but also to show constant approval. He jibbed at nothing, accused no one, defended no one; in his eyes, everyone was in the right. He therefore counted no longer as a man, but merely as a digestive apparatus. In the course of her long tirade, the Présidente admitted to her cousin – with a certain cautiousness of statement – that she was ready to accept almost blindly any candidate for her daughter's hand. Even a man of forty-eight would suit her book so long as he had an income of twenty thousand francs.

'Cécile has turned twenty-three, and if by bad luck she had to wait till she was twenty-five or twenty-six, it would be exceedingly difficult to find her a husband. People begin to wonder why a young person of that age has remained on the shelf for so long. In our social circle there's already too much tittle-tattle about her situation. We have used up all the commonplace excuses: "She's very young. – She's too fond of her parents to leave them. – She's happy at home. – She's particular and wants to marry into a good family." People are beginning to laugh at us, I am sure of that. Besides, Cécile is tired of waiting: the poor child is suffering.'

'From what?' was Pons's artless query.

'Can't you see?' her mother replied, with the tartness of a duenna. 'It vexes her to see all her friends getting married before she does.'

'And yet, cousin,' said the old musician, meekly, 'in what way have things changed since I last had the pleasure of dining here, for you to be thinking of men of forty-eight for Cécile?'

'Just this,' the Présidente retorted. 'We were to have an interview with a Judge of Appeal, who has a tidy fortune and a son thirty years old, for whom Monsieur de Marville would have obtained – it would have cost something – a post as chief clerk in the Audit Office. The young man is already there as a supernumerary. Well, we have just learnt that this young man has been fool enough to run off to Italy with a "duchess" – of the popular ballroom variety. It's as good as saying "No thank you". And we have been refused a young man whose mother is dead, who already enjoys an income of thirty thousand francs and will inherit a fortune from his father. And so you must excuse us, dear cousin, for feeling out of humour. You have come at a really critical moment.'

Just as Pons was racking his brains for one of those obsequious replies which always occurred to him too late when he was with hosts who intimidated him, Madeleine came in, handed a short missive to the Présidente and waited for an answer. This is how it read:

If we made out, dear Mamma, that this note was sent from the Law Courts by my father, telling you to bring me for dinner to his friend's for further talks about my marriage, Cousin Pons would go away; and we could carry out our plan to go to the Popinots.

'Who brought this note from my husband?' asked the Présidente in a sharp tone of voice.

'A court messenger,' was the arid Madeleine's bare-faced reply – it was this elderly Abigail's way of telling her mistress that she herself had hatched this plot in concert with Cécile, who had lost patience.

'Tell him that my daughter and I will be there at half-past five.'

*

56

Once Madeleine had left the room, the Présidente looked at Pons with that false geniality which has the same effect on a sensitive mind as a mixture of vinegar and milk has on an epicure.

'My dear cousin, dinner is ordered. Do have it without us, for my husband has written to me from the Court-room to tell me that the marriage project is being taken up again with the judge I mentioned, and we are going to dine there . . . You know we don't need to stand on ceremony with you. Just make yourself at home. You see how open I am with you; we have no secrets from you. You would not wish, I am sure, to stand in the way of my little angel's marriage.'

'On the contrary, cousin, I only wish I could find her a husband myself. But in the circle I live in . . .'

'You are right, it's not very likely,' the Présidente rudely interrupted. 'Well then, will you stay here? Cécile will keep you company while I get dressed.'

Cruelly hurt as he was by the way the Présidente had set about reproaching him for his poverty, he was still more dismayed at the prospect of remaining alone with the servants.

'But I can dine elsewhere, cousin,' said the simple fellow.

'Why do that? . . . Dinner is ready. The servants would eat it.'

At this horrible remark, Pons drew himself up with a start as if an electric current had passed through him. He gave his cousin a chilly bow and went to pick up his spencer. Cécile's bedroom door, which opened into the ante-room, was ajar, so that by looking straight into a mirror Pons was able to see the girl shaking with laughter and speaking to her mother in the language of nods and grimaces, which made it clear that the old artist was being meanly taken in. Pons slowly walked downstairs, almost in tears: he was being expelled from this house without knowing why.

'I'm too old now,' he said to himself. 'Age and poverty are so ugly that people find them horrible. I'll never go anywhere again without being invited.' – A heroic resolve!

The kitchen door on the ground-floor, facing the lodge, often remained open, as happens in buildings which the owners occupy themselves, while the street door is always kept closed.

Thus it happened that Pons could hear the laughter of the cook and manservant, to whom Madeleine was recounting the trick they had played on him; for she had not imagined that the poor man would make so prompt a retreat. The manservant expressed loud approval of this deceit practised on a regular guest who, he said, never gave him more than a three-franc piece as an annual tip.

'That's all very well,' the cook remarked; 'but if he takes the huff and doesn't come here, good-bye to the three francs the rest of us might have got on New Year's Day . . .'

'Rubbish, how would he know?' was the manservant's retort to the cook.

'Who cares?' added Madeleine. 'If he does find out sooner or later, what does it matter to us? The masters in the houses where he dines find him such a bore that he will be thrown out everywhere.'

At this moment the old music-master called out to the concierge: 'Open the door, please.' This doleful cry was received in deep silence in the kitchen.

'He was listening,' said the manservant.

'What does it matter?' Madeleine retorted. 'Bad luck for him, good luck for us. The stingy old beggar's done for.'

The poor man, who had missed none of this kitchen conversation, heard this parting shot too. He walked home through the streets in the same state of mind an old man would have been in after a desperate tussle with footpads. He hurried along in fits and starts, muttering to himself, for his wounded self-respect urged him on as a straw is puffed away by a blustering gale. Finally, not knowing how he got there, he arrived at five o'clock at the Boulevard du Temple. But – a most unusual thing – he had lost all appetite for food.

And now, if the reader is to understand what a revolution in Pons's flat his return at such an hour was going to cause, he needs the enlightenment we promised about Madame Cibot.

6. The Concierge Species – male and female

THE rue de Normandie is one of those streets in which you might feel you were in a provincial town. Grass thrives there, a passer-by is a rare occurrence, and everybody knows everybody else. The houses date from the time of Henri IV, when it was planned that every street in this quarter should be named after a province, and that a handsome square at the centre should be dedicated to France itself. The idea of a 'Quartier de l'Europe' was merely a repetition of this plan. In every sphere, including that of speculative building, plagiarism is rife. The house inhabited by the two musicians was once a town house built between courtyard and garden; but the front part of it, which gave on to the street, had been put up during the heyday of popularity which the Marais district enjoyed during the last century. In this former town house the two friends occupied the whole of the second storey. Both portions of this house belonged to a Monsieur Pillerault, a man of eighty, who left the running of it to a Monsieur and Madame Cibot – they had been his lodge-keepers for twenty-six years. Now, since a porter in the Marais quarter is not paid enough for him to live on what his lodge brings him in, the worthy Cibot eked out his five per cent on rents, and his perquisite of one log per load of wood, with what he could earn by his own toil: he was, like many concierges, a tailor. As time went on, Cibot had given up working for master-tailors; for, by virtue of the reputation he had gained among the shopkeeper class in that area, he enjoyed the unchallenged privilege of patching, invisibly mending and reconditioning every suit of clothes within a radius of three streets. The lodge itself was spacious and salubrious, with a bedroom leading from it. And so the Cibot establishment was considered one of the luckiest by the concierge gentry in the district.

Cibot was a little man of stunted growth and almost olive complexion thanks to his constant squatting, cross-legged, on a table level with the lattice window looking out on to the street. His occupation brought him in about two francs a day. Although he was fifty-eight, he kept on working; but fifty-eight is the best time of life for house-porters; they have grown into their lodges, which have become as much a part of themselves as its shell is for an oyster. And besides, *they are known to everyone in the quarter*!

Madame Cibot, formerly oyster-girl – a comely one – at the Cadran Bleu, had, at twenty-eight, given up her post for love of Cibot, after sampling all those incidental liaisons which wait upon a comely oyster-girl. Comeliness is short-lived among working-class women, especially when they spend their days, espalier-wise, outside a restaurant entrance. Hot gusts from the kitchen buffet and coarsen their features; leavings from bottles of wine, shared with the waiters, seep through to their complexion; and no bloom is more quickly over than the bloom of a comely oyster-girl. Fortunately for Madame Cibot, lawful wedlock and life as a concierge occurred in time to preserve her good looks. She remained a fitting model for a Rubens canvas, and still kept a sort of virile beauty which her rivals in the rue de Normandie insulted by calling her a 'fat lump'. Her flesh-tints could be compared with the appetizing glaze on pats of Isigny butter; and notwithstanding her plumpness she displayed an incomparable nimbleness in carrying out her duties. Madame Cibot was reaching the age when women of her type are obliged to shave, which amounts to saying that she was forty-eight. A portress complete with moustache is one of the surest guarantees of law and order that a landlord can desire. If Delacroix could have seen Madame Cibot in stately pose, ordering arms with her broomstick, he would certainly have made a Bellona of her!

The situation of the Cibots – spouse and consort, if we may adopt the Public Prosecutor's style – was, in a strange manner, one day destined to affect that of the two friends.

Therefore the historian, to give a true picture, is obliged to go into some detail concerning the lodge. The whole building brought in some eight thousand francs, for it consisted of three complete flats of double depth giving on to the street, and three flats in the old mansion between the courtyard and the garden.

In addition, a scrap-iron merchant named Rémonencq occupied a shop giving on to the street. This Rémonencq, who a few months earlier had promoted himself to the status of dealer in curiosities, was so well aware of Pons's standing in bric-à-braquerie that, whenever the musician came in or went out, he saluted him from the inside of his shop. So then, the five per cent on rents brought in about four hundred francs per annum to the Cibots, who moreover paid nothing for lodging and fuel. And since Cibot's wages amounted on an average to seven or eight hundred francs a year, husband and wife had an annual income of sixteen hundred francs, gratuities included, and they spent every penny of it, for they lived better than working-class people usually do. 'You only live once,' La Cibot used to say – she had been born during the Revolution and so, as can be seen, she did not know her catechism.

From her contact with the Cadran Bleu, this portress with her tawny eyes and haughty stare had retained some skill in cooking, which made her husband a subject of envy among his fellows. That is why, being ripe in years, and verging on old age, the Cibots had not so much as a hundred francs' savings to their credit. They dressed well and fed well, and also commanded in their neighbourhood the respect due to twenty-six years of scrupulous honesty. Though they had nothing saved up, they 'nn... owed not a sou to nn... anybody' – that is how Madame Cibot put it, for she lavished 'n's' in her discourse, and told her husband: 'You're nn ... an ... nn ... angel!' Why this indigence? As well ask why Madame Cibot cared nothing for the promises of religion. They were both proud of living in the public eye, of the esteem they enjoyed within a radius of six or seven streets, of the fact that their 'proprietor' allowed them autocratic rule over the house; but in secret they groaned at the thought of having no private income. Cibot complained of aches in his hands and legs, and Madame Cibot deplored the fact that her poor husband still had to work at his age. The day will come when a concierge, after thirty years of such existence, will accuse the Government of injustice and demand to be awarded the Legion of Honour! Whenever they learned through local gossip that such and such a servant-girl, after eight or ten years in her job, had been left an annuity of a hundred francs, they went round wailing from lodge to lodge: and that gives some idea of the envy which gnaws away at those who follow the humblest professions in Paris.

'It's a shame! *We* shall never get mentioned in a will! No such luck! And yet we are more use than any house-maid. *We* can be trusted. *We* collect the rents. *We* keep our weather eye open. But they treat us no better than dogs, and that's a fact!'

'You've got to take the rough with the smooth,' Cibot would say as he brought in a coat for mending.

'If I'd left Cibot in charge and taken a job as a cook,' cried Madame Cibot as she chatted with a neighbour with her hands on her ample hips, 'we'd have thirty thousand francs put by. I've made a mess of my life, just so that I could live warm and cosy in a nice lodge, and not go short of anything.'

*

When, in 1836, the two friends took over jointly the second floor of the former mansion, they brought about a sort of revolution in the Cibot *ménage*. In this way: Schmucke, as well as his friend Pons, was in the habit of taking on the porter or portress of the buildings in which he lodged, to do the house-work. And so the two musicians were of one mind when they moved to the rue de Normandie in arranging for Madame Cibot to become their housekeeper at a rate of twenty-five francs a month, of which each paid half. By the end of one year, this most efficient portress reigned supreme over the two old bachelors, just as she reigned over the house of Monsieur Pillerault, great-uncle of Madame la Comtesse Popinot. Their business was her business, and she called them 'her two gentle-men'. In short, when she found that the two 'Nutcrackers' were as docile as sheep, easy to get on with, very trusting, just a couple of children, her plebeian kind-heartedness prompted her to protect, adore and serve them with such genuine devotedness that she scolded them on occasions and defended them against all the swindling which in Paris makes household expenses mount up. For twenty-five francs a month, the two bachelors, without premeditation and without suspecting it, got themselves a mother. In their simple-hearted way the two musicians, when they came to realize Madame Cibot's sterling worth, showered praise and thanks on her, and gave her little seasonal tips which strengthened the bonds of this domestic alliance. Madame Cibot was a thousand times better pleased to be appreciated at her face value than to receive her pay: such an attitude, once noticed, always adds a bonus to wages. For half the usual cost Cibot ran errands, repaired their clothes, and did all he could in his line for the service of his wife's 'two gentlemen'.

Finally, from the second year onwards, a new factor – mutual friendship – came to tighten the link between second floor and lodge. Schmucke struck a bargain with Madame Cibot which suited both his slothfulness and his desire to live without responsibility. For thirty sous a day or forty-five francs a month, Madame Cibot undertook to provide lunch and dinner for Schmucke. Pons, finding that his friend thus got a very satisfactory lunch, made a similar bargain: lunch for himself at eighteen francs a month. This system of supply brought about ninety francs a month into the Cibots' takings, and transformed the two tenants into inviolable beings – angels, cherubs, divinities. It is very doubtful whether even the King of France – a good judge in such matters – is looked after as well as the two 'Nutcrackers' then were. The milk they drank came out of the can undiluted, and they had a free perusal of the newspapers from the first and third floors, whose tenants were late risers and would have been told, in case of inquiry, that the papers had not come. Moreover Madame Cibot kept the flat, their clothes, the landing – everything in fact – as clean as a Flemish interior.

As for Schmucke, he basked in unhoped-for happiness. Madame Cibot made life easy for him. He paid her about six francs a month for doing his laundry; and she also did his mending. His tobacco cost him fifteen francs a month. These three kinds of expenditure made up a monthly total of sixty-six francs; multiplied by twelve, that makes seven hundred and ninety-two francs. Add to that two hundred and twenty francs rent and taxes, and you have one thousand and twelve francs a year. Cibot made Schmucke's clothes for him, and on the average this last provision amounted to a hundred and fifty francs. And so this profound philosopher lived on twelve hundred francs a year. How many European people whose sole ambition is to come and live in Paris will be agreeably surprised to know that one can live happily there on an income of twelve hundred francs a year, in the rue de Normandie, under the wing of a Madame Cibot!

Madame Cibot was stupefied when she saw Pons coming home at five in the evening. Such a thing had never happened before, and what is more, her 'gentleman' did not see her and gave her no greeting.

'My goodness, Cibot,' she said to her husband, 'either Monsieur Pons has become a millionaire or he has gone mad!'

'It looks like it,' said Cibot, and the coat-sleeve, into which he was letting what is called a 'gore', in tailors' parlance, fell from his grasp.

7. 'The Two Pigeons': a fable come true

At the moment when Pons was mechanically making his way into the house, Madame Cibot was putting the last touches to Schmucke's dinner. This dinner consisted of a kind of stew whose aroma permeated the entire courtyard: the remains of a joint of boiled beef bought from a cookshop whose owner did some trade in left-overs, hashed up in butter with thin slices of onion until the meat and onions soaked up the butter, so that this concierge's fare looked quite like a freshly fried dish. La Cibot had lovingly concocted it for sharing between her husband and Schmucke, and it went in company with a bottle of beer and a morsel of cheese: it answered the needs of the old German music-master. And you may take it that Solomon in all his glory dined no better than Schmucke. Sometimes it would be this same dish of boiled beef with onions *en fricassée*, sometimes remnants of *poulet sauté*, sometimes a cold beef salad with parsley, or fish served up with a sauce of La Cibot's own invention – a mother could unsuspectingly have eaten her own child with this – and sometimes venison, all depending on the quality and quantity of food sold off by the boulevard restaurants to the man who ran the cookshop in the rue Boucherat. Such was Schmucke's ordinary fare, and he was content to eat, without comment, anything set before him by the 'goot Matame Cipot'. And, as time went on, the good Madame Cibot had reduced this menu until it cost her no more than a franc to produce.

'I'm off to find out what has happened to the poor dear man,' Madame Cibot told her husband, 'for Monsieur Schmucke's dinner is piping hot.'

She covered the deep earthenware dish with a coarse china plate; then, in spite of her years, she got to the friends' flat at the instant when Schmucke was letting Pons in.

'Vat is wronk, my goot frient?' asked the German, alarmed at the affliction he saw written on Pons's face.

'I'll tell you all about it; but I've come home to dine with you . . .'

'Tine viss me! Tine viss me!' cried Schmucke in ecstasy, 'put zet is impossible,' he added as he remembered how much his friend was given over to gastrolatry.

The old German then noticed that Madame Cibot was there, exercising her legitimate right as their housekeeper to eavesdrop. Seized with one of those inspirations which only flash out from the heart of a true friend, he went straight to the portress and took her out on to the landing.

'Matame Cipot, ze goot Pons lofs only goot sinks. Go to ze Catran Pleu unt orter a choice little tinner: anshoffies, macaroni: in fact, a meal vorzy of Lucullus.'

'What's that mean?' asked Madame Cibot.

'Vell, it means plain roast feal, a goot fish, a pottle of port vine: eferysink zat is most tasty, like rice croquettes and smoket pacon. Pay for it, say nossink, and I gif you all ze money pack in ze mornink.'

Schmucke re-entered the flat, gleefully rubbing his hands, but little by little his face took on a look of stupefaction as he listened to his friend's account of the woes which had so suddenly swooped down on him. Schmucke tried to console Pons with a picture of polite society as he saw it. Paris was an ever-raging tempest; the men and women in it were whirled around in a kind of frenzied waltz; one should expect nothing of society, which has eyes only for outward show, and not, he said, for 'vat zere iss insite'. For the hundredth time he told how, year by year, the only three school-girl pupils whom he had really loved, who had cherished him, for whom he would lay down his life, who even paid him a small pension of nine hundred francs, each one contributing an equal share of about three hundred francs, had so completely forgotten, from year to year, to come and see him, and were so carried away in the current of Parisian life that for three years they had been out when he paid them a visit. (As a matter of fact, Schmucke used to pay his visits to these great ladies at ten in the morning.) In short, the said pension came every quarter through a notary.

'Unt yet,' he continued, 'zey haf hearts of golt. In a vort, zey are my little Saint Cecilias, scharmink vomen, Matame te Portentuère, Matame te Vantenesse, Matame tu Tillet. I only see zem in ze Champs-Elyssées, vizout zem seeink me. Unt yet zey lof me much, and I coult go to lif viz zem, unt zey vould pe fery plisst. I coult stay in zeir country-house, put I like much pesser to pe viz my frient Pons, pecausse I can see him ven I vish unt efery tay.'

Pons took Schmucke's hand between his own, and the clasp he gave it was fully expressive of his heartfelt emotion. They remained thus for several minutes, like lovers meeting again after a long separation.

'Tine here efery tay,' continued Schmucke, who, inwardly, was blessing the Présidente for her harshness. 'Look! Ve vill go pric-à-prackink togezzer, unt, ze defil vill nefer show his hornss insite our house.'

To indicate how much heroism was contained in this phrase 've vill go pric-à-prackink togezzer' it must be made plain that Schmucke was crassly ignorant in the knowledge of bric-à-brac. It needed all the motive force of his friendship for him to avoid breakages in the drawing-room and study given over to Pons for his art collection. Schmucke was wholly devoted to music: he composed it for his own pleasure, and he gazed at all his friend's baubles as a fish supplied with a complimentary ticket would gaze at a flower-show in the Luxembourg gardens. The respect he showed to these wonderful creations was due to the respect Pons himself manifested as he dusted his treasures. 'Yes, it iss fery pretty' was his response to his friend's expressions of admiration, just as a mother responds by meaningless patter to her baby's gestures before he has learned to speak. Seven times, since the two had set up house together, Schmucke had seen Pons bartering one time-piece for another, and gaining by the exchange. At this period, Pons was the owner of Buhl's most magnificent clock, an ebony one in his first manner, inlaid with copper and decorated with carvings. Buhl had two styles, just as Raphael had three. In the first he blended copper with ivory; in the second, sacrificing his convictions, he went in for tortoise-shell, performing wonders in order to outstrip his competitors who had invented tortoise-shell marquetry. Now

Schmucke, in spite of Pons's learned demonstration, could not perceive the slightest difference between the splendid clock in Buhl's first manner and the many others which succeeded it. And yet, in order to make Pons happy, he took more care of these 'pauples' than Pons himself. Let us not then be astonished at the fact that Schmucke's inspired remark was potent enough to soothe Pons in his despair, for the German's 'Ve vill go pric-à-prackink togezzer' meant this: 'If you will take your dinners here I will put money into bric-à-brac.'

'Dinner is served, gentlemen,' Madame Cibot announced with remarkable aplomb.

It is easy to understand Pons's surprise when he saw and savoured the dinner which Schmucke's affection had conjured up. The kinds of sensation he felt, rare enough in a life-time, are not due to that steady devotion by means of which two men are for ever conveying to each other: 'I am simply your second self.' No, they arise when one compares the happy experiences of intimate family life with the cruelty inflicted by life in society. Society is thus ceaselessly forging anew the bonds between two friends or two lovers, when two great souls have united in love or friendship. And so Pons wiped away two big tears, and Schmucke, in his turn, was obliged to dry his eyes. They spoke not a word, but their mutual love was the greater for that, and they exchanged expressive little nods which acted like balm on Pons's feelings, wounded as they were by the gravel which the Présidente had introduced into his heart. Schmucke was rubbing his hands hard enough to take the skin off them, for there had occurred to him one of those bright ideas which astonish a German whose brain, normally congealed by the respect he pays to sovereign princes, has hatched one out spontaneously.

'My poor Pons,' he began.

'I can guess what you are going to say: you want us to dine together every day . . .'

'If only I vass rich enough to feet you like zis efery tay,' was the good German's melancholy reply.

And then Madame Cibot, to whom, from time to time, Pons presented tickets for the Boulevard theatres – this fact put him as high in her affections as her boarder Schmucke – came out with the following proposal:

'Goodness gracious,' she said, 'for three francs, wine not included, I can do both of you a dinner which will make you lick your plates as clean as soap and water could make them.'

'Ze fact iss,' answered Schmucke, 'zet I tine pesser on vat Matame Cipot cooks for me zen ze people who eat ze kink's stew.' So high were his hopes that the otherwise respectful German went so far as to imitate the irreverence of the scurrilous newspapers by casting a slur on the fare served up at the royal table.

'Is that so?' said Pons. 'Very well, I'll try it tomorrow.'

When he heard this promise, Schmucke leapt from one end of the table to the other, dragging with him the cloth, the dishes and the carafes, and clasped Pons in an embrace comparable to that of one gas uniting with another for which it has chemical affinity.

'Vat happiness!' he cried.

'Monsieur Pons will dine here every day,' Madame Cibot, much moved, proudly exclaimed.

Knowing nothing of the occurrence to which she owed the fulfilment of her ambition, the excellent Madame Cibot went down to her lodge and burst in as impetuously as the opera-singer Josépha when she makes her entry in *Wilhelm Tell*. She threw down the plates and dishes and called out:

'Cibot, run along to the Turk's Head and get two small coffees, and tell the cook's boy they're for me.'

Then she sat down, laid her hands on her sturdy knees and staring through the window at the wall opposite the house, she said: 'This very evening, I'm going to consult Ma'me Fontaine.'

*

Madame Fontaine was a fortune-teller who read the cards for all the cooks, chambermaids, footmen and porters in the Marais district.

'Since these two gentlemen came to the house, we have put two thousand francs into the savings-bank. In eight years, that's lucky! Had I better not make anything out of Monsieur

Pons's dinners but rather get him fond of home life? Ma'me Fontaine's hen will tell me.'

Seeing that Pons and Schmucke, as far as she knew, had no heirs, Madame Cibot had for the past three years cherished the hope that she might be mentioned in her two gentlemen's wills, and her zeal increased twofold thanks to this covetousness, a much later growth than her moustaches, which until now had betokened nothing but probity. By dint of dining out every day, Pons had eluded the complete enslavement to which the portress aimed to reduce 'her gentlemen'. The vague ideas of beguilement which flitted through Madame Cibot's head had shied at the nomadic life led by the old wandering minstrel-cum-collector; but after his memorable dinner, they crystallized into a formidable plan. A quarter of an hour later, she re-appeared in the dining-room armed with two cups of excellent coffee reinforced with two liqueur glasses of *kirschwasser*.

'Lonk lif Matame Cipot!' exclaimed Schmucke. 'She has guesst vat I vantet.'

The parasite in Pons gave vent to a few lamentations, but he yielded to his friend's blandishments as does the carrier pigeon to the cooing of the nesting dove, and the two friends went out together. Schmucke was reluctant to leave his friend alone in the state to which the Camusot household, mistresses and servants, had reduced him. He knew Pons well, and was aware that as he sat in his conductor's chair in the orchestra-pit, he might be assailed by such horribly gloomy reflections as might ruin the salutary effect of his return to the nest. So when he took Pons home about midnight, he walked arm-in-arm with him, and like a lover escorting a cherished mistress, he showed Pons the spots where the pavement ended or began again, and warned him whenever they came to a gutter. How he wished for a pavement as soft as cotton, for a blue sky, for Pons to be able to hear the strains of angelic music which he himself was hearing! He had won his way into the hitherto inaccessible reaches of this man's heart!

For a matter of three months, Pons dined with Schmucke every day. But to begin with he was obliged to deduct eighty francs a month from his outlay on bric-à-brac, for he had to disburse some thirty-five francs on wine as well as the forty-five francs his dinners cost him. Moreover, in spite of Schmucke's attentiveness and his Teutonic jokes, the old artist pined for the choice dishes, the liqueurs, the excellent coffee, the small talk, the insincere civilities, the varied company and the scandal-mongering in the houses he had frequented. As a man goes downhill in life, he cannot break with the habits he has indulged in for thirty-six years. A cask of wine costing one hundred and thirty francs dispenses a liquid which, to a gourmet, lacks nobility; and so, whenever Pons raised his glass to his lips, a thousand poignant regrets welled up as he remembered the exquisite wines his hosts had been accustomed to serve. There-fore, when three months had gone by, the excruciating pain which had almost broken Pons's sensitive heart was dulled, and henceforth he thought only of the agreeable side of social life. Not otherwise does an elderly gallant yearn for a discarded mistress, guilty though she may be of countless infidelities! Although he did his best to conceal the deep melancholy which consumed him, the old musician seemed visibly to be suffering from one of those unaccountable maladies whose origin is moral rather than physical.

To explain this nostalgia due to a broken habit, it will suffice to relate one of those thousand trivialities which have the same effect as the meshes of a coat of mail: they press in on the soul like a network of steel. One of the keenest pleasures in Pons's former mode of living (indeed one of the real joys of a man who dines at other people's tables) had been the *surprise*, the gastro-nomic effect of an exceptional dish, a delicacy triumphantly served up by a hostess intent on imparting a really festive air to the dinner she is giving. Pons missed this gourmet's delight. Madame Cibot was in the habit of proudly announcing the dishes she was about to serve, and Pons could never look for-ward to the occasional thrill of something unexpected, some-thing which formerly, in our grandparents' household, went by the name of a 'covered dish'. This was a mystery to Schmucke. Pons was too polite to complain, but if there is a more lamen-table thing than misunderstood genius, it is a stomach whose yearnings are left unsatisfied. Unrequited love – a theme over-exploited in drama – is based on an inessential need; for, if we are spurned by one of God's creatures, we can give our love to

God, who can heap treasures upon us. But an unrequited stomach! . . . no suffering can be compared to this, for good living comes first! Pons yearned for certain kinds of *crème*, each one a poem; for certain white sauces, every one a masterpiece; for certain dishes of truffled poultry, all ravishing to taste; and above all for those Rhenish carp which are only found in Paris, and with such delicious seasoning. On certain days Pons exclaimed: 'O Sophie!' as he thought of the Comte Popinot's cook. A stranger who heard him sighing like that would have imagined that the good man was thinking of an absent mistress, but he had something more rare in mind: a succulent carp, with a sauce which was clear in the sauce-boat but thick upon the tongue, a sauce which was worthy of the Montyon prize! And so the memory of the dinners he had eaten made the orchestra-conductor lose a lot of weight: he was stricken with gastric nostalgia.

*

At the beginning of the fourth month, about the end of January, 1845, the young flautist – called Wilhelm, like practically every German, and Schwab, to differentiate him from the other Wilhelms, though it did not differentiate him from the other Schwabs – thought fit to enlighten Schmucke about the conductor's state of health, which was causing sore concern in the theatre. This happened on the day of a first performance in which the instruments played by the old German music-master were included.

'The poor old fellow is on the decline,' said Wilhelm Schwab, pointing to Pons as he stepped up to his stand with a mournful air. 'There's something wrong with him. He looks unhappy. The swing of his baton is getting weak.'

'Von is always like zat at sixty,' replied Schmucke. Like the mother in the *Canongate Chronicles* who gets her son shot through contriving to enjoy his company for another twenty-four hours, Schmucke was capable of sacrificing Pons for the pleasure of having him to dinner every day.

'Everybody in the theatre is anxious, and, as our leading dancer, Héloïse Brisetout, has pointed out, he now makes scarcely any noise when he blows his nose.'

The old musician's long and cavernous nose, when he blew it, usually let out such a blare into the handkerchief that he appeared to be playing the horn. This blast was the cause of the most constant reproaches levelled against Pons by the Présidente.

'I voult gif many sinks to pe aple to amusse him,' said Schmucke. 'He is loosink all interest in life.'

'Indeed,' said Wilhelm Schwab, 'Monsieur Pons seems to be so much above the rest of us poor folk that I didn't dare invite him to my wedding ... I'm getting married ...'

'Marriet? How?' asked Schmucke.

'Oh, it's all above board,' replied Wilhelm, interpreting Schmucke's odd question as a piece of banter whose import would never have occurred to that perfect Christian.

'Come, gentlemen, take your places!' cried Pons, eyeing his little army in the orchestra-pit after hearing the stage-manager's bell.

They played the overture to *The Devil's Betrothed*, a fairy-play which was to run to two hundred performances. At the first interval, Wilhelm and Schmucke found themselves together in the deserted orchestra pit. The temperature in the theatre had risen to thirty degrees Réaumur.

'You haf a story to tell me,' said Schmucke to Wilhelm.

'Yes ... You see that young man in the proscenium? ... Do you recognize him?'

'Not in ze least.'

'Ah, that's because he's wearing yellow gloves and radiating opulence. Anyway, he's my friend Fritz Brunner from Frankfurt-am-Main.'

'The man who uset to vatch ze playss from ze orchestra, near you?'

'The very same. Isn't it hard to believe in such a metamorphosis?'

The hero of the promised story was one of those Teutons in whose faces are blended both the sombre raillery of Goethe's Mephisto and the good nature to be found in Auguste Lafontaine, that novelist of blissful memory; cunning and guilelessness, commercial ruthlessness and the calculated nonchalance of a member of the Jockey Club; but above all, that disgust with life which put a pistol into the hands of Werther, vexed as he was with the German princelings more than with Charlotte. He was a genuinely typical German figure: much sharp practice and much simplicity; stupidity and courage; a knowledgeableness productive of boredom; experience of the world which the slightest piece of childishness could nullify; excessive indulgence in beer and tobacco; and yet, to give piquancy to all these antitheses, a demoniacal sparkle in his fine, tired blue eyes. Tricked out with all a banker's elegance, Fritz Brunner offered to the gaze of the whole auditorium a head of Titian hair, bald on top, but with a few curly, auburn locks on either side which riotous living and poverty had spared him so that he could keep the right to pay a barber on the day his ship came home. His face, once a fresh and comely countenance such as painters give to Jesus Christ, had taken on crude tones to which red whiskers and a tawny beard had imparted an almost sinister note. His conflict with the vexations of life had clouded the clear blue of his irises. In short, the constant self-prostitution which life in Paris entails had blurred his gaze and put shadows round those eyes into which, long ago, a mother had fondly looked so as to catch the divine response of his glance. This young-old man, precocious in worldly wisdom, was the handiwork of a stepmother.

And here begins the curious story of one of Frankfurt-am-Main's prodigal sons: the oddest and strangest event that ever came about in that sedate but central city.

8. Prodigal sons from Frankfurt-am-Main don't always end up with the husks of the swine

HERR GIDEON BRUNNER, Fritz's father, one of those Frankfurt-am-Main innkeepers who, in complicity with the bankers, cut legally authorized slits in tourists' wallets – an honest Calvinist to boot – had married a converted Jewess, whose dowry helped him to lay the foundations of a fortune. This Jewess died, leaving her son Fritz, aged twelve, under the guardianship of his father and the supervision of a maternal uncle, a Leipzig furrier, the head of the firm of Virlaz and Company. Brunner senior was forced by this uncle, who was not so soft as his furs, to invest young Fritz's inheritance – quite a respectable sum in standard marks – in the firm of Al-Sartchild, and to keep his fingers out of it. To recoup himself for such Jewish intransigence, the elder Brunner married again, alleging the impossibility of running a large hotel unaided by a woman's eye and arm. He took to wife the daughter of another innkeeper – a pearl of a woman, so he thought. But he had had no experience of life with an only daughter, idolized by her father and mother. The second Frau Brunner was just what German girls can be when they are ill-natured and flighty. She squandered his money, and avenged the first Frau Brunner by giving her husband a home life which made him the unhappiest man known throughout the territory belonging to the free city of Frankfurt-am-Main – in which city, it is said, the millionaires are about to pass a municipal law constraining their wives to love them and them alone. Being German, she relished the different kinds of vinegar which in Germany are commonly called Rhenish wines. She loved fancy goods from Paris. She loved riding. She loved clothes. In fine, the only costly article she did not love was other women. She took a dislike to little Fritz, and would have driven this youthful product of Calvinism and the Mosaic Law mad if he had not had Frankfurt for a cradle and the Leipzig firm of Virlaz for guardian. But Uncle

75

Virlaz, given over to his furs, only looked after the standard marks, and left the boy to his stepmother's tender mercy.

This hyena was so much the more furious with the cherubic son of the handsome first Frau Brunner because, though she puffed and strained like a railway-engine, she could produce no offspring. With diabolic cunning, this wicked woman launched young Fritz, at twenty-one, into a career of dissipation unusual among Germans. She hoped that English ponies, Rhenish vinegar and Gretchens à la Goethe would destroy the Jewess's child and his fortune: for Uncle Virlaz had left his little Fritz a fine inheritance just when the latter attained his majority. Roulette in the spas and wine-bibbers (Wilhelm Schwab among them) demolished the Virlaz capital; but the young prodigal son lived on as a providential warning to the elder sons of Frankfurt-am-Main, where every family still holds him up as a bogey to frighten their children and keep them on the strait and narrow path, to confine them to their steel counters lined with standard marks. However, far from dying in the bloom of youth, Fritz Brunner had the satisfaction of seeing his stepmother buried in one of those delightful cemeteries which enable the Germans, under the pretence of honouring their dead, to abandon themselves to their unbridled passion for horticulture. Thus the second Frau Brunner predeceased her progenitors, leaving her spouse so much the worse off for the money she had drawn from his coffers and the hard labour she had imposed on him: at the age of seventy-seven this innkeeper, a man of herculean constitution, found himself as much diminished as if he had been undermined by a course of Borgia poisoning. The fact of not inheriting from his wife after bearing with her for ten years turned him into a second Heidelberg ruin, but one which was kept in repair by the bills his clients paid: just so is the Heidelberg *Schloss* itself kept in repair to fan the enthusiasm of those tourists who come in flocks to feast their eyes on those beautiful, well-maintained remains. To the Frankfurt people this predicament was as serious as bankruptcy, and they used to point to him with the remark:

'That's what comes of marrying a bad woman who leaves you nothing, and bringing your son up like a Frenchman!'

In Italy and Germany, Frenchmen are the cause of every

misfortune, a target for every bullet; yet they manage to rub along.

The owner of the Grand Hôtel de Hollande was not content to vent his spleen only on his guests, whose bills were proportionate to his grievance. When his son had spent all his money, Gideon, regarding him as the indirect cause of all his woes, denied him food and drink, hearth and home, and even tobacco. And that, in a German parent, an innkeeper to boot, is as far as paternal malediction can go. The local authorities, taking no account of Gideon's initial injustices to his son, and deeming him to be one of the most unfortunate citizens of Frankfurt-am-Main, took his side. They banished Fritz from the territory of that free city on a trumped-up charge. In Frankfurt justice is not wiser or more humane than elsewhere, even though this city is the seat of the German Diet. Rarely does a magistrate dealing with crime and bad luck work upstream to find out who had held the urn from which the first trickle of water poured out. Brunner consigned his son to oblivion – and his son's friends followed suit.

Reader, if only this story could have been played out in front of the prompter's box to that gathering in whose midst journalists, social 'lions' and a handful of Paris ladies were speculating about the antecedents of this Teuton, this deeply tragic figure who had loomed up as the sole occupant of a stage-box, before a Parisian élite immersed in a first performance, it would have been a much finer production than the fairy-play *The Devil's Betrothed*, even though it would have been the two-hundred-thousandth staging of that sublime parable first enacted in Mesopotamia three thousand years before Christ.

Fritz went on foot to Strasbourg, but there he met with something the Prodigal Son did not find in the realms of Holy Scripture; and herein is revealed the special vocation of Alsace, so rich in generous hearts, for showing the German people how fine a combination of French wit and German stability can be. A few days previously, Wilhelm had come into his parents' money and now owned a hundred thousand francs. He welcomed Fritz with open arms, open heart and open purse. To describe the moment when Fritz, dust-laden, penniless and in a well-nigh leprous condition, crossed the Rhine and made the acquaintance of a genuine twenty-franc piece in the hand of a real friend, would be like trying to write an ode – such an ode as only a Pindar, writing in Greek, could pour forth to revive the embers of friendship in the human race. Put the names of Fritz and Wilhelm beside those of Damon and Pythias, Castor and Pollux, Orestes and Pylades, Dubreuil and Pemjah, Schmucke and Pons and all those imagined names which we give to the two friends from Monomotapa (for La Fontaine, that man of genius, made shadowy, unreal abstractions of them). Add these two fresh names to all these examples, and you will be doing them justice, the more so because Wilhelm ate up his inheritance with Fritz's aid, just as Fritz had drunk down his own with Wilhelm's help; and of course they also puffed it away – in every known brand of tobacco.

These two friends, strange to say, squandered all their money in the Strasbourg beer-houses, in the most stupid and vulgar manner, in the company of ballet dancers from the Strasbourg theatre and Alsatian girls whose little brooms were worn down to the handle. And every morning they said to each other: 'We really must call a halt, settle down, do something with what we have left!'

'Oh well,' said Fritz, 'let's enjoy ourselves today. But tomorrow . . . certainly tomorrow . . .'

In the life of spendthrifts, today is an egregious fop, but tomorrow is an egregious poltroon, overawed by his predecessor's courage. Today is the *capitano* of old-fashioned comedy; tomorrow is the Pierrot in our pantomimes. When they had come down to their last thousand-franc piece, the two friends took seats on the stage-coach and so came to Paris, where they lodged in the attic of the Hôtel du Rhin, in the rue du Mail, as sub-tenants of Graff, who had once been Gideon Brunner's head-waiter. Fritz got a clerk's job at six hundred francs a year with a firm of bankers, the Keller brothers – on a recommendation from Graff, the well-known tailor's brother. The latter took Wilhelm on as bookkeeper. He provided the pair of prodigal sons with these two unremunerative posts in memory of his apprenticeship at the Grand Hôtel de Hollande. These two facts, a rich friend acknowledging a poor one, and a German hotel-keeper showing kindness to a couple of down-at-heel fellow-countrymen, will induce some people to believe that this story is fictitious. All facts look so much the more like fairy-stories because, in our time, fairy-stories take unconscionable pains to look like the truth.

Fritz, a clerk with six hundred francs a year, and Wilhelm, a book-keeper with the same wages, found out how hard life can be in so meretricious a city as Paris. And so, in 1837, when they had been there for a year, Wilhelm, who had a pretty talent for flute-playing, joined the orchestra conducted by Pons in order to be able now and then to spread a little butter on his bread. As for Fritz, he was only able to eke out his pay by developing the financial acumen inborn in a scion of the Virlaz stock. Yet, for all his perseverance, and perhaps because of his talent, the exile from Frankfurt only rose to two thousand francs by 1843. But that heaven-sent stepmother, Indigence, did for these two young men what their own mothers had not been able to do: she taught them thrift, the ways of the world and life; she put them through that hard and stringent course of education which she dispenses in the form of whippings to great men, all of whom have had an unhappy childhood. Fritz and Wilhelm were common enough types, and they were not attentive to all the lessons she gave them. They did their best to fend off her blows; they found that her bosom was stony and her arms scraggy; and they failed to identify her with that beneficient Fairy Bountiful who yields to the blandishments of men of genius. None the less, they came to realize the full value of my lady Fortune, and undertook to clip her wings if ever again she flitted past their door.

*

'Well, Papa Schmucke,' Wilhelm continued, after lengthily narrating this story to the pianist, in German, 'I can tell you the rest in a nutshell. Brunner senior is dead. Without his own son or Herr Graff, in whose house we live, knowing a word about it, he had been one of the promoters of railroads in Baden. He made enormous sums out of that, and his estate amounts to four millions! No more flute-playing for me after tonight; had this not been a first performance, I should have left several days ago, but I didn't want to leave a gap in the score.'

'Zat iss goot, younk man,' said Schmucke, 'put who iss it you marry?'

'The daughter of our host Herr Graff, who owns the Hôtel du Rhin. I have been in love with Fraülein Émilie for seven years, and she has read so many 'immoral' novels that for my sake she has refused every proposal of marriage, without knowing how things would turn out. This young lady is very rich, for she is the sole heiress of the Graff tailoring firm in the rue de Richelieu. Fritz is going to give me five times the amount we squandered together in Strasbourg – five hundred thousand francs! He is putting a million francs into a banking house, in which Herr Graff the tailor is also investing five hundred thousand francs. My fiancée's father is letting me use her marriage portion for the same purpose – two hundred and fifty thousand francs – and he is coming in for the same sum. So the house of Brunner, Schwab and Company will have a capital of two and a half million francs. Fritz has just bought fifteen hundred thousand francs' worth of shares in the Banque de France, as a backing for our account. And that does not include all Fritz's fortune: he still has his father's houses in Frankfurt, which are valued at a million, and he has already let the Grand Hôtel de Hollande to a cousin of the Graffs.'

'You look viz satness at your frient,' replied Schmucke, 'you are tchealous off him?'

'I'm not jealous of him, but *for* him – for his happiness. Is that the face of a contented man? I fear the effect Paris may have on him. I wish he would do what I am doing. The old Adam may revive in him. Of the two of us, he is by no means the more steady-minded. His clothes, his opera-glasses – all that worries me; he has eyes only for the loose women in the audience. If you only knew what a job it is to get Fritz married! The idea of paying court to a young lady appals him. He needs to be flung into family life, as the English fling criminals into eternity.'

During the commotion which marks the close of all first performances, the flautist invited the conductor to his wedding-party. Pons joyfully accepted. Schmucke then saw a smile dawn on his friend's face for the first time in months. He took him back to the rue de Normandie in profound silence, for Pons's elation showed him how deep-seated was the malady gnawing at his vitals. That so noble-hearted and unselfish a man, one of such great feeling, should be a prey to such weakness! This simply stupefied the stoical Schmucke, for he recognized that he would have to give up the pleasure of seeing his 'goot Pons' opposite him at table every day – for the greater happiness of Pons himself. He was not sure he could bring himself to this sacrifice: the thought of it drove him out of his wits.

*

The haughty silence maintained by Pons in his retreat on the Aventine Hill of the rue de Normandie had necessarily made its impression on the Présidente, though she lost no sleep for being delivered of her parasite. She and her charming daughter surmised that her little Lili's pleasantry had got home to her cousin. But her husband showed some concern. The stout little Président Camusot de Marville, whose judicial preferment had made him portentous, admired Cicero, liked the Comic Opera better than the Théâtre des Italiens, sorted out the merits of the various actors, and conformed slavishly to current tastes. He quoted all the articles of the Ministerial press as if he had written them himself, and when he pronounced an opinion, he paraphrased the ideas of the Councillor who had spoken before him. We know well enough the chief traits of this magistrate's character. His position obliged him to take a serious view of everything, and he laid great store by family ties. Like most husbands completely ruled by their wives, the Président made in trivial matters a show of independence which his wife respected. For a month or so, he accepted the Présidente's trite explanations of Pons's withdrawal, but in the end he found it curious that the old musician, a friend of forty years' standing, had ceased his visits, and particularly after bestowing so considerable a present as Madame de Pompadour's fan. Le Comte Popinot had recognized it as a masterpiece, and it brought the Présidente compliments which were exceedingly flattering to her vanity – even at the Tuileries Palace, where this toy was passed from hand to hand. Her attention was drawn to the lovely workmanship in its ten ivory radials, each one of them adorned with inconceivably exquisite carvings. A Russian lady (Russians always behave as if they were at home) offered the Présidente, in the Comte Popinot's house, six thousand francs for this amazing fan. It amused her to think that it had fallen into such hands, for admittedly it was fit for a duchess.

'There's no denying,' said Cécile to her father the day after this offer was made, 'that poor Cousin Pons is very knowing about such silly trifles.'

'Such silly trifles!' the Président exclaimed. 'Why, the State is about to pay a hundred thousand francs for the late Councillor Dusommerard's collection and to go halves with the City of Paris in spending nearly a million on the purchase and repair of the Hôtel de Cluny for the housing of such "silly trifles". Such "silly trifles", my dear child, are often the only relics we have of vanished civilizations. An Etruscan jar, a necklace, sometimes worth forty or fifty thousand francs respectively, are "silly trifles" which reveal the perfection that had been reached by the arts at the time of the siege of Troy, and prove that the Etruscans were Trojans who had taken refuge in Italy!'

This was the kind of humour the Président favoured; he liked to be heavily ironical at his wife's and daughter's expense.

'The sum total of knowledge required for assessing these "silly trifles", Cécile,' he continued, 'is the science known as archaeology. Archaeology comprises architecture, sculpture, painting, the goldsmith's craft, ceramics, cabinet-making (a completely modern art), lace-making, tapestry; in short all the products of human workmanship.'

'So Cousin Pons is a learned man?' said Cécile.

'By the way, why do we never see him here these days?' asked the Président, in the tone of a man who is worried by a host of little facts, taken in but forgotten for a time, which suddenly, to borrow a sportsman's phrase, 'bunch up' into a solid bullet.

'He must have taken offence at some supposed slight,' answered the Présidente. 'Perhaps I didn't make enough fuss when he gave me the fan. As you know, I'm not very up in art ...'

'You, one of Servin's most promising pupils!' the Président exclaimed, 'you don't know Watteau?'

'I know David, Gérard, Gros and Girodet, and Guérin, and Monsieur de Forbin, and Monsieur Turpin de Crissé . . .'

'You ought to have . . .'

'What ought I to have done, Monsieur?' asked the Présidente with a Queen of Sheba look.

'You ought to have known about Watteau, my dear. He's in great favour today,' replied the Président with a meekness which showed he was duly aware of all he owed to his wife.

This conversation had taken place a few days before the first performance of *The Devil's Betrothed*, when the whole orchestra had been struck by Pons's sickly appearance. But by then the people accustomed to having Pons at their table and using him as an errand boy had all begun to inquire about him, and in the circles in which the old man moved disquiet had spread, all the more serious because people had taken stock of him at his conductor's stand. Despite the care with which Pons, while taking his walks, avoided any of his former acquaintances whom he might see in the offing, he nevertheless came face to face one day with the former Minister, the Comte Popinot, in the shop kept by Monistrol, a well-known and enterprising dealer in the newly constructed Boulevard Beaumarchais: a man Pons had mentioned to the Présidente not long before, a man whose wily enthusiasm sends up the price of curios every day – they are getting so scarce, it is said, that one can no longer lay hands on them.

'My dear Pons, why don't we ever see you these days? We miss you very much, and Madame Popinot is wondering why you have deserted us.'

'Monsieur le Comte,' the old fellow replied, 'I have been led to realize in one of the houses I visit – a kinsman's – that people of my age are out of place in society. I never did get much of a welcome there, but at any rate I hadn't yet been insulted . . . I have never asked for anything,' he said, with all the pride of an artist. 'In return for a few civilities, I often made myself useful to my hosts. But it seems I was mistaken; I had to be at everybody's beck and call to pay for the honour of dining with friends and relatives . . . Well, I have resigned from my post as hanger-on. In my flat, I can find every day what I have been offered at no one's table – a real friend.'

These words, uttered with all the bitterness that the old artist was still capable of conveying by tone and gesture, so impressed the Peer of France that he drew the worthy musician to one side.

'Oh, come, old friend. What's the matter? Can't you tell me in confidence what has hurt your feelings? You won't mind my saying that in my house we have always treated you with consideration.'

'You are the only exception,' said the old man. 'Besides, you are an important person, a statesman, and your many duties would be an excuse for everything, if excuse were needed.'

In the end, under the influence of that diplomatic tact which Popinot had acquired in the handling of men and affairs, Pons told his tale of woe in regard to the Marville household. Popinot felt so keenly for the victim of such ill-treatment that he went home immediately and told Madame Popinot all about it. This excellent and worthy woman made representations to the Présidente as soon as she met her. The ex-Minister for his part said a few words on the subject to the Président. Then the Camusots de Marville had it out together in a family session. Although Camusot was by no means master in his own house, his remonstrances were too well founded *de jure* and *de fatto* for his wife and daughter not to acknowledge their pertinence. Both of them ate humble pie and blamed the servants. The latter were summoned and brow-beaten, and only obtained forgiveness by making a full avowal which clearly showed the Président how right Pons had been in keeping away. Like all lords and masters under their wives' thumb, the Président marshalled all his marital and magisterial majesty, declaring to his servants that they would be dismissed, and would thus lose all the benefits which their long service with him might entail, if henceforth his cousin Pons and all others who did him the honour of visiting him were not treated with the same respect as himself. This remark drew a smirk from Madeleine.

'You have indeed,' said the Président, 'only one chance to save yourselves. You must apologize and make your peace with him. You will go and tell him that your remaining here depends entirely on him. I will turn you all out if he does not forgive you.'

84

9. Pons brings the Présidente something better than a fan

THE next day, the Président set out fairly early in order to pay his cousin a visit before his legal sessions began. The arrival of Monsieur le Président de Marville, announced by Madame Cibot, was quite an event. Never in his life had Pons received such an honour, and he sensed that amends were forthcoming.

'My dear cousin,' said the Président, after the usual exchange of civilities, 'I now know the reason for your withdrawal. Your conduct increases, if that were possible, my esteem for you. I will just say one word about all this. My servants are under notice. My wife and daughter are in despair. They are anxious to see you to explain their behaviour. In this affair, cousin, one person is blameless – an old judge. Do not punish me then for the escapade of a silly girl who was intent on dining with the Popinots, above all since I have come to make our peace with you, acknowledging that we are entirely in the wrong. A friendship of thirty-six years' standing, even if it has been impaired, has still some claims. Come now, make peace with us by coming to dine with us this evening.'

Pons stammered out a wordy reply and ended by telling his cousin that he was booked that evening for the engagement party of a member of his orchestra who was throwing up his duties as flautist in order to take up banking.

'Very well, come tomorrow evening.'

'My cousin la Comtesse Popinot has honoured me with an extremely amiable written invitation.'

'The day after tomorrow then,' the Président went on.

'The day after tomorrow my chief flautist's partner, a German by the name of Brunner, will be returning the hospitality he is receiving today from the engaged couple.'

'Your company is certainly agreeable enough for people to compete for the pleasure of having you,' said the Président. 'Very well, next Sunday, eight days from this instant, as the lawyers say!'

'That day we are dining with Monsieur Graff, the flautist's prospective father-in-law.'

'Very well, make it Saturday. Between now and then there will be time for you to calm down a little girl who has already shed many tears over her bad behaviour. Our Lord asks only for repentance. Would you be sterner than our eternal Father with my poor little Cécile?'

This touched Pons's softer feelings, and he took refuge in over-polite phrases before seeing the Président out. An hour later, the Président's domestic staff arrived at his flat. They were like all servants, cowardly and glib. They wept! Madeleine took Pons aside and was resolutely abject.

'It's all my fault, but you know how fond I am of you,' she said, bursting into tears. 'You must put this unhappy incident down to the vengefulness which was raging inside me. *We shall lose our pensions!* . . . Monsieur Pons, I was out of my senses, and I should not like my fellow-servants to suffer for my folly. I can see now that I was not destined to belong to you. I have argued it out with myself. I had got above myself. But I am still fond of you, Monsieur Pons. For ten years I have thought of nothing but the happiness of making you happy and looking after everything here. It was a lovely prospect for me! Oh, if only you knew how much I care for you! But you must have guessed that from my spiteful deeds. If I were to die tomorrow, what would they find among my belongings? A will in your favour, Monsieur Pons . . . yes, Monsieur, in my trunk, underneath my jewellery.'

By twanging on this chord, Madeleine brought the old bachelor to that pleasurable self-complacency which is always evoked by the idea of having inspired a passion, even an unwelcome one. After generously absolving Madeleine, he showed mercy to everyone else by promising to persuade his cousin the Présidente to keep all her servants on. It afforded unspeakable pleasure to Pons to see himself reinstated in all his wonted enjoyments without having demeaned himself. Society had made advances to him, and this was a sop to his personal dignity; but when he disclosed his triumph to his friend Schmucke he was sorry to see him saddened and full of unspoken doubts. Nevertheless, noting the sudden change in Pons's physiognomy, the kindly German shared his joy and decided to forgo the happiness he had derived from having his friend entirely to himself for nearly four months. As for Pons – mental ills have a tremendous advantage over physical ones in that, having been caused by the thwarting of a desire, they are instantaneously cured once that desire is fulfilled – on that happy morning, Pons was transfigured. The gloomy, moribund old man gave way to the self-satisfied Pons who not so long before had carried the Marquise de Pompadour's fan to the Présidente. But Schmucke fell to pondering deeply over this phenomenon which he failed to understand, for real stoicism will never fathom the why and wherefore of French sycophancy. Pons was a true Frenchman of the Empire period, a compound of eighteenth-century courtesy and that devoted respect for woman of which ballads like *Partant pour la Syrie* make so much. Schmucke buried his disappointment deep in his heart and strewed it with the flowers of his Teutonic philosophy; but in a week his face turned sallow, and Madame Cibot had to use guile to call in the local doctor. The latter diagnosed a possible *icterus*, and Madame Cibot was flabbergasted by this learned synonym for common or garden jaundice!

It was probably the first time that the two friends had dined out together, but for Schmucke it was like taking a trip back to Germany. In fact Johann Graff, the proprietor of the Hôtel du Rhin, his daughter Émilie, the tailor Wolfgang Graff and his wife, Fritz Brunner and Wilhelm Schwab were all Teutons. Pons and the notary were the only Frenchmen admitted to the banquet. The tailor and his wife, who owned a splendid mansion in the rue de Richelieu, between the rue Neuve des Petits Champs and the rue Villedo, had brought up their niece themselves, for her father had – not unreasonably – wished to shelter her from contact with the varied types of people who come and go in hotels. This worthy couple, who loved the child as if she had been their own daughter, were allotting the ground floor of their house to the bridal pair. There also the banking house of Brunner, Schwab and Company was to be installed. And since these arrangements had been made about a month before, in order to allow time for Brunner, the author of all this felicity, to collect his heritage, the well-known tailor had had the happy

87

pair's flat richly decorated and furnished. The banking house offices had been fitted out in the wing which linked a magnificent block of rented flats to the former town house between the courtyard and the garden.

*

As they made their way to the rue de Richelieu, Pons obtained from Schmucke (whose mind was on other things) the detailed story of the modern Prodigal Son in whose interests death had killed the fatted calf, namely the innkeeper. Pons, now reconciled with his nearest relations, was instantly seized with the desire to make a match between Fritz Brunner and Cécile de Marville. By a stroke of chance, the notary employed by the brothers Graff turned out to be the son-in-law and successor of Cardot, who had once been assistant head clerk in the latter's office. Pons had often dined at his house.

'How good to see you, Monsieur Berthier,' said the old musician, offering his hand to his former amphitryon.

'How is it that you no longer give us the pleasure of dining with us?' asked the notary. 'My wife has been anxious about you. We saw you at the opening performance of *The Devil's Betrothed*, and our anxiety made us inquisitive.'

'Old men are touchy,' Pons replied. 'They make the mistake of being a century behind the times. But how can they help that? They have quite enough to do to represent their own century – they can't belong as well to the one which is only awaiting their demise.'

'True,' said the notary, with a subtle air, 'one can't cope with two centuries at one and the same time.'

'Tell me,' said the old fellow, drawing the young notary into a corner, 'why don't you get my cousin Cécile de Marville married?'

'Why not indeed?' the notary replied. 'In this century, now that luxury has made its way even into the lodges of concierges, young men think twice about joining their lot with that of the daughter of a presiding judge in the Royal Court of Paris, when her dowry only amounts to a hundred thousand francs. In the social class to which Mademoiselle de Marville's husband will belong, the woman who will cost her husband only three thousand francs a year has yet to be found. The interest on such a dowry could scarcely pay for the future wife's cosmetics. A bachelor with an income of fifteen to twenty thousand francs can live in a cosy mezzanine. Society doesn't expect him to spread himself. He can manage on one servant and devote all his money to his enjoyments. The only appearances he has to keep up are his tailor's concern. He has all the match-making mammas bustling around, and he lords it over the fashionable world of Paris. On the other hand, a wife demands a well-furnished house; she commandeers the carriage when she goes to the theatre; she expects a box, whereas a bachelor only has a single seat to pay for. In a word, she becomes the show-piece and she herself spends the money which, as a bachelor, the man had to himself. Suppose a couple have thirty thousand francs to live on: in our present society, the rich bachelor has become a needy fellow who has to consider even the cost of going to the races. And when children come, they are hard-up. Since Monsieur and Madame de Marville are only in their early fifties, "expectations" have to be postponed for fifteen or twenty years. No bachelor is inclined to make such long-term investments, and arithmetical calculations are such a canker in the hearts of these irresponsible young men who dance the polka with easy-going girls in the popular ballrooms that all eligible young males study both sides of the question without needing to consult us lawyers. Confidentially, Mademoiselle de Marville leaves her suitors so emotionally undisturbed that they are able to think the matter out and take all these anti-connubial considerations into account. If some young man, in his right mind and enjoying an income of twenty thousand francs, is thinking *in petto* of some marriage project which will meet his ambitions, Mademoiselle de Marville is not the answer to his prayer.'

'But why not?' asked the bewildered musician.

'Just because almost all bachelors, even if they are as ugly as you and myself, my dear Pons, have the impertinence to demand a dowry of six hundred thousand francs and girls of good family, beautiful to look at, very intelligent, very well brought-up, with no blemishes: in short, perfect.'

'So my cousin will find it difficult to get a husband?'

'She will remain a spinster until her parents decide to settle

Marville on her as a marriage portion. If they had been willing to do that, she would already be Madame la Vicomtesse Popinot ... But here comes Monsieur Brunner. I am going to read out the Articles of Association for the Brunner firm, and then the marriage contract.'

Once the introductions were made and compliments exchanged, Pons was asked by the relations to witness the contract. He listened while the deeds were read out; and after that, at about five-thirty, they went through into the dining-room. The dinner was one of those sumptuous repasts which business people provide when they take time off from business. It also bore witness to the close contact existing between the hotel proprietor and the most expensive caterers of Paris. Never had Pons and Schmucke partaken of such fare. There were dishes to send you into raptures: such delicious vermicelli as had never been tasted before: fried smelts which dissolved in the mouth: a *ferra* from Geneva in a real Genevese dressing: and a sauce for plum-pudding which would have astonished the London doctor who is said to have invented it. They rose from table at ten o'clock in the evening. The variety of Rhenish and French wines they had drunk would have amazed our native dandies, for no one can conceive how much liquid a German can absorb while remaining calm and peaceful. You must dine in Germany to see bottle succeeding bottle as wave succeeds wave on a beautiful Mediterranean shore, and vanishing as if Germans were as absorbent as sponges or stretches of sand. But harmony reigns: there is no French rowdiness, and conversation remains as smooth as a moneylender's patter: faces become flushed by imperceptible degrees, like those of betrothed damsels in the frescoes of Cornelius or Schnor. Reminiscences pour leisurely forth like the smoke from tobacco pipes.

At about ten-thirty, Pons and Schmucke were sitting on a bench in the garden, with the ex-flautist between them, and they had come round, they scarcely knew how, to the mutual revelation of their characters, opinions and misfortunes. While this hotch-potch of confidential communications went on, Wilhelm spoke with vinous energy and eloquence of his desire to see Fritz married.

'What do you think of this idea for your friend Brunner?'

said Pons, turning to Wilhelm: 'a charming young person, reasonable, twenty-four, belonging to a highly distinguished family. The father holds one of the most eminent magisterial posts. She will have a dowry of a hundred thousand francs and expectations of a million.'

'Wait a bit!' answered Schwab, 'I'm going to put it to Fritz this very minute.'

And the two musicians saw Brunner and his friend circle round the garden, pacing to and fro in front of them, listening to each other in turn. Pons was a trifle bemused. He was not quite intoxicated, but the ideas which passed through his brain were as light as the skull which contained them was heavy. He gazed at Fritz Brunner through the diaphanous mist which wine engenders, and tried to detect in his facial expression some aspiration to family bliss. Not long after, Schwab introduced his friend and associate to Monsieur Pons, and Fritz thanked the old man for deigning to take such trouble on his behalf. A conversation ensued: the two bachelors, Schmucke and Pons, sang the praises of married life and, without any malicious intent, hazarded the pun that 'marriage was the end of man'. When ices, tea, punch and cakes were served in the flat destined for the engaged couple, hilarity reached a climax among these respectable businessmen – almost all of them drunk – when they learned that the sleeping partner of the banking house was thinking of following his working partner's example.

At two in the morning, Schmucke and Pons made their way home along the boulevards, lost in philosophical divagations about the harmonious disposition of events on this earth.

*

The next day Pons went to visit his cousin the Présidente, full of joy at the thought of returning good for evil. Poor, dear, candid soul! Sublime magnanimity, as each one of us will agree, for do we not live in the century of the Montyon Prize, awarded to those who do their duty, although they are only following the precepts of the Gospel?

'Oh, they will be tremendously obliged to their hanger-on!' he told himself as he turned into the rue de Choiseul.

Any man less wrapped up in self-satisfaction, any man of the world, any wary man would have kept an observant eye on the Présidente and her daughter on re-visiting their home. But this poor musician was a child, a simple-minded artist, with as much faith in moral goodness as he had in artistic beauty. He was delighted at the fuss that Cécile and the Présidente made of him. Poor simpleton! For twelve years he had been watching vaude-villes, comedies and dramas. He should have had no illusions about the play-acting which goes on in social life: yet he could not recognize humbug when he saw it. Those who frequent polite circles in Paris and have realized how desiccated in body and soul the Présidente was, how avid for worldly honours, how exasperated at having kept her virtue, how hypocritical in religion, how arrogant in character, accustomed as she was to ruling the roost in her house, can imagine what secret hatred she bore her cousin after putting herself in the wrong. Any show of friendliness therefore on the part of the Présidente and her daughter concealed a formidable craving for vengeance, clearly only deferred. For the first time in her life, Amélie had been on the losing side in a conflict with a husband she usually dominated – and she had to simulate affection for the author of her defeat! There is nothing analagous to such a situation except certain hypocrisies which last for years in the Sacred College of Cardinals or the chapter-houses of abbots and priors. At three o'clock, just as the Président arrived home from the Courts, Pons had scarcely finished recounting the marvellous details of his meeting with Brunner, the previous night's ban-quet which had lasted till morning, and also everything to do with this same Frederick Brunner. Cécile had come straight to the point. She had inquired about Frederick's clothes, his height, his appearance, the colour of his hair and eyes, and after surmising that he looked quite distinguished, she expressed approval of his generosity.

'Fancy giving five hundred thousand francs to his com-panion in misfortune! Oh, Mamma, I shall have a carriage and a box at the *Italiens*!' And Cécile looked almost pretty at the thought that all her mother's ambitions for her were about to be fulfilled and that she would no longer have to go on hoping against hope.

As for the Présidente, she made just one remark: 'Dear little girl, we'll have you married in a fortnight.' – All mothers call their daughters 'little girl', even when they are twenty-three!

'All the same,' said the Présidente, 'we must have time to collect information. Never will I give away my daughter to a nobody.'

'As regards information,' the old artist replied, 'Berthier is in charge of the legal side. As for the young man, my dear cousin Amélie, you know what you told me. Well, he's over forty, and he's half bald. He's looking for family life as a haven of refuge, and I did not discourage him: it's a natural thing to want.'

'All the more reason for inspecting Monsieur Frederick Brunner,' retorted the Présidente. 'I don't want to give my daughter to a valetudinarian.'

'Well, cousin, you can take stock of my candidate, within five days if you like, for, in view of your requirements, one interview would be enough.'

Cécile and the Présidente made a gesture of delight.

'Frederick is quite a distinguished connoisseur, and he has asked me to let him inspect my little collection,' Cousin Pons replied. 'You have never seen my pictures or my antiques. Come along as ladies brought by my friend Schmucke. In that way you will make the acquaintance of the prospective bride-groom without committing yourselves, and Frederick needn't have any idea who you are.'

'Splendid!' cried the Présidente.

It may be guessed what attentions were lavished on the para-site, once so scorned. That day, the poor man was indeed the Présidente's cousin. The happy mother, submerging her hatred under a flood of joy, mustered kind glances, smiles and compli-ments which sent the old fellow into raptures because of the good he was doing and the future he saw looming ahead of him. Was he not sure of getting, in the homes of Brunner, Schwab and Graff, yet more dinners like the one he had had at the signing of the marriage-contract? He could look forward to a rosy existence – a wonderful succession of 'covered dishes', gastronomic surprises and exquisite wines!

'If our cousin Pons can help us to bring off this affair,' said the Président to his wife when Pons had gone, 'we must settle an income on him equivalent to his conductor's salary.'

'Certainly,' said the Présidente. And Cécile was commissioned – provided she approved of the young man – to persuade the old musician to accept this humiliating munificence.

Next morning, the Président, avid for authentic proof of Monsieur Frederick Brunner's affluence, went to see the notary. Forewarned by the Présidente, Berthier had summoned his new client, Schwab the banker and ex-flautist. Everyone knows what great respect is paid to social distinctions in Germany, where a woman is *Frau General, Frau Hofrat, Frau Advokat*; and dazzled at the prospect of his friend contracting such an alliance, Schwab was as smooth as a collector trying to outwit a dealer.

'What matters most is this,' said Cécile's father to Schwab: 'since I shall contract to hand over my Marville estate, I should want to make her a settlement in trust. Then Monsieur Brunner would invest a million in land in order to round off Marville. Thus a marriage-settlement would be constituted which would ensure my daughter's future, and that of her children, against the hazards of banking.'

Berthier stroked his chin and said to himself, 'The Président's getting on nicely!'

When Schwab had had the working of a settlement in trust explained to him, he came out strongly in his friend's favour. This provision would fulfil the desire to which he had heard Fritz give voice – that of finding some arrangement which would prevent him from ever again falling into penury.

'At this very moment twelve hundred thousand francs' worth of farms and grazing-land are being put up for sale,' said the Président.

'A million francs' worth of Bank of France shares will be enough,' said Schwab, 'to guarantee the solvency of our banking house. Fritz does not want to put more than two million francs into business. He will do what you ask, Président.'

When the Président told the two women this news, they were almost beside themselves with joy. Never had so rich a catch swum so obligingly into the matrimonial net.

'You will be Madame Brunner de Marville,' said the father to his daughter, 'for I shall obtain leave for your husband to add this name to his own; and later he will take out naturalization papers. If I am made a Peer of France, he will succeed me!'

The Présidente spent five days getting her daughter ready. On the day of the interview she dressed Cécile herself and rigged her out with her own two hands, taking as much care as the Admiral of the 'Blue Fleet' took to fit out Queen Victoria's pleasure yacht when she set off on her journey down the Rhine.

On their side, Pons and Schmucke cleaned and dusted Pons's museum, the flat and the furniture, with all the nimbleness of seamen making the Admiral's flagship spick and span. Not a speck of dust remained on the wood carvings. All the bronzes were refulgent. The glass frames of the pastels gave a clear view of the works of Latour, Greuze and Liautard, the illustrious painter of 'The Chocolate-Girl', a miraculous specimen of a pictorial art which, alas, was so ephemeral. The inimitable enamel of the Florentine bronzes was glistening. The stained-glass windows were resplendent with their exquisite tints. Every object had its own particular brilliance and its special theme to delight the soul in that concert of masterpieces organized by two musicians who were each of them poets in their own way.

10. A German whimsy

THE women were clever enough to avoid the embarrassment of making a formal entry; and so, in order to choose their ground, they were the first to arrive. Pons introduced Schmucke to his relations, to whom he seemed mentally deficient. They had no thought for anything but this fiancé with four millions, and, philistines as they were, they paid scant attention to Pons's exhibition of his treasures. They threw a casual glance at Petitot's enamels set out on a background of red velvet in three wonderful frames. The floral studies of Van Huysum and David van Heim, Abraham Mignon's insects, the canvases of Van Eyck and Albrecht Dürer, the genuine works of the elder Cranach, the Giorgione, the Sebastiano del Piombo, the Backuysen, the Hobbema, the Géricault – all the pick of rare paintings – nothing stirred their curiosity, for they were waiting for the solar deity who was to light up these riches. None the less, they were impressed by the loveliness of certain Etruscan jewels and the solid value of Pons's snuff-boxes. To humour him, they were handling and gushing over some Florentine bronzes when Madame Cibot ushered in Monsieur Brunner. They did not turn round, but made use of a splendid Venetian mirror, set in a massive carved ebony frame, in order to scrutinize this Phoenix among suitors.

Previously schooled by Wilhelm, Fritz had made the best he could of his few remaining hairs. He was wearing smart trousers of a soft, subdued shade, a supremely elegant waistcoat cut in the latest fashion, a shirt with drawn thread-work made of Frisian hand-woven linen, and a blue cravat with white pin-stripes. His watch-chain and the knob of his cane had been bought from Florent and Chanor. As for his coat, Graff himself had cut it from his finest cloth. His suede gloves betokened the extravagance of a man who had already squandered his mother's fortune. From the sheen on his polished boots the two women could have guessed he had come in the light open carriage-and-pair typical of a banker, even if they had not already heard it rumbling along the rue de Normandie.

When a banker of forty emerges after twenty years from the cocoon of a rake, he uses his eyes. Brunner's powers of observation were all the more keen in that he was well aware of the advantage a German can draw from a show of naïveté. That morning he wore the pensive air of a man faced with the alternative of taking to family life or continuing his bachelor dissipation. This cast of countenance, in a gallicized German, appeared superlatively romantic to Cécile. She looked upon this scion of Verlaz stock as a replica of Goethe's Werther. Is there any girl who does not make a little romance of her wedding preliminaries? Cécile regarded herself as the happiest of women when Brunner, at the sight of those magnificent antiques, the product of forty years' patient searching, waxed enthusiastic, and, to Pons's great satisfaction, was the first person to appreciate them at their true value.

'He's a real poet!' thought Mademoiselle de Marville. 'He thinks they are worth millions.' A poet is a man who doesn't haggle over expense, leaves his wife to look after the capital, can be easily led and kept amused with trifles.

Every pane in the two windows of Pons's room was of Swiss stained glass. Each one of them was worth a thousand francs, and he possessed sixteen of these masterpieces, for which in our days connoisseurs seek far and wide. In 1815 these panes had cost from six to ten francs. As for the sixty pictures in this superb collection – all of them masterpieces, all genuine, not one of them touched up – only the heated atmosphere of an auction room could reveal what they were worth. Each picture was girt with a resplendent frame of untold value, and every style was represented: Venetian frames with the elaborate ornamentation of present-day English plate; Roman frames remarkable for what artists call *flafla*; Spanish frames with their audacious scroll-work; Flemish and German frames with their naïve-looking figures, shell-work frames inlaid with pewter, copper, mother-of-pearl and ivory; ebony frames; boxwood frames; frames in all the styles from Louis XIII to Louis XVI; in short, a unique collection of all the finest examples. Pons, luckier in this than the curators of the Dresden and

Vienna museums, had in his collection a frame by the famous Brustolone, the Michelangelo of wood-carving.

Naturally, Madame de Marville had to have each fresh curio explained to her. She sought initiation in the understanding of these marvels from Brunner. She uttered such naïve exclamations and seemed so delighted for Frederick to tell her the value and beauty of this or that painting, sculpture or bronze that the German thawed completely; his face became youthful again. In the end, both parties went farther than they intended in this first encounter, which was still, in theory, only a chance meeting.

The viewing lasted three hours. Brunner offered a hand to Cécile to help her downstairs. As she went down each step with decorous slowness, Cécile, still talking art, expressed astonishment at her prospective fiancé's admiration of Pons's knick-knacks.

'So you think that everything we have been looking at is worth a lot of money?'

'Indeed, Mademoiselle, if your respected cousin would sell me his collection, I would give him eight hundred thousand francs for it this very evening, and I should be doing very well. The sixty canvases alone would reach a higher sum in a public sale.'

'I believe it if you say so,' she replied; 'and it must be true, for that is what has monopolized your attention.'

'Oh, Mademoiselle!' exclaimed Brunner, 'my sole answer to that reproach is this: I am going to ask your lady mother for permission to come to your house, just for the happiness of seeing you again.'

'Isn't my little girl clever!' thought the Présidente, following hard on her daughter's heels.

'That will give us great pleasure, sir,' she replied out loud. 'I hope you will come at dinner-time with our cousin Pons. My husband will be delighted to make your acquaintance ... Thank you, cousin.'

She gave such an expressive squeeze to Pons's arm that the sacramental phrase 'We are friends for life' could not have said more. And the melting glance she cast at Pons as she said: 'Thank you, cousin' was as good as an embrace.

After seeing the young lady into her carriage, and after the hired brougham had disappeared into the rue Charlot, Brunner discussed bric-à-brac with Pons, but the latter talked only of matrimony.

'So you don't see any obstacle?' said Pons.

'I don't know,' replied Brunner. 'The girl is nothing to get excited about, and the mother's a bit prim. We'll see.'

'A fine fortune in prospect,' remarked Pons. 'More than a million . . .'

'We shall meet on Monday,' interjected the millionaire, 'and if you would like to sell your collection of pictures, I wouldn't mind giving you five or six hundred thousand francs for them.'

'Oh,' said the good Pons, surprised to learn how rich he was, 'I could never part with the things which bring me happiness. I would only sell my collection for delivery after my death.'

'Well, we shall see . . .'

'That sets two transactions going,' said the collector; but his mind was on the marriage project. Brunner took his leave of Pons and rattled off in his splendid turnout. Pons watched the little brougham speeding away without noticing Rémonencq, who was smoking his pipe on the doorstep.

*

That very evening the Présidente went to talk over the matter with her father-in-law, and she found the Popinot family there. In her desire to satisfy a little grudge – very natural in a mother who had previously failed to capture a son and heir – Madame de Marville hinted that Cécile was making a splendid match. 'Who's the happy man?' – this question was on everybody's lips. Then, thinking she was letting nothing out of the bag, the Présidente gave so many hints and half-revelations – which moreover Madame Berthier confirmed – that the following remarks were made next day in that middle-class Elysium in which Pons used to perform his gastronomical exercises:

'Cécile de Marville is going to marry a young German setting up as a banker out of sheer disinterestedness, for he has a capital of four millions. He's a hero straight out of a novel, a real Werther, charming, good-hearted, with all his wild oats sown. He has fallen madly in love with Cécile. Love at first

99

sight! And that is certain, because Cécile had to compete with all the painted Madonnas in Pons's collection', etc., etc.

Two days later, a few persons came to congratulate the Présidente – but in fact to find out whether the goose with the golden eggs really existed. The Présidente played wonderful variations on the following theme (mothers might find them useful, as in former days we found *The Model Secretary* useful): 'A marriage is only concluded,' she said to Mme Chiffreville, 'when one leaves the registry-office and the church; and as yet we are only at the interview stage. So I rely on your friendship not to tell anyone of our hopes.'

'You are very lucky, Madame la Présidente. Marriages are difficult to arrange nowadays.'

'Well, after all, it's a matter of luck. Marriages are often made in this way.'

'So you are getting Cécile married after all?' asked Madame Cardot.

'Yes,' answered the Présidente, well aware of the spite behind the words 'after all'. 'We were rather particular, and that is what delayed us in getting Cécile settled. But we have found what we wanted: plenty of money, a personable man, amiable and easy to get on with. And my little darling deserves it. Monsieur Brunner is a charming and distinguished bachelor. He likes the very best things. He knows the ways of the world. He is infatuated with Cécile – really in love with her. And, in spite of the three or four millions he possesses, Cécile is willing to take him . . . We were not aiming so high, but why boggle at such advantages? . . . It's not the money, but the affection my daughter has inspired that decides us,' said the Présidente to Madame Lebas. 'Monsieur Brunner is in such a hurry that he wants to be married as soon as the law permits.'

'Isn't he a foreigner?'

'Yes, Madame, but I confess I am very happy. Monsieur Brunner is a man of charmingly delicate feeling. I shall be gaining, not a son-in-law, but a son. You can scarcely imagine how eager he is to marry on a trust settlement basis – such a safeguard for prospective families! He is buying twelve hundred thousand francs' worth of pasture-land which will one day be added to Marville.'

The next day there were similar variations on the same theme. For instance, Monsieur Brunner became a man of great distinction, doing everything in a most distinguished manner. Money did not matter with him, and if Monsieur de Marville could arrange for him to take out naturalization papers (after all, the Ministry of Justice owed the magistrate this little concession), his son-in-law could be made a Peer of France. By now the Brunner fortune was beyond calculation: he sported the finest horses and the finest carriages in Paris. And so forth.

The pleasure the Camusots took in broadcasting their expectations bore witness to the unexpectedness of their triumph.

Immediately after the interview at Pons's flat, Monsieur de Marville, prompted by his wife, persuaded the Minister of Justice, his Chief Justice and the Attorney-General to dine with him on the day when this phoenix of sons-in-law was to make his appearance. All three of these important persons accepted, even though invited at such short notice. Each one of them was aware of the role the paterfamilias expected them to play, and they came to his help with pleasure. In France, succour is very willingly given to mothers who are trying to net a rich son-in-law. The Comte and Comtesse Popinot also lent themselves to the impressiveness of the occasion, although they thought that the invitation was in bad taste. There was a total of eleven guests. Cécile's grandfather, Camusot senior, and his wife, were bound to attend this gathering, since its purpose was, through the prestige of the guests, to get Monsieur Brunner definitely committed. As we have seen, he was cried up as one of the richest German capitalists, a man of taste (he was in love with the 'little girl'), and a rival to-be of such bankers as Nucingen, the Keller brothers, du Tillet, etc.

'This is our at-home day,' said the Présidente with studied simplicity as she introduced her other guests to the man she already regarded as her son-in-law. 'Just an intimate little gathering. First of all, my husband's father who, as you know, is to be promoted to the peerage. Also Monsieur le Comte and Madame la Comtesse Popinot – their son was not in a sufficiently wealthy position to marry Cécile, but none the less we are good friends. Our Minister of Justice, our Chief Justice, and our Attorney-General. In short, only our friends. We shall have to dine rather late because my husband never leaves the Court before six o'clock.'

Brunner gave Pons a meaning look, and Pons rubbed his hands as if to say: 'You see what our friends, my friends, are like!'

With feminine skill the Présidente thought of something to say in private to her cousin, so as to leave Cécile alone with her Werther. Cécile chatted away volubly, and managed to draw Frederick's attention to a German dictionary, a German grammar, and a copy of Goethe which she pretended to be hiding.

'Ah, you are learning German?' cried Brunner, colouring up.

Only Frenchwomen know how to lay this kind of trap. 'Oh,' she replied, 'how unkind you are! . . . It isn't nice of you to be so curious about my secret belongings. I want to read Goethe in the original, and have been learning German for two years.'

'Then this grammar-book must be very difficult to follow,' was Brunner's ingenuous remark, 'for there are not more than ten pages cut.'

Cécile was embarrassed, and she turned her head away to hide her discomfiture. But a German finds it hard to resist such proofs of the interest he inspires, and he took Cécile's hand, turned her round to face him again, and gazed at the bashful girl like a fiancé in a novel by that chaste writer, the late Auguste Lafontaine.

'You are adorable!' he exclaimed.

Cécile tossed her head roguishly as if to say: 'But what about you? Who could help liking you?'

'Mamma, we are getting on fine!' she whispered in her mother's ear, as the latter came back with Pons.

The atmosphere reigning in a family on such an evening baffles description. Everyone was happy to see a mother fastening her hooks into an eligible son-in-law. Congratulations – cryptic or elliptic – were proffered, both to Brunner who pretended not to understand, to Cécile who understood only too well, and to the Présidente, who was on the look-out for compliments. The blood tingled in Pons's ears, and all the gas-jets in the footlights of his theatre seemed to be flaring up before his eyes when Cécile told him in a whisper, and with the most ingenious tactfulness, of her father's intention to settle a life income of twelve hundred francs per annum on him. The old man was firm in his refusal, basing it on the information Brunner had given him about the high value of his furniture.

The Minister, the Chief Justice, the Attorney-General, the Popinots and all their guests with business to attend to went off. There soon remained only Monsieur Camusot senior and Cardot, the retired notary, with his son-in-law Berthier. The worthy Pons, now that the family was left to itself, gave clumsy thanks to the Président and his wife for the offer Cécile had just made to him. Simple-hearted people are just like that: they do not stop to think things out. Brunner interpreted the income thus offered as being a sort of payment for services rendered: his Hebrew instincts were aroused, and he assumed an attitude indicative of the more than frosty withdrawal of a man counting his gold.

'My collection or the price it fetches will always belong to your family, whether I do a deal with our friend Brunner or whether I keep it,' said Pons, as he informed the astonished family that he had such valuable assets.

Brunner noticed the flutter of approval that passed through all these philistines in favour of a man passing from a state of presumed indigence to one of wealth. He had already noticed how completely Cécile, the idol of the household, was spoiled by her father and mother, and thereupon he took pleasure in rousing these respectable *bourgeois* to exclamations of surprise.

'I told Mademoiselle Cécile that Monsieur Pons's pictures were worth that sum to me. But judging by the value which rare objects of art have acquired, no one could foretell the price this collection would reach at a public sale. The sixty pictures alone would fetch a million – several of them are worth fifty thousand francs each.'

'Your heir will be a lucky person,' said the notary to Pons.

'I shall leave everything to my cousin Cécile,' the old fellow replied, still emphasizing the family tie.

There was a general stir of admiration for the old musician.

'She will be a very rich heiress,' said Cardot as he smilingly took his departure.

The gathering was thus reduced to Camusot senior, the Président and his wife, Cécile, Brunner, Berthier and Pons, for everyone supposed that a formal demand for Cécile's hand was about to be made. It turned out that, as soon as these persons were alone together, Brunner asked a question which struck the parents as a promising beginning: 'Am I right in believing,' asked Brunner, addressing the Présidente, 'that Mademoiselle is an only child?'

'Certainly,' the Présidente proudly replied.

'There will be no rival to stand in your way,' added the good Pons, in an endeavour to bring Brunner to the point.

Brunner's face clouded over, and an ominous silence brought a strange chill to the atmosphere. One would have thought that the Présidente had confessed that her 'little girl' was an epileptic. The Président, judging that his daughter had better not stay, made Cécile a sign which she understood: she left the room. Brunner remained mute. They all scrutinized one another. The situation became embarrassing. The elder Camusot, a man of experience, led the German into the Présidente's bedroom under the pretext of showing him the fan which Pons had discovered, for he guessed that some difficulty was arising. He gave a silent hint to his son, his daughter-in-law and Pons to leave him alone with the bridegroom-elect.

'Here is the masterpiece,' said the old silk-mercer as he handed over the fan.

'It's worth five thousand francs,' replied Brunner after looking it over.

'Did you not come here, Monsieur,' asked the future Peer of France, 'to ask for my grand-daughter's hand in marriage?'

'Yes, Monsieur,' said Brunner, 'and I beg you to believe that no match could be more gratifying to me. I shall never find a more beautiful young lady, one more amiable and more suitable than Mademoiselle Cécile. But . . .'

'Ah, no "buts", please,' said Camusot senior, 'or at any rate tell us straight away how you translate these "buts", my dear sir.'

'Monsieur,' continued Brunner gravely, 'I am very glad that no engagements have been undertaken on either side, for the fact of her being an only child, which everyone but myself values so much – believe me, I was quite ignorant of it – is an absolute impediment . . .'

'What, Monsieur,' cried the old man in stupefaction, 'you regard a tremendous advantage as a disqualification? This is an extraordinary line to take, and I should like to have your reasons.'

'Monsieur,' the German went on, unperturbed, 'I came this evening intending to ask the Président for his daughter's hand. I wanted to guarantee Mademoiselle Cécile a brilliant future by offering her all she would have consented to accept of my fortune. But an only daughter is a child whom her parents' indulgence accustoms to doing as she pleases and whose will has never been crossed. What goes on here is the same as in several families in which, some time ago, I was able to take note of the worship that is paid to these heavenly creatures: not only is your grand-daughter the idol of the household, but also Madame la Présidente wears the . . . you know what I mean! Monsieur, I saw my father's home turned into an inferno for this very reason. My stepmother, the cause of all my misfortunes, an only daughter, an object of worship, the most charming of fiancées, became a fiend incarnate. I don't doubt that Mademoiselle Cécile would prove an exception to the rule. But at forty I am no longer a young man, and the difference of age between us involves difficulties which would prevent me from giving happiness to a young person who is used to seeing the Présidente doing everything she wants and listening to her as if she were an oracle. What right have I to demand a change in Mademoiselle Cécile's ideas and habits? Instead of having a father and mother ready to satisfy her slightest whims, she would be up against the selfish habits of a man of forty. If she stood firm, the man of forty would have to give way. And so I act as a gentleman would act, and withdraw. Moreover, I wish to take the entire blame on myself, if by chance it becomes necessary to explain why I made only one visit here.'

'If those are your motives, Monsieur,' said the future Peer of France, 'however singular they may be, they are not implausible . . .'

'Monsieur, do not doubt my sincerity,' continued Brunner, interrupting him heatedly, 'for if you can name a penniless girl from a large family, who has been well brought up but has no money of her own, as is frequent with French girls, provided that her character can stand surety for her, I will marry her.'

During the silence which followed this declaration, Frederick Brunner left Cécile's grandfather, returned to the drawing-room to take polite leave of the Président and of his wife, and withdrew. Cécile, a silent observer of her Werther's mode of departure, was deathly pale: she had been hiding in her mother's dressing-room, and had overheard everything.

'Rejected!' she whispered to her mother.

'But for what reason?' the Présidente asked her embarrassed father-in-law.

'For the ingenuous reason that an only daughter is a spoilt child,' the old man answered. 'And he's not entirely wrong in this case,' he added, seizing on the opportunity to blame his daughter-in-law, who had been causing him much annoyance for twenty years.

'This will be the death of my daughter, and *you* will have killed her,' said the Présidente to Pons, holding her daughter up, for Cécile thought it becoming to justify this assertion by drooping into her mother's arms.

The Président and his wife dragged her to an armchair, and there she completed her faint. Her grandfather rang for the servants.

11. Pons under a landslide of gravel

'I CAN see through the plot this person has hatched,' said the outraged mother, pointing to Pons.

Pons started up as if the trumpet blast of Judgement Day had sounded in his ears.

The Présidente's eyes were like twin pools of green bile. 'Monsieur,' she continued, 'you decided to do us a wrong in return for an innocent jest. Can anyone believe that this German is in his right mind? Either he is your accomplice in an atrocious act of vengeance, or he is a lunatic. I hope, Monsieur Pons, that in future you will spare us the displeasure of seeing you in a house on which you have tried to bring shame and dishonour.'

Pons stood there like a statue, stared down at a rose-pattern in the carpet, and twiddled his thumbs.

'What! You are still here, ungrateful monster,' cried the Présidente, turning round. She pointed to Pons and told the servants: 'Neither my husband nor myself will be at home, if ever this gentleman calls again ... Jean, go and fetch the doctor ... And you, Madeleine, get some smelling-salts.'

The Présidente considered that the reasons put forward by Brunner were only a cover for others he had not divulged; but that only made the breaking-off of the marriage more definite. With a swiftness of thought typical of women in critical situations, Madame de Marville had seized on the only means for countering this rebuff. Holding fast to her hatred for Pons, she had converted a mere feminine suspicion into a fact. Generally speaking, women have their own system of beliefs and moral code. They accept as reality everything which serves their interests and their passions. The Présidente carried this even farther. She spent the whole evening hammering her own conviction into the Président's head, and by next morning the magistrate was persuaded of his cousin's guilt. Every reader will regard the Présidente's conduct as horrible; but in similar circumstances any mother would follow Madame Camusot's example and prefer to sacrifice an outsider's good name to that of her daughter. The method might be different, but it would be directed to the same end.

The musician rushed downstairs, but his pace was slow as he walked through the streets to his theatre, which he entered in a daze. He went to his stand in a daze and conducted the orchestra in a daze. During the intervals, he gave such vague replies to Schmucke's inquiries that Schmucke concealed his anxiety, thinking that Pons was out of his mind. To so childlike a mentality as that of Pons, the scene which had just taken place assumed the proportions of a catastrophe. To have reawakened fearful hatred in persons whose happiness he had tried to ensure meant that his whole existence was turned upside down. He had at last come to discern what deadly hostility was recorded in the Présidente's glance, gestures and tone of voice.

The next day, Madame de Marville made an important decision: the circumstances demanded it and the Président concurred. They resolved to give the Marville estate, the house in the rue de Hanovre and a hundred thousand francs to Cécile as a marriage portion. In the course of the morning, the Présidente called on the Comtesse Popinot, realizing the necessity of meeting such a discomfiture by settling her daughter's marriage once and for all. She told her of the appalling vengeance and frightful mystification engineered by Pons. It all seemed credible enough when the Popinots learnt that Brunner's pretext for breaking off the match had been the fact of Cécile being an only child. Finally the Présidente artfully dangled before their eyes the advantage of being a 'Popinot de Marville' and getting an enormous dowry. As property prices go in Normandy, this estate, at a rent of two per cent, was worth about nine hundred thousand francs, and the house in the rue de Hanovre was reckoned as being worth two hundred and fifty thousand francs. No right-minded family could turn down such an alliance, and so the Comte Popinot and his wife gave their consent. Whereupon, as people concerned about the honour of the family they were joining, they promised to help in accounting for the catastrophe of the previous day.

Then, at the house of the same Camusot senior, Cécile's

grandfather, in front of the same people who had been present a few days earlier and for whose benefit the Présidente had chanted her litanies in praise of Brunner, this same Présidente, whom no one dared to question, bravely went ahead with her task of explaining.

'Really,' she said, 'you can't be too careful today when it comes to marriages, and above all when you are dealing with foreigners.'

'Why, Madame, what has happened?' asked Madame Chiffreville.

'Haven't you heard of our adventure with the man Brunner, who had the audacity to aspire to Cécile's hand? . . . the son of a German innkeeper, the nephew of a rabbit-skin merchant.'

'You don't say! And yet you're so wide-awake! . . .' one lady said.

'These adventurers are so cunning! But Berthier put us wise to all that. This German's best friend is a sorry individual who plays the flute! He's in league with a man who runs a lodging-house in the rue du Mail and a family of tailors . . . We learnt that he has lived a most dissolute life, and no fortune is big enough for a ne'er-do-well who has already squandered his mother's inheritance.'

'How unhappy your daughter would have been with him!' said Madame Berthier.

'But how did he get into touch with you?' asked old Madame Lebas.

'Through a piece of vengefulness on the part of Monsieur Pons. He introduced that fine gentleman to us in order to make a laughing-stock of us. His name is Brunner, that is to say *Fountain* – and they passed him off as a very grand person! His health is ruined; he's bald; he has very bad teeth. And so I distrusted him as soon as I set eyes on him.'

'But what of the great fortune you said he possessed?' a young woman shyly asked.

'It's much less than it was made out to be. The tailor's family, the hotel-keeper and he have all scraped the barrel in order to set up a banking-house . . . What is a bank in its beginnings, nowadays? – a passport to ruin. A woman could go to bed a millionairess and wake up without a penny to bless herself with. One word with this ill-bred person, one glance at him, and our minds were made up. One can see by his gloves and his waistcoats that he belongs to the working-classes: a German cook-shop keeper for a father, no refinement of feeling, a beer-drinker, a man – just imagine, Madame! – who smokes twenty-five pipes a day! I still shudder to think of what my little Lili's lot would have been. Heaven has preserved us from that. And Cécile didn't take to him at all ... Could we have expected such a hoax on the part of a relative who was always in and out of our house, and who had dined with us three times a week for twenty years? A man we overwhelmed with kindnesses, and yet so cunning an actor that he declared Cécile was his heiress in front of the Keeper of the Seals, the Attorney-General and the Chief Justice! This Brunner and Monsieur Pons had agreed to pretend that each of them was worth millions ... Oh no, I assure you, ladies, every one of you would have been taken in by a hoax which only a man of the theatre could devise!'

Within a few weeks the Popinots and the Camusots, united in one family, together with their hangers-on, had won an easy victory in social circles, for there was no one to stand up for the wretched Pons: that sly, miserly parasite, that wolf in sheep's clothing, henceforth buried under a weight of scorn, written off as a viper nourished in the family bosom, an extraordinarily wicked man, a dangerous mountebank, best consigned to oblivion.

*

About one month after the pseudo-Werther had made his refusal of marriage, poor Pons for the first time left his bed, to which a nervous fever had confined him, and walked along the sunlit boulevards leaning on Schmucke's arm. No one in the Boulevard du Temple laughed at the two 'Nutcrackers', so visibly stricken was the one and so touching was the other's concern for his convalescent friend. By the time they reached the Boulevard Poissonnière, the colour had returned to Pons's face as he breathed in the air which is so bracing in city thoroughfares; for so vital a fluid abounds in crowded centres that in Rome it has been noticed that there is no malaria in the loathsome Ghetto swarming with Jews. Perhaps also the sight of what had formerly afforded him pleasure, the great spectacle Paris offers, was having its effect on the sick man. When they came to the Théâtre des Variétés Pons left Schmucke. Hitherto they had walked side by side, but occasionally the convalescent quitted his friend in order to inspect the latest novelties displayed in the shops. He thus found himself face to face with the Comte Popinot, whom he accosted in the most respectful manner, the former Minister being one of those people for whom Pons had the greatest esteem and veneration.

'I must say, Monsieur,' was the stern response given by the Peer of France, 'I do not understand how you can be so tactless as to salute a person allied to the family on which you tried to bring shame and ridicule by perpetrating an act of vengeance such as only a theatrical entertainer could invent. Please understand, Monsieur, that from now on we can have absolutely no dealings with one another. My wife the Comtesse shares the indignation which everyone in society feels with regard to your behaviour towards the Marvilles.'

The ex-Minister went his way, leaving Pons thunderstruck. When passion is at work, when justice, politics or great social forces are in operation, no heed is paid to the condition of those they strike at. Under family pressure to overwhelm Pons, the statesman did not notice the physical weakness of this redoubtable enemy.

'Vat iss ze matter, my poor frient?' cried Schmucke, turning as pale as Pons himself.

'I have just had another dagger in my heart,' replied the poor man, leaning on Schmucke's arm. 'I think that God alone has the right to do good, and that is why all those who take His duties on themselves are so cruelly punished.'

This piece of sarcasm, coming from an artist, was a supreme effort on the part of this excellent creature to dispel the dismay he saw written on his friend's face.

'I pelief zet iss true,' was Schmucke's simple answer.

Pons, who had received no invitation to Cécile's wedding from either the Camusots or the Popinots, could conceive of no explanation. In the Boulevard des Italiens he saw Monsieur Cardot coming towards him. Forewarned by the way the Peer of France had addressed him, he took care not to bring this eminent person to a halt, although, the previous year, he had dined at his house once a fortnight; he merely raised his hat to him. But the Mayor and Deputy of Paris threw an indignant glance at Pons without returning his greeting.

'Do go and ask him what they all have against me,' said Pons to Schmucke, who knew every detail of the disaster which had befallen the poor man.

'Monsieur,' said Schmucke to Cardot, with some delicacy, 'my frient Pons hass peen ill in pet, and I expect you haf not recognizet him.'

'I certainly have.'

'Put vat haf you to plame him for?'

'Your friend is a monster of ingratitude. If he has got over his illness, it is because, as the proverb says, weeds grow in spite of everything. People have good cause for mistrusting artists: they are as wily and treacherous as monkeys. Your friend tried to dishonour his own family, to ruin a girl's reputation just to get his own back for an innocent jest. I don't want anything more to do with him. I shall try to forget that I ever knew him or that he still exists. And that, Monsieur, is the feeling of every member of my family, his own family, and all those who used to do the man the honour of welcoming him . . .'

'Put, Monsieur, you are a fair-mintet man, unt, if you vill permit me, I vill explain eferysink.'

'Be his friend still, if you feel like it,' retorted Cardot. 'That's for you to decide, sir; but leave it at that, for I feel bound to tell you I shall regard as equally blameworthy those who seek to excuse or defend him.'

'To tchustify him?'

'Yes, for his conduct is as unjustifiable as it is unspeakable.'

With this parting shot, the Deputy of the Seine constituency stalked on without waiting to hear another syllable.

'I have already two representatives of public authority against me,' said Pons with a rueful smile, after Schmucke had reported these savage imprecations to him.

'Eferyvon iss against us,' replied Schmucke dolefully. 'Let us take ourselfs off, so zat ve vill not meet any ozzer plockheats.'

This was the first time in his life that Schmucke, always as mild as a lamb, had ever uttered such words. Never before had his almost angelic gentleness been ruffled. He would have met any personal misfortune with an ingenuous smile. But to see such ill-treatment meted out to his sublime Pons, this unknown Aristides, this uncomplaining genius, this unsoured nature, this soul of goodness, this heart of gold, filled him as full of choler as Molière's Alceste, and he called Pons's amphitryons 'plockheats'! Such a reaction, in so mild a disposition, was equivalent to all the fury of Orlando! With sage foresight, Schmucke shepherded Pons back towards the Boulevard du Temple, and Pons let himself be guided along, for the stricken man's condition was like that of a wrestler after innumerable throws. Fate had decided that the poor musician should have everything in the world against him. There was to be no element lacking in the avalanche that was rolling over him: the House of Peers, the Chamber of Deputies, his family, strangers, the strong, the weak and the innocent!

In the Boulevard Poissonnière, as they were returning home, Pons saw coming towards him the daughter of that same Monsieur Cardot, a young woman who had had enough unhappiness in her life to incline her to indulgence. A lapse from virtue which had been hushed up had made her her husband's slave. Of all the hostesses who had him to dinner, Madame Berthier was the only one Pons addressed by her Christian name, Félicie. This gentle creature seemed put out at meeting cousin Pons – though they were not related by blood, he was accepted as 'cousin' by the relatives of the second wife of his cousin, Camusot senior – but she was unable to avoid meeting the moribund Pons, and came to a halt in front of him.

'I did not think you were a bad man, cousin; but if only one quarter of all I have heard said about you is true, you are a very deceitful person . . . Please do not make any excuses,' she went on hurriedly as she saw Pons making gestures of protest. 'It's no use, for two reasons: one is that I have no right to accuse, judge or condemn anyone, since I know by my own experience that those who appear to be grievously in the wrong may have some grounds for self-justification. The other is that your arguments would be of no avail, for Monsieur Berthier, who drew up the marriage contract between Mademoiselle de Marville and the Vicomte Popinot, is so incensed with you that if he knew that I had spoken a single word to you, he would be angry with me. Everybody is against you.'

'So I see, Madame,' the poor musician replied in moved tones and respectfully raised his hat to the notary's wife.

Then he plodded along painfully to the rue de Normandie, leaning so heavily on Schmucke's arm that it was plain to the old German that he was manfully fighting against physical collapse. This third encounter was as it were the verdict pronounced by the lamb which rests at the feet of God. Wrath in this angel of the poor, this symbol of the people, was heaven's final utterance. The two friends arrived home without exchanging a word. In certain predicaments, having a friend by one's side is a thing which can only be *felt*: spoken consolation merely turns the knife in the wound and shows how deep it has gone. As can be seen, the old pianist had a genius for friendship and the delicate touch of those who, having suffered a great deal themselves, are conversant with the ways of suffering.

This walk was to be the last the good Pons ever took. He stumbled from one sickness into another. Since he was of a bilious-sanguine temperament, the bile invaded his bloodstream and he had a violent attack of hepatitis. These two successive ailments being the only ones he had ever had, he knew of no doctor. And so the sympathetic and devoted Madame Cibot – her first impulses were always excellent, and even maternal – sent for the local doctor.

*

In every quarter of Paris there exists a practitioner whose name and habitation are known only to the lower classes, the shopkeepers and the concierges, who in consequence call him 'our local doctor'. This doctor bleeds people and attends confinements. In medicine he is the equivalent of the 'maid of all work' sought for in the advertising periodicals. He has to be kind to the poor, his long experience as a practitioner gives him a fair amount of competence, and he is usually well liked. Dr Poulain, whom Madame Cibot brought to see Pons, and whom Schmucke recognized, listened inattentively to the old musician's complaints: Pons had spent the whole night scratching his skin which had lost all sensitivity. The condition of his eyes, which had yellow rings round them, tallied with this symptom.

'You have had some severe disappointment in the last two days,' the doctor said to his patient.

'I have, alas!' said Pons.

'You have the disease which this gentleman nearly had,' he said, pointing to Schmucke. 'Jaundice, in fact ... But it's nothing serious,' he added, writing out a prescription.

However soothing this last remark, the doctor had given his patient one of those Hippocratic glances in which the death-sentence, although covered with a veil of conventional com-miseration, can always be divined by observant people desirous of knowing the truth. And so Madame Cibot peered inquisitively into the doctor's eyes and did not misinterpret either the tone of his pronouncement or the deceptive expres-sion on his face. She followed him out on to the landing.

'So you think it's not serious?' she asked him.

'My dear Madame Cibot, your gentleman is a doomed man, not on account of the bile which has invaded his bloodstream, but because he is so low in spirits. However, if he were well looked after, your patient might still pull through. But he would have to be got out of here and taken away for a change of scene.'

'And where's the money coming from?' asked the concierge. 'He's only his job to live on, and his friend here makes do with the scraps of pension paid to him by some great ladies – for services rendered, so he says. Very charitable ladies! It's a couple of children I've had on my hands these nine years.'

'My life is spent watching people die, not of disease, but of that grave and incurable injury – shortage of money. In how many garrets am I not obliged, far from charging a fee for my visit, to leave a franc or two on the mantelpiece!'

'Poor dear Monsieur Poulain! ...' said Madame Cibot. 'Oh, if only you had a hundred thousand francs a year like some of the skinflints you see around – *limbos* of Satan that's what they are! ... you'd be like the good Lord Himself on earth!'

The doctor who, through the esteem in which the concierge confraternity of the neighbourhood held him, had managed to build up a little practice which just kept body and soul together, raised his eyes to heaven, and thanked Madame Cibot by making a grimace worthy of Tartuffe.

'So you say, my dear Monsieur Poulain, that if we looked after him well, our dear patient would get better?'

'Yes, if his morale isn't too low after the vexation he has suffered.'

'The poor man! Who could have vexed him so? He's a good man . . . and there's no one on earth who comes up to him except his friend, Monsieur Schmucke . . . I'm going to find out what it's all about. And the people who have done such damage to my gentleman are going to get the rough edge of my tongue.'

'Listen to me, my dear Madame Cibot,' said the doctor, who by now was stepping through the *porte cochère*. 'One of the chief symptoms of your gentleman's disease is to keep on getting impatient over trifles. And as he's not likely to be able to afford a nurse, you'll have to take care of him yourself. And so . . .'

'Is it Monsieur Pons you are talking about?' It was the scrap-iron merchant, pipe in mouth, who broke in with this question. And he got up from the corner-post beside the door to join in the conversation between the concierge and the doctor.

'It is, Papa Rémonencq,' Madame Cibot replied.

'Well, he's richer than Monsieur Monistrol and all the big owners of curiosity shops. I know enough in that line of business to tell you that the dear man has a gold-mine of treasures.'

'Why, I thought you were taking me in the other day when I showed you all that old junk while my two gentlemen were out!'

In Paris the very paving-stones have ears, and doorways have tongues, the window-bars have eyes: there is no greater danger than gossiping at front entrances. The tail-end of a conversation, like the postscript of a letter, may be as dangerously indiscreet both for those who let themselves be overheard as for those who overhear it. The truth of this observation, which our narrative is about to illustrate, is confirmed by the following anecdote.

12. 'Why, what a god is gold!'

ONE day, one of the best hairdressers of Imperial times – even the men took great care of their hair in that period – was leaving a house in which he had just finished his work on a pretty woman's hair, and in which all the well-to-do tenants were his clients. Among them there flourished a confirmed bachelor strictly guarded by a housekeeper who detested her master's heirs. This man, not so young as he had been, had fallen seriously ill and had just been the subject of a consultation between some of the most highly rated doctors – they had not yet been christened 'the princes of medical science'. These doctors happened to come out at the same time as the hairdresser, and, as they took leave of one another on the threshold of the main entrance, they were letting science and truth out of the bag and chatting together as doctors do once the farce of a consultation is over. 'He's as good as dead,' said Dr Haudry. 'Short of a miracle, he hasn't a month to live,' added Desplein. The hairdresser overheard these words. Like all hairdressers, he was on confidential terms with the servants. Under the promptings of monstrous cupidity, he immediately climbed up again to the not-so-young man's flat, and promised the housekeeper-mistress a sizeable bonus if she could persuade her master to invest a large part of his possessions in a life-annuity. Among the possessions of this moribund bachelor – he was fifty-six and, thanks to his amorous jousts, looked three times that age – was a magnificent house in the rue de Richelieu, then worth two hundred and fifty thousand francs. The hairdresser coveted this house, and it was sold to him in return for a life-annuity of thirty thousand francs. This happened in 1806. The hairdresser, now retired and seventy years old, is still paying this annuity in 1846. As for the not-so-young man, now ninety-six, in his dotage, and married to his housekeeper, he may still hold out for quite a time. The hairdresser had handed thirty thousand francs to the housekeeper, and so this property has cost him over a million: true, the house is worth between eight and nine hundred thousand francs today.

Following the hairdresser's example, the Auvergnat had overheard Brunner's final remarks to Pons on his doorstep, on the day of the meeting between Cécile and that paragon among fiancés, and the desire had taken him to get into Pons's museum. Rémonencq was on good terms with the Cibots, and before long they had let him into the flat while the two friends were out. Dazzled at the sight of such wealth, Rémonencq saw the chance of 'a nice bit of business', and that means, in dealer's slang, a fortune to pillage; he had been pondering over it for five or six days.

'I wasn't being funny,' he replied to Madame Cibot and Dr Poulain. 'We'll have a chat about it. If this good gentleman wants an annuity of fifty thousand francs, I'll slip you a hamper of good wine if you can . . .'

'Do you mean that?' the doctor asked Rémonencq. 'An annuity of fifty thousand francs! . . . Why, if the old chap is as rich as that, with me to tend him and Madame Cibot to nurse him, he may get well again. Liver diseases only trouble people with very strong constitutions.'

'Did I say fifty? Why, a gentleman standing there, on this very doorstep, offered him seven hundred thousand francs – no less – for the pictures alone!'

Hearing Rémonencq make this declaration, Madame Cibot threw a strange glance at the doctor, and a diabolic thought kindled a sinister gleam in her tawny eyes.

'Come, don't let's listen to such nonsense,' the doctor continued, though he was glad enough to know his client would be able to pay for the calls he intended to make.

'But doctor,' said Rémonencq, 'the gentleman is in bed, and if our dear Madame Cibot would let me bring my expert along, I'm sure I could get the money in a couple of hours – seven hundred thousand francs, even . . .'

'That's enough, my friend,' replied the doctor. 'Now, Madame Cibot, take care never to cross the patient. You must be forbearance itself, for he'll get irritated and tired at everything, even the attention you give him. You must expect him to find fault with everything you do.'

'He's going to be a handful,' said the concierge.

'Look now, get this clear,' the doctor went on, in an authoritative tone of voice. 'Those who look after Monsieur Pons will have his life in their hands. And I'm coming to see him every day, perhaps even twice a day. He will be the first on my round.'

The doctor had suddenly passed from the profound indifference he normally felt for the lot of his impecunious patients to a most tender solicitude, now that he saw that the speculating Rémonencq was in earnest about the possibility of Pons possessing a fortune.

'I'll treat him like a king,' replied Madame Cibot with feigned enthusiasm.

The concierge waited until the doctor had turned into the rue Charlot before resuming her conversation with Rémonencq. The scrap-iron merchant was finishing his pipe with his back against the door-frame of his shop. This posture was not accidental, for he was anxious to intercept the concierge as she came back.

This shop, which had once been a coffee-house, was still as the Auvergnat had found it when he took over the lease. You could still read 'Café de Normandie' on the signboard usually found above all shop-windows. The Auvergnat had persuaded some apprentice house-decorator to paint – free of charge, no doubt – the following legend on the blank space under 'Café de Normandie': 'Rémonencq, dealer in scrap-metal and second-hand goods'. It was done with an artist's brush and in black lettering. Naturally the mirrors, tables, stools, shelves and all the coffee-house furniture had been sold. For six hundred francs a year Rémonencq had rented the shop, a bare shell, the back premises, the kitchen and a single mezzanine bedroom, in which the head waiter had formerly slept, the flat attached to the Café de Normandie having been let separately. Of the original gaudy decoration favoured by the bar-keeper nothing remained except the plain green wallpaper in the shop and the strong iron bars and bolts on the shop-front.

*

Rémonencq had settled there in 1831, after the Revolution of July. He began by displaying cracked door-bells and dishes, old iron, old pairs of scales, and weights rendered obsolete by the new metric laws, which the State alone fails to observe, since it keeps in currency pennies and halfpennies dating from the reign of Louis XVI. After that the Auvergnat, a match for any five other Auvergnats, bought up sets of kitchen utensils, old frames, old copper, chipped china. His shop was filled and emptied so many times that by imperceptible degrees it made the same sort of progress as some of our contemporary music-halls have made: the goods it sold improved in quality. The scrap-iron merchant adopted the safe and prodigious system which some gamblers follow: he went on doubling his stakes. The effects of this system are obvious to onlookers thoughtful enough to study the arithmetical progression by which the stock in these intelligently managed shops increases in value. Tin-ware, old-fashioned lamps and potsherds give place to frames and bronzes. Then comes porcelain. Temporarily a mortuary for cheap daubs, the shop soon becomes a museum for works of art. One fine day the grimy window-panes are cleaned and the inside is redecorated. The Auvergnat gives up wearing corduroys and short jackets and puts on a frock-coat. He looks like a dragon guarding a treasure. He has master-pieces all round him. He has become an astute connoisseur. Customers' stratagems no longer take him in; he knows all the tricks of the trade. There he is, the monster, like an old madam amidst the bevy of girls she offers for sale. The beauty and marvels of art mean nothing to this man, who is simultaneously subtle and vulgar, figuring out the profit he is going to make and browbeating ignoramuses. He has become quite an actor and feigns attachment to his canvases and his inlays; or he pleads poverty, lies about the prices he has paid and offers to show you his bills of sale. He changes shape like a Proteus. He is everything by turns . . . a cheap-jack, a bumpkin, a lumpkin, a Scrooge, a stooge and a clown.

Before three years were over, Rémonencq had on view some fairly fine clocks, pieces of armour and old pictures. During his absences he left his shop in charge of a very fat, ugly woman, his sister, who at his summons had come on foot from her native province. The female Rémonencq, a kind of idiot with a blank stare, dressed like a Japanese idol, never came down a farthing from the prices her brother prescribed. She also took over the household duties and solved the apparently insoluble problem of thriving on the fogs of the Seine. Rémonencq and his sister lived on bread and herrings, potato-peelings and scraps of vegetables culled from the rubbish-bins which restaurant keepers leave beside their doorways. The pair of them together did not spend, with bread thrown in, more than twelve sous a day: and the Rémonencq woman earned this by her sewing and spinning.

Rémonencq had first come to Paris to take on a street-porter's job, and from 1825 to 1831 he pushed a handcart round for curio-dealers in the Boulevard Beaumarchais and for tin-smiths in the rue de Lappe. The history of his beginnings as a salesman is the normal one with curio-dealers. There are four breeds of men – Jews, Normans, Auvergnats and Savoyards – who have the same instincts and get on by the same methods. They spend nothing, make small gains, heap up interest and profits; such are the clauses in their charter. And this charter really exists.

By this time Rémonencq, now on good terms with his erstwhile employer Monistrol, and doing business with the big dealers, went rummaging throughout Paris and its outlying parts, and that, as you know, comprises a radius of some forty lcagues. After plying his trade for fourteen years, he had sixty thousand francs and a well-stocked shop to his credit. Having no overheads, and remaining in the rue de Normandie where he paid next to nothing in rent, he sold his goods to the dealers and was content with modest profits. He conducted all his affairs in the Auvergne patois which in France is called *charabia*. He had one favourite dream: he wanted to set up on one of the boulevards. He wished to become a rich curio-dealer so that one day he might bargain directly with collectors. And indeed, he had in him the makings of a redoubtable haggler. His face was the colour of dust: it was always coated with a compound of iron filings and sweat, for he did everything himself. That made his physiognomy all the more inscrutable, because the habit of physical toil had endowed him with the stoical impassivity of the old soldiers of 1789. In physical appearance

Rémonencq was short and thin; his small eyes, closely set like those of a pig, with their chilly blue tint, revealed the concentrated avidity and sly cunning of a Jew, minus the mock humility which Jews combine with a deep contempt for Christians.

There was a relationship of patron and protégé between the Cibots and the Rémonencqs. Madame Cibot was convinced of the latters' extreme poverty, and sold them, at a fabulously cheap price, the left-overs from Schmucke's and the Cibots' own table. The Rémonencqs paid half a sou for a pound of dry crust and crumb, and even less for a bowl of potatoes. The wily Rémonencq was not supposed to be carrying on business on his own account. He was still working for Monistrol, and said he was ground down by rich dealers; and so the Cibots were sorry for the Rémonencqs. After eleven years Rémonencq had not yet outworn his corduroy coat, waistcoat and trousers; but these garments, to which Auvergnats are partial, were riddled with holes, which Cibot had patched up free of charge. As can be seen, all Jews do not come from the ghetto.

'Are you making fun of me, Rémonencq?' asked the concierge. 'Can Monsieur Pons really own such a fortune and live as he does? You wouldn't find a hundred francs in his flat.'

'Collectors are all like that,' replied Rémonencq sententiously.

'So you honestly think that my gentleman has seven hundred thousand francs' worth of stuff?'

'In pictures alone. There's one of them . . . why, if he wanted fifty thousand francs for it I'd squeeze myself dry to get the money. You know those little frames in enamelled copper and red velvet with portraits inside them? Well, they're enamels by Petitot, and that gentleman in the government, the one that used to make scent, he buys things like that for three thousand francs apiece!'

'And there are thirty of them in the two cases!' said the concierge, with bulging eyes.

'There you are then, just think what a treasure he owns!'

Madame Cibot's head swam, and she spun right round. All at once the idea came to her of getting a mention in good Pons's will, just like all the servant-mistresses whose life-annuities had excited so many people's cupidity in the Marais district. She saw herself living in a country cottage in a village not too far from Paris, taking great pride in her poultry and her garden. She would end her days there, waited on like a queen – and her dear Cibot too! A good man, spurned and unappreciated like all good men, he richly deserved to be happy!

The concierge's sudden right-about-turn made Rémonencq feel sure of success. For a *chineur* – the word for a bargain-hunter, from the word *chiner* which means to go searching for bargains and make profitable deals with ignorant owners – the difficulty lies in getting a foot inside private houses. A *chineur*, or 'knocker', invents all the unimaginable tricks of Molière's most resourceful valets, all the cajolery of his serving-maids, in order to gain admittance into a respectable person's domicile: play-acting worthy of the stage, and always based on the rapacity of domestics. The latter, particularly in rural or provincial posts, in return for thirty francs' worth of money or merchandise, will engineer deals from which a knocker makes a profit of one or two thousand francs. For instance, there is a certain service of old Sèvres, in soft paste, whose manner of acquisition, if the story were told, would reveal all the wiles which diplomats practised at the Congress of Munster, all the stratagems brought into play at Nymwegen, Utrecht, Ryswick and Vienna. In fact the knockers do better than that, for they are more frankly comic than the negotiators of treaties. Knockers have methods which dive as deep into the abysses of personal interest as those which ambassadors strain after so painfully in order to bring about the dissolution of the most solidly cemented alliances.

'I've got her nicely worked up,' Rémonencq told his sister as he saw Madame Cibot resume her seat on a frayed rush-bottomed chair. 'And that's why I'm going to talk it over with the only man who knows his way about, our Jew, our good Jew, who only charged us fifteen per cent for the money we borrowed.'

Rémonencq had read La Cibot's mind. With women of her mettle, to will is to act. They stop at nothing to reach their ends. In a flash they pass from the strictest probity to the direst villainy. Probity – and incidentally, all our sentiments – should be divided into two sorts: negative and positive. The negative kind is that of people like the Cibots, who stay honest so long as no opportunity of enrichment comes their way. The positive kind is that of people who can wade knee-deep in temptation without succumbing to it – the sort of probity bank messengers need.

Through the sluices of self-interest which Rémonencq's diabolic remark had opened, a flood of evil intentions rushed into the concierge's mind and heart. She went up, in fact she flew up from her lodge to the flat of her two gentlemen, and, with a mask of tenderness on her face, opened the door of the room in which Pons and Schmucke were busy lamenting. When he saw their housekeeper come in, Schmucke made a sign to her not to say a word in the sick man's presence about the doctor's real opinion: for, like the true friend he was, the sensitive German had read a warning message in the doctor's eyes. She responded with another nod, expressive of deep concern.

'Well, my poor dear gentleman, how are you feeling?' asked La Cibot.

She planted herself at the foot of the bed, with her hands on her hips and her gaze resting gently on the sick man: but what golden glints flashed forth from her eyes! An observant on-looker would have found her glance as terrifying as the glance of a tiger.

'Oh, very poorly,' Pons answered, 'I've no appetite at all. Oh, the vanity of social life!' he exclaimed as he pressed Schmucke's hand, which was holding his. His friend was sitting beside his bed, and doubtless the sick man had been talking to him about the cause of his illness. 'I should have done much better, my dear Schmucke, to have taken your advice – to have dined at home every day since we set up house together: to have given up society which is now rolling over me like a cart-wheel over an egg – and for what reason?'

'Come, come, my good gentleman, it's no use complaining,' said La Cibot. 'The doctor told me how things are.'

Schmucke plucked at the concierge's dress.

'After all, you can get over it, but only if you're well looked after ... Don't worry, you've got a good friend by your side, and – I'm not bragging – a woman who'll care for you as if you were her first-born child. I got Cibot on his legs again when he was so bad you could tell Dr Poulain had given him up and was well-nigh pulling the sheet over his face, as you might say, and making out the death certificate! . . . Well, thank the Lord you're not that bad, though you're bad enough . . . You trust to me . . . I'll pull you through with these two hands . . . Keep still now, don't toss about like that.'

She drew the blanket over the sick man's hands.

'Now, now, my lamb,' she said, 'Monsieur Schmucke and me, we'll spend all our nights nursing you, so we will. You'll be treated better than a prince. And anyway, you've enough money to afford anything you need to make you better. I've just been working it out with Cibot – he'd be helpless without me, poor dear man! . . . Well, I've made him see things my way, and as we both care so much about you, he's willing for me to stay here at night. And for a man like him that means a big sacrifice, I can tell you, because he's as loving now as he was when we were first married. I just don't know what comes over him! It must be the lodge, you know, always being side by side, I mean . . . Keep the bedclothes on,' she cried, rushing to the head of the bed and pulling the blankets up again over Pons's chest. 'If you won't be good, if you don't do every mortal thing the doctor tells you – and mark my words, he's like the good Lord himself treading this earth – I'll wash my hands of you. You've got to do as you're told!'

'Inteet, yess, Matame Cipot! He vill certainly to vat you say,' answered Schmucke. 'He vants to lif for ze sake of hiss goot frient Schmucke.'

'And you mustn't get into tantrums,' added Madame Cibot. 'You're likely enough to do that with the complaint you've got, without getting impatient and making things worse. The Lord sends us our troubles, my dear good gentleman; and pays us out for our sins . . . and I bet you've got some nice little ones to blame yourself for!'

The sick man shook his head in denial.

'Oh, get along with you! You must have had a girl or two when you were young. You've had your little fling. I wouldn't mind betting there's some little love-child somewhere about, with nothing to live on. You're a bad lot, you men ... You have your fun, and then, whoosh! – off you go. Never a thought for anything, not even while the baby's still being suckled! ... Us poor women! ...'

'But no one has ever loved me except my mother and Schmucke,' said poor Pons sadly.

'Nonsense! You're no saint! You were young once and you must have been a good-looking lad at twenty. I wouldn't have said no myself to a kind man like you.'

'I have always been as ugly as a toad,' said Pons despairingly.

'Oh, you're just being modest – I'll say that for you, you *are* modest.'

'No, no, my dear Madame Cibot. I tell you again, I have always been ugly, and have never been loved.'

'A man like you?' said the concierge. 'Are you trying to fool me into believing, here and now, that at your age you're still an innocent? Come off it; you, a musician, a man of the theatre! Even if a woman told me a tale like that, I wouldn't believe it.'

'Matame Cipot, you're makink him cross,' cried Schmucke, noticing that Pons was writhing like a worm under his bedclothes.

'You be quiet too! You're just a couple of old rakes. You aren't prize beauties, but as the saying goes: "Ugly as sin, there's still a way in!" Cibot managed to get one of the prettiest oyster-girls in Paris to fall for him, and he's not a patch on you. You're a nice pair, you are! Come on now, you've had your bit of fun, and the Lord's taking it out of you for leaving your children in the lurch, like Abraham ...'

Overwhelmed as he was by this spate of words, the sick man still had strength enough to make another gesture of protest.

'But never mind, you'll still live to be as old as Methusalem.'

'Can't you leave me in peace?' Pons cried out. 'I have never known what it is to be loved ... I've never had any children. I'm alone in the world.'

'Is that Gospel truth?' said the concierge. 'You're such a kind man, and women, it's a fact, always fall for kindness; that's what draws them. I'd have sworn that when you were young and hearty ...'

'Take her away,' whispered Pons to Schmucke. 'She's driving me mad.'

'Anyway, Monsieur Schmucke, he's sure to have some children . . . You're all the same, you old bachelors.'

'*I?*' cried Schmucke, springing to his feet. 'Nefer haf I . . .'

'Go on now, I suppose you'll be telling me you've no heirs either! And that the pair of you just popped up like mushrooms.'

'Zet iss enough! Leaf ze room!' replied Schmucke. And the good German heroically seized Madame Cibot round the middle and dragged her into the drawing-room, paying no heed to her cries.

13. A treatise on the occult sciences

'HERE, you're not going to get rough with a woman at your age!' bawled out La Cibot, struggling in Schmucke's grip.

'Schtop shoutink!'

'And you the best of the two!' La Cibot replied. 'Oh, what a fool I was to talk about love to a pair of old men who've never had anything to do with women! It's heated your blood, you monster!' she cried as she saw the angry gleam in Schmucke's eyes; 'Help! Help! Police! I'm being assaulted!'

'You are a stupit voman!' the German replied. 'Tell me now vat tit ze toctor say?'

'A nice way to treat me,' said the weeping woman, now released. 'And me ready to go through fire and water for both of you. Well, it's right what they say: you never know with men till you've tried. It's gospel truth! My poor Cibot wouldn't maul me about like that . . . and me as good as a mother to you! I've no children myself, and only yesterday I was saying to Cibot: "My dear, the Lord knew what He was about when He sent us no children. I've got two children upstairs" . . . That's what I said, may God strike me dead if I didn't!'

'Tell me, vat tit ze toctor say?' Schmucke asked again, stamping with rage for the first time in his life.

'All right, I'll tell you what he said,' answered Madame Cibot, beckoning Schmucke into the dining-room. 'He told me that our poor dear darling invalid is likely to die if he's not well looked after. But I'm still here, even if you have treated me like a brute. You *were* a brute, you know, and I thought you were so gentle. You do go for the women then, after all! Fancy wanting to tumble one, at your age, you wicked old rascal!'

'Vicket rascal? Vill you not unterstant zat Pons iss ze only person I lof?'

'All right then. Keep your paws off me, see?' she said to Schmucke, breaking into a smile. 'You'd better watch out:

128

Cibot would break a man's neck if he caught him playing about with his wife.'

'Haf a goot care of Pons, my little Matame Cipot,' pleaded Schmucke, and his hand reached out to hers.

'There you go, at it again!'

'Pleass listen! I vill leaf you all I haf if ve can safe him.'

'All right, I'll go to the chemist to get him what he needs. And remember, Monsieur Schmucke, him being ill is going to cost quite a bit: how are you going to manage?'

'I vill work hart. I vant Pons to pe caret for like a prince.'

'He shall be, my good Monsieur Schmucke. And look, don't worry about anything. Cibot and me have two thousand francs saved up. You can have them, and I tell you it won't be the first time I've dipped into my savings for you two.'

'Vat a kint voman!' exclaimed Schmucke, wiping his eyes. 'Vat a heart of golt!'

In melodramatic tones La Cibot replied: 'Dry those tears. They do me honour, and I ask for no other reward. I am the least self-seeking of God's creatures ... But don't you go back in there with your eyes wet. Monsieur Pons will think he's worse than he is.'

Moved by this delicate thought, Schmucke finally took hold of Madame Cibot's hand and pressed it.

'Now go easy!' said the one-time oyster girl; and she threw a tender glance at Schmucke.

'Pons,' said the kindly German as he went back into the bedroom, 'she is an antchel, Matame Cipot. She talks much for an antchel, but she *iss* an antchel.'

'Do you think so?' the sick man replied, shaking his head. 'I've lost all my faith in people this last month. After all my misfortunes, God and yourself are all I trust in.'

'Get pesser,' cried Schmucke, 'unt ve vill lif all sree togezzer like kinks.'

*

The concierge rushed back breathless to her lodge. 'Cibot,' she called out, 'my love, our fortune's made! My two gentlemen have no heirs, no natural children, nothing! Think of that! I'm going straight to Ma'me Fontaine to get her to read the cards and tell me how much we shall have coming to us.'

'Wife,' replied the little tailor, 'don't reckon on stepping into a dead man's shoes if you don't want to go bare-foot.'

'Now don't you pour cold water down my back!' she said, giving Cibot a friendly tap. 'Monsieur Poulain says Pons is done for. And we're going to be well off. I'll see to that! You get on with your stitching and look after the lodge. You won't have to go on with it very long. We'll retire into the country, to Batignolles. A fine house, a fine garden . . . You'll enjoy growing things, and I'll have a maid!'

'Well now, neighbour, how are things going up there?' asked Rémonencq. 'Have you found out what the collection's worth?'

'Oh no, not yet. You can't rush things like that, my good neighbour. I've been finding out more important things.'

'More important! What could be more important than that?' exclaimed Rémonencq.

'Here, my lad, leave me to steer the boat,' said the concierge with some firmness.

'But just think! With thirty per cent out of seven hundred thousand francs you'd live snug for the rest of your life.'

'Don't worry, Papa Rémonencq! When the time comes to find out what it will all fetch, the stuff the old man has stacked up, we'll see about that!'

*

The concierge went to the chemist's to get the doctor's prescriptions made up, but decided to postpone her consultation with Madame Fontaine till the next day. She expected to find the sibyl's oracular faculties fresher and in better form if she arrived quite early, before anybody else – for people queued up to consult Madame Fontaine.

After forty years' rivalry with the celebrated Mademoiselle Lenormand, who had recently died, Madame Fontaine was now the undisputed oracle of the Marais. It is difficult to imagine how important fortune-tellers are to the lower classes of Paris, or what a tremendous influence they exert in helping illiterate persons to make up their minds. For cooks, concierges, kept women, workmen and all those people in Paris who live on their hopes, come to consult those privileged beings who possess the strange, inexplicable power of foretelling the future. Belief in the occult sciences is much more widespread than is imagined by scientists, barristers, notaries, doctors, magistrates and philosophers. The lower classes have ineradicable instincts; and among these instincts, the one that is so stupidly called 'superstition' is as much in the blood of the working classes as it is in the minds of their betters. In Paris, more than one statesman has recourse to card-readers. To unbelieving minds, judicial astrology (an extremely quaint combination of terms) is merely the exploitation of an inherent curiosity, one of the strongest urges implanted in us by nature. And so sceptics completely deny the relationship which divination establishes between human destinies and the configuration resulting from the seven or eight principal methods which judicial astrology utilizes. But the occult sciences, like so many phenomena of nature, are spurned by sceptics or materialist philosophers, that is to say by those who cleave solely to solid, visible facts, to the results shown by the retorts and balances of modern physics and chemistry. None the less, these sciences persist; the practice of them goes on, though without making any progress, because for the last two centuries they have no longer been cultivated by the finest minds.

If we consider only the practical side of divination, to believe that previous events in a man's life and the secrets known to him alone can be directly represented by the cards he shuffles and cuts, and which are then stacked by the fortune-teller in accordance with some mysterious rites, is to believe the absurd. But this criterion of absurdity once ruled out the harnessing of steam; it still rules out aerial navigation; it ruled out many inventions: gunpowder, printing, the telescope, engraving and also the most recent great discovery of our time, the daguerreotype. If anyone had come and told Napoleon that a man or a building is incessantly and continuously represented by a picture in the atmosphere, that all existing objects project into it a kind of *spectre* which can be captured and perceived, he would have consigned him to Charenton as a lunatic, just as Cardinal Richelieu consigned Salomon de Caux to Bicêtre when that martyred Norman put within his grasp a tremendous victory over nature: navigation by steam. And yet that is what

Daguerre's discovery proved! Now, if God, for the benefit of certain clairvoyants, has imprinted every man's destiny in his physiognomy – taking this word as applying to every bodily characteristic – why should not the human hand sum up that physiognomy in itself, since the hand comprises human action in its entirety and is its sole means of manifestation? Hence palmistry. And does not society itself, in this respect, follow God's example? To foretell the events of a man's life from the study of his hand is not, for someone endowed with the faculties of a seer, a more extraordinary feat than telling a soldier he is going to fight, a barrister that he is going to plead a cause, a cobbler that he is going to make boots or shoes, a farmer that he is going to manure and plough his land. Let us take a still more striking example: genius is a sort of immaterial sun whose rays give colour to everything passing by. Cannot an idiot be immediately recognized by characteristics which are the opposite of those shown by a man of genius? An ordinary man goes almost unnoticed. Most observant people, students of nature in Parisian society, are able to tell the profession of a passer-by as they see him approach. Today the mysteries of the witches' sabbath, so graphically depicted by sixteenth-century painters, are no longer mysteries. The Egyptians, male and female, the ancestors of our gypsies, that strange nation which had its origins in India, merely administered hashish to their clients. The phenomena produced by this preparation perfectly well account for the ridings on broomsticks, the exits from chimneys, the *tangible visions*, so to speak, of old hags transformed into young women, the frantic dances and the entrancing music which made up the fantasies familiar to the so-called devil-worshippers.

Nowadays so many attested and authenticated facts have emerged from the occult sciences that the time will come when these sciences will be professed as chemistry and astronomy are professed. Just now, when so many professorial chairs are being set up in Paris – chairs in Slavonic, in Manchurian studies, and in literatures so *unprofessable* as those of the North; chairs which, instead of offering instruction, stand in need of it themselves; chairs whose titular holders eternally grind out articles on Shakespeare or the sixteenth century – is it not a matter of surprise that, under the name of anthropology, the teaching of occult philosophy, one of the glories of the old-time university, has not been restored? In this respect Germany, so great and yet so immature a country, is a step ahead of France, for there that science *is* professed: it is much more useful than the many kinds of 'philosophies' which are all identical.

That certain beings should have the power to discern future facts in the causative germ, as the great inventor discerns an industry or a science in an effect of nature which the common man does not perceive, is no longer one of those violent exceptions which cause a stir: it is the effect of a recognized faculty, one which might well turn out to be a certain somnambulism of the spirit. Although this proposition on which the various means of deciphering the future are based may seem absurd, the fact is there. We should note that the prediction of important future events is not, to the seer, a more extraordinary feat than divining the past. In the sceptical mode of thought the past and the future are equally unknowable. If events which have happened have left traces, it is reasonable to suppose that events to come have their roots in the present. If a fortune-teller can give you minute details about facts in your earlier life which are known to you alone, it follows that he can tell you the events which existing causes will bring forth. The spiritual world is cut, so to speak, to the pattern of the material world; the same sequence of cause and effect must therefore be operative in both, with differences appropriate to their diverse fields of activity. Just as physical objects do in fact project themselves on to the atmosphere so that it retains the 'spectre' which the daguerreotype can fix and capture, in the same way ideas, which are real and active creations, imprint themselves on what we must call the 'atmosphere' of the spiritual world, produce effects in it and live on in it *spectrally* (one must coin words in order to express unnamed phenomena); if that be granted, certain creatures endowed with rare faculties are perfectly capable of discerning those forms or traces of ideas.

As for the means employed to arrive at *visions*, that is the most easily explained miracle, once the consultant's hand arranges the objects by whose aid the hazards of his life are set forth before him. In fact, everything in the real world is linked together. Every movement in it corresponds to a cause, every cause is bound up with the whole; and consequently the whole is represented in the slightest movement. Rabelais, the greatest of modern minds, the man who summed up in himself Pythagoras, Hippocrates, Aristophanes and Dante, said three centuries ago: 'Man is a microcosm.' Three centuries later Swedenborg, the great Swedish prophet, was to say that 'the earth is a man'. Thus the prophet and the precursor of incredulity met together in the greatest of formulas. In human life, as in the life of our planet, all that happens is 'fated' to happen. The most trivial, the most insignificant 'accidents' are predetermined. Therefore great matters, great designs, great thoughts in life are necessarily reflected in the most trivial acts, and with such fidelity that, if some conspirator cuts and shuffles a pack of cards, he will be writing in them the secret of his conspiracy, to be read by the seer known as a gypsy, a fortune-teller, a charlatan, etc. . . . As soon as you admit fatality, that is to say, the enchainment of causes, judicial astrology attains validity and becomes what it was in former ages, a vast science comprising as it does the deductive faculty which made Cuvier so great; but its exercise is spontaneous, instead of being pursued, as it was with that outstanding genius, night after night, in the scholarly seclusion of his study.

Judicial astrology – divination – reigned for seven centuries, not as today, over the masses, but over the foremost minds – kings and queens and men of substance. One of the greatest sciences of antiquity, animal magnetism, emerged from the occult sciences, just as chemistry emerged from the alchemist's furnaces. Craniology, physiognomy and neurology emerge from them no less: and the illustrious creators of these apparently new sciences made only one mistake, that which all discoverers make, of constructing a hard and fast system from isolated facts whose generative cause still eludes analysis. One fine day the Catholic Church and modern philosophy came to an agreement with the judiciary to proscribe, persecute and ridicule the mysteries of the Kabbala, and a regrettable gap of a hundred years interrupted the reign and study of the occult sciences. None the less the masses, and also many intelligent people, particularly women, continue to pay tribute to the mysterious powers possessed by those who are able to peep behind the veil of the future. They go to them to purchase hope, courage, strength – virtues which it is the prerogative of religion to confer. And so this science is still practised, though not without some risk. For today sorcerers, shielded as they are from all forms of torture through the tolerance due to the eighteenth-century Encyclopedists, are only subject to the petty jurisdiction of the police-courts, and then only when they have recourse to fraudulent operations, or intimidate their 'clients' in order to extort money, thus laying themselves open to the charge of deceptive practices. Unfortunately such practices and, only too often, serious felony accompany the exercise of this sublime faculty. And this is why: the admirable gifts which go to the making of a clairvoyant are found, as a rule, in people whom one might describe as 'brutish'. Such 'brutish' individuals are the chosen vessels into which God pours the elixirs which astonish mankind. From such raw material prophets come forth, such as Saint Peter and Peter the Hermit. Whenever mental energy subsists in its entirety, remains a compact whole, is not fragmented into conversations, intrigues, literary activities, scientific speculations, administrative efforts, inventive conceptions and warlike pursuits, it is liable to emit effulgences of prodigious intensity: they are pent up, just as an uncut diamond holds in reserve the sparkle of its facets. Let some circumstance arise, and this intelligence bursts into flame: it has wings to cover distances, it has the all-seeing eyes of a god. Yesterday it was mere carbon; today, thanks to the unknown fluid coursing through it, it is a scintillating diamond. Sophisticated people, with every facet of their intelligence abraded, can never, unless by one of those miracles which God sometimes permits, display this superlative power. And so soothsayers, male and female, are nearly always mendicants who have never exercised their mental powers, creatures of seemingly coarse texture, stones rolled along in the torrent of indigence and the gutters of life, in which they have expended nothing but physical suffering. In short the prophet or the seer is a man like Martin the Ploughman, who terrified Louis XVIII by telling him a secret which he alone as king could know; or a woman like Mademoiselle Lenormand; a former cook like Madame Fontaine; an almost cretinous Negress; a herdsman living with his cattle; a fakir squatting beside a shrine, one who, by mortifying the flesh, gives his spirit possession of all the incalculable power of the somnambulistic faculties.

It is in Asia that, from time immemorial, the heroes of the occult sciences have been found. Often, then, these people who in their normal state simply remain what they are – for to some extent they perform the functions of chemical and physical bodies conducting electricity, now inert metals, now ducts replete with mysterious fluids – these people, when they return to their normal selves, give themselves up to practices and calculations which lead them to the police-courts; nay even, like the notorious Balthazar, to the assize courts or the penitentiary. And a final proof of the immense power that cartomancy exerts over the common people is the fact that the life and death of our unfortunate musician depended on the horoscope that Madame Fontaine was going to cast for Madame Cibot.

Certain repetitions are unavoidable in a history so considerable and so laden with details as a complete account of French society in the nineteenth century. But here it is unnecessary to depict Madame Fontaine's squalid abode, since it has already been described in *The Unwitting Play-Actors*. We need only observe that Madame Cibot entered Madame Fontaine's house in the rue Vieille-du-Temple for all the world like an *habitué* of the Café Anglais repairing to that restaurant for lunch. Madame Cibot was a very old client, and had often brought along both young people and her cronies, all of them eaten up with curiosity.

*

The old servant who acted as receptionist to the fortune-teller opened the door of the sanctuary without forewarning her mistress.

'Ah! it's Madame Cibot! ... Come in,' she added, 'She's quite alone.'

'Well, my dear, what brings you here so early in the morning?' asked the old witch. She was then seventy-eight and deserved to be so called, for her external appearance was worthy of one of the Fates.

'My head's all in a whirl. Do me the big pack,' cried La Cibot. 'My fortune's at stake . . .' She explained the situation she was in, and begged for a prediction relevant to her sordid hopes.

'Do you know what the tarot pack means?' asked Madame Fontaine in solemn tones.

'No, I've never been able to afford the whole box of tricks . . . It costs a hundred francs! . . . All very fine, but how would I come by them? But today I've simply got to have it!'

'I don't often work it, dearie,' replied Madame Fontaine, 'I only do it for well-off people on great occasions, and it costs them five hundred francs. You see, it tires me, it wears me out. The *Spirit* churns me all up inside, in my stomach. It's like going to what they used to call the witches' sabbath.'

'But I tell you, good Ma'me Fontaine, it's to do with my whole future.'

'Ah well, you've had many a consultation with me, and as a favour to you I'll give myself up to the Spirit!' replied Madame Fontaine – and she showed on her ravaged face an expression of genuine terror.

She got up from the dirty old rocking-chair by her fireside and went over to the table, which was draped with a green cloth so threadbare that you could count the strands. On the left side of it was a sleeping toad of extraordinary dimensions, and next to it, in an open cage, a black hen with ruffled feathers.

'Ashtaroth! Here, my son!' she said, and with a long knitting needle she gave the toad a gentle tap on the back: it looked at her with a knowing eye.

'And you, Mademoiselle Cleopatra! Wake up!' she continued, administering a light tap on the old hen's beak.

Then Madame Fontaine withdrew into herself and remained quite still for a few seconds. She looked like a corpse. Her eyes turned upwards until only the whites were visible. Then she stiffened and, in a hollow voice, said: 'Here I am!'

Mechanically she scattered some bird-seed for Cleopatra, and then took up her tarot pack, shuffled it convulsively, and handed it to Madame Cibot to cut – but with a deep sigh. Madame Cibot felt cold shivers go down her back as this cadaverous figure in her filthy turban and sinister dressing-gown peered at the grains of seed which the black hen was pecking up and called to her toad Ashtaroth to hop over the cards spread out on the table. Only great credulity can give rise to great emotion. Annuity or no annuity? As Shakespeare said, that was the question.

14. A character from Hoffmann's Tales

SEVEN or eight minutes went by while the sorceress opened a book of spells and read aloud from it in a sepulchral voice. She studied the grains the hen had left and the path the toad was taking as it hopped away. Then, with the whites of her eyes still showing, she scanned the cards and made out their meaning.

'You will get what you want!' she said. 'And yet nothing will turn out as you think. You will have a great deal of intriguing to do. But you will reap the reward of your labours. You will behave very badly, but it will be with you as it is with all those who tend sick persons and covet a share in the money they leave. In this evil task you will have the support of important people ... Later on the pangs of death will bring you to repentance, for in the village to which you will retire with your second husband you will be murdered for your reputed fortune – murdered by two escaped convicts, a short man with red hair and an old man with no hair at all ... There, my daughter, you are free to take action, or to leave well alone.'

The inner excitement which had been kindling torches in the sunken eyes of this skeleton, outwardly so cold, died down. When the prognostication was finished, Madame Fontaine seemed to be quite dazed, and looked for all the world like a somnambulist coming out of a trance. She gazed around her with a bewildered air. Then she recognized Madame Cibot and seemed surprised to see the stark horror imprinted on her face.

'Well, my daughter,' she said in tones quite different from those she had used while uttering her prediction, 'are you satisfied?'

Madame Cibot gazed in stupefaction at the sorceress and could find no reply.

'Well, you asked for the tarot pack! I have treated you as an old acquaintance. You need only pay me a hundred francs.'

'Is Cibot going to die?' cried the concierge.

'Why, have I told you some very horrible things?' asked Madame Fontaine with great ingenuousness.

'That you have!' said La Cibot, pulling a hundred francs from her pocket and placing them on the edge of the table. 'I'm going to be murdered!'

'Ah! There you are! You wanted the tarot pack! ... But don't worry. Not all the people die whom the cards mark out for murder.'

'Then tell me, can I get out of it, Ma'me Fontaine?'

'My dear good woman, how do *I* know? You wanted to knock at the door of the future, and I released the latch, that's all – and *he* came!'

'*He*? Who's *he*!' asked Madame Cibot.

'Why, the *Spirit* of course!' the sorceress retorted testily.

'Good-bye, Ma'me Fontaine!' cried the concierge. 'Little did I know what the big pack was like. You've given me a real scare, I can tell you!'

The servant escorted the concierge to the landing and said:

'Madame Fontaine doesn't get into that state twice in a month. It might knock her out, the strain of it tires her so much. Now she's going to eat some cutlets and then go to sleep for three hours.'

As La Cibot walked off down the street, she made what all clients make of any sort of consultation: she accepted every part of the prophecy which suited her purposes and discounted the predictions of misfortune. Next day her mind was quite made up. She decided to do everything she could to get rich by laying her hands on part of the Pons collection. And so for some time she gave no thought to anything except working out a plan of campaign. There is a phenomenon we explained above, namely the concentration of inner resources in all coarse-grained people, who, instead of using up their intelligential faculties, like people who move in society, in day-to-day expenditure, find them ready at hand, strong and powerful, at the moment when that formidable weapon, the *idée fixe*, comes into play in their minds. This phenomenon was made manifest in La Cibot to a superlative degree. An *idée fixe* can produce miracles for prisoners intent on escape, and also in the realm of feeling: so this mere concierge, under the spur of covetousness, became as resourceful as a Baron de Nucingen faced with the prospect of ruin, as nimble-witted (under the mask of stupidity) as that alluring adventurer La Palférine.

A few days later, about seven in the morning, she saw Rémonencq opening his shop and sidled up to him like a cat.

'How can we find out,' she asked him, 'what the things piled up in my gentlemen's flat are worth?'

'That's easy enough,' the curio-dealer replied in his frightful *charabia*. 'You play fair with me and I'll get you a valuer, a decent fellow who'll tell you what the pictures are worth to a penny.'

'And who's he?'

'Monsieur Magus, a Jew who's no longer in business except for pleasure.'

The name of Elias Magus is too well-known in the *Human Comedy* to need introducing. He had retired from trading in pictures and *objets d'art* and, as a dealer, had adopted the procedure that Pons had followed as a collector. The celebrated valuers – the late Henry, Messieurs Pigeot and Moret, Thoret, Georges and Roehn, in fact, the experts of the Louvre Museum – were as babes compared with Elias Magus, who could pick out a masterpiece from under the grime of centuries, who knew every school and the signature of every painter.

This Jew, who had come to Paris from Bordeaux, had given up business in 1835 without giving up his squalid appearance: that he maintained, in accordance with the habits of most Jews, so faithful to its traditions does this race remain. In the Middle Ages, persecution forced the Jews to disarm suspicion by going about in rags, perpetually complaining, whining and pleading poverty. What was once a necessity has become, as is always the case, an ingrained racial instinct, an endemic vice. By dint of buying and selling diamonds, dealing in pictures and lace, rare curios and enamels, delicate carvings and antique jewellery, Elias Magus had come to enjoy an immense untold fortune, which he had acquired through this kind of commerce, nowadays so important. In fact, in the last twenty years the number of dealers has multiplied ten times in Paris, that city in which all the curios in the world manage to come together. As for pictures, they are sold in only three cities: Rome, London and Paris.

Elias Magus lived in the Chaussée des Minimes, a short and narrow street leading to the rue Royale. There he owned an old mansion which he had bought in 1831 for a song, as they say. This splendid building contained one of the most sumptuous of the apartments decorated during the reign of Louis XV, for it had been the residence of the Baron de Maulaincourt, that famous President of the Board of Excise who had built it himself. Its situation had saved it from devastation during the Revolution. If the old Jew had decided, in breach of Israelite practice, to become a house-owner, you may be sure he knew what he was about. The old man was ending up – as we all do – by carrying an obsession to the point of mania. Although he was as miserly as his late friend Gobseck, he had surrendered to the admiration aroused in him by the masterpieces he dealt in: but his taste had become more and more refined and exacting, developing into one of those passions which only kings can indulge, provided they are rich and lovers of the arts. Like Frederick William of Prussia, who had no use for grenadiers who were less than six feet tall, and spent extravagant sums in order to buy such men for his living museum of grenadiers, the retired dealer only fell in love with faultless canvases, those which had remained exactly as the master had painted them and were of first-class workmanship. And so Elias Magus never missed any of the big sales, ransacked all the markets and travelled all over Europe. His cold heart, dedicated to Mammon, warmed at the sight of a masterpiece, just as a sated libertine is roused by the sight of a lovely girl and devotes himself to the quest for women of flawless beauty. In his search for perfection, such admiration, for this Don Juan of the picture-gallery, was a source of enjoyment superior to that of a miser gloating over his gold. He lived in a harem of beautiful paintings!

These great works, housed as the children of royalty should be, filled the whole of the first floor in the mansion which Elias Magus had had most splendidly restored. At the windows hung curtains of the finest Venetian gold brocade. On the floors were laid the most superb carpets ever woven in the Savonnerie workshops. His pictures – numbering about a hundred – were enclosed in the most splendid frames, which had all been intelligently regilded by the only gilder in Paris whom Elias regarded as conscientious, namely Servais. The old Jew himself had taught Servais to use English gold-leaf, which is infinitely superior to that produced by the French gold-beaters. In the art of gilding, Servais is equal to Thouvenin in the art of bookbinding: both of them are in love with their craft. The windows of these apartments were protected by shutters lined with sheet-iron. Elias Magus occupied two attic rooms on the second floor; they were poorly furnished, with his own shoddy and tattered garments scattered about them, and they smelt of the ghetto, for he was finishing his days in conformity with the habits of a lifetime.

The ground floor was entirely given over to such pictures as the Jew was still buying and selling, and the storage of crates from far and wide. It also contained an immense workshop in which Moret, the cleverest of our picture-restorers and one of those who ought to be employed at the Louvre, worked almost exclusively for him. In addition there were the rooms occupied by his daughter, the fruit of his old age; a beautiful girl, like all Jewesses who reincarnate the Asian type in all its purity and nobility. Noémi was guarded by two fanatically devoted Jewish serving-maids, but her chief guard was a Polish Jew named Abramko, a man who had been implicated in the Polish risings – a marvellous find for Elias Magus, who had come to his rescue as a mere matter of speculation. Abramko was the concierge of this silent, gloomy and deserted mansion, and the lodge he occupied was protected by three remarkably ferocious dogs: a Newfoundland, a Pyrenean mountain-dog and an English bull-dog.

Elias used to go off on his travels with no misgivings; he lived in complete tranquillity of mind, and had no fears for the safety either of his daughter, who was his paramount treasure, or of his pictures, or of his gold. This sense of security was based on the following carefully pondered precautions. Every year Abramko was paid two hundred francs more than the previous year; he was to receive nothing at his master's death, but the latter was training him in the practice of usury throughout the district. Abramko never opened the main door to anyone before peering through a spy-hole fitted with stout iron bars. This doorkeeper was as strong as Hercules and worshipped Magus as Sancho Panza worshipped Don Quixote. The dogs were kept chained up all day long, and had not a morsel of food. But at night time Abramko let them loose, and the cunning old Jew had arranged that they should take up their stance, one in the garden, at the base of a post with a piece of meat fastened to the top, the second in the courtyard under a similar post, and the third in the great hall on the ground floor. You will understand that these dogs, already prompted by instinct to guard the house, were themselves kept under guard by the pangs of hunger. Not for the most alluring bitch would they have abandoned their vigil at the base of their greasy poles; they only moved away to go sniffing here and there. Should an intruder appear, all three dogs imagined that he was after their food – and this was only brought down to them in the morning when Abramko woke up. This infernal device had one tremendous advantage: the dogs never barked; Elias's ingenious training had made them savage, and they had become as crafty as Mohicans. There had been an occasion when some malefactors, emboldened by the prevailing silence, were reckless enough to suppose that they could 'clean out' the Jew's money chest. The man who was selected to lead the attempt scaled the garden wall and got ready to climb down inside, while the bulldog, who had heard him quite well, bided his time. As soon as the man's foot was within reach of the dog's jaws, he bit it clean off and ate it. The thief had enough stamina to get back over the wall and to hobble away on the stump of his leg before falling unconscious into his comrades' arms; and they carried him away. The *Police-Court Gazette* did not fail to report this delightful 'Paris-by-Night' episode, but it was taken to be no more than a piece of journalism.

Magus was then seventy-five, and quite capable of reaching his century. Though rich, he lived like the Rémonencqs. His total budget, including what he lavished on his daughter, amounted to three thousand francs a year.

No mode of existence could be more methodical than his. He rose at daybreak and munched some bread rubbed with garlic, and that kept him going till dinner-time. Dinner, monastically

144

frugal, was a family affair. Between getting up and midday this monomaniac spent his time walking to and fro among the masterpieces with which his apartments were adorned. He dusted everything, furniture and pictures alike, never flagging in admiration. Then he went down to his daughter's rooms to enjoy the intoxication of paternal bliss, before setting off on his business in Paris – attending sales, visiting exhibitions, and so on. When a masterpiece was available within his terms, he came to life: here was a trap to set, a deal to bring off, a battle to win. He resorted to every conceivable trick in order to get his new Sultana cheaply! Magus had his own map of Europe with every masterpiece marked on it, and at every relevant spot he had co-religionists who kept their eyes open on his behalf in return for a commission – but the reward was meagre for the amount of vigilance entailed!

Where are the two lost Raphael pictures so persistently searched for by Raphael enthusiasts? Magus has them! He owns the original of Giorgione's *Portrait of his Mistress* – the woman who caused this painter's death. Other supposed originals are merely copies of this famous canvas, worth half a million francs according to Magus himself. This same Jew owns Titian's masterpiece, *The Entombment of Christ*, which was painted for Charles V of Spain and sent by the great artist to the great emperor with a letter in Titian's own hand-writing pasted underneath the picture. He owns another original work by the same artist – the maquette which served as a model for all his portraits of Philip the Second. The ninety-seven remaining pictures are all of equal power and distinction. And so Magus scoffs at our Paris Museum, with which the sunlight plays havoc, gnawing away at the finest canvases as it streams through window-panes whose action is equivalent to that of burning-glasses. The only possible picture galleries are those with ceiling lighting. Magus himself used to open and close the shutters in his museum. He took as much care and pains with his pictures as he did with his daughter, the only other idol he worshipped! Certainly this fanatical lover of pictures was well versed in all that pertains to the pictorial art. He held that masterpieces had a life of their own: they changed from day to day: their beauty depended on the light which brought out their tints. He talked about them as the Dutch florists used to talk about their tulips. He would come and look at some particular picture at the time of day when the great work was resplendent in all its glory, when the atmosphere was clear and pure.

He was himself like an animate picture in the midst of all these inanimate ones, this little old man in his shabby frock-coat, ten-year-old waistcoat and dirty trousers; with his bald head, his sunken cheeks, his white quivering porcupine beard, his aggressive pointed chin, his toothless mouth, the canine gleam in his eyes, his bony shrivelled hands, his obelisk nose, his cold rough skin – gloating over these lovely creations of genius! The sight of a Jew with a three-million treasure around him will always be one of the finest spectacles the human race can offer. Our great actor, Frédérick Lemaître, superb as he is, cannot rise to poetry like this. Of all the cities in the world, Paris is the one which harbours the greatest numbers of such strange figures, so devoted to their particular religion. The *eccentrics* in London always grow tired of their enthusiasms in the end, just as they grow tired of life itself, whereas your Parisian monomaniac goes on living with his fantasy in blissful spiritual concubinage. In Paris you will often come upon people like Pons or Elias Magus. They dress like tramps, and have their heads in the clouds like the permanent secretary of the French Academy. They look as if they cared about nothing and were devoid of feeling. They never turn round to look at a woman or gaze in a shop-window. You would think their ambling progress haphazard, purposeless and brainless, and wonder to what strange tribe of Parisians they belonged. The answer is this: they are millionaires, collectors, the most impassioned men on the face of the earth: men quite capable of venturing into the miry regions of the police-courts in order to lay hands on a cup, a picture or a rare exhibit – Elias Magus himself had actually had this experience once in Germany.

Such then was the expert to whose house Rémonencq furtively escorted La Cibot. Rémonencq was in the habit of consulting Magus every time he met him in the street; and on several occasions the Jew had induced Abramko to lend money to this erstwhile street-porter, for he knew he could depend upon him. Since the Chaussée des Minimes was only a stone's throw from the rue de Normandie, the two conspirators took only ten minutes to get there.

'You're going to meet the richest of the retired antique dealers in Paris,' said Rémonencq, 'the greatest expert in town.'

Madame Cibot was stupefied when she found herself in the presence of a little old man wearing a greatcoat which would scarcely have been worth taking to Cibot for repair. He was watching a painter who was busy restoring pictures in a cold room on the spacious ground floor. She trembled when the old man's glance fell on her: his eyes were as coldly malevolent as those of a cat.

'What do you want, Rémonencq?' he asked.

'I'd like to have some pictures valued, and you are the only person in Paris who can tell a poor old tinker like me how much he can pay for them when he's not rolling in money like you!'

'Where are they?'

'This is the concierge who looks after the gentleman who owns them. I have arranged with her to . . .'

'What's his name?'

'Monsieur Pons!' said La Cibot.

'Don't know him,' replied Magus with an ingenuous air as his foot softly pressed the foot of the picture-restorer.

The latter was Moret, the painter: he was aware of the value of Pons's collection, and his head had jerked up at the name. Only in the presence of Rémonencq and such a woman as La Cibot could the Jew have risked giving this cautionary hint. In one glance – a goldsmith's scales would not have been more accurate than his appraisal – he had summed up the moral worth of the concierge. Neither of the visitors could know that the good Pons and Magus had often bared their fangs at one another. In fact, these two fanatical collectors were mutually envious, and that is why the old Jew's heart had just missed a beat. He had never hoped for a chance of getting inside so well-guarded a harem! The Pons collection was the only one in Paris which could vie with the one Magus possessed. Twenty years earlier than Pons, the Jew had conceived the same idea, but Pons had always been an amateur buyer, and his museum remained closed to Magus as it was to Dusommerard. Pons and Magus were equally secretive in their heart of hearts. Neither of them relished the celebrity for which the owners of *objets d'art* are usually avid. So the prospect of inspecting the poor musician's splendid collection afforded the same delight to Elias Magus as a connoisseur of women would feel if he managed to steal into the boudoir of a friend's beautiful and jealously secluded mistress. The great respect shown by Rémonencq to this odd creature, and the spell which this undoubtedly forceful, even mysterious personality inevitably cast upon her, reduced the concierge to obedience and pliancy. La Cibot dropped the autocratic tone of voice which she used in her lodge for dealing with tenants and her 'two gentlemen'; she accepted Magus's stipulations and promised to take him to the Pons museum that very day. This was tantamount to introducing the enemy into the heart of the citadel and plunging a dagger into Pons's heart. For the last ten years he had forbidden the woman to let anyone whatsoever set foot in his salon. He always carried the keys about with him, and La Cibot had obeyed him so long as she had shared Schmucke's opinion on the value of bric-à-brac. Indeed, by regarding these treasures as 'knick-knacks' and deploring Pons's mania, Schmucke had infused his contempt for such antiquated lumber into the concierge's mind, and by so doing had safeguarded the Pons museum against all intrusion for a very long period.

Now that Pons was bedridden, Schmucke was taking his friend's place in the theatre and boarding-schools. The poor German could only see his friend in the mornings and at dinner, since he was trying to cope with everything and to keep all their joint clientele. But this task called on every ounce of his strength, so overwhelming was the sorrow he felt. Seeing the poor man so sad, his schoolgirl pupils and the theatre staff, all of whom he had informed of Pons's sickness, were continually asking him for news, and the pianist's affliction was so great that even those who were really unconcerned accorded him the same show of sympathy as people in Paris usually accord to the greatest catastrophes. The kindly German's vital strength was as much undermined as that of Pons. He had a double burden of suffering – his own grief and his friend's sickness. And so he went on talking of Pons during half of every lesson he gave. His teaching was subject to such naïve interruptions, as he paused to wonder how Pons was getting on, that his pupils found themselves merely listening to explanations of Pons's malady. Between two successive lessons he would rush back to the rue de Normandie to spend a quarter of an hour with Pons. And yet, appalled as he was by the depletion of the resources they held in common, alarmed as he was by Madame Cibot's now fortnight-old habit of swelling the sick-room expenses as much as she could, the piano-teacher's anxiety was kept in control by such courage as he would never have thought he could muster. For the first time in his life his mind was set on earning money so that the household should not go short. Whenever a pupil, genuinely moved by the plight of the two friends, asked Schmucke how he could bear to leave Pons quite alone, he replied, with the superior smile of a gullible man:

'Matemoiselle, ve haf Matame Cipot! A treashure! A tchewel! She looks after Pons as if he vere a printce!'

Now when Schmucke went trotting off to his work, La Cibot remained in command both of the flat and Pons. The latter had eaten nothing for a fortnight. He lay there inert. Madame Cibot herself had to lift him up and deposit him in an easy-chair while she made his bed. How could he have kept an eye on this self-styled guardian angel? Naturally, the visit she had paid to Elias Magus had occurred while Schmucke was at home for lunch.

She had returned so as to be there just as the German was taking his leave of the patient, because, since the likely extent of Pons's fortune had been revealed to her, she was reluctant to leave the old bachelor and she sat over him like a broody hen. She used to settle herself in a comfortable armchair at the foot of his bed, and regale him with all the gossip such women have on tap. She became wheedling, soft-spoken, attentive and fussy. And, as we shall see, she used Machiavellian tactics in order to gain ascendancy over the poor man's mind.

15. Tittle-tattle and tactics – elderly concierge style

LA CIBOT had been frightened by the predictions of Madame Fontaine's tarot pack, and had promised herself she would use gentle methods and resort merely to moral villainy in order to get her name in her master's will. Having had no idea for ten years of the value of Pons's collection, she credited herself with ten years of devoted, honest and disinterested service, and she proposed to convert this valuable asset into cash. Since the day when Rémonencq had with one word hinted at golden prospects and thereby hatched out in this woman's heart a serpent – the lust for wealth – which had been contained in its shell for twenty-five years, this creature had been feeding it on all the noxious ferments which work deep down in the heart. We shall see how she carried out the advice which this serpent whispered in her ear.

'Well, has our cherub had a good drink? Is he any better?' she asked Schmucke.

'He iss not vell, tear Matame Cipot, he iss not vell!' And the German wiped away a tear.

'Come on now, my dear gentleman! You're getting too worried about it yourself. You have to take things as they come. Even if Cibot was on his deathbed, I shouldn't take on the way you do. After all, our cherub's as strong as a horse. And then, you see, it seems he's lived clean. You just don't know how long people who've lived clean last out. He's in a bad way, sure enough, but I'll look after him so well I'll pull him through. Don't fret. Go back to your work. I'll keep him company, and see that he takes every pint of his barley-water.'

'If it vere not for you, I shoult vorry myself to deass,' said Schmucke, showing the trust he placed in this good housekeeper by clasping her hands in his.

La Cibot was wiping her eyes as she came into Pons's bedroom.

'What's the matter, Madame Cibot?' asked Pons.

'Monsieur Schmucke has made me all upset,' she replied. 'He's been crying so much you might be dead and gone! I know you're very poorly, but you're not that far gone, and there's no need to be crying over you. Gracious me, what a fool I am to get so fond of people and make more fuss of them than I do of Cibot! When all's said and done, I don't mean a thing to you. Mother Eve's the only relation we have in common. But all the same I get so bothered when I think of you, and that's a fact. I'd have my hand cut off – the left one of course – to see you coming and going like you used to, eating well and doing the dealers down. If the Lord had blessed me with a child, I don't believe I'd have been so fond of him as I am of you, so there! Have a good drink, my pet; come on, empty the glass. Drink it up now. Remember what the doctor said: "If he wants to keep out of the churchyard, he's got to drink as many bucketfuls as the water-seller takes round in a day." Come on then, drink it up! . . .'

'But my good Cibot, I'm drinking such a lot that my stomach's all awash . . .'

'There, that's finished,' said the concierge as she took away his glass. 'That's what'll put you to rights! Monsieur Poulain had another patient like you, who had no one to wait on him. His children left him to himself, and he was so ill that his disease carried him off just because he wouldn't drink . . . So you see you've got to drink, dearie! . . . He's been in his grave these two months. Don't you know that if you died, my dear gentleman, you'd carry off good Monsieur Schmucke with you? Honestly, he's just like a baby. Oh, how he loves you, the sweet lamb – more than any woman ever loves a man. He won't eat or drink. He's got as thin as you this last fortnight, and you're nothing but skin and bone. It makes me jealous when I'm so fond of you too. But I don't go that far, oh no, I haven't lost my appetite. I'm up and downstairs all day, and I get so weak in the legs, come nightfall, I'm fit to drop – just like a lump of lead. And there am I neglecting my poor man for your sake, leaving Mademoiselle Rémonencq to get him his meals, and they're so bad he does nothing but grumble. And then I tell him straight he must be ready to suffer for other people's sake, and you're too ill to be left to yourself . . . In fact, you aren't well enough to do without a nurse. But you can take it from me I wouldn't stand a nurse here, when I've spent the last ten years doing for you . . . And besides, nurses do nothing but gorge themselves. They eat enough for a dozen, and you've got to give them wine, sugar and make them cosy with foot-warmers and the like. What's more, if their patients don't put them down in their will, they rob them! You call in a nurse this very day, and tomorrow you'll find a picture or something else missing . . .'

'Oh, Madame Cibot!' cried Pons, quite beside himself. 'Don't leave me! . . . Don't let anyone take anything! . . .'

'Trust me!' said La Cibot. 'While there's strength left in me I'll be here . . . don't worry. Didn't Monsieur Poulain want to call a nurse in? – Maybe *he* has an eye on your treasures. I soon put him to rights! "I'm the only person Monsieur Pons wants," I told him. "We're both used to one another's ways." And he shut up. Nurses are thieves, no less. I can't stand them. I could tell you something about their scheming ways. For instance, there was an old gentleman . . . mind, it was the doctor himself told me about it . . . Well, a certain Madame Sabatier . . . thirty-six she was . . . she used to keep a shoe-shop near the Law Courts – you remember the line of shops that they pulled down there? . . .'

Pons gave an affirmative nod.

'You do? . . . Well then, this woman couldn't make ends meet, and why? Because her man drank like a fish, and he died of spontaneous *imbustion*. She was a good-looking woman, I must say, but she got nothing out of that, though I've heard it said that she had a few affairs with the barristers there. Well, she was down on her luck and took to nursing women in labour. And then she happened to take on an old gentleman; if you don't mind me saying so, he had trouble with his water-works, and they pumped it out of him like out of a well. He needed so much attention that she used to sleep on a camp-bed in his room. Would you believe such a thing? I know what you'll say: "Men are that selfish they have no respect for women." Anyway, there she stayed all the time, livening him up, telling him tales, jabbering away with him just like you and me do, don't we? . . . She found out that his nephews – the poor man had some nephews – were no better than monsters and were causing him no end of vexation, and in point of fact it was them that were making him ill. Well, then, dearie, she saved his life and he married her, and they've got a lovely little boy, and Ma'me Bordevin, the butcher's wife in the rue Charlot – she's a relation of this lady – stood at the font for him. Bit of luck for her, eh? I'm a married woman, but I never had a baby, and I can tell you it's Cibot's fault, he loves me too much – I could manage it if I wanted . . . Enough said . . . And what would we have done with a family, Cibot and me, without a penny to bless ourselves with, which is what comes of living an honest life for thirty years, my dear good gentleman! But I don't care. I've never taken a farthing from anybody else. I've never done anybody wrong. Look now, suppose, as you might say, seeing you'll be back on your pins in six weeks' time and taking a stroll along the boulevard, suppose you were to put me in your will. Well, I wouldn't rest till I'd given it back to your rightful heirs, I'd be so afraid to have money I hadn't earned with the sweat of my brow. You'll say to me: "Ma'me Cibot, don't make such a to-do about it. It's your deserts, you've looked after us two gentleman as if we were your children, you saved us a thousand francs a year." – It's a fact, Monsieur Pons, in my situation there's many a cook who'd have put ten thousand francs in her stocking already. – Suppose anybody said to me: "It's only right that this worthy gentleman should leave you some money to live on." Well then, I'd say "No!" I'm not self-seeking. I just can't think how women can do good for what they can get out of it. That's not doing good, is it, Monsieur? I'm no church-goer, I've no time for it, but my conscience tells me what's right . . . Don't wriggle about like that, my pet! Stop scratching! Goodness me, how yellow you're getting! So yellow you're well-nigh brown . . . Funny how a man can turn as yellow as a lemon in three weeks. – Being honest's all the riches poor people can have, and they must have something after all. Now let's suppose you were on your last legs, I'd be the first to tell you you ought to leave all your belongings to Monsieur Schmucke. It's what you owe him, he's all the family you can boast of. He's as fond of you, he is, as a dog is of his master.'

'You're right!' said Pons. 'He's the only person in all my life who has ever loved me.'

*

'Oh, Monsieur Pons!' Madame Cibot exclaimed. 'That's not a kind thing to say! What about me? Do you think I don't love you?'

'I don't say that, my dear Madame Cibot.'

'That's all very fine! You treat me like a drudge, just an ordinary cook, as if I hadn't any feelings at all. Goodness me! Work yourself to skin and bone for two old gentlemen. Rack your brains to give them every comfort – and there I've been ransacking a dozen grocers' shops and getting told off for it, just to find you a nice bit of Brie, and trudging to market to get you a bit of fresh butter! . . . Spend all your time looking after things . . . never in ten years have I broken or chipped a single piece of crockery . . . Fuss over them like a mother. And all the thanks you'll get is a "my dear Madame Cibot"! It only shows I don't matter a scrap to an old gentleman I've cared for as if he were a prince of the blood. Napoleon's own son, the King of Rome, wasn't cared for any better. It's a sure thing, he wasn't cared for as you are – didn't he go and die just when he was coming of age? Monsieur Pons, you don't treat me as you ought. You've no gratitude! Just because I'm only a poor caretaker. Lord help me, you're like the rest of them, you think we're no better than dogs . . .'

'But, my dear Madame Cibot . . .'

'Come to that, you who've got learning, you tell me why we're treated like that, us caretakers. Why do people think we've no feelings? Why do we get laughed at in these times when there's all this talk of everybody being equal? Aren't I as good as any other woman? Me that used to be one of the best-looking women in Paris and was talked about as the lovely oyster-girl, and never a day went by but I was proposed to morning, noon and night! And could be still, if I was so minded! Look now, Monsieur Pons, you know that little shrimp of a man, that rag-and-bone merchant down below? Well, supposing I was a widow, he'd marry me with his eyes shut, for he's kept them open quite a lot so far, looking me up and down.

"What lovely arms you've got, Ma'me Cibot," he says to me. "Last night I dreamt they were nice bread rolls and I was spread over them like a pat of butter!" ... Take a look, Monsieur Pons. There's arms for you!'

She rolled up one sleeve and displayed the finest arm imaginable, as white and fresh as her hands were red and chafed: a chubby, round, dimpled arm! Drawn from its coarse woollen sheath as a sword is drawn from its scabbard, it might well have dazzled even Pons, though he was too shy to let his gaze linger on it.

'What's more,' she continued, 'the sight of them brought more customers to the Cadran Bleu than the oysters I used to open. Well, they belong to Cibot, and I'm wrong to neglect the poor man. One word from me, and he'd jump over a cliff ... and I'm neglecting him for your sake, Monsieur Pons, and all you can do is to call me "my dear Madame Cibot". And there's nothing I wouldn't do for you!'

'Please do listen to me,' said the sick man. 'I can't call you "Mother" or "Wife".'

'No, never again in all my days will I let myself get attached to anybody!'

'But let me speak!' continued Pons. 'Be reasonable. It was Schmucke I was talking about in the first place.'

'Ah! Monsieur Schmucke! There's a good-hearted man if you like! Now *he's* fond of me because he's poor. It's the rich that have no feeling, and you're rich. Very well, call in a nurse, and see what a dance she'll lead you! She'll be buzzing round you like a bumblebee ... The doctor will tell her that you must have a lot to drink, and she'll only give you solids! She'll bring you to your grave so as to rob you. You don't deserve to have a "dear Madame Cibot" like me! ... There we are then: when Monsieur Poulain comes back you can ask him to get you a nurse!'

'For God's sake listen to me!' shouted the exasperated Pons. 'When I spoke of my friend Schmucke I wasn't referring to women. I know very well that you and Schmucke are the only people who have any kindness in their hearts for me.'

'Now don't get so worked up,' exclaimed La Cibot, swooping down on Pons and thrusting him back in his bed.

'After all, how could I help being fond of you?' said poor Pons.

'So you really are fond of me? There then, there then, forgive me, Monsieur Pons,' she said, weeping and wiping her eyes. 'Yes indeed, you're fond of me just as you might be fond of a servant, that's all – the sort that gets a pension of six hundred francs thrown at her . . . like throwing a bone to a dog!'

'Madame Cibot!' cried Pons. 'What do you take me for? How little you know me!'

'Ah well! You'll get fonder of me still,' she went on in response to a glance from Pons. 'You'll come to love your good fat Cibot like a mother, won't you? Well, so you ought. I'm your mother and you're my children, both of you. Oh, if only I knew the people who've vexed you so, I'd soon get myself landed in the dock or the lock-up, I'd tear their eyes out, I would . . . People like that ought to have their heads chopped off! And even that's too good for such scum! You that's so kind and affectionate! A heart of gold, that's what you have! The Lord made you and put you in the world to make some woman happy . . . And believe me, you *would* have made her happy . . . It's plain to see you were cut out for that . . . The first thing I said to myself when I saw how it was between you and Monsieur Schmucke, I said: "Monsieur Pons has missed his way in life! He was meant to be a good husband." Tell me now, you *do* like women, don't you?'

'Indeed I do,' said Pons. 'But I've never had anything to do with them.'

'You don't say!' cried La Cibot. She put on a provocative air, moved nearer to him and took him by the hand. 'So you don't know what it's like to have a mistress who'll do all she can, and more, to make her lover happy? Who'd have believed it! Well, if I were you I wouldn't like to pop off to the next world before I'd had the greatest enjoyment you can get out of this one! You poor ducky! If I was still what I used to be, take my word for it, I'd give Cibot the go-by for you! Why, with a nose like yours – you've a first-rate nose! – what have you been doing all this time, you poor cherub? . . . Now you'll be telling me it's not every woman that goes for the right sort of man.

It's a shame, they make such a mess of choosing a man, it's enough to make you cry. I thought you had mistresses by the dozen – dancers and actresses and duchesses, you spent so much time out! It's a fact, whenever I saw you going off, I said to Cibot, I said: "There's Monsieur Pons off for a nice bit of fun!" On my oath, that's what I said, I thought the women just fell for you! Love's what you were made for . . . Bless your heart, I could tell that the first night you had dinner at home. How pleased you were at giving Monsieur Schmucke such a treat! And the next day he was still in tears about it: "Matame Cipot, he haf tinet viz me!" and there was I blubbing about it too! And remember how down he was when you started your gallivanting again and went and dined out. The poor man! I've never seen him so low. Well, you're quite right to leave him your money. After all, he's as good as a whole family to you, the dear good man! . . . Don't forget that, or the Lord won't have you in Heaven. He only lets in those who've done well by their friends and left them a nice bit of money to live on.'

*

Pons made vain efforts to reply, but La Cibot swept on like a hurricane. One can turn off the cock of a steam-engine, but it will always be beyond the power even of genius to arrest the flow from a concierge's tongue.

'I know what you'll be telling me next!' she went on. 'But bless you, Monsieur Pons, it doesn't kill a man to make a will when he's taken ill. If I were you – just in case – I wouldn't leave the poor lamb unprovided for, and him as harmless as any sucking dove. He's as innocent as a babe. You can't let him be fleeced by money-grubbing lawyers and a pack of thieving relations! Look here, has a single one of them been to see you in the last three weeks? . . . And you're minded to leave them your money? You know, don't you, that folks are saying that what you've got here is well worth bothering about?'

'I know that,' said Pons.

'Rémonencq does some second-hand dealing, and he knows you're a private collector. Well, he says he'd settle no less than thirty thousand francs on you if you'd leave him your pictures. There's an offer! Why not take it? I thought he was fooling me when he said that ... Anyway, you ought to put Monsieur Schmucke wise to what all these things are worth. He'd be taken in like a five-year-old. He's no notion of what they would fetch, all your fine bits and pieces. He's so little idea, he'd give them away for next to nothing – if so be he didn't keep them all his life out of love for you ... Though, I doubt if he'll outlast you – when you die he'll die too. Never mind, there's me to look after him! Cibot and me, we'll stand by him through thick and thin.'

Pons was moved by this appalling gabble, which seemed to be prompted by the genuine feeling natural to simple working people.

'Dear Madame Cibot,' he replied, 'what would have become of me without you and Schmucke?'

'You may well say that. We're the only friends you have on earth. But two kind hearts are better than any families. Don't talk to me about families! It's like fine talk, as the old actor said: you can make what you like of it, good or bad ... Where are they anyway, your relations? ... I've never set eyes on them.'

'It's through them that I'm laid up like this!' exclaimed Pons out of the bitterness of his soul.

'Oh then, you've got some relations!' said La Cibot, starting up from her chair as if she had suddenly found herself sitting on a red-hot poker. 'Well, a nice lot they are. Relations! What! You've been at death's do for three weeks – three weeks this morning – and they haven't been to inquire about you! That's a fine way to behave! ... Why, if I were in your place, I'd sooner leave my money to a foundling hospital than give them a farthing!'

'Well, you see, my dear Madame Cibot, I intended to bequeath all I possess to my second cousin, the daughter of my first cousin, Président Camusot – you know, the magistrate who came here one morning nearly two months ago.'

'Oh yes, the stocky little man who sent his servants along to ask you to forgive them ... for the silly trick his wife played on you. That lady's-maid was asking me questions about you. The stuck-up old piece! I'd have liked to have given her velvet cloak a good dusting with my broom-handle. Fancy a lady's-maid flaunting herself in a velvet cloak! Take my word for it, the world's turned topsy-turvy. What's the good of having revolutions? It's all very well for the idle rich to have their two dinners a day if they can afford it. But I say the law's no good: nothing's sacred if the King doesn't keep people in their place. Are we all equal, or are we not? If we are, no lady's-maid ought to have a velvet cloak when I have to go without one – me, a respectable woman that's been honest for thirty years ... A fine state of things, I do declare! You should show what you are by what you wear. A lady's-maid is a lady's-maid. A concierge is a concierge, like me, Ma'me Cibot. Why does an army officer wear pips on his shoulders? To show what his rank is. Listen, shall I tell you the solemn truth about all that? The country's going to the dogs ... Things were different under the Emperor, weren't they, Monsieur Pons? And so I said to Cibot: "Mark my words, husband, people that let their lady's-maids go about in velvet cloaks are people with hearts of stone ... "'

'Hearts of stone, that's it exactly!' Pons replied. And he poured all his troubles and vexations into Madame Cibot's ears. In return she launched out into abuse of the Camusots and displayed the most emphatic sympathy at every word in his sorry tale. In the end she burst into tears!

This sudden familiarity between the old musician and Madame Cibot is explicable enough if one imagines a bachelor's predicament when he is seriously ill for the first time in his life, lying on a bed of pain, alone in the world, face to face with himself the whole day long and finding the time drag all the more because he is at grips with the unspeakable sufferings caused by hepatitis, which throws a dark shadow on even the brightest of lives. Also, robbed of his numerous occupations, he misses all the sights which Paris affords free of charge, and falls into a black depression such as Parisians alone experience.

This deep and gloomy solitude, the attacks of pain which lower both moral and physical vitality, the emptiness of existence: all this induces a bachelor, particularly one who is inclined to be weak in character, sensitive of soul, and credulous, to cling to the person who waits on him as a drowning man clings to a straw. That is why Pons listened so avidly to La Cibot's gossip. Schmucke, Madame Cibot and Dr Poulain were the whole of mankind for him; his room was the whole wide world. Sick people in general concentrate their attention on the narrow sphere their eyes encompass; their egoism is of such limited range that it is subordinated to the persons and things inside a single room. What then could be expected of an old bachelor with no attachments, one who had never known a woman's love? Three weeks had been enough to bring Pons – at certain moments – to regret not having married Madeleine Vivet! And so, during the same three weeks, Madame Cibot had been acquiring an enormous ascendancy over the sick man's mind. He felt he would be lost without her, for in Schmucke the unfortunate invalid only saw a replica of himself. La Cibot's prodigious artfulness – though she herself was scarcely aware of this – consisted in giving expression to certain ideas which were passing through Pons's own mind.

'Ah! Here's the doctor,' she said on hearing the doorbell ring. And, knowing full well that the visitors were the Jew and Rémonencq, she left Pons to himself.

'Don't make any noise, gentlemen,' she said to them. 'He mustn't notice a thing! He's terribly cantankerous about his collection.'

'A quick look round will do,' the Jew replied. He had come provided with his magnifying glass and a lorgnette.

16. Corruption in conference

THE room containing the greater part of the Pons collection was one of those ancient salons such as the architects employed by the French nobility designed: twenty-five feet wide, thirty feet long and thirteen feet high. Pons's pictures, sixty-seven in all, were all hung on the four walls of this salon which was panelled in white and gold. But Time had softened the white to yellow, and the gold to red, and these mellowed tones did not spoil the effect of the canvases. Fourteen statues rising from pedestals by Buhl stood in the corners of the room or between the pictures. Ebony sideboards, all richly and regally carved, lined the lower portions of the walls to elbow height. These sideboards contained the curios. In the middle of the room, a row of carved wood credence tables displayed the rarest products of human art: ivories, bronzes, wood-carvings, enamels, goldsmith's work, porcelains and so forth.

Once the Jew was in this sanctuary, he went straight to four masterpieces which he recognized as the finest in this collection, by great masters not represented in his own. They meant as much to him as those rare plants which send a naturalist off on his voyages, from west to east, through tropical countries, deserts, pampas, savannahs and virgin forests. One was a Sebastiano del Piombo, the second a Fra Bartolommeo della Porta, the third a Hobbema landscape, the last a female portrait by Dürer: four pictorial gems! In the art of painting Sebastiano del Piombo is, as it were, a brilliant node in which three schools converge, each contributing its outstanding qualities. A Venetian painter, he moved to Rome and there acquired the technique of Raphael under the direction of Michelangelo, who wanted to set him in opposition to Raphael and so use one of his own pupils to pit himself against that sovereign pontiff of art. In consequence this easy-going genius made a fusion of Venetian colour, Florentine composition and Raphaelesque technique in the few pictures he deigned to paint, the cartoons for which, it is said, were drawn by Michelangelo himself. And so one can see the peak of perfection reached by this man with his three-fold technique, when one studies the Louvre portrait of Baccio Bandinelli, which, without losing by the comparison, can be set beside Titian's *Man with a Glove*, the *Portrait of an Old Man* in which Raphael blended his own artistic perfection with that of Correggio, and Leonardo da Vinci's *Charles VII*. These are four pearls of the same water, the same orient, the same roundness, the same sheen, the same pricelessness. Human art can go no further. It surpasses nature, which gave but momentary existence to the originals. One work by this great but incurably indolent genius, this immortal master of the palette, was in Pons's possession: a *Knight of Malta at Prayer*, painted on slate, having a freshness, a finish, a depth far superior to the qualities which the Baccio Bandinelli portrait displays. The Fra Bartolommeo, depicting *The Holy Family*, would have been attributed to Raphael by many connoisseurs. The Hobbema would have fetched sixty thousand francs at a public sale. As for the Albrecht Dürer, this *Portrait of a Woman* was similar to the famous Nuremberg *Holzschuer*, which the Kings of Bavaria, Holland and Prussia tried several times, unsuccessfully, to buy for two hundred thousand francs. Does it represent the wife or daughter of the Ritter Holzschuer, Dürer's friend? This appears to be a safe conjecture since the woman in Pons's collection is posed in such a way as to suggest a companion picture, and the painted coat of arms is similarly arranged in both portraits. Finally the subscription *aetatis suae XLI* agrees exactly with the age shown in the portrait so piously preserved by the Holzschuer family at Nuremberg – of which an engraving has recently been completed.

Elias Magus had tears in his eyes as he scanned these four masterpieces, one by one.

'I will give you a commission of two thousand francs for each of these pictures if you can get them for me for forty thousand francs,' he whispered in La Cibot's ear. She was stupefied at the prospect of such an unexpected fortune.

Elias Magus's admiration or, to be more exact, his delirious ecstasy, had so disturbed his intelligence and his habitual cupidity that, as can be seen, the Jew in him was quite submerged.

'What about me?' asked Rémonencq, who had no knowledge of pictures.

'Every one of them is up to the same standard,' the Jew's whispered answer, with its quick suggestion, came at once: 'Get me any ten of these pictures and your fortune is made.'

This trio of thieves were still exchanging glances, each yielding in his own way to that most intense of all delights – satisfaction at the prospect of imminent gain – when the sick man's voice rang out in echoing tones:

'Who's there?' cried Pons.

'Monsieur Pons, lie down again,' said La Cibot, rushing to Pons's bed and pushing him back on to it. 'What next! Do you want to kill yourself?... Well, it wasn't Monsieur Poulain after all. It's only kind Rémonencq, so anxious about you that he's come for news of you. You're so well-liked that everybody in the building is all in a flutter about you. What's worrying you?'

'But it sounds as if there are several of you,' said the sick man.

'Several! The idea! What's got into your head? My goodness, you'll soon be going out of your mind. Here, see for yourself.'

La Cibot made quickly for the door and opened it, motioning Magus to withdraw, and beckoning Rémonencq forward.

'Well, my dear sir,' said the Auvergnat, thus ushered in by La Cibot. 'I've come to ask about you. The whole house is in a state about you. Nobody likes the idea of a death on the premises. And another thing: old Monistrol – you know him well – asked me to tell you that if you need money he'll be ready to oblige you.'

'He's only sent you to have a look at my trinkets,' said the old collector in sour and suspicious tones.

Those who suffer from diseases of the liver almost always contract a special and fleeting antipathy: their irascibility singles out some particular object or person. Now Pons had got it into his head that people had designs on his treasures and his mind was set on watching over them. At frequent intervals he had been sending Schmucke to make sure that no one had slipped into his sanctuary.

'You certainly have a fine collection,' was Rémonencq's astute reply. 'It might well attract the *chineurs*' attention. I don't know a thing about valuable antiques, but they do say that you, sir, are a great expert, and although I'm not much of a judge, I'd shut my eyes and buy anything from you ... if it so happened you needed any money now and then, for nothing costs more than these cursed diseases. Take my sister now: she used to have giddy turns, and in less than a fortnight she spent thirty sous on quackeries, and she'd have got over it just the same ... Doctors are rogues and they take advantage of our ailments to ...'

'Good day to you, Monsieur, and thank you,' replied Pons to the scrap-iron merchant, casting anxious glances at him.

'I'll see him out,' La Cibot whispered to her patient. 'So that he can't touch anything.'

'Yes, please do!' answered the patient with a grateful look.

She closed the bedroom door, and that reawakened Pons's suspicions. She found Magus stock-still in front of the four pictures. Such immobility, such admiration can only be understood by those whose souls are open to supreme beauty, to the ineffable emotion aroused by perfection in art: those who will stand for hours on end in the Louvre contemplating Leonardo's *Mona Lisa*, Correggio's *Antiope*, Titian's *Mistress*, Andrea del Sarto's *Holy Family*, Domenichino's *Children among Flowers*, Raphael's little cameos and his *Portrait of an Old Man*, all of them of immeasurable artistic value.

'Don't make any noise as you go out!' she said.

The Jew withdrew slowly, walking backwards, gazing at the pictures with the lingering look of a lover saying good-bye to his mistress.

*

The steadiness of his contemplation had put ideas into La Cibot's mind, and so, when the Jew had reached the head of the stairs, she tapped his scrawny arm.

'Four thousand francs for each of those pictures, or nothing doing!'

'I'm a poor man,' said Magus. 'It's just love, just love of art, my dear, that makes me want these pictures.'

164

'You're as hard as nails, my lad,' said the concierge, 'and I can guess what love like that means. Anyhow, if you don't promise me sixteen thousand francs this very day in Rémonencq's hearing, it'll be twenty thousand tomorrow.'

'I'll make it sixteen,' replied the Jew, appalled by the concierge's greed.

'What's a Jew's promise worth?' La Cibot asked Rémonencq.

'You can take his word for it,' replied the scrap-iron merchant. 'He's as honest as I am myself.'

'Well, how about you? If I get you some of them to sell, what'll *you* give me?'

'Half shares in the profits,' was Rémonencq's prompt reply.

'I prefer hard cash straight away. I'm not a businesswoman,' she retorted.

'You've a wonderful head for figures!' said Elias Magus with a smile. 'You would make a fine saleswoman.'

'I'm ready to go in with her, lock, stock and barrel,' said the Auvergnat, taking hold of La Cibot's plump arm and giving it a vigorous pat. 'I don't ask her to put money into it, only her good looks! You're silly to stick to your cross-legged Turk and his needle! Can a miserable little porter put a good-looking woman like you in money's way? What a figure you'd cut in a shop on the boulevards, with antiques all around you, chattering away with amateurs and twisting them round your little finger! Say good-bye to your lodge when you've made your pile in this affair, and just think what we can do working together!'

'Make my pile!' exclaimed La Cibot. 'I wouldn't steal a pennyworth of stuff here, understand that, Rémonencq. Everybody round here knows I'm an honest woman, see!' Her eyes were blazing.

'Calm down!' said Elias Magus. 'Our friend from Auvergne seems to admire you far too much to want to insult you.'

'Wouldn't she bring in the customers!' cried the Auvergnat.

Madame Cibot was mollified.

'Be fair to me, my friends,' she continued, 'and judge for yourselves what my position is here. I've been wearing myself out the last ten years for those two old bachelors and never been paid back in anything but words. Ask Rémonencq. I've

165

been feeding those two old sticks at a loss. I've been losing twenty to thirty sous a day at it. All I've laid up has gone on them. I'll swear that on my own mother's grave, and she's the only parent I ever knew. As true as I stand here in God's own daylight, may my next cup of coffee poison me if I'm a farthing out in my reckoning! Well, there's a man who's going to die right enough, and he's the best off of those two old fogies I've treated like my own children. Would you credit it, my dear sir? I've been telling him these last three weeks that he's ripe for the churchyard, and Monsieur Poulain has given him up. And the old skinflint hasn't said a word about mentioning me in his will, no more than he would a total stranger. Take my word for it, if we want our due we've got to take it, sure as I'm an honest woman. Some hope there'd be from his heirs, I don't think! Look now, I've got to speak my mind: they're dirty rogues, every one of them.'

'True enough,' replied Elias with a sly grimace. 'It's people like us,' he added with a glance at Rémonencq, 'who are the most reliable.'

'Let me explain,' La Cibot went on. 'It's not you I'm talking about. As the old actor said, "pressing company is always accepted". I swear those two men already owe me nigh on three thousand francs, and what little I've got has already gone on medicine and their little wants. Suppose they don't take any account of what I've paid out for them! . . . I'm such a fool, I'm so honest I don't dare mention it to them. Well then, my dear sir, you who are in business, would you advise me to see a lawyer? . . .'

'A lawyer!' cried Rémonencq. 'You know more than all the lawyers put together.'

The sound of a heavy body falling on to the flagstones in the dining-room echoed through the wide spaces of the stairway.

'Oh, my goodness!' cried La Cibot. 'What's that? It sounds as if it's Monsieur Pons who's just had a nasty tumble.'

She gave a push to her two accomplices and they hurried briskly downstairs. Then she turned round, dashed into the dining-room and found Pons in his shirt, stretched full-length on the floor, in a faint. She put her arms round him, lifted him up as if he weighed no more than a feather, and carried him to his bed. When she had laid the unconscious man down she set to work reviving him by burning feathers under his nose and moistening his temples with eau de Cologne. Once she saw that his eyes were open and that he had recovered consciousness, she stood over him with her arms akimbo.

'No slippers! Nothing on you but a shirt! You might have caught your death! And why do you distrust me, Monsieur Pons? If that's how things are, it's all over between us. Fine thanks I get, after serving you for ten years and putting money of mine into your housekeeping, so that all I've got has gone to save poor Monsieur Schmucke any worry, and him going up and down the stairs crying his eyes out . . . And that's all the thanks I get! You come spying on me . . . The Lord has paid you out, and so He should! And me straining my insides to carry you back and maybe rupturing myself for the rest of my days . . . Oh my goodness, I've left the door open . . .'

'Who were you talking to?'

'That's a fine thing to ask! La Cibot exclaimed. 'The very idea! I'm your slave, am I? Have I got to tell you everything I do? You just take this in: if you plague me like this, I'm clearing out! You can get a nurse in.'

Appalled at this threat, Pons unwittingly showed La Cibot exactly how far she could go in holding this sword of Damocles over his head.

'It's my liver!' he said in piteous tones.

'That's all very well!' was La Cibot's surly reply.

She went off, leaving Pons in a state of confusion, full of remorse, admiring the strident devotion of his sick-bed attendant, heaping reproaches upon himself, and not realizing the terrible harm his fall on to the flagstones of the dining-room had done him, or how much it had aggravated his disease.

*

La Cibot caught sight of Schmucke as he came upstairs.

'Do come in, Monsieur Schmucke. There's bad news, very bad. Monsieur Pons is going out of his mind! Just think, he got out of bed with nothing on and tried to follow me, but he fell down full-length on the floor in there. And it's no use asking him why . . . He doesn't know . . . He's in a bad way. I never did a thing to make him so violent, except I might have given him ideas when I was talking to him about his early loves. You never know where you are with men. Old rakes every one of them ... I never ought to have made him look at my arms – his eyes were shining like carbuncles ...'

Schmucke was listening to Madame Cibot as though she were talking double Dutch.

'I gave myself such a strain that I shan't get over it for the rest of my days!' she added, making a pretence of suffering acute pain, with the thought of exploiting an idea which a slight feeling of muscular fatigue had suggested to her. 'Why am I such a fool? When I saw him lying flat like that I picked him up and put him back to bed, just as if he were a baby. And now I've ricked my back. I feel terrible, I'm going downstairs. You must look after the patient. I'm going to send Cibot to fetch the doctor to me. I'd rather die than become a cripple.'

She clutched the bannisters and lumbered downstairs with a great many contortions and plaintive groans, which startled all the other tenants and brought them out on to their landings. Schmucke was supporting the suffering caretaker, shedding tears and telling the story of her devotion. The whole house, the whole district, soon heard of Madame Cibot's splendid heroism: she was supposed to have given herself a terrible wrench by lifting up one of the 'Nutcrackers'. Schmucke came back to Pons and told him what a fearful plight their factotum was in. They looked at one another and said: 'What will become of us without her?'

Seeing how much Pons's condition had been worsened by his rash sortie, Schmucke had not the heart to scold him.

'Zet curset pric-à-prac! I voult razer purn it zen loose my frient!' he exclaimed when Pons told him the cause of the accident. 'Vy mistrust Matame Cipot, when she lents us her safinks? It vass not goot, put your dissease iss to plame.'

'Ah, what a disease!' said Pons, 'I know I'm not myself. I don't want you to suffer for it, my dear Schmucke.'

'Scolt no von put me!' said Schmucke, 'unt leafe Matame Cipot alone!'

Dr Poulain took only a few days to dissipate Madame Cibot's alleged infirmity, and in the Marais this cure, regarded as miraculous, gave extraordinary lustre to his reputation. In Pons's household he attributed this success to the sick woman's excellent constitution and, to the great satisfaction of the two 'Nutcrackers', she resumed her service with them after a week. This event increased a hundredfold the influence, or rather the tyranny, which the concierge wielded in the two men's abode. In the course of that week they had incurred debts, but it was she who paid them. She took advantage of this circumstance to obtain from Schmucke – with consummate ease – an IOU for the two thousand francs which she said she had lent them.

'What a fine doctor he is, Monsieur Poulain!' said La Cibot to Pons. 'He'll save you all right, my dear gentleman. Didn't he keep me out of my coffin? My poor dear man thought I was done for. Well now, Monsieur Poulain must have told you that when I was lying in bed, I never gave a thought to anything but you. "Dear God," I said, "take me, but spare my dear Monsieur Pons."'

'Poor dear Madame Cibot, you nearly became a cripple for my sake.'

'It's a fact. But for Monsieur Poulain, I'd be fitted out with the pinewood shirt that's waiting for all of us. As the old actor said, we've all got to come a cropper. No use making a fuss about it . . . How did you get on without me?'

'Schmucke looked after me,' the sick man replied. 'But our cash-box and our customers are the worse for it. I just don't know how he managed.'

'Ton't vorry, Pons!' cried Schmucke. 'Papa Cipot hass peen our panker.'

'Not a word about that, my dear lamb!' cried La Cibot. 'It's as if you were both our children. After all, our savings are in good hands with you. You're more dependable than the Bank of France. As long as we've a crust of bread to eat, you'll get half of it . . . It's not worth talking about . . .'

'Poor Matame Cipot!' said Schmucke as he left the room.

'Would you credit it, my cherub,' said La Cibot, seeing how troubled the sick man looked. 'While I lay there, well-nigh at my last gasp – I was looking Death in the face, you know – what vexed me most was the idea of leaving you to look after your two selves with never a helping hand, and leaving my poor

Cibot without a brass farthing . . . I've got hardly anything put by. I'm only telling you this in case I popped off and because of Cibot. He's an angel if ever there was one! Just think, the poor man coddled me as if I were the Queen of France. He wept bucketfuls over me! . . . But I knew I could depend on you, and that's the honest truth. I said to him: "Cibot, my gentlemen won't ever let you starve."'

Pons made no response to this attack *ad testamentum*, and the concierge waited in silence for a word from him.

'I will recommend you to Schmucke,' the sick man said at last.

'Ah well!' cried the concierge, 'I'm sure you'll do whatever's right. I put my trust in you and your kind heart. Don't let's ever talk of that; it makes me feel ashamed, it does, my cherub. Just think about getting well again. You'll outlive the lot of us.'

Madame Cibot was seized with deep and heartfelt anxiety, and she made up her mind to draw her master out on the question of the legacy he was intending to leave her. But by way of preliminary, that very evening, after giving Schmucke his dinner – he had taken to eating at his friend's bedside since the latter's illness – she went off to consult Monsieur Poulain at his house.

17. How all careers begin in Paris

DR POULAIN lived in the rue d'Orleans in a little ground-floor flat consisting of an ante-room, a sitting-room and two bedrooms. A pantry next to the ante-room and communicating with the doctor's bedroom had been converted into a consulting-room. A kitchen, a servant's bedroom and a small cellar were included in these rented quarters which were situated in one wing of a house – an immense construction built during the Empire on the site of an old mansion – of which the garden still remained and was shared by the tenants of the three ground-floor flats.

The doctor's flat had undergone no change for forty years; paint, wallpaper and decoration were all redolent of Imperial times. Forty years of grime and smoke had tarnished the mirrors and their frames, the patterns on the wallpaper, the ceilings and the paint. This tiny habitation, although it was in the heart of the Marais district, cost one thousand francs a year in rent. The doctor's seventy-year-old mother, Madame Poulain, was in occupation of the second bedroom for the rest of her mortal span. She worked for some breeches-makers, sewing gaiters, buckskins, braces, belts, in short everything pertaining to this kind of garment, which is more or less out of fashion today. Her time was taken up with looking after the house and her son's only maid, and so she never went out, but took the air in the tiny garden, to which she stepped down through the french window of the drawing-room. At her husband's death, twenty years before, she had sold his breeches-maker's stock and goodwill to his chief journeyman, who reserved enough work for her to earn about thirty sous a day. She had sacrificed everything to her only son's education, wishing at all costs to raise him to a social status higher than that of his father. Proud of her Aesculapius and believing he had a fine future before him, she was happy to care for him, to economize for his sake, dreaming only of his well-being, and bringing intelligence to the aid of love, which all mothers are not able to do. Thus Madame Poulain, remembering that she had been a humble seamstress, was anxious not to harm her son or expose him to ridicule or contempt, for the good woman larded her discourse with s's as Madame Cibot did with n's. She made a point of keeping to her room on the few occasions when distinguished patients came for a consultation, or when his college or hospital friends turned up. Never, therefore, had the doctor had any occasion to feel ashamed of his mother, whom he venerated, and whose heroic tenderness fully compensated for her lack of education. The sale of the breeches-making business had brought in about twenty thousand francs. In 1820 the widow had invested them in Government stock, and she had no other private means than the eleven hundred francs' interest she drew from them. And so, for a long time, their neighbours had been accustomed to seeing the doctor's and his mother's linen hanging out in the garden. All the laundering was done inexpensively by the maid and Madame Poulain. This domestic economy did considerable harm to the doctor, for people could not credit him with talent when they saw he was so poor. The eleven hundred francs' interest paid the rent. For the first few years the needlework done by Madame Poulain, a worthy, stout little woman, had covered all the expenses of this needy household. After twelve years of perseverance along his stony path, the doctor was now earning one thousand crowns per annum, so that henceforth Madame Poulain had about six thousand francs a year at her disposal. For anyone familiar with Paris, this was barely enough to live on.

The drawing-room, which served as a waiting-room for patients, was meanly furnished with a common type of mahogany sofa upholstered in flowered yellow Utrecht velvet, four armchairs, six upright chairs, a console and a tea-table left them by the defunct breeches-maker – he had chosen them all himself. The clock, still enclosed in its glass globe, and standing between two Egyptian candelabra, was in the shape of a lyre. You would wonder how they could have contrived to make the window-curtains survive so long, for they were of yellow calico, printed with rose-patterns, from the Jouy factory. Its owner, Oberkampf, had received the Emperor's compliments in 1809 for similarly atrocious products of the cotton industry. The consulting-room was furnished in the same style, with furniture from the paternal bedchamber. It was meagre, poor and cold. What patient could trust the skill of a doctor without repute, and who still had no decent furniture, in an age when advertisement is all-powerful and even the lamp-posts in the Place de la Concorde are gilded over to console the poor by persuading them that they are affluent citizens?

The ante-room was used as a dining-room. The maid worked in it when she was not busy in the kitchen or keeping the doctor's mother company. On entering the building, one sensed the respectable poverty which reigned in this dreary flat, whose tenant was absent half the day, as soon as one noticed the russet muslin curtains at the window of this room giving on to the courtyard. One could guess at the contents of the cupboards: scraps of musty pie, chipped platters, long-serving corks, table-napkins lasting the whole week, in short all the squalid but excusable objects one finds in small Parisian homes, fit only to pass from there into the rag-and-bone merchant's sack. That is why, in such times as ours, when money is the preoccupation of every mind and the topic of every conversation, the thirty-year-old doctor, whose mother had no social relationships, was still a bachelor. Not once in ten years had he met with the slightest incitement to a romance among the families to which his profession gave him access, for he practised his art in a sphere in which everyone led the same kind of existence as he did. He only came upon households like his own, those of clerks and minor civil servants and small manufacturers. His richest clients were butchers, bakers and the big retailers in the quarter; people who, as a rule, put down their cures to nature, so that they need only pay him a couple of francs for his visits, which he made on foot. For a doctor a cab is even more necessary than a knowledge of medicine.

A commonplace and uneventful life ultimately affects the most adventurous spirit. A man shapes himself to his lot and accepts the humdrum nature of life. And so, after ten years in practice, Dr Poulain still carried on with his Sisyphean labours, having shaken off the despair which had embittered his early days. None the less he cherished a dream. All people in Paris have their dreams; Rémonencq was indulging in a dream, and La Cibot had hers. Dr Poulain hoped to be called in to some rich and influential patient: he would infallibly cure this patient, and then use the credit so gained to obtain a post as senior doctor in a hospital, as a prison health-officer, as a consultant to the boulevard theatres or to a Civil Service department.

Incidentally, this was how he had obtained his post as municipal health officer. La Cibot had brought him to, and he had cured, Monsieur Pillerault, the owner of the house in which the Cibots were concierges. Monsieur Pillerault, great-uncle of Madame la Comtesse Popinot, the Minister's wife, had taken an interest in the young man whose undivulged poverty he had divined on paying him a visit of gratitude. Pillerault had solicited from his great nephew the Minister, who revered him, this post which the doctor had held for the last five years, and the slender emoluments had come just in time to prevent him from taking the drastic step of emigrating – and for a Frenchman to have to leave France is a lugubrious prospect. Dr Poulain duly went to thank the Comte Popinot, but since the illustrious Bianchon was this statesman's physician, the aspirant realized that he had no chance of practising in that family. The unfortunate doctor had vainly cherished the hope of obtaining the patronage of one of the influential Ministers, one of those dozen or more playing-cards which royal hands have been shuffling for the last sixteen years on the green baize of the Cabinet table. But he found himself still immersed in the Marais quarter, where he was now making a living among poor and lower-middle-class people and writing out death certificates, an occupation which brought him in twelve hundred francs a year.

Dr Poulain had not been without distinction as a houseman; he had become a prudent practitioner; he was not lacking in experience. Besides, he had no scandalous deaths to account for, and he was able to study all forms of disease *in anima vili*. Judge what bitterness welled up within him! In consequence, the expression on his naturally long and melancholy face was sometimes fearsome. Insert into a piece of yellow parchment the burning eyes of a Tartuffe and the sour grimace of an Alceste, and then imagine the gait and attitude of this man and the way he looked about him. He regarded himself as being as good a doctor as the illustrious Bianchon, but felt that an iron hand was holding him down in this dingy milieu! He could not refrain from comparing his fees – ten francs on a lucky day – with the five or six hundred francs which Bianchon pocketed. Does this not help one to imagine all the resentment which a so-called democratic régime inspires? Moreover, this man with his frustrated ambitions had no cause for self-reproach. He had already made one bid for fortune by inventing laxative pills similar to those of Morisson. He had entrusted the exploitation of them to a friend of his hospital days, a house-doctor who had become a pharmacist. But the pharmacist, having fallen in love with a dancer at the Ambigu-Comique, had gone bankrupt, and, since the patent for the invention of these laxative pills had been registered under the pharmacist's name, this great discovery had enriched the latter's successor. The sometime house-doctor had gone off to Mexico, that El Dorado, and taken with him one thousand francs of poor Poulain's savings. All that the latter got out of it was to be branded as a usurer by the dancer, when he went to her to ask for his money to be returned. Not a single well-to-do patient had come forward since he had had the good luck of curing old Pillerault. And so Poulain plodded round the whole of the Marais quarter on foot like a lean cat, and, out of twenty visits, only about two might earn him a couple of francs. The client who paid well was, in his eyes, that bird of fantasy known in all parts of the globe as the 'white blackbird'.

A briefless junior barrister and a young doctor without patients are the two most notable examples of that respectable despair peculiar to the city of Paris: that mute and cold despair which wears a frock-coat, the sort of black trousers with glossy seams which call to mind the zinc on a garret roof, a shiny waistcoat, a hat piously cared for, old gloves and a calico shirt. An elegiac poem, sombre as the solitary confinement cell in a state prison! Other kinds of indigence, such as those suffered by poets, artists, actors and musicians, derive some cheer from the joviality natural to the Arts, from the irresponsibility of that Bohemian life on which genius embarks before retiring into creative solitude. But these two men in black coats, who go about their business on foot and belong to two professions which see only the diseased or disreputable side of life: these two types of men, exposed as they are to the humiliations of their early struggles, acquire sinister, challenging casts of countenance; in their eyes you see pent-up resentment and ambition waiting to erupt like smouldering fires ready to burst into flame.

When two men who were friends as students happen to meet again after twenty years, the one who has become rich tries to avoid his former comrade if the latter has remained poor. He cuts him dead, appalled by the gulf which destiny has interposed between them. One of them has coursed through life on the spirited steed of good fortune or in the golden haze of success. The other has crawled along underground in the Paris sewers and wears the stigmata of his journey. How many of the doctor's former friends drew aside when they caught sight of his frock-coat and waistcoat!

We can now easily understand how skilfully Dr Poulain had played his part in the comedy of La Cibot's 'dangerous injury', for one can divine covetousness and ambition wherever they appear. Finding no lesion in any of the concierge's organs, admiring the regularity of her pulse and the perfect ease of her movements, and hearing her loud groans, he realized that self-interest alone prompted her claim to be at death's door. Since the swift cure of an allegedly serious illness was sure to spread his fame throughout the district, he exaggerated La Cibot's supposed hernia and undertook to rectify it by means of timely treatment. In short he subjected the concierge to spurious remedies and a fictitious operation. His efforts were crowned with complete success! He ransacked the arsenal of Desplein's extraordinary cures in order to find an exceptional case; he then applied it to Madame Cibot, modestly attributed its happy result to the great surgeon, and professed to have followed his method. To such bold shifts do professional men resort in the earlier stages of their career. Any ladder will serve to help them on to their particular stage. But everything wears out, even the rungs of a ladder, and the beginners in each profession can scarcely find enough wood to fashion into steps. At certain moments Parisians are refractory to success. Tired of putting people on pedestals, they sulk like spoilt children, and will worship no more idols. Or rather, truth to tell, there are sometimes not enough men of talent to excite infatuation. Lacunae occur in the matrix from which the ore of genius is extracted: when this happens, your Parisian stops short, reluctant to be for ever prizing and lionizing mediocrities.

*

Bursting in with her usual abruptness, Madame Cibot surprised the doctor at table with his old mother, eating a lambs'-lettuce salad – the cheapest there is – having nothing for dessert except a thin wedge of Brie, a meagre plateful of figs, nuts and raisins (with plenty of stalks among them) and a dish of cheap, withered apples.

'Don't go away, Mother,' said the physician, holding Madame Poulain back by the arm. 'It's Madame Cibot. I told you about her.'

'My respects, Madame. Your servant, Monsieur,' said La Cibot, taking the chair which the doctor offered her. 'Ah! this is your mother, doctor? She must be very happy to have so clever a son. He saved my life, Madame. He snatched me from the jaws of Death.'

Widow Poulain thought Madame Cibot a charming woman when she heard her thus singing her son's praises.

'I came to say, dear Monsieur Poulain, between you and me, that poor Monsieur Pons is in a very bad way. I wanted a word with you about him.'

'Let us go to the drawing-room,' said the doctor, making a sign to Madame Cibot in order to draw her attention to the maid's presence.

Once in the drawing-room, La Cibot lengthily unfolded her situation with regard to the two 'Nutcrackers'. She repeated – with embellishments – the story of her loan, and told of the tremendous services she had rendered for ten years to Messieurs Pons and Schmucke. To hear her, one would have supposed that these two old men could never have survived without her maternal attention. She adopted the pose of a guardian angel, and uttered so many lies, watered with tears, that in the end Madame Poulain was much moved.

'You will understand, my dear Monsieur Poulain,' she said by way of conclusion, 'that I simply must know where I stand as to Monsieur Pons' intentions about me, in case he happened to die. I do hope he won't, because having these two innocents to care for is what I live for. All the same, if I lose one of them, I'll look after the other. That's how Nature has made me – to take on a mother's cares. I don't know what I'd do if I hadn't someone to be interested in, someone to mother ... And so, if Monsieur Poulain is willing, he could do me a service which I'd be very thankful for, and speak for me to Monsieur Pons. Goodness me! Is a thousand francs' life pension too much? ... I ask you? It's as good as putting it into Monsieur Schmucke's pocket ... Anyhow, our dear patient told me he would recommend me to the poor German gentleman, and so it looks as if he's minded to make him his heir ... But what good is a man who can't string two ideas together in French? And in any case he's quite capable of going off to Germany, he'll be so desperate over his friend's death.'

'Dear Madame Cibot,' the doctor replied, assuming a grave demeanour. 'Such matters are not a doctor's concern, and I should be barred from my profession if I were known to have meddled with the testamentary disposition of one of my clients. The law does not allow a doctor to accept a legacy from his patient ...'

'How stupid the law is!' La Cibot retorted. 'What could stop me from sharing my legacy with you?'

'I will go further,' said the doctor. 'My professional conscience would forbid me to speak to Monsieur Pons about his death. In the first place, he is not in such great danger as that. In the second place, such a conversation coming from me would cause a shock which might do him real harm and so bring on his death.'

'But,' exclaimed Madame Cibot, '*I* make no bones about telling him to put his affairs in order, and he's none the worse for it. He's used to it! Have no fear!'

'Say no more, dear Madame Cibot! ... Such things are not a doctor's business. They are for lawyers to deal with ...'

'But my dear Monsieur Poulain, supposing Monsieur Pons asked you outright what his position is, and whether he hadn't better take precautions. Now then, would you refuse to tell him it would be a good thing, if he wants to get well again, to get everything tied up . . . Then you could slip in a little word for me . . .'

'Oh, if he speaks to me about making a will, I certainly will not dissuade him.'

'Very good, then, that's settled,' cried Madame Cibot. 'I came to thank you for taking care of me,' she added, slipping into his palm a screw of paper containing three gold coins. 'That's all I can manage at the moment. Oh, if I were rich, you would be too, Monsieur Poulain. You, God's own image in this wicked world! . . . Madame Poulain, your son is an angel!'

La Cibot got up, Madame Poulain bade her an affable good-bye, and the doctor showed her out to the landing. And there a glimmer of infernal enlightenment came to this fearful Lady Macbeth of the streets! She realized that the doctor was bound to be her accomplice, because he had accepted a fee for a fictitious ailment.

'Why now, my dear Monsieur Poulain,' she said, 'now you have put me right after my accident, would you refuse to save me from poverty? A few words would do it.'

The doctor felt as if he had allowed the Devil to seize him by the forelock and twist it round the red nail of his pitiless claw. Frightened at the prospect of losing his integrity for so slight a cause, he responded to this diabolic idea by one no less diabolic.

'Listen to me, my dear Madame Cibot,' he said, bringing her indoors again and leading her to his surgery. 'I will pay you the debt of gratitude I incurred when you got me my post on the town-council!'

'We'll share the proceeds,' she promptly replied.

'What do you mean?' asked the doctor.

'The inheritance,' the concierge replied.

'You don't know me,' the doctor retorted, taking the pose of a Valerius Publicola. 'No more talk about that. I have an old college friend, a very intelligent fellow, and we are so much the more bound to one another because we have both had the same mischances in life. While I was studying medicine, he was learning his law. While I was a houseman, he was engrossing documents in a solicitor's office – Maître Couture. He was a cobbler's son, I am the son of a breeches-maker. He hasn't found anyone to take much interest in him, and he hasn't put by any capital either. If you don't get somebody interested in you, you don't get capital. He was only able to make a start in a provincial practice at Mantes. Now provincial people can't understand the way a Parisian's mind works, and they made a lot of fuss about my friend's way of doing things.'

'Dirty rascals,' cried Madame Cibot.

'Quite so,' the doctor continued. 'They combined against him, and he was forced to sell his practice for something he did which seemed to put him in the wrong. The public attorney got mixed up in all this; this magistrate was a native of that region, and so he sided with the local people. So this poor fellow, who's even worse off than I am, and more out-at-elbow, and has the same sort of house I have (his name is Fraisier), took refuge in our district. He's a barrister, but he has come down to pleading before the petty sessions and the local police-court. Go to no. 9, walk up the stairs, and on the third-floor landing you will find, in gold lettering, on a small square of red morocco: MONSIEUR FRAISIER, BARRISTER-AT-LAW. Fraisier specializes in the legal troubles of such folk as concierges, journeymen and all the poor people in the quarter – and his fees are moderate. He's an honest man, for I needn't tell you that he's smart enough, if he were a rogue, to be going about in a carriage. This evening I'll have a word with my friend Fraisier. Call on him tomorrow morning. He knows Monsieur Louchard, the district bailiff; Monsieur Tabareau, bailiff to the justice of the peace; Monsieur Vitel, the justice of the peace* himself; and Monsieur Trognon, the notary. He has already made his name among the most reputable legal men in the quarter. If he takes on your case, and if you can get Monsieur Pons to accept him as legal adviser, you may be sure he will be entirely with you. One other thing: do not, as you did with me, propose transactions which will wound his sense of honour. Then,

*For convenience, this term is used throughout for *juge de paix*: a paid magistrate who deals with minor civil and criminal cases.

when it comes to acknowledging his services, I will be your go-between.'

Madame Cibot cast a shrewd glance at the doctor.

'Isn't he the man who got Madame Florimond, the haberdasher in the rue Vieille-du-Temple, out of the nasty fix she was in over her lover's inheritance?'

'That's the man,' said the doctor.

'Wasn't it horrible,' cried La Cibot, 'that after Monsieur Fraisier had got her a two thousand francs' annuity, after she'd refused to marry him as he wanted, she thought she'd done her duty by him by giving him a dozen holland shirts, two dozen handkerchiefs, et cetera, in fact a whole outfit of clothes!'

'My dear Madame Cibot,' said the doctor, 'the outfit was worth a thousand francs, and Fraisier, who was just setting up in the quarter, needed it. Besides, she paid his expenses without question . . . That case brought a good many more to Fraisier, and now he has plenty to do. But in my line of business I have the same kind of clients . . .'

'It's only the good people who suffer in this world,' replied the concierge. 'Well, thank you and good-bye, kind Monsieur Poulain.'

And here begins the drama, or if you prefer, the terrible comedy of the death of a bachelor delivered over by the force of circumstances to the rapacity of covetous people assembled round his bed: people who, in this case, were aided and abetted by the all-consuming passion of a maniacal lover of pictures, the avidity of the egregious Fraisier, who will make you shudder when you see him at work in his den, and the greed of an Auvergnat capable of anything, even crime, in order to launch out in business. This comedy, for which the preceding part of the story has served to some extent as a curtain-raiser, has moreover, as its actors, all the characters who up to now have occupied our stage.

18. A 'man of law'

THE debasement of words is one of the peculiarities of social behaviour which it would take volumes to explain. Write to a solicitor and call him a 'man of law', and you will offend him as much as you would offend a wholesale dealer in colonial produce if you addressed him by letter as 'Monsieur So-and-So, grocer'. A fairly large number of people in society, who ought to understand at least these niceties of good breeding, since they understand nothing else, are still ignorant of the fact that the designation 'man of letters' is the cruellest insult one can offer to an author. The word *'monsieur'* is a shining example of the life and death of words. *'Monsieur'* means 'my lord'. This title, once so weighty, and nowadays reserved for kings by the transformation of *'sieur'* into *'sire'*, is given to all and sundry. And yet the use of *'messire'*, which is merely another form and synonym of the word *'monsieur'*, provokes articles in Republican journals when it happens to be used in a burial licence. Now magistrates, councillors, jurists, judges, advocates, notaries, attorneys, bailiffs, counsels, procurators and pleaders are all varieties of men falling into the classification of those who administer justice or whose work is concerned with it. The two lowest rungs of the ladder are occupied by the practitioner and the 'man of law'. The 'practitioner', commonly known as the bailiff's man, is only incidentally an officer of the law. His business is to ensure that judgments are carried out; he is, as regards civil jurisdiction, a make-shift executioner. As for the man of law, he suffers the contumely peculiar to the profession. He is to the law what the man of letters is to literature. Among all the professions in France, a rivalry rages which has found appropriate terms of disparagement. Each way of life has its own vocabulary of insults. The contempt involved in the words 'man of letters' and 'man of law' does not apply in the plural. You may talk of 'men of letters' and 'men of law' without wounding anyone's feelings. But in

Paris every profession has its dregs – individuals who pull it down to the level of the man in the street and the proletariat. Thus the 'man of law', the small pettifogger, still exists in certain quarters, just as one still finds, round about the Central Market, the small short-term moneylender who is to the big banks what Monsieur Fraisier was to the confraternity of attorneys. Strangely enough, the working classes are as afraid of the officials of the courts as they are of the fashionable restaurants. They have recourse to the small legal fry as automatically as they go to the wine-shops for a drink. To keep to one's own level is the general rule in each different social sphere. Only exceptional people like to reach above their own rank, do not feel abased in the presence of their superiors, and assert themselves, as the former watch-maker Beaumarchais did when he deliberately dropped the watch of a great lord who was trying to humiliate him. But self-made men like Beaumarchais, especially those who are able to disguise their humble beginnings, are notable exceptions.

The next day, at six in the morning, Madame Cibot was in the rue de la Perle, eyeing the abode of her future legal adviser, our Monsieur Fraisier, man of law. It was one of those houses inhabited by erstwhile lower-middle-class people. You entered it from an alley. The ground floor was partly taken up by the porter's lodge and the premises of a cabinet-maker whose workshops and showrooms encumbered a small inner courtyard. It was divided into two portions by the alley and the well of the staircase, into which saltpetre and damp had eaten. The whole house appeared to be suffering from leprosy.

Madame Cibot made straight for the lodge, where she found one of Cibot's cronies, a cobbler, his wife and their two young children, housed in a space of ten square feet to which light penetrated from the little courtyard. It was not long before the most cordial understanding was established between the two women, once La Cibot had stated her profession, given her name and spoken of her house in the rue de Normandie. After a quarter of an hour taken up with gossip, during which time Monsieur Fraisier's concierge was preparing breakfast for her cobbler and her two children, Madame Cibot brought the conversation round to the tenants and mentioned the man of law.

'I have come to see him on business,' she said. 'One of his friends, Doctor Poulain, has recommended me to him. Do you know Doctor Poulain?'

'You bet I do!' said the concierge of the rue de la Perle. 'He saved my baby's life. Croup is what he had.'

'He saved my life too, Madame. What sort of man is this Monsieur Fraisier?'

'He's the sort of man, my dear lady,' said the concierge, 'who isn't at all keen at the end of the month to pay for the postage on his letters.'

This answer sufficed for the intelligent Madame Cibot. 'You can be both poor and honest,' she remarked.

'I should hope so,' replied Fraisier's concierge. 'We ourselves may not be rolling in gold, nor in silver, nor even in copper, but we don't owe a farthing to anybody.'

La Cibot felt at home with this kind of language.

'Anyway, my dear,' she went on, 'I can put my faith in him, eh?'

'That you can! When Monsieur Fraisier takes a liking to somebody, I've heard Madame Florimond say, there's nobody to compare with him.'

'Why didn't she marry him then?' La Cibot promptly demanded. 'Didn't he get her a lot of money? Quite a catch for a small haberdasher, who was kept by an old man, to get a barrister as a husband!'

'You want to know why?' said the concierge, leading La Cibot into the alley. 'You're going up to see him, aren't you, Madame? . . . Well, once you get into his office, you'll find out why.'

*

The staircase drew its light from sliding windows giving on to a little court. It was clear that except for the owner and the egregious Fraisier, the other tenants were manual workers. The muddy stairs bore the marks of every known trade, strewn as they were with brass chippings, broken buttons, scraps of gauze and shreds of esparto straw. The final remark of Fraisier's concierge had excited Madame Cibot's curiosity and naturally decided her to consult Dr Poulain's friend, but to accept his services only if he made a favourable impression.

'I sometimes wonder how Madame Sauvage can keep on her job with him,' commented the concierge as she followed Madame Cibot. 'I'm coming up with you, Madame,' she added, 'as I'm taking the landlord his milk and newspaper.'

When La Cibot arrived at the second floor above the *entresol*, she found herself in front of a most shabby-looking door. The paint, of a dubious red, was coated, over an area of several inches, with that murky grime which clients' hands deposit on it in the course of time: the kind with which, in elegant apartments, architects have tried to cope by fitting glass panels above and beneath the keyholes. The grille in this door, blocked up with a scabby crust rather like that invented by restaurant-keepers to give a look of age to their 'vintage' bottles, served no other purpose than to justify its being taken for a prison-cell door, and also tallied with the clover-leaf ironwork, formidable hinges and stout nail-heads. These fittings must have been designed by some miser or some pamphleteer at odds with the whole world. The drain into which the household slops were discharged added its quota of nauseous odours to the stairway, whose ceiling was everywhere decorated with arabesques – such weird ones! – traced in candle-smoke. The bell-pull, at the end of which hung a dirty olive-shaped grip, rang a little bell whose feeble timbre betrayed a crack in the metal. Every object in this hideous picture contributed some feature in keeping with the whole.

La Cibot heard the thud of a heavy step and the wheezy breathing of a hefty woman, and Madame Sauvage appeared. She was one of those hags divined by Adrian Brauwer when he painted his *Witches setting out for the Sabbath*: a woman five feet six inches tall, with the face of a trooper, and much more of a beard than La Cibot. She was unhealthily corpulent and wore an appalling dress of cheap printed cotton, with a Madras scarf tied round her head; her hair was still in curl-papers made of the printed forms which her master received gratis; from her ears hung something resembling gold carriage-wheels. In her hand this female Cerberus held a battered tin saucepan from which milk was slopping over and adding one more smell to the stairway – not that it was conspicuous, in spite of its nauseating sourness.

'Anything I can do for you, Meddem?' asked Madame Sauvage. And, doubtless considering La Cibot too well dressed, she darted a menacing look at her, all the more murderous in that her eyes were naturally bloodshot.

'I've come to see Monsieur Fraisier, from his friend, Dr Poulain.'

'Come in, Meddem,' replied Madame Sauvage. Her suddenly amiable demeanour proved that she had been forewarned about this early morning visit.

And so, after dropping a stage curtsey, Monsieur Fraisier's half-masculine domestic threw open the door of the office, which looked out on to the street, and in which the former attorney of Mantes was sitting. This office was an exact replica of one of those tiny chambers occupied by third-class bailiffs. The filing-cabinets in them are of blackened wood: the files are so ancient that they have grown beards like those of lawyers' clerks; the red tape hangs down in a sorry way; the boxes smell of the frolics of mice, and the floor is grey with dust and the ceiling yellow with smoke. The mantelpiece mirror was tarnished; the cast-iron fire-dogs supported a slow-burning log; the clock, a modern marquetry piece, was worth sixty francs and had been bought at some bankrupt sale; the sconces on either side of it, though they affected, with little success, a rococo elegance, were made of zinc, and the paint on them had peeled off here and there to reveal the bare metal. Monsieur Fraisier, a shrivelled and sickly looking little man with a red face covered with spots which spoke of impurities in the blood, who moreover was constantly scratching his right arm, and whose wig, pushed far back on his head, incompletely concealed a sinister-looking, brick-coloured cranium, rose from the cane armchair in which he had been sitting on a green leather cushion. Assuming an amiable air and a fluting tone of voice, he said as he offered her a chair:

'Madame Cibot, I think?'

'Yes, Monsieur,' the concierge replied, with none of her usual self-assurance. She was alarmed by the sound of his voice, which was scarcely less dissonant than that of the doorbell, and by the hard scrutiny she received from the harsh, greenish eyes of her prospective legal adviser. And the office reeked so strongly of Fraisier that you might have thought that a pestilence reigned in the very atmosphere. Madame Cibot now understood why Madame Florimond had never become Madame Fraisier.

'Poulain has told me about you, my dear lady,' said the man of law, in those affected accents which are commonly called 'genteel', but which remained as sharp and thin as a local wine.

At this point Fraisier endeavoured to drape his person to advantage by bringing up over his bony knees, which were cased in very threadbare duffel, the two flaps of an old printed calico dressing-gown, the padding of which was taking the liberty of pushing out through a number of rents; but the weight of the wadding pulled the flaps away and exposed a flannel jerkin blackened with age. With an air of self-complacency, he drew tightly around him the girdle of this rebellious dressing-gown in order to emphasize his waspish waist-line. Next he picked up the fire-tongs and brought together two charred sticks which had stayed apart for a long time like a pair of quarrelsome brothers. Then an idea suddenly struck him and he drew himself up.

'Madame Sauvage!' he cried.

'What is it?'

'I am not at home to anyone.'

'God help me, I know that!' replied the virago in an aggressive tone of voice.

'She's my old nurse,' said the man of law to La Cibot, revealing some embarrassment.

'Was her milk as sour then as her looks are now?' asked the former beauty-queen of the Central Market.

Fraisier laughed at this quip and bolted the door to make sure that his housekeeper could not come in and interrupt La Cibot's confidential utterances.

'Well now, Madame, tell me what your business is,' he said, sitting down and still trying to bring his dressing-gown around him. 'Anyone recommended to me by the only friend I have in the world can count upon me absolutely . . . absolutely!'

Madame Cibot talked for half an hour without the lawyer allowing himself to make the slightest interruption. He had the rapt air of a young recruit listening to a veteran of the Guard.

His silence and deference, the attention he seemed to be paying to this spate of chatter – samples of which have been furnished in the scenes between La Cibot and poor Pons – caused the mistrustful concierge to jettison some of the misgivings which had assailed her at the sight of so many sordid details.

*

When La Cibot had finished and was waiting for advice, the little lawyer, whose green eyes, dotted with black specks, had been studying his future client, was taken with what is commonly called a 'churchyard cough' and had recourse to an earthenware bowl half-filled with a herbal decoction which he gulped down.

'But for Poulain,' said Fraisier in response to his visitor's glance of maternal solicitude, 'I should be dead already, my dear Madame Cibot. But he says he will put me right again.'

He seemed to have lost all memory of his client's confidences, and she was in half a mind to take her leave of a person who seemed to have one foot in the grave.

'Madame, in cases of inheritance, before going any further, I need to know two things,' continued the former attorney of Mantes with a solemn air. 'Firstly, is the inheritance large enough to bother about? Secondly, who are the legal heirs? Inheritances may well be counted as the spoils of war, but there is an enemy to contend with: the rightful heirs!'

La Cibot told him about Rémonencq and Elias Magus and informed him that these two wily confederates valued the collection of pictures at six hundred thousand francs.

'Would they buy them at that price?' asked the former attorney of Mantes. 'Because, you see, Madame, legal men are sceptical about pictures. A picture is either two francs' worth of canvas or a painting which will fetch a hundred thousand francs. Now paintings worth a hundred thousand francs are known far and wide – and what miscalculations have been made about all of them, even the most famous ones! A well-known financier, with a much vaunted, much visited gallery – engravings had been made of his pictures, think of that! – was supposed to have spent millions on it. He died – as people do. Well, his genuine Old Masters didn't sell for more than two hundred thousand francs! You would have to bring those two gentlemen to me. . . . And now, what about the heirs?'

And Fraisier returned to his pose as a listener. When he heard Président Camusot's name pronounced, he gave a nod accompanied by a grimace which put La Cibot very much on the *qui vive*. She made an effort to interpret what she read on the forehead and atrocious physiognomy of the man; but she only found herself scrutinizing what gamblers call a 'poker-face'.

'Yes, my dear sir,' La Cibot repeated, 'my gentleman, Monsieur Pons, is the Président Camusot de Marville's own cousin – he dins it into me a dozen times a day. The first wife of Monsieur Camusot the silk-merchant . . .'

'Who's just been made a Peer of France . . .'

'Was a Mademoiselle Pons, Monsieur Pons's first cousin . . .'

'Actually they are second cousins . . .'

'Well, by now they are nothing at all to one another. They've fallen out.'

Monsieur Camusot de Marville, before coming to Paris, had for five years been President of the Tribunal at Mantes. Not only was he still remembered there, but he had also kept in touch, for his successor, that very member of the bench with whom he had been in closest contact while he was there, was still presiding over the Tribunal and consequently knew Fraisier through and through.

'Do you know, Madame,' asked Fraisier when La Cibot had stemmed the torrent by closing the red sluice-gates of her mouth, 'do you know that your chief adversary would be a man who can send people to the scaffold?'

The concierge leapt up in her chair like a jack-in-the-box.

'Calm yourself, my dear lady,' Fraisier went on. 'It's quite understandable that you shouldn't know what it means to be a President of the Chamber of Indictment in the Royal Court of Paris, but you ought to have known that Monsieur Pons had a legal heir by consanguinity. Monsieur le Président de Marville is your sick man's one and only heir. True, he is only a collateral in the third degree, and this means that Monsieur Pons, as the law goes, can leave his fortune to anyone he wishes. Another thing that you don't know: at least six weeks ago Monsieur le Président's daughter married the eldest son of Monsieur le

Comte Popinot, Peer of France, recently Minister of Agriculture and Trade, one of the most influential figures in present-day politics. This marriage alliance makes the Président even more redoubtable than he is as ruler of the Assize Court.'

Madame Cibot trembled at the sound of the word 'Assize'.

'Yes, he's the man who can send you there,' continued Fraisier. 'Ah, my dear lady! You don't know what a Scarlet Robe can do! It's bad enough to have a mere Black Gown against you! Here am I, ruined, bald, nearly dead. Well, it's because, unwittingly, I came up against a mere Public Prosecutor. I was forced to sell my practice for next to nothing, and thought myself quite lucky to get away with the loss of all I had. Had I tried to resist, I could not have kept my status as a barrister. Yet another thing you don't know: if you only had Monsieur le Président Camusot to deal with, that wouldn't matter. But note also that he has a wife . . . ! And if you came face to face with her, you'd shake in your shoes, just as if you were already at the foot of the scaffold. Your hair would stand on end. The Présidente is vindictive enough to devote ten years to inveigling you into a trap which would cost you your life! She manages her husband like a child whipping a top! In her time she has brought a charming young man to suicide in the Conciergerie prison. She completely whitewashed a count who was indicted for forgery. She almost managed to get one of the most distinguished aristocrats at Court declared a lunatic. Finally, she won a stand-up fight against Monsieur de Granville, the Procurator General . . .'

'The man who lived in the rue Vieille de Temple, at the corner of the rue Saint-François? . . .'

'The very same. They say she intends to get her husband made Minister of Justice, and I wouldn't swear she won't bring it off . . . If she took it into her head to send us both to the Assize Court and from there to the galleys, I – mark you, I'm as innocent as a new-born babe – I would apply for a passport and go off to the United States. I know too much about the ways of the law. Now then, my dear Madame Cibot, in order to marry her daughter to the young Vicomte Popinot, who will be, so they say, your landlord Monsieur Pillerault's heir, the Présidente has stripped herself of all her property, so that at present the Président and his wife are reduced to living on his official salary. Do you imagine, dear lady, that in these circumstances Madame le Présidente is going to give the cold shoulder to your Monsieur Pons's inheritance? Why, I would rather face guns loaded with grape-shot than find myself up against such a woman!'

'But why?' said La Cibot. 'They've fallen out.'

'What does that matter? All the more reason. You might kill a relative to satisfy a grievance. That's something. But it's a real pleasure to grab his money!'

'But the poor man is dead set against all his legal heirs. He keeps on telling me about those people. I remember their names, Monsieur Cardot, Monsieur Berthier and the rest. They've squashed him like an egg under a cartwheel.'

'Would you like to be smashed to bits in the same way?'

'My goodness, my goodness!' cried the concierge. 'Oh, Ma'me Fontaine was right when she said I'd find obstacles in my way. But she said things would work out all right.'

'Listen, dear Madame Cibot ... You may well get some thirty thousand francs out of this affair. But give up the idea of getting the legacy ... Monsieur Poulain and I were talking yesterday about you and your problem.'

At that Madame Cibot gave another jump.

'What's the matter now?' asked Fraisier.

'Well, if you knew all about my problem, why did you let me chatter away like a magpie?'

'Madame Cibot, I knew all about your problem, but I knew nothing about Madame Cibot! All my clients have their little peculiarities.'

At this point Madame Cibot cast a singular glance at her future counsel, one in which all her mistrust was plain to see. Fraisier intercepted this glance.

19. Fraisier makes things clear

'I WILL continue,' said Fraisier. 'Well now, it was you who put our friend Poulain in touch with old Monsieur Pillerault, great-uncle of Madame la Comtesse Popinot. And that's one of the things that give you a claim to my devoted service. Mark this: Poulain visits your landlord once a fortnight, and he has learnt all the relevant facts from him. This retired tradesman attended his great-grand-nephew's wedding (the Popinots have expectations from this uncle, who has certainly an income of about fifteen thousand francs per annum, and for the last twenty-five years has been living like a hermit, spending scarcely three thousand francs a year) – and he told Poulain the whole story of the marriage. It appears that all this turmoil was caused by no other than your precious old musician, who tried out of spite to bring the Président's family into disrepute. You have to listen to both sides of a question, you know. Your sick man protests his innocence, but everyone thinks he's a monster . . .'

'I shouldn't be surprised if he was!' cried La Cibot. 'Just imagine, I've been helping him out for ten years. He's had all my savings. He knows it and he just won't put me in his will . . . It's a fact, Monsieur, he just won't; he's as stubborn as a mule. I've been talking to him about it for a fortnight, and the old fraud won't budge an inch. Not a word can you get out of him; he just stares at you. All he told me was that he would recommend me to Monsieur Schmucke.'

'So he proposes to make a will in Schmucke's favour?'

'He'll leave him every penny.'

'Listen, my dear Madame Cibot, in order to make up my mind about this, if I'm to think out a plan of action, I should have to know Monsieur Schmucke, inspect the chattels comprising the inheritance, and have a talk with the Jew you told me about. And so you must let me manage the affair.'

'I'll think it over, my good Monsieur Fraisier.'

'*Think it over!* What do you mean?' said Fraisier. There was all the venom of an adder in his glance. He returned to his normal manner of speech. 'Look now. Am I or am I not your legal adviser? Let's get this clear.'

La Cibot felt that he was reading her thoughts, and a chill went down her spine.

'I have every confidence in you,' she replied, realizing she was at the mercy of a tiger.

'We advocates are well used to being betrayed by our clients. Just consider your position: it's a splendid one. If you follow my advice in every particular, you will get – I guarantee you this – thirty or forty thousand francs out of his inheritance. But there's a reverse side to this lovely medal. Suppose it comes to the Présidente's ears that Monsieur Pons's inheritance is as much as a million, and that you want to pare it down a bit? . . . There are always informers,' he added by way of parenthesis, 'ready to pass on news like that.'

This parenthesis, preceded and followed by a pause, brought a shudder to La Cibot, for it immediately occurred to her that Fraisier himself might well be the informer.

'My dear client, it would only take them ten minutes to prevail upon good Monsieur Pillerault to dismiss you from your lodge, and give you two hours to clear out.'

'A fat lot I should care!' said La Cibot assuming the stance of a Bellona. 'I should stay on with my two gentlemen as their confidential servant.'

'And when they saw that, they would lay a trap for you, and one fine morning, you'd find yourself in the lock-up, you and your husband, with a capital charge hanging over you.'

'What, me!' cried La Cibot. 'I've never lifted a brass farthing from anybody! Me? Me?'

She went on for five minutes, and Fraisier studied this great artiste as she performed the solo part in her concerto of self-praise. His air was cold and mocking; his glance went through La Cibot like a stiletto; he was laughing to himself, and his dusty wig was twitching. Robespierre, the Lucius Cornelius Sulla of France, must have looked like that when he was composing verses in the intervals of signing death-sentences.

'How could they? Why should they? And on what grounds?' she asked by way of conclusion.

'You would like to know how they could bring you to the guillotine?'

La Cibot went as pale as death, for this sentence felt like the knife of judgement crashing down on to her neck. She looked at Fraisier in bewilderment.

'Listen carefully, my dear child,' continued Fraisier, repressing the thrill of satisfaction which the sight of his client's terror had given him.

'I'd rather throw the whole thing up,'-she muttered, and she tried to rise from her chair.

'Keep your seat. You must learn of the danger you are in. It's for me to enlighten you,' said Fraisier in commanding tones. 'You lose your job with Monsieur Pillerault – no doubt about that, is there? You take service with these two gentlemen. Very good. That means a declaration of war between you and the Présidente. You'll stop at nothing to lay your hands on this inheritance and get what pickings you can.'

La Cibot made a gesture of dissent.

'Oh, I don't blame you, that's not my job,' said Fraisier in answer to this silent protest. 'You'll be involving yourself in a fight and you'll take it further than you think. An idea goes to one's head, and one hits out . . .'

Madame Cibot bridled, and made another gesture of denial.

'Come, come, old lady,' Fraisier continued with nauseating familiarity. 'You'd stop at nothing . . .'

'The very idea! Do you take me for a thief?'

'Come along now, Mamma. You have a receipt from Monsieur Schmucke which didn't cost you much . . . See here, my beauty, you're at confession now, and you mustn't deceive your confessor, particularly when this confessor can see right through to your heart!'

La Cibot was terrified at the man's perspicacity and now knew the reason why he had listened to her with such deep attention.

'Well then,' continued Fraisier. 'You can take it for granted that the Présidente isn't going to let you lead the field in the succession stakes. You will be watched – spied upon. You get

Monsieur Pons to put you in his will. Then, one fine day, the police come along. They pounce on some decoction or other and find arsenic in it. You and your husband are arrested, tried and condemned for attempting to murder Monsieur Pons in order to draw the legacy ... There was a poor woman at Versailles whose defence I undertook. She was as truly innocent as you would be in such a case. Things were just as I'm telling you, and so the utmost I could do was to save her life. The wretched woman was sentenced to twenty years' penal servitude, and she's doing her stretch in Saint-Lazare.'

Madame Cibot's terror was at its height. Deadly pale, she gazed at the wizened little green-eyed man as a poor Moresco girl, denounced for her loyalty to her religion, might have gazed at the Inquisitor as she heard herself being condemned to the stake.

'Do you mean then, my kind Monsieur Fraisier, that if I left things to you and trusted in you to watch over my interests, I should get something out of it and have nothing to fear?'

'I guarantee you thirty thousand francs,' said Fraisier, with the air of a man who knows what he is talking about.

'After all, you know how fond I am of dear Dr Poulain,' she went on in her most fawning tones. 'It was he that told me to come and see you, and such a nice man wouldn't send me here to be told I was going to be guillotined for poisoning people.'

She melted into tears; the idea of being guillotined had put her in such a tremble that her nerves were twitching and her heart was in the grip of terror. She lost her head. Fraisier was enjoying his triumph. When he had noticed his client's hesitation, he had seen the affair being taken out of his hands, and he had set out to tame La Cibot, terrify her, stupefy her, get her in his power, bound hand and foot. The concierge had entered his office like a fly blundering into a spider's web and she was to remain there, immeshed and entangled – a meal served up for this little lawyer's ambition. From this affair, in fact, Fraisier hoped to draw sustenance for his old age, easy circumstances, happiness and consideration. During the whole of the previous evening he and Poulain had been weighing the whole matter up and carefully studying its ins and outs. The doctor had given his friend a sketch of Schmucke's character and their nimble wits had weighed every hypothesis and examined all possible expedients and dangers. In a burst of enthusiasm Fraisier had exclaimed: 'There's a fortune in it for both of us!' He had promised Poulain a post as Medical Officer in a Paris hospital, and he had promised himself that he would become the justice of the peace in his *arrondissement*.

To be a justice of the peace! For Fraisier, an eminently capable man and a Doctor of Law, though a penniless one, this ambition was so rough a chimaera to ride that his thoughts lingered over it like a junior counsel dreaming of a judge's robes or an Italian priest dreaming of the triple tiara. It amounted to an obsession. The then justice of the peace, Monsieur Vitel, in whose court Fraisier conducted his pleas, was an old man of seventy-nine, failing in health, and thinking of retirement. Fraisier talked to Poulain about the prospect of succeeding him, and Poulain talked to Fraisier about the wealthy heiress whose life he was going to save as a prelude to marrying her.

Few people are aware of the covetousness which any public office involving residence in Paris arouses. Everyone yearns to live in Paris. If the Excise authorities have a licence to confer for the retail of tobacco and postage-stamps in Paris, a hundred woman rise up as one person and work upon all their friends to obtain it for them. A probable vacancy in one of the twenty-four Inland Revenue posts sets a host of ambitions seething in the Chamber of Deputies! All such posts are conferred in the King's Council and are State appointments. Now the salary of a justice of the peace in Paris amounts to six thousand francs a year; keeping the court records is a responsibility which brings in a hundred thousand francs. It is one of the most sought-after posts within the magisterial orbit. Fraisier as justice of the peace and friend of a chief medical officer could see himself making a rich marriage and also finding a bride for Poulain. They were going to work hand in hand.

*

Night had rolled down its leaden shutters over all the calculations of the sometime attorney of Mantes, and a formidable plan had germinated in his mind: an intricate plan, fraught with intrigue and profitable results. La Cibot was the pivot on which this dream was to turn. And so any rebelliousness in this woman, a mere tool, had to be crushed. No such possibility had been foreseen, but the former attorney had just brought the recalcitrant concierge to his feet by marshalling all the forces his venomous nature could assemble.

'My dear Madame Cibot, conquer your fears,' he said, taking her hand.

The feel of his hand, cold as a serpent's skin, produced a terrible impression on the concierge. It set up a physical reaction which calmed her down. She felt that Madame Fontaine's toad, Ashtaroth, was less dangerous to handle than this man with his red wig and his corncrake voice, this alchemist's vial of poison.

'Don't think that I am wrong in rousing your alarm,' continued Fraisier after taking note of the fresh shudder of repulsion which went through La Cibot's frame. 'The incidents responsible for Madame la Présidente's terrible reputation are so well known in the Law Courts that you may consult anyone you like on that score. The great nobleman who was almost put under judicial interdiction is the Marquis d'Espard. The man she saved from the galleys is the Marquis d'Esgrignon. The rich handsome young man with brilliant prospects who was to have married a young lady belonging to one of the foremost families of France, and who hanged himself in his prison cell, was the celebrated Lucien de Rubempré. His case caused a commotion throughout all Paris. There also an inheritance was in question – that of the notorious Esther, who left several millions. The young man, a poet, was accused of poisoning her because she had bequeathed all her wealth to him. He was away from Paris when the girl died, and he didn't even know he was her heir. Could there be any greater proof of innocence? Well, after being questioned by Monsieur Camusot, the young man hanged himself in gaol ... Justice is like the practice of medicine: it has its victims. With the first, one dies for Society; with the second, for Science.' He said this with a hideous smile. 'Well, you see that I know the risk you run. The law has already ruined me, a poor obscure little advocate. My experience has cost me dear: it is wholly at your service.'

'My goodness, no, thank you,' said La Cibot. 'I'll have nothing to do with it. I must put up with ingratitude . . . I only wanted my due . . . I've thirty years' honest living behind me, Monsieur. My Monsieur Pons says he will recommend me to Monsieur Schmucke in his will. Well, I'll end my days in peace with that kind German.'

Fraisier saw he had gone too far and disheartened La Cibot. So he had to wipe out the unhappy impression he had made on her.

'Let's not take a gloomy view,' he said. 'Go along home in complete peace of mind. Be sure we'll see that you come safe into port.'

'But what must I do then, my good Monsieur Fraisier, to get an income and . . .'

'And keep your conscience clear?' he broke in quickly. 'Why, that's just what lawyers are for. One can't get anything in such cases unless one abides by the terms of the law . . . You don't know the law: I do . . . With me, you can keep on the windy side of it. You'll have peaceful possession as far as your fellow creatures are concerned. As for your conscience, that's your affair.'

'Well then, tell me what to do,' went on La Cibot, now pacified and full of curiosity.

'I can't yet. I haven't studied the ways and means, only the obstacles. To begin with, you must push on with the will. But first of all let's find out to whom Pons is going to leave his possessions . . . Suppose he left everything to you! . . .'

'Not a chance! He doesn't like me. Oh, if only I'd known beforehand what his knick-knacks were worth, and if only I'd known what he's told me about not having had any love-affairs I'd be without a care today.'

'Never mind,' said Fraisier. 'Carry on! Dying people are taken with queer whims, my dear Madame Cibot. They disappoint many people's expectations. Let him make his will; then we shall see what to do. But the first thing is to value the articles comprising the inheritance. So put me in touch with the Jew and the man Rémonencq; they'll be very helpful to us ... Trust me completely, I'm entirely on your side. I'm a friend to my clients through thick and thin, once they treat me as a friend. Either a friend or an enemy: that's how I am.'

'Very well, I'll put myself in your hands,' said La Cibot. 'And what about your fee?... Monsieur Poulain said...'

'Never mind that now,' said Fraisier. 'See that you keep Poulain at the sick man's bedside. He's one of the most honest, the most loyal souls I know; and you see we must have a man we can trust. Poulain's a better man than I am. I have become ill-natured.'

'You do seem to be,' said La Cibot, 'but I'd put my trust in you, I would...'

'So you should! ... Come and see me whenever anything crops up, and after all, you have your wits about you. All will go well.'

'Good-bye, my dear Monsieur Fraisier. I hope you'll soon be better... Your servant.'

Fraisier took his client back to the door, and there, as she herself had done the day before with the doctor, he said his last word:

'If you can get Monsieur Pons to ask for my legal advice, that would be a big step forward.'

'I'll try.'

'Old lady,' he continued, drawing her back into his office, 'I'm on good terms with Monsieur Trognon, the notary – the one in our quarter. If Monsieur Pons hasn't a notary, tell him about this one. Get him to engage him.'

'I understand,' answered La Cibot.

As she went out the concierge could hear the swish of a dressing-gown and the thud of heavy feet trying to step lightly. Once more alone and back in the street, she walked along for a time and was soon able to think for herself again. Although she had not recovered from the shock of this consultation and was still terrified at the prospect of the scaffold, the Law Courts and the judges, she came to a very natural decision – one which was going to put her, secretly, at odds with her terrible counsellor.

'After all,' she asked herself, 'do I need partners? I'll feather my own nest, and after that I'll take anything they offer me to work for them . . .'

This resolution, as we shall see, was destined to hasten the demise of the unfortunate musician.

20. La Cibot at the theatre

'WELL now, dear Monsieur Schmucke,' said La Cibot as she entered the flat. 'How is our dear, cherished patient doing?'

'Not vell,' the German replied. 'Hiss mint hass peen vanterink all ze night.'

'What was he talking about?'

'Foolish sinks! He vantet to leaf me all hiss fortune, put so zet I sell nossink . . . unt he vass veeping, ze poor man! It mate me fery sat.'

'He'll get over that, dearie,' replied the concierge. 'I've kept you waiting for your breakfast. It's after nine o'clock. But don't be cross with me. I've had such a lot to do, you see . . . about your concerns. The fact is, we've nothing left, and I've been getting some money.'

'Vere tit you get it?'

'At Uncle's.'

'Vat uncle?'

'The pop-shop.'

'Pop-shop?'

'Oh the dear man, isn't he a simple one! No really, you're just a saint, an angel, a blessed innocent. You should be put in a glass case, as the old actor said. What! You've been in Paris these twenty-nine years, you've lived through the July Revolution, and you've never heard tell of the pawnbroker's, where they lend you cash on your bits and pieces . . . I've popped my silver spoons and forks – eight of them with thread design. Well, it can't be helped. Cibot'll have to make do with Algiers metal: it's quite good style, as they say. And don't go telling our poor cherub about that. It would only get him all bothered and turn him yellow; he's touchy enough as it is. Let's pull him through first, and then we'll see about it. After all, there's a time and a place for everything. You've got to take the rough with the smooth, haven't you . . . ?'

'You kint voman! You goot-heartet soul!' said the poor

musician, taking La Cibot's hand and laying it against his heart, his face working with emotion.

The angelic creature raised her eyes to heaven, so as to show the tears swimming in them.

'Don't take on so, Papa Schmucke! You really are funny! Fancy making such a fuss! I'm only an old working-woman, and I wear my heart on my sleeve. I've got one, you know,' she added, slapping her bosom, 'just like you two have, and you've got hearts of gold...'

'I to not feel funny,' said the musician. 'No inteet, to sink off him hafink so much sorrow, veepink tears of ploot and zen leafink zis vorlt pehint, it iss preakink my heart. If Pons tie, I tie also.'

'Lord help us, I shouldn't be surprised, you're taking it so hard. Listen, my duckling...'

'Tucklink? Vass iss zet?'

'Well then, my poppet...'

'Puppet?'

'My petsy then, if you like that better.'

'Zet iss not clear eizer.'

'Well anyhow, let me look after you. Be advised by me, or else, if you go on like this, I'll have two sick people on my hands sure and certain. The way I see it, we've got to share jobs here. You'll have to give up your lessons in town: you get all done up and then you're no good for anything here, and there's a lot of sitting-up to be done with Monsieur Pons getting worse all the time. I'm going off this very day to tell all your customers you're ill... That makes sense, doesn't it? From now on, you can spend your nights sitting up with our poor lamb, and you can go to bed from five in the morning till two in the afternoon, let's say. I'll do the hardest jobs, the day ones. I've got to give you lunch and dinner, care for the patient, get him out of bed, change him, give him his medicine... You see, the way I'm slaving now, I shan't last out a fortnight. We've both been on edge for a month. And what would you do if I got knocked up?... You too, you're in a shocking state after sitting up all last night with Monsieur Pons...'

She shepherded Schmucke to the looking-glass to show him how altered he was.

'So then, if you're of the same mind as me, I'm going to give you your breakfast double-quick. Then you'll mind our dearie till two o'clock. But you must give me a list of your customers, and I'll soon settle that. That'll get you a fortnight off. When I get back you can go and lie down and take it easy till this evening.'

The suggestion was such a wise one that Schmucke agreed to it there and then.

'Mum's the word with Monsieur Pons. You know he would think he was done for if we told him straight out that he's giving up the theatre and his lessons for a time. The poor gentleman would imagine he'd never get his pupils back – as if it mattered! Dr Poulain says we won't pull our pet through if we don't keep him as quiet as possible.'

'Fery goot! Fery goot! Get ze preakfast unt I vill make ze list and gif you ze attresses. You are qvite right, I coult not holt out!'

One hour afterwards, La Cibot put on her Sunday best and sailed off like a great lady – to Rémonencq's amazement. She was determined to cut a dignified figure as the confidential representative of the two 'Nutcrackers' in carrying out her mission to all the young ladies' seminaries and all the private houses where the musicians' pupils lived.

There would be no point in recording the diversified gossip, the variations on a single theme performed by La Cibot for the benefit of the headmistresses and families she visited. It will suffice to report the scene which took place in the 'illustrious' Gaudissart's managerial bureau, to which she obtained admission, though not without considerable difficulty. Theatre directors in Paris are better guarded than kings and ministers. The reason why strong barriers are raised between them and other mortals is easy to comprehend: kings have only to ward off ambition, whereas theatre directors have to contend with the *amour-propre* of artistes and authors.

La Cibot got over all the hurdles thanks to a sudden amity established between herself and the theatre door-keeper. Concierges can pick one another out of a crowd, like all members of one and the same profession. Each calling has its own shibboleths as well as its grievances and stigmata.

'Ah, Madame! You are the caretaker of this theatre,' La Cibot had said. 'I am only a humble concierge in a house in the rue de Normandie, where your orchestra conductor Monsieur Pons lives. What wouldn't I give to be in your shoes, watching the actors, the dancers and the authors coming in and out! As the old actor said, yours is the top rung in our profession.'

'How is dear Monsieur Pons getting on?' asked the concierge.

'He's not getting on a bit. All of two months it's been since he last got out of bed, and mark my words, he'll be carried out feet first!'

'Oh dear! That will be such a loss.'

'It will that. Now, I've come from him to explain his position to your director. So do try and get him to see me, my dear.'

'A lady on behalf of Monsieur Pons!' It was thus that the commissionaire attached to the director's office announced Madame Cibot after the theatre concierge had put her case to him. Gaudissart had just come in to supervise a rehearsal, and it turned out that there was no one waiting to catch him, and that actors and authors were late in arriving. So he beckoned La Cibot in with a sweeping Napoleonic gesture.

This commercial traveller of former times, now in charge of a popular theatre, had been treating his partners in the concern as a man treats his lawful spouse – that is to say he deceived them. In consequence, his rise in financial importance was writ large on his person. Having grown stout and portly and acquired the ruddy countenance which comes of good cheer and prosperity, he had undergone a real metamorphosis: he now looked like a successful pill-merchant.

'I'm on the way to becoming a Croesus!' he said in an effort to be the first to laugh at himself.

'Did you say Crease-us or Fleece-us?' retorted Bixiou, who often understudied for him with the leading dancer, the celebrated Héloïse Brisetout.

In fact, the once 'illustrious' Gaudissart ran his theatre solely and uncompromisingly in his own interests. After forcing his way in as joint author of several ballets, plays and vaudevilles, taking advantage of his collaborators' ever-pressing needs, he

bought up their share in them. These plays and vaudevilles –
always billed to appear with successful dramas – brought
Gaudissart a fair number of gold coins *per diem*. He also
trafficked – by proxy – in the sale of tickets, and as he had
allotted himself a certain number of these as director's perquisites, he was able to levy a tithe on all the takings. These
three ways of collecting directorial imposts, and in addition,
the sale of theatre boxes, and bribes from untalented actresses
keen on getting walking-on parts and flaunting themselves as
queens and pages, so swelled out his third share of the profits
that his sleeping partners, on whom the other two thirds
devolved, drew scarcely a tenth part of the proceeds. None the
less, this tenth part still brought them fifteen per cent interest
on their capital. And so, Gaudissart, on the strength of this
fifteen per cent dividend, made great talk of his intelligence,
his probity and his zeal, and pointed out how lucky his partners
were. When the Comte Popinot, with some show of concern,
asked Monsieur Matifat, General Gouraud, Matifat's son-in-
law, and Célestin Crevel if they were pleased with Gaudissart,
Gouraud, now a Peer of France, replied:

'They say he fleeces us, but he does it with such wit and good
humour that we are satisfied.'

'Like the cuckold in La Fontaine's story – delighted to get a
thrashing!' said the former Minister with a smile.

Gaudissart was putting his capital to use in ventures outside
the theatre. He had shrewdly appraised the Graffs, Schwabs and
Brunners and invested in the railway enterprise now being
launched by this firm. Concealing his astuteness behind the
bluff jauntiness of the libertine and the voluptuary, he appeared
to be concerned only with dissipation and flashy attire. But he
kept an eye on everything, and exploited the immense business
experience he had acquired as a commercial traveller. This
self-made man who seemed not to take himself seriously lived
in a sumptuous flat which his scene-painter had fitted out with
great care and in which he gave suppers and parties to well-
known figures. Fond of display, and liking to do things on a
grand scale, he made himself out to be an easy-going man, and
he seemed so much the less dangerous because he had kept up
the 'patter' as he called it, of his former occupation, though

it was overlaid with stage slang. And since theatre people are not addicted to mincing words, he borrowed enough wit from the green-room (it has its own brand of wit) and seasoned it with enough of the commercial traveller's lively pleasantries to pass himself off as a superior man. Just now he was thinking of selling his theatre licence and, to quote his expression, 'passing on to higher activities'.... He wanted to be a railway director, a man of consequence, an administrator, and marry Mademoiselle Minard, the daughter of one of the richest mayors of Paris. He hoped to be elected to the Chamber of Deputies on the strength of his own 'speciality' and, with Popinot's patronage, to end up in the Council of State.

'To whom have I the honour of speaking?' asked Gaudissart, fixing his managerial gaze on La Cibot.

'Monsieur, I am Monsieur Pons's confidential friend.'

'Well, how is he, the dear old chap?'

'Bad, very bad, Monsieur.'

'Dear me! Dear me! I'm sorry to hear it ... I must go and see him. There aren't many men like him.'

'Very true, Monsieur, he's a real cherub ... I can't think how a man like him came to take up with the theatre.'

'Why, Madame,' said Gaudissart, 'the theatre is a school for the reform of morals ... Poor Pons! ... Upon my word, there ought to be special kinds of feeding-stock to keep up the supply of men like that – an exemplary man, and such talent! When do you think he will be able to start work again? Unfortunately, the theatre's like a stage-coach: full or empty, it must leave on time. Every evening the curtain goes up at six o'clock; it's no use being sorry for people. That won't supply us with the music we want... Tell me, what's the position?'

'Alas, kind sir!' said La Cibot, pulling out her handkerchief and wiping her eyes. 'It's a terrible thing to say, but I believe we're going to be unlucky enough to lose him, even though we're caring for him like the apple of our eye, Monsieur Schmucke and me ... What's more, I've come to tell you that you mustn't reckon any more on getting dear Monsieur Schmucke back – he never gets a night's sleep – and there it is ... You can't help keeping on as if there was still some hope and trying to snatch the dear, worthy man from the grave . . . But the doctor says there's no hope . . .'

'What's he dying of?'

'Vexation, jaundice, liver, not to speak of lots of family worries.'

'And of his doctor,' said Gaudissart. 'He should have called in Dr Lebrun. He's the theatre doctor and there would have been no bill.'

'Monsieur Pons has a doctor straight from Heaven. But what can the cleverest doctor do when he's up against all that?'

'I really did need those two excellent "Nutcrackers" to do the music in my new fairy-play.'

'Is there anything I can do instead?' asked La Cibot, with all the naïveté of a Simple Simon.

Gaudissart burst out laughing.

'Monsieur, I'm their confidential agent, and there are many things that these gentlemen . . .'

At the sound of Gaudissart's laughter, a female voice cried out:

'If you're laughing, it means I can come in, darling.' And the leading dancer bounded into the office and flung herself down on its only settee. It was Héloïse Brisetout, wrapped in a gorgeous multicoloured wrap.

'What's making you laugh? Is it this lady? What job's she come for?' asked the dancer, treating La Cibot to one of those glances – from one artiste to another – which would make a good subject for a painting.

Héloïse was well up in literary circles, a prominent figure in the Bohemia of the time, on close terms with all the prominent artistes, elegant, smart and graceful. She had more wit than leading dancers usually have. As she put these questions she took a sniff from a phial of heady perfume.

'Madame,' said La Cibot, 'one good-looking woman's no worse than another, and just because I don't sniff up pestiferous smells out of bottles and plaster brick-dust on my cheeks . . .'

'With what Nature has already put on yours, my dear, it would be gilding the lily,' said Héloïse, glancing sideways at her director.

'I'm a respectable woman . . .'

'Hard luck. It isn't all that easy, I assure you, to be a kept woman! I'm one, Madame, and I'm doing splendidly.'

'No credit to you! You can give yourself airs and wear all the colours of the rainbow, you still won't get the gentlemen round you as I used to, Meddem! And you'll never be a patch on the lovely oyster-girl of the Cadran Bleu . . .'

The dancer sprang to her feet, stood to attention and brought the back of her hand to her forehead like a private saluting a general.

'What,' said Gaudissart. 'Are you the lovely oyster-girl my father told me about?'

'If that's so, both the cachucha and the polka must be too up-to-date for you, Madame. Madame must be over fifty!' said Héloïse. She assumed a theatrical pose and declaimed the line from Corneille:

'Cinna, let us be friends! . . .'

'That's enough, Héloïse. This lady can't compete with you. Leave her alone.'

'Could this lady be the *new* Héloïse that Rousseau wrote about?' asked the concierge, with mock innocence and much sarcasm.

'Not bad, you old stager!' exclaimed Gaudissart.

'Very stale,' said the dancer. 'That joke's got whiskers on it. Try something more up to date, you old stager . . . or have a cigarette.'

'You must excuse me, Madame,' said La Cibot. 'I've too much on my mind to go on bandying words with you. I've two very sick gentlemen on my hands. And to feed them and save them trouble, I've had to pawn my husband's clothes this morning. Look, here's the ticket.'

'Oh, now we're going all melodramatic!' cried the fair Héloïse. 'What's it all about?'

'This lady,' La Cibot continued, 'flounces in here like . . .'

'Like a leading dancer,' said Héloïse. 'I'm prompting you. Get on with it, Meddem!'

'That will do, I'm in a hurry,' said Gaudissart. 'Enough of this fooling, Héloïse. This lady is the confidential agent of our poor conductor who's at death's door. She's just come to tell me we can't expect him here any more. I'm in a fix.'

'Oh, the poor man! We ought to give him a benefit performance.'

'He'd be ruined!' said Gaudissart. 'The next day he might have to turn over five hundred francs to the alms-houses. They don't recognize any charitable causes in Paris other than their own . . . Here, my good woman, since you're competing for the prize for this year's good deed . . .'

Gaudissart rang, and the commissionaire promptly appeared.

'Tell the cashier to send me a thousand-franc note. Sit down again, Madame.'

'Oh, the poor woman's in tears! . . .' cried the dancer. 'It's a shame . . . Come on, old lady, we'll go and see him, cheer up – See here, you old Chink,' she said to the director, drawing him aside. 'You want me to take the leading dancer's part in the *Ariana* ballet. You're getting married, and you know I can put a spoke in your wheel!'

'Héloïse, my heart is copper-bottomed like a frigate.'

'I'll show her the children you've fathered on me. I'll borrow some.'

'I've told my fiancée about you and me . . .'

'Be a nice boy, give Pons's job to Garangeot. The poor fellow has talent. He's down on his luck. Do that and I'll keep quiet.'

'You might wait till Pons is dead . . . The old chap may still get over it.'

'Oh, no, Monsieur,' La Cibot broke in. 'He hasn't been in his right mind since last night. He's just raving. He won't last long, I'm sorry to say.'

'In any case, let Garangeot fill in the gap,' said Héloïse. 'All the press is on his side.'

At this moment the cashier came in with two five-hundred-franc notes.

'Hand them over to this lady,' said Gaudissant. 'Good-bye, my good woman. Take good care of the dear man, and tell him I'll come and see him to morrow . . . or the next day . . . as soon as I can.'

'Man overboard!' cried Héloïse.

'Oh, Monsieur, people with hearts like yours are only to be found in the theatre. May God bless you!'

'What account is that to go on?' asked the cashier.

'I'll sign a chit, you can put it down in the gratuities account.'

Before leaving, La Cibot made a fine curtsey to the dancer, and her ear caught the following question put by Gaudissart to his former mistress:

'Is Garangeot capable of composing the music for our ballet *The Mohicans* in a matter of twelve days? If he can manage that he can take over Pons's job.'

*

The concierge, reaping a better reward for such a disservice than if she had done a good deed, withheld all the payments due to the two friends. She had also robbed them of their means of existence in the eventuality of Pons recovering his health. In a few days time this perfidious manoeuvre was to bring about the desired end: the sale of the pictures coveted by Elias Magus. In order to carry out this initial spoliation, she had to hoodwink the terrible collaborator she had engaged, the advocate Fraisier, and ensure absolute discretion on the part of Magus and Rémonencq.

As for the Auvergnat, he had gradually become a prey to one of those passions conceived by uneducated people, such as come up to Paris with a set of notions inspired by the isolation of country life; the ignorance of these primitive creatures and the brutishness of their desires converts such notions into *idées fixes*. Madame Cibot's beauty and her market-place brand of wit had been the object of the second-hand dealer's attentions, and he had it in mind to filch her away from Cibot and live in concubinage with her: a sort of bigamous union more frequent than one imagines among the lower classes in Paris. But day by day the noose of avarice tightened its hold on Rémonencq and ended by stifling his reasoning faculties. And so, reckoning that the commission which La Cibot would extract from Magus and himself would amount to forty thousand francs, he moved forward from misdemeanour to felony and aimed to get her as his lawful wife. His purely mercenary attachment, lengthily ruminated as he leaned against the doorway smoking his pipe, eventually brought him to the point of wishing for the little tailor's death. In this way his capital would be almost tripled, and he told himself what an excellent saleswoman La Cibot would make and what a fine figure she would cut in a splendid shop on the boulevard. This twofold covetousness intoxicated Rémonencq: he would rent a shop in the Boulevard de la Madeleine and stock it with the finest articles from the Pons collection. But then, after basking in these dreams of a golden future and watching millions of francs curling skywards from the bowl of his pipe, he used to wake up and find himself face to face with the little tailor sweeping up the courtyard, entry and street, at the moment when he himself was opening up his shop-front and laying out his wares – for, since Pons had fallen ill, Cibot had taken over the functions which his wife had allotted to herself. So the Auvergnat regarded this stunted little tailor with his sallow, almost coppery complexion as the only obstacle to happiness, and he began to wonder how to get rid of him. This growing passion filled La Cibot with pride, for she was reaching the time of life when women begin to realize that it is possible to grow old.

One morning then, on rising, La Cibot studied Rémonencq with a thoughtful gaze, as he was setting out the paltry articles in his shop-window; she decided to find out how far his infatuation would go...

The Auvergnat came up to her and said:

'Well now, are things going the way you want?'

'It's you I'm bothered about,' replied La Cibot. 'You'll be getting me talked about,' she added; 'the neighbours will spot you goggling at me with your sheep's eyes.'

She passed through the door and dived into the depths of Rémonencq's shop.

'What an idea!' said the Auvergnat.

'Here, I want to talk to you,' she said. 'Monsieur Pons's lawful heirs are going to get moving and they could cause us a lot of trouble. God alone knows what would happen to us if they saw dealers nosing about the place like dogs after a bone. I can only get Monsieur Schmucke to sell a few pictures if you're keen enough about me to keep it secret – so dead secret you wouldn't breathe a word about where they came from or who sold them – not even with a rope round your neck. It's like this: once Monsieur Pons is dead and buried, if they find fifty-three pictures instead of sixty-seven, nobody will know how many there were. And besides, Monsieur Pons might have sold some of them while he was still alive, and nobody can gainsay that.'

'That's all right for me,' answered Rémonencq. 'But Monsieur Magus will want regular receipts.'

'God help you, you'll get your receipt too! You don't think I'd be the one to write them out? Monsieur Schmucke'll do that. But you tell your Jew,' she added, 'to keep as mum as you.'

'We'll be as silent as the grave. It's part of our job. Now look, I can read, but I can't write, and that's why I need a capable woman, one with schooling, like you! . . . Well now – here was I with never a thought but laying up a bit for my old age, and blessed if I aren't hankering after some little Rémon-encqs! . . . Come on now, get rid of your Cibot!'

'Why, here's your Jew coming,' said the concierge. 'We can get things settled now.'

'Well, my dear lady,' said Elias Magus, who was in the habit of coming along once every three days, very early, to find out when he could buy his pictures. 'Where do we stand?'

'Have you had anybody talking to you about Monsieur Pons and his knick-knacks?' asked La Cibot.

'Yes,' replied Magus, 'I've had a letter from a queer sort of lawyer, who looks to me like a small-time busybody, and as I distrust such people, I didn't answer. Three days later he came to see me and left his card. I told my concierge I should never be in when he called!'

'You're a lovely old Jew,' said La Cibot, who was little used to such cautiousness as Magus had shown. 'Well, my chicks, in a few days' time I'll get Monsieur Schmucke to sell you seven or eight pictures – ten at the most. But on two conditions. One is, mouths tight shut. It's Monsieur Schmucke who'll have sent for you, you see, Monsieur Magus. It's Monsieur Rémon-encq who'll have brought you to Monsieur Schmucke as a buyer. In short, whatever comes of it, I've nothing to do with it. Will you pay forty-six thousand francs for the four pictures?'

'I will,' answered the Jew with a sigh.

'All right then,' the concierge continued. 'And here's my second condition. You'll hand over forty-three thousand to me, and you'll be buying them from Monsieur Schmucke for three thousand francs. Rémonencq will buy four for two thousand francs and hand on the surplus to me . . . But that's not all. See here, my dear Monsieur Magus: when that's all over, I'm going to put a fine bit of business in your way, the two of you, on condition the three of us share the proceeds. I'll take you to that lawyer or, more likely, he'll come to us. You'll value everything Monsieur Pons has at the price you're able to pay, so that Monsieur Fraisier can be sure how much the succession is worth. But he mustn't come here before our little sale. Understand?'

'I understand,' said the Jew. 'But it will take time to inspect the goods and fix a price.'

'You can have half a day. Trust me, I'll see to that. Talk it over between yourselves, my friends. There you are then: the job will be done the day after tomorrow. I'll go and have a talk with Monsieur Fraisier – he knows everything that goes on here through Dr Poulain. It's no end of trouble keeping that customer quiet.'

Half-way between the rue de Normandie and the rue de la Perle, La Cibot met Fraisier coming to see her, so impatient was he to learn what he called 'the basic facts'.

'What a surprise!' she said. 'I was on my way to your house.'

Fraisier complained about Elias Magus refusing to see him, but the concierge dimmed the gleam of suspicion which was dawning in the lawyer's eye by telling him Magus had been away, and that in two days' time she would arrange a meeting for them in Pons's flat, where they could settle the value of the collection.

'Be open and above board with me,' was Fraisier's answer. 'It's more than likely that the interests of Pons's heirs will be entrusted to me. In such circumstances, I shall be in a much better position to serve you.'

He said this so sharply that La Cibot quaked. This starveling lawyer must surely be working for his own ends, just as she was working for hers. She was not wrong in her conjecture. The advocate and the doctor had gone to the expense of ordering a brand-new suit for Fraisier, so that he could present himself in respectable garb at the house of Madame la Présidente Camusot de Marville. The time needed for the making of this suit was the only reason for delaying the interview on which the prospects of the two friends depended. After visiting Madame Cibot, Fraisier was intending to go to his tailor to try on his coat, waistcoat and trousers. He found these garments finished and ready. He went back home, put on a new wig, and set off in a hired cab, at about ten in the morning, for the rue de Hanovre, where he hoped to obtain an audience with the Présidente. Fraisier in white cravat, yellow gloves, new wig and scented with toilet-water looked like a measure of poison in a crystal phial with a white leather stopper – everything about it is neat, the label and even the thread round the stopper, but it appears no less dangerous for that. His self-assertive air, his pimply face, his scrofulous skin, his green eyes, and the savour of viciousness which his person exuded, cast a chill like clouds moving across a blue sky. In his office, under La Cibot's gaze, he had been the common knife, a murderer's tool of trade. Now, at the Présidente's door, he was the elegant poniard a young lady keeps in a little display-cabinet.

21. *The Fraisier* blossoms forth*

A GREAT change had taken place in the rue de Hanovre. Neither the Vicomte and Vicomtesse Popinot, nor the ex-Minister and his wife, would dream of letting the Président and Présidente move from the house they had made over to their daughter as a marriage portion, and into a rented flat. And so the Président and his wife settled in on the second floor, now vacated by the old lady, who wanted to live in the country for the rest of her life.

Madame Camusot kept on Madeleine Vivet, her cook and her manservant, and found herself back in the straitened circumstances of her early married years, though this poverty was alleviated by the fact that she had no rent to pay for her four-thousand-francs flat, and also by Camusot's salary of ten thousand francs a year. This *aurea mediocritas* in itself was distasteful to Madame de Marville, who aspired to financial means proportionate to her ambitions.

Moreover the transfer of all their estates to their daughter meant that the Président had forfeited his property qualification for election to the Chamber of Deputies. Now Amélie was not the sort of woman who would readily forgo her plans: she aimed at getting her husband into the Chamber, and by no means despaired of securing the Président's election in the constituency to which Marville belonged. For two months, therefore, she had been pestering Baron Camusot (the new Peer of France had been raised to this dignity) to make over to his son an advance of one hundred thousand francs on his patrimony in order, as she said, to purchase a small domain enclaved within the Marville estate, one which, when taxes had been paid, would bring in about two thousand francs. She and her husband would thus have a home of their own, they would be near their children, and the Marville property would be rounded off and correspondingly enlarged. In her talks with

*In French, *fraisier* = strawberry-plant.

215

her father-in-law, the Présidente laid emphasis on the sacrifice she had had to make for her daughter's marriage, and she asked the old man if he really had the heart to debar his eldest son from the highest magisterial honours which could only be accorded to a man holding a strong position in the Chamber; her husband would be capable of seizing such a position and hence of inspiring respect in the Ministers.

'Those gentry give you nothing unless you twist their cravats round their necks until their tongues are hanging out,' she exclaimed. 'An ungrateful lot . . . think what they owe to Camusot! By pressing for the July Ordinances, he raised the House of Orléans to the throne!'*

The old man averred that he had strained his resources by investing in railways, and although he admitted that the suggested donation was necessary, he postponed making it until the shares went up, as he expected they would.

The Présidente had been plunged into despondency by this half-promise, which she had extorted from him a few days ago. It was doubtful whether the former owner of Marville would be able to stand for the next elections, since the property qualifications only became valid after a year.

Fraisier had no difficulty in obtaining access to Madeleine Vivet. These two vipers had been hatched from the same egg and recognized their kinship.

'Mademoiselle,' said Fraisier, in sugary tones, 'I would request a moment's audience with Madame la Présidente on a matter which affects her personally and has to do with her financial situation. It is a question of an inheritance . . . Be sure you tell her this . . . I have not the honour of being known to Madame la Présidente, and so my name would mean nothing to her . . . As a rule I do not leave my consulting-room, but I know what deference is due to a presiding magistrate's lady, and I have taken the trouble to come in person, the more so because the affair brooks no delay.'

So couched, this request, repeated and amplified by the lady's-maid, naturally met with a favourable response. It was

* These reactionary Ordinances provoked the revolution which sent Charles X into exile. The argument is, of course, a specious one. You might as well say that by starting a fire in your house you help the firemen!

a critical moment for the two ambitions embodied in Fraisier; and therefore, despite the intrepidity of this little provincial solicitor, so overbearing, so harsh, so incisive, he felt what military leaders feel at the beginning of a battle on whose issue a whole campaign depends. As he passed into the little salon in which Amélie was awaiting him, he experienced an effect which no sudorific, however potent, had yet been able to produce on an epidermis clogged up by a nauseating disease and resistant to remedies: he felt a slight sweat down his back and on his forehead.

'Well, even if I don't make my fortune,' he said to himself, 'I am saved, for Poulain promised I should recover my health the day I started perspiring.'

'Madame,' he said on seeing the Présidente, who was in morning dress. Fraisier halted and bowed to her with the obsequiousness which, in legal circles, is an acknowledgement of the superior status of the person addressed.

'Be seated, Monsieur,' said the Présidente, at once recognizing in him a member of the legal confraternity.

'Madame la Présidente, if I have taken the liberty of approaching you over a matter of material interests which concerns Monsieur le Président, it is because I am certain that Monsieur de Marville, occupying the high position he does, would be likely to allow things to take their course and thus lose seven or eight hundred thousand francs: a sum which few ladies, who in my view are much better versed in private affairs than the most capable magistrates, would consider unimportant . . .'

'You mentioned an inheritance . . .' the Présidente interrupted. Dazzled at the mention of such a sum and trying to conceal her astonishment and satisfaction, Amélie was acting like a reader impatient to find out how a novel ends.

'Yes, Madame, an inheritance which is lost to you – entirely lost – but one which I can and shall recover for you . . .'

'Pray proceed, Monsieur,' said Madame de Marville coldly, as she examined Fraisier from head to foot with an appraising eye.

'Madame, I am aware of your eminent capabilities, since I was once at Mantes. Monsieur Lebœuf, the President of Assizes in that town, a friend of Monsieur de Marville, will be able to furnish him with information about me.'

The Présidente gave a shrug which was so bluntly significant that Fraisier was obliged to insert a parenthesis into his exordium.

'So distinguished a lady as you will understand straight away why I am beginning by talking of myself. It is the shortest cut to the inheritance.'

The Présidente responded to this delicate remark with a silent gesture.

'Madame,' continued Fraisier, taking this gesture as an authorization to go on with his story. 'I was an attorney at Mantes, and all my prospects depended on the post I held, for I had bought the practice of Monsieur Levroux – you knew him, no doubt? . . .'

The Présidente nodded.

'. . . With borrowed capital and about ten thousand francs of my own. For six years previously I had been senior clerk to Monsieur Desroches, one of the most competent attorneys in Paris. Well, I was unlucky enough to incur the displeasure of the Public Prosecutor in Mantes, Monsieur . . .'

'Olivier Vinet.'

'Precisely, Madame, the Attorney-General's son. He was paying court to a young person . . .'

'Really?'

'. . . Madame Vatinelle. She was very pretty and attractive . . . when I was there. She was kind to me: *inde irae*,' Fraisier continued. 'I was energetic, I wanted to pay back the loans from my friends and get married. I needed cases, and I looked round for them. I was soon handling more business on my own than the rest of the law officials. Well then, I found myself up against all the attorneys, notaries and even the bailiffs in Mantes. They looked for ways of harming me. You know, Madame, that in our redoubtable profession, when a man is marked for destruction, it doesn't take long. They found out I was acting as counsel on both sides of a case. Slightly unprofessional, but it's done in Paris in certain conjunctures: attorneys take in one another's washing. Not, however, at Mantes. Monsieur Bouyonnet, to whom I had already done a good turn of that kind, egged on by his colleagues and encouraged by the Public Prosecutor, gave the game away . . . You see I am hiding nothing. There was a general hue and cry. I was a scoundrel, a greater blackguard than Marat. They forced me to sell out and I lost everything. I came back to Paris, and tried to build up a practice here; but my health was undermined, and I was not fit to work even for two solid hours out of the twenty-four. Today I have only one ambition – a paltry one. Sooner or later, Madame, you will be the wife of a Keeper of the Seals, or perhaps of a senior Judge of Appeal. I, poor puny creature that I am, have no other desire than to obtain a post in which I can peacefully end my days, a post to vegetate in; I want to be a justice of the peace in Paris. It would be a trifling matter for you and Monsieur le Président to obtain me this appointment – you must cause the present Keeper of the Seals sufficient embarrassment for him to be anxious to oblige you . . .

'. . . But that is not all, Madame,' he added as he saw the Présidente stirring as if she were about to break in. 'I have a friend, a doctor, in attendance on the old man from whom Monsieur le Président ought to inherit. You see I am coming to the point . . . This doctor, whose cooperation is indispensable, is in a similar situation to myself: he has talent, but no luck! . . . It was through him that I learnt how your interests are being encroached upon. At this very moment the die may already be cast and the will which disinherits the Président made . . . This doctor seeks an appointment as senior medical officer in a hospital or as a consultant to the Royal Colleges. To put it briefly, you understand, he needs a position in Paris equivalent to the one I am seeking . . . Pardon me for treating of such delicate matters, but there must not be the slightest ambiguity in this respect. I would add that the doctor is a man of high repute and great skill – he saved the life of Monsieur Pillerault, the great-uncle of your son-in-law the Vicomte Popinot. So then, if you will be so good as to promise me these two posts – that of justice of the peace for myself and a medical sinecure for my friend – I will take it upon myself to secure the heritage almost intact. I say *almost* intact, because it will be saddled with obligations which the legatee will have to incur towards certain persons with whose help we cannot dispense.

You will only carry out your promises when I have carried out mine.'

*

The Présidente, who for the last few minutes had had her arms folded like a person forced to listen to a sermon, unfolded them, looked at Fraisier and said:

'Monsieur, you have the merit of clarity as regards everything that concerns yourself, but you leave my side of things in the dark.'

'Two words will suffice to make everything clear, Madame. Monsieur le Président is the sole heir – collaterally – of Monsieur Pons. Monsieur Pons is very ill. He is about to make his will – he may have done so already – in favour of a German friend of his named Schmucke: a considerable legacy, amounting to more than seven hundred thousand francs. In three days time I hope to have completely accurate information about the figure . . .'

'If that is so,' the Présidente murmured – she was thunderstruck on hearing how high the figure might reach – 'I made a great mistake in quarrelling with him and heaping abuse upon him . . .'

'No, Madame, for were it not for that quarrel he would be as chirpy as a sparrow and would outlive us all.'

'The ways of Providence are inscrutable; let us not look into them too closely,' he added in order to mask the odiousness of the reflection he had just made. 'After all, we legal practitioners see the positive side of things. You must realize, Madame, that Monsieur de Marville, occupying the important position he does, would not and could not do anything in the present situation. He is at mortal odds with his cousin. You no longer receive Pons; you have blackballed him from society. No doubt you had excellent reasons for doing so; but the man is ill and he's leaving his possessions to his only friend. A Président in the Royal Court of Justice cannot cavil at a properly drawn-up will made in such circumstances. But between you and me, Madame, when one is legally entitled to an inheritance of seven or eight hundred thousand francs – who knows? a million perhaps – when one is the only heir recognized by the law, how disagreeable it is not to recover one's due!... Only, in the effort to achieve this end, one gets involved in disreputable manoeuvres which are very difficult, very delicate; one has to be in touch with such lowly-placed people, servants, underlings; one has to press them so hard, that no solicitor, no notary in Paris could see such a business through. It needs a briefless barrister like me: a man of real, solid capacity, whose assiduity can be reckoned on, and whose regrettably precarious position is on a level with that of such people. In my district I deal with the affairs of the lower middle classes, working men, the common people... Yes, indeed, Madame, that is the level to which I have sunk thanks to the enmity of a public attorney who is now a deputy public prosecutor in Paris – just because he cannot forgive me for being more competent than himself... I know you, Madame, I am fully cognizant of the reliability of your protection, and in the service I can render you I foresee the end of my misfortunes and success for my friend Dr Poulain!'

The Présidente remained absorbed in thought. This was a moment of terrible anguish for Fraisier. Vinet, one of the orators of the centre party in the Chamber of Deputies, an Attorney-General of sixteen years' standing, ear-marked ten years since for the post of Chancellor, and the father of the public prosecutor of Mantes who for a year had been a deputy public prosecutor in Paris, was at daggers drawn with the vindictive Présidente. Nor did this haughty Attorney-General hide his scorn for Président Camusot. Fraisier was ignorant, and was to remain ignorant of these circumstances.

'Is that all you have on your conscience – the fact of having been counsel for two opposing litigants?' she asked, looking Fraisier straight in the eye.

'Madame la Présidente can consult Monsieur Lebœuf. He was well-disposed towards me.'

'Are you sure that Monsieur Lebœuf will give a favourable account of you to Monsieur de Marville and the Comte Popinot?'

'I can answer for that, especially since Monsieur Olivier Vinet is no longer at Mantes, for between ourselves, the very proximity of that little magistrate was a cause of misgiving to the worthy Lebœuf. Moreover, with your permission, Madame la Présidente, I will go to Mantes to see Monsieur Lebœuf myself. It will cause no delay. I shall not be able to ascertain the amount of the inheritance for two or three days. I must not tell you, I am obliged to conceal from you, the strings I have to pull. But is not my success guaranteed by the reward I expect for my entire devotion to your interests?'

'Very well. Win Monsieur Lebœuf's goodwill, and if – which I doubt – the inheritance is as considerable as you make out, I promise you the two posts. But only if you succeed – that goes without saying.'

'I shall succeed, Madame. One thing however: will you have the goodness to summon your notary and your solicitors as soon as I need them? Will you give me written authority to act in the Président's name? Will you tell these gentlemen to follow out my instructions and do nothing on their own initiative?'

'Yours is the responsibility,' the Présidente solemnly answered. 'Yours too must be the plenary powers ... But is Monsieur Pons seriously ill?' she asked with a smile.

'Well, Madame, I honestly think he would recover, above all since he has so conscientious a doctor as Poulain. This friend of mine, Madame, is only an innocent onlooker whom I am using in your interests: he is quite capable of pulling the old musician through. But the concierge who is looking after the sick man would willingly thrust him into his grave in order to get thirty thousand francs ... No, she wouldn't kill him: she won't give him arsenic. That would be too charitable. She'll do more than that, she will commit moral murder by trying his patience a thousand times a day. Poor old man; in quiet, peaceful country surroundings, well-tended, with friends to make a fuss of him, he'd get better. But under the constant nagging of a scold who, in her youth, was one of the thirty 'comely oyster-girls' whose praises were sung throughout Paris – grasping, voluble, domineering – a woman who keeps on worrying him to leave her a substantial legacy, the sick man will inevitably contract hardening of the liver; gall-stones are forming at this very moment, and the extraction of them will entail an operation which he will not be able to stand ... The doctor – a splendid person – is in a frightful predicament. He really ought to have this woman dismissed.'

'But she's a vixen, a monster,' cried the Présidente, adopting her gentle, fluting tone of voice. Fraisier was inwardly amused at the thought of sharing this particular affectation with the Présidente. He well knew what value to assign to these soft modulations of a naturally grating voice. Her hypocrisy reminded him of a judge who is the hero of a story by Louis XI – the latter's authorship is indicated in the final sentence. This magistrate was blessed with a wife cut to the same pattern as Socrates's wife. But he was less of a philosopher than Socrates, and so he had salt mixed with his horses' oats and stopped their water ration. One day, when his wife was riding alongside the Seine to their country house, these thirsty beasts dragged her off with them into the river – and the magistrate gave thanks to Providence for relieving him of his spouse in so 'natural' a way. At this moment Madame de Marville was giving thanks to her Maker for putting Pons in the care of a woman ready to rid her of him in so 'respectable' a way.

'I would not,' she declared, 'accept a million acquired by indelicate means . . . Your friend should enlighten Monsieur Pons and get the concierge dismissed.'

'In the first place, Madame, Messieurs Schmucke and Pons regard this woman as an angel: it's my friend they would dismiss. In the second place, this dreadful oyster-woman is the doctor's benefactor – she recommended him to Monsieur Pillerault. He urges this woman to be extremely gentle with the sick man; but his injunctions only serve to show this creature how to aggravate his complaint.'

'What does your friend think of my cousin's condition?'

'In six weeks his estate will be up for probate!' So apt was Fraisier's reply, and so lucid his assessment of her motives, no less greedy than those of La Cibot, that Madame de Marville gave a start. Her eyes dropped.

'Poor man!' she said, in a vain attempt to put on an expression of sadness.

'Madame, you may have a message for Monsieur Lebœuf. I shall take the train to Mantes.'

'Yes, wait here. I will write him an invitation to dine with us tomorrow. I must get in contact with him in order to repair the injustice from which you have suffered.'

Once the Présidente had left him, Fraisier already saw himself as a justice of the peace. He was transformed. He looked twice his size. He was filling his lungs with deep draughts of happiness and the balmy breeze of success. From the springs of that mysterious force, will-power, from its divine essence, he was drawing fresh and heady gulps. Like Rémonencq he felt capable of committing any crime to achieve his ends – so long as nothing could be proved against him. He had gone ahead boldly with the Présidente, putting forward possibilities as facts, making unwarranted assertions with the sole aim of persuading her to let him salvage this inheritance and so earn her goodwill. Representing two persons who were immeasurably eager to escape from immeasurable indigence, he now spurned the idea of maintaining his revolting establishment in the rue de la Perle. He counted on getting a retainer of three thousand francs from La Cibot and five thousand from the Présidente. With this he could acquire a suitable flat. And finally, he would be able to fulfil his obligation to Dr Poulain. Some kinds of men are full of hatred and bitterness and inclined to malevolence through suffering and ill-health: yet they can go just as violently to the opposite extreme of benevolence. Richelieu, for example, was no less kind as a friend than he was cruel as an enemy. So grateful was Fraisier for the help Poulain had given him that he would willingly have let himself be cut in pieces for him.

The Présidente came in again with a letter in her hand, and, before he was aware of her return, she scrutinized this man who was looking forward so much to a happy life and a comfortable income. She found him less ugly than when she had first inspected him. After all, he was going to be useful, and a convenient tool is always looked on with greater favour than one who is serving another's interest.

'Monsieur Fraisier,' she said, 'you have proved that you are a man of intelligence, and I believe you are capable of speaking your mind.'

Fraisier's answering gesture was more eloquent than words.

'Well,' the Présidente continued, 'I want a candid answer to this question. Are Monsieur de Marville and myself likely to be compromised by the steps you are about to take?'

'I should not have come to see you, Madame, if there were any likelihood of my one day bespattering you with mud, even so little as would stand on a pin-head. Even so tiny a speck would seem as big as the moon. You are forgetting, Madame, that if I am to become a justice of the peace in Paris, I have to satisfy you first. I have had one lesson in my life, too hard a one for me to risk qualifying for a similar drubbing. One word in conclusion, Madame: every step I take will be submitted to you beforehand for your consideration.'

'Very good. Here is the letter for Monsieur Lebœuf. I shall now await information about the value of the inheritance.'

'That's the essential thing,' said the subtle Fraisier as he bowed low to the Présidente with as much grace as his physiognomy would permit.

'How providential!' thought Madame Camusot de Marville. 'I shall be rich! Camusot will be elected deputy, for if I give Fraisier a free hand in the Bolbec constituency, he will get a majority of votes for us. What a useful tool he will be!'

'How providential!' thought Fraisier, as he walked downstairs. 'What a fine partner Madame Camusot will make! I could do with a wife like her! Now I must get to work!'

And he set off for Mantes, where he had to gain the good graces of a man he scarcely knew. But he was counting on Madame Vatinelle who, alas, had been responsible for all his misfortunes. Troubles arising out of love are often as it were the protested bill of exchange drawn by an honest debtor: they bear interest!

22. A warning to old bachelors

THREE days later, while Schmucke was asleep – Madame Cibot and he had already shared out the burden of nursing and watching over the patient – she had had what she called a 'set-to' with poor Pons. It is worth while calling attention to a regrettable peculiarity about hepatitis. Sick people suffering from a more or less serious liver disease are inclined to impatience and bad temper, and these fits of anger give them temporary relief; just as, in a bout of fever, a man feels he has enormous strength at his command. The bout passes off, and prostration ensues – *collapsus* as the doctors call it – and then the enfeeblement which the organism has undergone is appreciated in all its gravity. Likewise, in liver diseases, particularly those brought on by great mental distress, after these passionate outbursts the patient sinks into a condition of debility the more dangerous because he is subjected to a strict diet. It is a sort of fever which disturbs the interaction of the humours, for its seat is neither in the blood nor the brain. This agitation, affecting the whole person, brings on a melancholy which induces self-hatred in the patient. In such a situation, anything can set up a dangerous irritation. In spite of the doctor's recommendations, La Cibot, a working-class woman with neither experience nor education, had no belief in this theory of the excitation of the nervous system by the humoral system. In her view Dr Poulain's explanations were just 'doctor's fads'. Like all the common people, she insisted on feeding Pons up, and, to stop her surreptitiously giving him ham, rich omelettes or vanilla chocolate, no less was needed than a stern admonition from the doctor:

'Give a single mouthful of anything whatsoever to Monsieur Pons, and you will kill him as surely as if you put a pistol to his head.'

The obstinacy of the lower orders in this respect is so great that the reluctance of sick people to go into hospital is due to

226

the popular conviction that hospitals starve their patients to death. The mortality caused by wives smuggling in food for their husbands is so high that doctors have had to insist on relatives being subjected to a very rigorous search on visiting days.

La Cibot, desirous of provoking a momentary quarrel with Pons – necessary for the realization of her more immediate project – told him about her visit to the theatre manager; nor did she leave out her 'squabble' with the dancer, Mademoiselle Héloïse.

'But why did you go there?' asked the sick man for the third time, having been unable to stem La Cibot's torrent of words.

'Anyway, when I told her off, this Mademoiselle Héloïse, she saw what I was made of and drew her claws in, and after that we were the best friends in the world. . . . Now you asked me what I was doing there,' she added, repeating Pons's question. Some garrulous people who have a genius for garrulity, gather up interruptions, objections and observations as reserve provision for further discourse – as if the supply of this could ever dry up!

'Well, I went there to get Monsieur Gaudissart out of a fix. He wants music for a ballet, and you're hardly in a state, dearie, to scribble anything down on music-paper and do the job . . . I heard him say right out that he'd call in a Monsieur Garangeot to set *The Mohicans* to music . . .'

'Garangeot!' cried Pons in a fury. 'Garangeot, who has no talent at all! Why, I refused to take him on as first violin! No doubt he's a man of wit who can write good music reviews, but I defy him to compose a tune . . . And where on earth did you get the notion of going to the theatre?'

'Aren't you a pig-headed old thing! . . . Look, ducky, don't boil over like a saucepan of milk . . . Now *could* you write music in the state you're in? Have you taken a peep at yourself in the looking-glass? Shall I bring you one? You're all skin and bone . . . You're as weak as a kitten . . . And you think you're able to write out the notes . . . when you can't even sign one for me . . . That reminds me, I must go up to the third-floor tenant. He owes us seventeen francs – it's worth picking up, seventeen francs: once the chemist is paid, we haven't twenty francs left!... So Monsieur Gaudissart had to be told... He looks a decent sort, and he's got a lovely name... He's a real hail-fellow-well-met character who'd suit me fine... He'll never have anything wrong with *his* liver... So I was bound to tell him how you were doing... What else could I do? You're in a bad way, and he's had to replace you for the time being...'

'Replace me!' cried Pons in a thunderous voice, sitting up in bed.

As a rule sick people, especially those already within the sweep of Death's scythe, cling to their posts with a frenzy as great as that of beginners trying to obtain them. And so, to the poor suffering man, the news of his being replaced sounded like a death-knell.

'But the doctor told me I'm getting on very nicely, that I shall soon be back to normal. You have killed me, ruined me, murdered me!...'

'Stuff and nonsense! Off you go again!' La Cibot exclaimed. 'That's right, I'm putting the rope round your neck! You're always saying nice things like that about me to Monsieur Schmucke, I'll bet, once my back's turned. I know very well what you mean, indeed I do!... You're an ungrateful old monster.'

'But you don't realize that if I take more than another fort-night to get better I shall be told, when I do get back, that I'm an old fogey, an old fossil, a back-number, antiquated, an Empire relic!' said the old man, so ill, and yet still so intent on living. 'Garangeot must have been toadying throughout the whole theatre from the box-office to the flies. He'll have been transposing the music for actresses who can't reach the high notes, licking Gaudissart's boots, persuading his cronies to cry up the whole cast in the newspapers. What's more, Madame Cibot, in a thieves' kitchen like that they'd think nothing of skinning a gnat for its hide. What demon took you there?'

'Goodness me, Monsieur Schmucke talked it over with me for a week. What do you expect? You think of nobody but yourself. You're so selfish you don't mind wearing people out who are trying to get you better!... But Monsieur

Schmucke has been at the end of his tether for a month; it's as if he was walking over red-hot coals; he can't go anywhere, he can't give his lessons or do his work in the theatre. Have you no eyes in your head? He watches over you every night as I do in the day. As sure as I stand here, if I sat up all night as I tried to at first when I thought you'd soon be all right, I'd have to sleep the day through. And who'd look after the cleaning and everything else? . . . What's the good of complaining? When you're ill, you're ill, and that's all there is to it . . .'

'Schmucke simply can't have thought of doing that.'

'So now you're saying I took it upon myself? Do you think we're made of iron? Look, if Monsieur Schmucke had gone on giving seven or eight lessons a day and then spending the evenings from half-past six to half-past eleven conducting, he'd have been dead in another fortnight. Do you *want* the dear man to die, and him ready to give his life's blood for you? I'll take my oath on it, nobody's ever known a patient like you. Where's your common sense? Have you taken it to the pawn-shop? Everybody here's killing themselves for you, we're doing the best we can, and all you can do is grumble . . . Do you want to drive us raving mad? . . . Me to begin with – I'm dead beat, and there's worse to come!'

La Cibot was free to go on ranting, since Pons was too angry to utter a word. He was rolling over and over in his bed, giving vent to half-inarticulate protests before sinking into a state of exhaustion. As always, once this stage was reached, the quarrel suddenly took an affectionate turn. La Cibot rushed over to the sick man, held his head, forced him to lie back and drew the blankets over him.

'Fancy getting yourself into such a state! Never mind, ducky, after all it's your liver to blame. That's what good Monsieur Poulain says. Come on now, quieten down. Behave like a good lad. You're the idol of everybody who comes near you, and even the doctor himself comes as often as twice a day. What would he say if he found you all worked up like this? You just get me wild . . . You ought to be ashamed of yourself . . . When you've Mamma Cibot to care for you, you ought to be kind to her . . . You go on talking and shouting, and you've been told not to! Talking puts you into a tantrum . . . And why

lose your temper? It's you that's in the wrong. You always rub
me up the wrong way. Look now, be sensible: Monsieur
Schmucke and myself – you're as dear to me as my own heart's
blood – we're acting for the best . . . So there, my cherub, it's
all right, see?'

'Schmucke would never have told you to go to the theatre
without consulting me . . .'

'Let's wake him, shall we, the poor dear man, sleeping like
the blessed angel he is, and see what he says about it?'

'Certainly not!' cried Pons. 'If my good tender Schmucke
took this decision, perhaps I'm more ill than I thought?' And
he cast a lamentably melancholy glance round the room at the
objects of art it contained. 'I shall have to say good-bye to my
pictures and all the things I've doted on . . . and to my wonderful Schmucke as well . . . Oh, can it be true?'

La Cibot, black-hearted actress that she was, dabbed her eyes
with her handkerchief, and this wordless reply plunged the sick
man into gloomy meditation. Prostrate under the blows
delivered at his two tenderest spots – social life and good health,
the loss of his livelihood and the prospect of death – he collapsed
so completely that he no longer had the strength to fly into a
rage. He lay there as dejected as a consumptive after a final
spasm of coughing.

'Look now, if you had any consideration for Monsieur
Schmucke,' said La Cibot, seeing that no fight was left in her
victim, 'you'd do well to send for the district notary, Monsieur
Trognon, a very decent man.'

'You're always talking about this man Trognon,' said the
patient.

'Oh well, him or anybody else, what's it matter, for all I'm
likely to get out of you!'

And she shook her head in proof of her contempt for riches.
Quiet reigned once more.

*

At this moment, awakened by hunger after sleeping for more
than six hours, Schmucke got up, entered Pons's room and
contemplated him for a while in silence – for Madame Cibot
had put a finger to her mouth and murmured: 'Hush!'

Then she stood up, drew near to the German, and said in a whisper:

'Thank the Lord, he's off to sleep. He's as cross as two sticks . . . It can't be helped; it's his disease he has to fight against.'

'Not at all. On the contrary, I am very patient,' the victim replied in a doleful tone which showed how utterly dejected he was. 'My dear Schmucke, she actually went to the theatre to lose me my job.'

He stopped short, and had not the strength to finish. La Cibot took advantage of this pause to make a sign to Schmucke indicating that Pons was going out of his mind, and said:

'Don't argue with him. It would kill him . . .'

'What's more,' Pons continued, gazing at the honest Schmucke, 'She makes out it was you who sent her.'

'It *vass* me,' replied Schmucke, heroically. 'It hat to pe . . . Say nossink! . . . let us safe you! . . . It iss matness to vear yourself out vorkink ven you haf a fortune . . . Get vell again, ve vill sell a pit off pric-a-prac unt ve will ent our dayss in some qviet corner, viz zis goot Matam Cipot . . .'

'She's talked you over!' said Pons in rueful tones. The sick man could not see Madame Cibot, who had taken her stance behind the bed to conceal from Pons the signs she was making to Schmucke: he thought she had gone.

'She's murdering me!' he added.

'Murdering you, am I,' she said with blazing eyes and arms akimbo. 'So that's the reward I get for fussing over you like a pet poodle. God in Heaven!'

She burst into tears and sank into a chair. This piece of tragic mummery had a disastrous effect on Pons's condition.

'Very well!' she said, getting up again and turning baleful eyes on the two friends: eyes full of hate, darting both fire and venom. 'I'm sick of doing no good here and wearing myself out. You'll have to get a nurse.'

The two friends exchanged terrified glances.

'It's all very well for you to look at each other like a couple of play-actors! My mind's made up. I'm going to ask Dr Poulain to find you a nurse. And we'll settle accounts. You'll pay me back the money I've laid out on you – I would never

231

have asked for it back – and to think I've just been to Monsieur Pillerault to borrow another five hundred francs . . .'

'It iss hiss tisseasse!' said Schmucke, rushing over to Madame Cibot and putting his arm round her waist. 'Haf patience viz him!'

'Oh, you're a blessed saint, and I'd let you walk over me as if I were dirt,' she said. 'But Monsieur Pons has never liked me. He hates the sight of me . . . Anyway, he might think I want to be put in his will . . .'

'Hush!' cried Schmucke. 'You vill kill him.'

'Good-bye, Monsieur Pons,' she said, going up to his bed and blasting him with a look. 'I don't wish you any worse than to get better. When you're nice to me again, and when you're ready to believe I do what's best for you, I'll come back! Till then I'll keep my distance . . . You were like my own child. But have children ever started going against their mothers? . . . No, Monsieur Schmucke, I won't hear a word . . . I'll bring you your dinner, and I'll serve *you*. But get a nurse in. Ask Monsieur Poulain for one.'

And out she went, slamming the door hard enough to shatter the frail and precious objects in the flat. Pons heard a rattle of china which, to his tormented soul, was like the *coup de grâce* administered to a man being broken on the wheel.

One hour later, La Cibot, instead of coming into Pons's bedroom, called out to Schmucke through the doorway, telling him his dinner was ready in the dining-room. The poor German came in with a pallid, tear-stained face.

'My poor Pons iss out of hiss vits,' he said, 'for he svears you are a vicket voman. It iss only hiss tisseasse,' he added, hoping to soften La Cibot without accusing Pons.

'Oh, I've had enough of his disease! Look, he's not my father, nor my husband, nor my brother, nor my child. He's got a grudge against me, and that's just about enough! Look at you now: I'd go through fire and water for you. But when you've given up your whole life, your whole heart, all your savings, neglecting your husband – Cibot's taken ill now – and then get called a wicked woman, it's too much to stand . . .'

'Too moch?'

'Yes, too much. Let's stop wasting words and come down to

simple facts. Here then: You owe me three months' wages – a hundred and ninety francs a month – that's five hundred and seventy. Then there's the rent I paid twice – here are the receipts – that makes six hundred francs, and the five per cent for me and the rates. That's a bit less than twelve hundred francs, then there's the two thousand francs, without interest, mind you! All told, three thousand one hundred and ninety-two francs . . . And remember, you'll have to find at least two thousand for the nurse, the doctor, the medicine and the nurse's keep – that's why I went out and borrowed a thousand francs from Monsieur Pillerault,' she added, producing the thousand-franc note which Gaudissart had given her.

Schmucke listened to this statement of accounts with very understandable stupefaction, for he knew as much about finance as a cat knows about music.

'Matame Cipot, Pons iss not in hiss right mint! Forgif him. Ton't gif up nursink him. Pe our goot antchell shtill . . . On my knees I pek you!' And the German threw himself down in front of La Cibot and kissed the hands of his tormentor.

'Listen, my kitten,' she said, pulling him to his feet and kissing his forehead. 'Cibot is ill in bed, I've just sent for Dr Poulain. That being so I must get my affairs in order. Besides, Cibot saw me coming in crying, and he fell into such a fury he won't let me set foot in here again. It's him that's demanding the money, and it's his money after all. Womenfolk have nothing to do with that. But if we give my man his money back, three thousand two hundred francs, he may calm down. It's all he owns, poor man, every bit he's saved after pinching and scraping for twenty-seven years, and he earned it with the sweat of his brow. He wants his money tomorrow, and there's no dodging out of it. You don't know Cibot: when he gets angry he'd murder anybody. Never mind, I might perhaps get him to agree for me to go on looking after the pair of you. Don't worry, I'll let him go on at me as much as he likes. I'll put up with it for love of you, you're such an angel.'

'No, no, I am tchust a poor man who lofs his frient unt voult gif his life to safe him . . .'

'But the money? . . . My good Monsieur Schmucke, supposing you didn't give me a penny, we still have to find three thousand for your day-to-day needs! My goodness, do you know what I would do if I were in your shoes? . . . I wouldn't stop to think about it, I'd sell seven or eight of those wretched pictures and fill up the gaps with some of those in your bedroom – the ones which have been put face backwards to save space. What's it matter whether it's one picture or another?'

'Vy to zet?'

'He's so sly! It's his disease. When he's well he's as mild as a lamb. He might very well get out of bed and go ferreting round. And if he happened to come into the dining-room, even though he's so weak he couldn't get over the threshold, he'd still find the same number of pictures.'

'Zet iss so!'

'But we'll tell him about the sale when he's all right again. And if you want to tell him, put all the blame on me; tell him I wanted paying off. After all, I've broad enough shoulders!'

'I cannot sell sinks vich to not pelonk to me,' the good German answered simply.

'Very well, I shall take you to court, you and Monsieur Pons.'

'It voult kill him!'

'Take your choice. Good heavens! Sell the pictures and tell him about it afterwards . . . You can show him the summons.'

That very day, at seven o'clock, Madame Cibot, after consulting a writ-server, asked Schmucke to come downstairs. The German found himself in the presence of Monsieur Tabareau, who called upon him to pay up. Schmucke, trembling from head to foot, muttered some sort of reply, but he and Pons were served with a summons to appear before the court and receive the order to pay. The sight of this man and the scrawl on the stamped paper had such an effect on Schmucke that he gave way.

'Sell ze paintinks,' he said with tears in his eyes.

The next day, at six in the morning, Elias Magus and Rémonencq each unhooked the pictures they had bought. Two formal receipts, correctly worded, ran thus:

I the undersigned, acting for and on behalf of Monsieur Pons, acknowledge receipt from Monsieur Elias Magus of the sum of two thousand five hundred francs for the four pictures sold to him, the said sum to be applied to the needs of Monsieur Pons. Of these pictures, one, attributed to Dürer, is the portrait of a woman; the second, of the Italian school, is likewise a portrait; the third is a Dutch landscape by Brueghel; the fourth is a Florentine picture of the Holy Family, painter unknown.

The receipt given by Rémonencq was similarly couched and included a Greuze, a Claude Lorrain, a Rubens and a Van Dyck, vaguely designated as being pictures of the French and Flemish schools.

'Ziss money almost makes me pelief zet zese tchimcracks are vorse somesink,' said Schmucke on receiving the five thousand francs.

'They *are* worth something,' said Rémonencq, 'I'd willingly give a hundred thousand francs for all that lot.'

The Auvergnat was asked to render the small service of replacing the eight pictures by others of the same dimensions, in identical frames: he chose them from the inferior pictures Pons had put in Schmucke's bedroom.

Once in possession of the four masterpieces, Elias Magus took La Cibot home with him on the pretext of settling accounts. But he pleaded poverty, found flaws in the paintings, asserted they would need new backings, and offered La Cibot a commission of thirty thousand francs. He induced her to accept them by waving in front of her some of those glistening scraps of paper on which the Bank of France inscribes the words MILLE FRANCS. Magus ordered Rémonencq to pay over a like sum to La Cibot as an instalment on the other four pictures, and had them deposited in his house. These four pictures seemed so magnificent to Magus that he could not bring himself to hand them back, and the next day he took a commission of six thousand francs to the second-hand dealer, who ceded the four canvases, duly receipted. Madame Cibot, the richer by sixty-eight thousand francs, once more stipulated absolute secrecy from her two accomplices, and asked the Jew to advise her how to invest this sum in such a way that no one would be able to pin the possession of it on her.

'Buy shares in the Orleans railway. They are thirty francs below par. You will double your capital in three years, and you'll have it in paper values which will go into a pocket-case.'

'Stay here, Monsieur Magus. I'm going to see the attorney acting for Monsieur Pons's family. He wants to know what price you'll give for all the stuff up there. I'll go and fetch him.'

'Pity she isn't a widow!' said Rémonencq to Magus. 'She'd suit me down to the ground. She's rolling in money.'

'She'll be better off still if she takes out shares in the Orleans railway: they'll be worth twice that in a couple of years,' said the Jew. 'All my little savings are in them, for my daughter's dowry . . . Let's have a stroll along the boulevards while we're waiting for the lawyer.'

'If the Lord would take Cibot to His bosom – he's ill already –' continued Rémonencq, 'I'd have a grand woman to manage my shop, and I could go in for a big line of business.'

23. Schmucke climbs to the mercy-seat of God

'How do you do, my good Monsieur Fraisier?' said La Cibot, adopting a fawning tone as she entered her legal adviser's office. 'What's this your concierge tells me about you leaving here?'

'It's true, my dear Madame Cibot. I am moving to Dr Poulain's house and taking the first-floor rooms over his. I'm trying to find two or three thousand francs to furnish it suitably: it's a pretty flat and has just been redecorated. As I told you, I have been entrusted with the Président de Marville's interests – and yours too . . . I am giving up as a legal factotum and registering my name on the barrister's roll, and I must have very smart premises for that. Only those who possess respectable furniture, with a library and so on, can be called to the bar in Paris. I am a doctor of law, I have kept my terms, and I already have powerful protectors . . . Well now, how are things progressing?'

'Perhaps you would accept what I've put by in the savings bank,' said La Cibot. 'It's not much – three thousand francs; it comes from twenty-five years' pinching and scraping . . . You could make me out a bill of exchange. That's what Rémonencq calls them. I'm ignorant; I only know what I've been told.'

'No, the rules of the bar do not allow barristers to sign bills of exchange. I will give you a receipt bearing interest at five per cent, and you will return it to me if I get you a twelve-hundred francs' annuity out of old Pons's estate.'

Caught in a trap, La Cibot said nothing.

'Silence gives consent,' said Fraisier. 'Bring it to me tomorrow.'

'Oh well, I don't mind paying you your fees in advance. It means I'm sure of getting my annuity.'

Fraisier gave an assenting nod. 'Now then, what's the position?' he asked. 'I saw Poulain last night. It appears you are driving your patient pretty hard. One more attack like yesterday's, and stones will form in his gall-bladder. Mind you're gentle with him, my dear Madame Cibot. You mustn't burden your conscience. It shortens one's days.'

'Leave me alone with your talk of conscience! . . . Are you going to start telling me about the guillotine again? Monsieur Pons is a pig-headed old man. You don't know what he's like! He puts me into such a state of aggravation! There isn't a worse man alive; his relations were right; he's foxy, spiteful, pig-headed . . . Anyway, Monsieur Magus is there, as I told you, and he's waiting for you.'

'Good! . . . I'll be along as soon as you. The amount of your annuity depends on the worth of this collection. If it's valued at eight hundred thousand francs, you'll get fifteen hundred francs a year. That's a fortune!'

'All right, I'll tell them to make a fair valuation.'

One hour later, while Pons was fast asleep after Schmucke had given him a sedative duly prescribed by the doctor – La Cibot had doubled the dose without Schmucke knowing it – the three gallows-birds, Fraisier, Rémonencq and Magus, were busy examining one by one the seventeen hundred objects comprising the old musician's collection. Schmucke having gone to bed, they had the place to themselves and were sniffing around like carrion crows round a corpse.

'Don't make a sound,' said La Cibot every time Magus went into raptures and argued with Rémonencq, as he informed him of the value of some fine piece of work.

It was heart-rending to see these four persons, each a prey to his own special kind of cupidity, gauging the value of the inheritance while the man whose death they were greedily anticipating was fast asleep. This valuation of the contents of the salon lasted three hours.

'On an average,' said the shabby old Jew, 'every object here is worth a thousand francs.'

'That would make seventeen hundred thousand francs!' exclaimed Fraisier in stupefaction.

'Not as far as I am concerned,' Magus continued with a chilly glint in his eyes. 'I would not give more than eight hundred thousand francs. You never know how long you'll have such articles on your hands ... Some real masterpieces don't sell for a matter of ten years, and so your purchase price is doubled if you take compound interest into account. But I'll pay cash down.'

'In the bedroom,' Rémonencq remarked, 'he has some stained glass, enamels, miniatures, and gold and silver snuff-boxes.'

'May we examine them?' asked Fraisier.

'I'll see if he's sound asleep,' said La Cibot. Then she beckoned the three birds of prey in.

Magus, with every hair in his white beard quivering, pointed back to the salon. 'That's where the masterpieces are,' he said. 'But here are the real treasures. And what treasures! Crowned kings haven't finer articles in their collections.'

Rémonencq's eyes, all aflame at the sight of the snuff-boxes, were shining like coals of fire. Fraisier, calm and cold as a coiled snake, had his flattened head thrust forward, and his pose was like that which painters give to Mephistopheles. Each of these three varieties of miser, thirsting for gold just as devils in hell thirst for the dew of paradise, directed his own special glance at the owner of so much wealth, for he had stirred in his sleep as if he were having a nightmare. Suddenly, under the diabolic glare of this triple gaze, the sick man opened his eyes and let out a piercing cry.

'Thieves! ... Look at them! ... Call the police! ... Help! ... Murder!'

Although he was awake, his dream evidently still hung over him: he was now sitting up, his eyes wide open in a blank stare, unable to move.

Elias Magus and Rémonencq made for the door, but they stood rooted to the spot when they heard Pons shout 'Magus here! ... I'm being tricked!' ... The instinct which prompted him to watch over his treasure was no less strong in him than the instinct of self-preservation, and it had awakened him.

'Madame Cibot, who is this man?' he cried out with a shiver at the sight of Fraisier standing there motionless.

'For heavens' sake, I couldn't turn him out of the house, could I?' she said, winking at Fraisier and motioning to him. 'This gentleman has just called here on behalf of your family.'

Fraisier could not repress a start of admiration for La Cibot's resourcefulness.

'That is so, Monsieur. I have come on behalf of Madame la Présidente de Marville, her husband and her daughter, to bring you their apologies. They heard of your illness by chance and would like to take charge of you themselves. They invite you to go to their Marville estate to recover your health. Madame la Vicomtesse Popinet, the little Cécile you love so well, will nurse you . . . She took your part against her mother and made her realize the mistake she had made.'

Pons was indignant. 'So my would-be heirs sent you here with the cleverest connoisseur, the finest expert in Paris, as your guide! . . .'

'That's stretching it a bit too far!' he continued with a maniacal laugh. 'You've come here to value my pictures, my curios, my snuff-boxes, my miniatures! . . . Value them! You've brought a man with you who is not only knowledgeable about everything, but is able to buy, as he's a millionaire ten times over . . . My kind relatives won't have long to wait for my inheritance,' he added with deep irony. 'They've given me a good nudge forward . . . And you, Madame Cibot, you call yourself my mother, and while I am asleep you let in dealers, my rival, and the Camusots! Get out, all of you!'

And the unhappy man, under the double stimulus of anger and fear, lifted his gaunt body out of bed.

'Take my arm, Monsieur Pons,' said La Cibot, rushing forward to prevent him from falling. 'Calm down then, those gentlemen have gone.'

'I want to see the salon,' said the moribund man.

La Cibot motioned to the three vultures to hurry off. Then she took hold of Pons, lifted him up like a feather, and put him back to bed in spite of his shouting. Seeing that the unhappy collector was utterly exhausted, she went to shut the door of the flat. Pons's three tormentors were still out there on the landing and, seeing them, she asked them to wait. She heard Fraisier make the following remark to Magus:

'Write me a letter signed by both of you in which you undertake to pay nine hundred thousand francs in cash for the Pons collection, and we shall be putting a fine piece of business in your way.'

Then he whispered one word, one single word which no one could overhear, in La Cibot's ear, and went down to the porter's lodge with the two dealers.

*

'Madame Cibot,' asked the unhappy Pons on her return, 'have they gone?'

'Have who gone?' she asked.

'Those men.'

'What men? . . . So you think you've been seeing men! No: you've just been having a bad attack of fever, so bad that if I hadn't been there you'd have thrown yourself out of the window, and you're still babbling about men . . . How long are you going on like that? . . .'

'What! There wasn't a man here who pretended he'd been sent by my family? Over there . . . a minute ago?'

'Off you go again, so pig-headed! My goodness, do you know where you ought to be put? In a lunatic asylum, that's where! . . . You and your men!'

'Elias Magus and Rémonencq were in here!'

'Oh, Rémonencq. Yes, you may have seen him. He came in to tell me about my poor Cibot – he's so ill I'm leaving you to stew in your own juice. Cibot comes first, that's for sure! When my man's ill nobody else matters to me. Try and keep quiet and get a couple of hours' sleep. I've sent for Monsieur Poulain and I'll bring him up here . . . Take your medicine and be sensible.'

'You say there was nobody in my room – over there – when I woke up just now?'

'Nobody! You must have seen Monsieur Rémonencq in your looking-glass.'

'You are right, Madame Cibot,' said the sick man, suddenly turning as docile as a sheep.

'That's the style! Now you're getting reasonable . . . Goodbye, my cherub. Keep quiet and I'll be back in a jiffy.'

As soon as Pons heard the door of the flat shutting, he mustered his remaining strength and dragged himself out of bed, muttering to himself:

'They're cheating me, robbing me! Schmucke's such a child he'd let anybody bamboozle him! . . .'

Eager to clear up the mystery – the terrifying scene he had just witnessed seemed too real to have been a hallucination – the sick man managed to reach his bedroom door. Painfully, he pushed it open and advanced into the salon; there the sight of his beloved pictures, statues, Florentine bronzes and porcelains put new life into him. In his dressing-gown, with his legs bare and his head in a whirl, the collector managed to walk along the two alleys marked out by the row of credence-tables and commodes which divided the salon into two parts. His expert eye ran over the exhibits: the count was complete, and his collection appeared to be intact. Then, as he was going back into his bedroom, he noticed that a Greuze portrait had been substituted for Sebastiano del Piombo's *Knight of Malta*. Suspicion flashed across his mind as lightning streaks across a stormy sky. He looked along the wall on which his eight best pictures had hung and found that others had been put in their place. Suddenly a veil of darkness blacked out the poor man's vision; he fainted and fell to the floor; his swoon was so complete that he remained there two hours. When Schmucke woke up and came out of his room to visit his friend, he discovered him lying there. With infinite pains, he lifted the unconscious man and put him back on his bed; but when he spoke to this semi-corpse all the reply he received was an icy stare, meaningless words and stammerings. Instead of losing his head, the poor German showed the highest heroism of which friendship is capable. Under the stimulus of despair, the childlike man had the sort of inspiration a mother or a mistress might have: he succeeded in finding some towels, heated them, wrapped some of them round Pons's hands and placed the rest on the hollow part of his stomach. Then he laid his hands on his friend's cold, damp forehead and summoned life back to it with an inflexibility of will-power worthy of Apollonius of Tyana. He pressed his lips on Pons's eyes with the fervour of a Madonna kissing the dead Christ in some *Pietà* carved by a great Italian sculptor in bas-relief. These devoted efforts, this influx of animation from one being to another, this discharge of a mother's or a lover's function, was crowned with complete success. After half an hour Pons was warm again and looked human once more; his eyes were no longer glazed and the heat of the towels had restored the power of movement to his limbs. Schmucke gave Pons a drink of melissa cordial mixed with wine; the life-blood coursed once more through his veins, and the light of intelligence shone forth once more on a brow from which all sentience had been banished. Pons then realized to what saintly devotion, to what power of friendship he owed his resuscitation.

'But for you I should have died!' he said as he felt his friend's tears dropping gently on to his face: Schmucke was laughing and weeping at one and the same time. When he heard these words which he had been awaiting in a delirium of hope – as potent as the delirium of despair – poor Schmucke, utterly exhausted, collapsed like a burst balloon. It was his turn to totter: he fell into an armchair, folded his hands in prayer and gave thanks to God. A miracle had just happened. He gave no credit for this to the efficacy of his own action, in itself a prayer, but only to the divine power he had invoked. And yet this miracle was due to natural causes. Doctors have often seen similar things happen. A sick person on whom affection is lavished, cared for by people who want him to live, can be saved, *caeteris paribus*, where a patient tended by hirelings would succumb. Doctors will not see that this is the result of involuntary magnetism: they attribute it to intelligent surveillance and strict adherence to their prescriptions. But many mothers well know what virtue there is in this fervent projection of unfaltering will-power.

'My wonderful friend! . . .'

'Zere iss no neet to talk: my heart vill reat your soughts. Tchust rest,' said the now smiling musician.

'Dear friend! Noble creature! Child of God whose life is with God! The one being who has ever loved me! . . .' said Pons. His speech was still spasmodic, but there were unwonted inflexions in his voice. He put his whole soul, which had so nearly fled, into these words, and they were almost as delightful to Schmucke as the joy of a woman's love.

'You must lif! You must lif! Unt I shall pe as shtronk as a lion! I shall vork for poss off us!'

'Listen, good faithful, adorable friend! Let me speak. Time

presses, for I'm as good as dead. I shall not get over these continual attacks.'

Schmucke wept like a child.

'Listen now and weep afterwards,' said Pons. 'As a Christian you must resign yourself to it. But I have been robbed – by La Cibot. Before I leave you I must enlighten you about the ways of the world – you know nothing about them. I have been robbed of eight pictures which were worth enormous sums.'

'Forgif me, it vass I who solt zem.'

'You?'

'Yes,' the poor German confessed. 'Ve vere serfet viz a writ.'

'A writ?... By whom?'

'Vait!...' Schmucke went to find the document the writ-server had left and brought it to him.

Pons gave a careful reading to this piece of legal jargon. When he had finished he dropped it and was silent for a while. This man, so closely observant of human handicraft, so negligent of human behaviour, was now able to disentangle every thread of the plot hatched by La Cibot. His keen artistic perceptions, the intelligence he had shown as a pupil of the Rome Academy, all his youthful awareness came back to him for a few instants.

'My good Schmucke, I want you to obey my orders as a soldier does. Listen! Go down to the lodge and tell that abominable woman that I wish to see the person sent to me by my cousin the Président. Tell her that if he refuses to come I intend to bequeath my collection to the Louvre. Tell her I want to make my will.'

Schmucke obeyed these instructions, but La Cibot responded to his opening words with a smile.

'My good Monsieur Schmucke, our patient had a bad attack of fever and thought he saw people in his room. I take my oath as an honest woman that nobody ever came from our dear patient's family.'

Schmucke returned with this reply and repeated it verbatim to Pons.

'She's more clever, more cunning, more crafty, more Machiavellian than I thought,' said Pons with a smile. 'She's a downright liar! Just imagine, this morning she brought a Jew here, one Elias Magus, with Rémonencq and a third person I don't know, one who's more horrible than the other two put together. She counted on my staying asleep so that they could value my collection. I happened to wake up and I saw the three of them testing the weight of my snuff-boxes. Finally the man I didn't know said that the Camusots had sent him – I had a few words with him ... That infamous woman now swears I was dreaming ... My dear Schmucke, I wasn't dreaming! ... I certainly heard that man speaking to me. The two dealers were alarmed and made themselves scarce ... I thought that La Cibot would go back on her words ... but my ruse was unsuccessful. Well, I'm going to lay another trap and the wicked hag will fall into it ... My poor dear friend, you take La Cibot for an angel, and for a month she's been plaguing me to death for her own greedy purposes. I tried not to believe that a woman who has been such a faithful servant for years could be so wicked, and this hesitation was my ruin ... How much were you given for my eight pictures?'

'Fife sousant francs.'

'God in Heaven! They were worth twenty times that!' cried Pons. 'They were the gems of my collection. I haven't time to start an action. In any case, you would get involved as the dupe of these rascals ... A law-suit would kill you! You don't know what the Law Courts are like. They are the sewers into which all moral infamy is poured. A good soul like you would be so horrified at such turpitude you would give up the struggle. Anyway, you'll be rich enough. Those pictures cost me four thousand francs, and I've had them for thirty-seven years ... But they've been surprisingly smart in the way they've robbed us. I'm on the brink of the grave, and from now on you will be my sole concern – you, the best man alive. Now I don't want you to be fleeced, for all that I own is yours. And that's why you must distrust everybody – and distrust has never been your strong point. No doubt God looks after you; but He might lose sight of you a moment, and they will swoop down on you like buccaneers on a cargo-ship. La Cibot is a monster. She's killing me, and you still think she's an angel! I want you to know her for what she is. Go and ask her to tell you of a notary who will draw up my will ... I'll catch her with her hands in the till.'

Schmucke was listening to Pons as if the *Book of Revelations* were being read out to him. That there could exist so perverse a creature as La Cibot must be if Pons were right, seemed to him like denying the existence of Providence.

'My poor frient Pons iss so ill,' said the German, going down to the lodge and addressing Madame Cibot again, 'zat he vishes to make hiss vill. Pleass sent for ze notary ...'

These words were spoken in the hearing of several other persons, for Cibot was in an almost desperate condition. Rémonencq, his sister, two concierges who had hurried along from neighbouring buildings, three housemaids from other flats in the house and the tenant of the first-floor front were standing about at the street door.

'You can go and get a notary for yourself,' cried La Cibot with tears in her eyes. 'You can get anybody you like to have your will drawn up ... With my poor Cibot at death's door I'm not going to leave him. I'd give all the Ponses in the world to save Cibot ... A man who's never given me a minute's vexation in thirty years of wedded life!'

She went in again, and Schmucke stood there completely taken aback.

'Sir,' said the first-floor tenant, 'is Monsieur Pons very ill then?'

His name was Jolivard, and he was a registry clerk in the Law Courts.

'He haf nearly tiet tschust now,' replied Schmucke in tones of great grief.

'There's a notary near here in the rue Saint-Louis: Monsieur Trognon,' observed Monsieur Jolivard. 'He's a district notary.'

'Would you like me to go and fetch him?' asked Rémonencq.

'I voult pe fery glat,' answered Schmucke. 'If Matame Cipot vill not vatch ofer my frient, I voult not leaf him in ze state he iss in.'

'Madame Cibot says he's going off his head,' said Jolivard.

'Off hiss heat?' Schmucke cried out in dismay. 'Nefer hass he been so lifely of mint, ant zet iss vat makes me vorry about his healss.'

All the people assembled together were listening to this conversation with a very natural curiosity which engraved it on their memories. Schmucke was unacquainted with Fraisier; nor was he in a state to take any notice of that satanic head, those glittering eyes. By dint of two words whispered in La Cibot's ear, Fraisier had been the prime mover in her bare-faced display of histrionics. It was probably beyond her powers to stage such a scene, but she had played her part with consummate skill. To make it appear that the dying man was out of his mind was one of the cornerstones in the edifice the man of law was constructing. The incident of that morning had been useful to Fraisier's purpose. Without his prompting perhaps, La Cibot, so great was her mental disturbance, would have contradicted herself at the moment when Schmucke, that poor innocent, had come down to lay the trap for her by asking her to recall the emissary of the Camusot family.

Rémonencq, witnessing Dr Poulain's arrival, asked nothing better than to make himself scarce. And he had good reason for this.

24. A testator's cunning

FOR over a week Rémonencq had been usurping the role of Providence, an activity singularly displeasing to the Law, which claims the sole right to act in its stead. Rémonencq wanted at all costs to rid himself of the only obstacle standing between him and happiness; and happiness, for him, meant marriage with the alluring concierge and the tripling of his capital. One day, as he watched the little tailor drinking some herbal tea, the idea had come to him of converting his indisposition into a mortal illness, and his experience as a vendor of scrap-metal had suggested a method for this.

One morning, while smoking his pipe, leaning against the door-frame of his shop, and dreaming of a fine emporium in the Boulevard de la Madeleine, with Madame Cibot presiding over it in gorgeous apparel, his eye fell on a heavily oxidized round plate of copper. The thrifty notion of cleaning this plate in Cibot's infusion suddenly occurred to him. He tied this plate, as round as a five-franc piece, to a small length of string; and while La Cibot was busy with 'her gentlemen', he came every day to inquire after his friend the tailor. During this few minute's visit, he let the copper disc soak in the liquid, pulling it out by the string as he went away. This slight addition of copper, coated with the deposit commonly known as verdigris, secretly introduced a noxious ingredient into the beneficial decoction, but in such homoeopathic proportions as to cause incalculable harm. This criminal homoeopathy produced the following results: after three days, poor Cibot's hair started falling out, his teeth trembled in their sockets, and the whole balance of his constitution was upset by these imperceptible doses of poison. Dr Poulain racked his brains when he noticed the effect of this decoction, for he was knowledgeable enough to realize that some destructive agent was at work. He surreptitiously took away a sample of the infusion and analysed it himself; but he found nothing in it, for on that particular day, by good luck, frightened at what he was doing, Rémonencq had not used the baneful disc. Dr Poulain settled the problem for himself and medical science by supposing that the tailor's blood was in process of decomposition, and that he was suffering from the effects of a sedentary life in a damp lodge, squatting on a table in front of a latticed window, taking no exercise and perpetually inhaling the emanations from a stinking gutter. For the rue de Normandie is one of those ancient streets with a runnel down the middle; the municipal authorities have installed no street fountains in it, and a noisome gutter sluggishly carries off all the household slops which filter through the cobbles and produce the kind of sludge peculiar to Paris.

As for La Cibot, she had been used to bustling about while her hard-working husband sat like a fakir in front of his window. His knees had become stiff, the blood only circulated in the upper portion of his body; his crooked spindly legs scarcely served as limbs any more. And so Cibot's extremely coppery complexion had for a long time seemed chronically unhealthy. To the doctor, the wife's robust health and the husband's sickliness appeared to be a natural result of their different occupations.

'What's wrong with my poor Cibot?' the concierge had asked Poulain.

'My dear Madame Cibot,' the doctor had replied. 'He is dying of a disease common among porters ... His general anaemia betokens an incurable poverty of the bloodstream.'

In the end Dr Poulain's early suspicions faded from his mind: such a crime would be unmotivated, bring no gain, further no one's interests. Who could want to poison Cibot? Not his wife, for Poulain had seen her tasting Cibot's decoction as she sugared it. A fairly large number of crimes escape the vengeance of society – in general, those which, like this one, afford no startling proof of any form of violence – bloodshed, strangulation, bruises, in short any clumsy method of disposal; but above all when the murder has no apparent incentive and has been committed by a member of the lower orders. A crime is always given away by its antecedents: hatred and a visible cupidity of which everyone around is aware. In the circumstances in which the little tailor, Rémonencq and La Cibot lived, no one except the doctor had any interest in inquiring into the cause of death. This sickly, sallow porter, having nothing to leave and adored by his wife, had no enemies. The dealer's motives and the passion which inflamed him were hidden from the light of day, like La Cibot's ill-gotten fortune. The doctor had a thorough knowledge of La Cibot and her feelings; he believed she was capable of tormenting Pons, but he knew she had no motive for committing murder, nor the initiative to carry it out. Moreover, she sipped a teaspoonful of the beverage every time the doctor came and whenever she gave a cup of it to her husband. Enlightenment could only have come through Poulain, but he put it down to some chance disease, one of those astonishing exceptions which make the practice of medicine so hazardous. And in fact, the little tailor, by reason of his stunted existence, was unfortunately in such general bad health that this imperceptible addition of copper oxide was destined to kill him. The attitude of neighbouring gossips was also such as to ward off suspicion from Rémonencq by the explanation they gave of his sudden decline.

'I've been saying so for a long time,' declared one of them. 'Monsieur Cibot wasn't at all well.'

'The man worked too hard,' said another. 'He wore himself out.'

'He wouldn't listen to me,' yet another neighbour exclaimed. 'I advised him to take a stroll on Sundays and not to work on Mondays. Two days a week's not too much time to take for relaxation.'

In short, local gossip, that common informer to which the law lends such an attentive ear via the police superintendent, that tyrant of the lower classes, put forward quite a satisfactory explanation of the little tailor's death. None the less, Poulain's thoughtful air and anxious eyes caused much embarrassment to Rémonencq. That is why he had so eagerly offered to fetch Monsieur Trognon, Fraisier's nominee, on Schmucke's behalf.

'I shall be back by the time the will is being drawn up,' Fraisier whispered to La Cibot. 'You must master your grief and keep a weather eye open.'

The little lawyer disappeared as lightly as a shadow. On the way he met his friend the doctor.

'Ah! Poulain,' he cried. 'All goes well. Things look promising! . . . I'll tell you about it this evening. Think out what post will suit you and you'll get it! And I shall be justice of the peace. Tabareau will no longer refuse me his daughter . . . As for you, depend upon it, I'll get you married to Mademoiselle Vitel, the grand-daughter of our present justice!'

Fraisier left Poulain to the stupefaction these heady words had aroused in him, darted into the boulevard and waved to an omnibus; ten minutes later this modern version of the stage-coach deposited him opposite the rue de Choiseul. It was nearly four. Fraisier was sure of finding the Présidente alone, because judges rarely leave the Palace before five.

Madame de Marville welcomed Fraisier with a courtesy which proved that, in accordance with the promise he had made to Madame Vatinelle, Monsieur Lebœuf had commended the former advocate of Mantes. Amélie showed almost feline friendliness to Fraisier – as the Duchesse de Montpensier must have done to Jacques Clément, the assassin of Henri III – for this little lawyer was a dagger in her hand. But when Fraisier showed her the joint letter in which Elias Magus and Rémonencq undertook to buy the whole of Pons's collection for nine hundred thousand francs in cash, the Présidente answered her agent with a look from eyes agleam with the contemplation of such a sum. To the lawyer it was like a wave of covetousness sweeping towards him.

'Monsieur le Président,' she said, 'has asked me to invite you to dinner for tomorrow. A family gathering. Our other guests will be Monsieur Godeschal, the successor of my solicitor Maître Desroches; also Berthier, my notary; also my son-in-law and my daughter . . . After dinner, you and I, the notary and the solicitor will have the little talk you asked for, and I will then give you your authorization. These two gentlemen will act on your suggestions as you have stipulated, and will see that the whole affair goes off satisfactorily. You will receive the power of attorney from Monsieur de Marville as soon as is necessary.'

'I must have it on the day of the decease.'

'It will be ready.'

'Madame la Présidente, if I am asking for power of proxy, if I do not want your solicitor to appear in this matter, it is much less in my interests than in yours . . . Once I give my services, I do so without reserve . . . In my turn, therefore, Madame, I ask for the same loyalty, the same confidence from my protectors – I do not venture to call you my clients. You may possibly think that by acting thus I am trying to get a finger in the pie. Certainly not, Madame. If dubious measures have to be taken – when inheritances are involved one gets carried along . . . particularly by so weighty a consideration as nine hundred thousand francs . . . Well now, you would not be able to disavow a man like Maître Godeschal, who is probity itself; whereas you could put all the blame on the shoulders of a miserable little agent . . .'

The Présidente eyed Fraisier with admiration.

'You could rise very high or sink very low,' she said. 'In your place, instead of aiming at virtual retirement as a justice of the peace, I should wish to become a public prosecutor – at Mantes . . . and make a great career.'

'Leave me to my own devices, Madame. The office of justice of the peace is merely a comfortable nag for Monsieur Vitel. I will make it my battle charger!'

This brought the Présidente to the final confidential communication she wanted to make to Fraisier.

'You appear to be so entirely devoted to our interests,' she said, 'that I am going to inform you about the difficulties of our position and our hopes. At the time when there was a marriage project between our daughter and an adventurer who is now a banker, the Président keenly desired to round off the Marville estate with various grasslands then on the market. As you know, we dispossessed ourselves of that fine residence in order to marry my daughter, but since she is an only child I am very anxious to acquire these remaining grasslands. These beautiful meadows have already been sold in part, and belong to an Englishman who is about to return to England after living there for twenty years. He built the most charming cottage in a delightful situation, between the Marville parklands and the pastures formerly belonging to the property; and in order to provide himself with a park, he bought back – at exorbitant prices – the stables, the plantations and the gardens. This residence, with its outbuildings, forms an independent unit in the countryside, and it borders on the walls of my daughter's park. Both grasslands and house could be bought for seven hundred thousand francs, the net return for the pastures being twenty thousand francs ... However, if Mr Wadman learns that we want to buy it, he will no doubt ask another two or three hundred thousand francs, for he will be down on his purchase price for that amount if, as is usual in rural transactions, the period of occupancy is left out of account.'

'Well, Madame, in my opinion you can be so sure the inheritance will come to you that I offer my services as purchaser on your behalf, and will see to it that you get the estate at the cheapest possible price by private treaty, a procedure often followed by dealers in property ... I will negotiate with the Englishman in that capacity. I am an expert in such matters. It was a speciality of mine in Mantes. I worked for Vatinelle, and so doubled the value of his practice.'

'Hence your *affaire* with little Madame Vatinelle! ... That notary must be quite rich by now.'

'Madame Vatinelle is a spendthrift ... And so, rest assured, Madame, I will serve up the Englishman to you in a lordly dish!'

'If you brought this about, you would have an eternal claim on my gratitude ... Good-bye, my dear Monsieur Fraisier, till tomorrow.'

As he went out, Fraisier saluted the Présidente with less servility than on the previous occasion.

'Dinner tomorrow with the Président de Marville,' he said to himself. 'Well now, I have these people in my pocket. However, in order to have the affair in complete control, I ought to act as counsel for the German – using Tabareau, bailiff to the justice of the peace, as my catspaw. That fellow Tabareau has refused me his daughter – an only child – but he'll give her to me if I am made justice of the peace. Mademoiselle Tabareau, a lanky girl with red hair and a weak chest, owns a house in the rue Royale which came from her mother. That property will make me eligible for the Chamber of Deputies! When her father dies, she'll have another six thousand francs' income. She's no beauty, but ye gods, any stepping-stone is good enough to cross over from nothing to eighteen thousand francs a year!'

And so, hurrying along the boulevards to the rue de Normandie, he gave free rein to his golden dream: he looked forward to the happiness of never being needy again; he thought of the marriage between Mademoiselle Vitel and his friend Poulain. He could see himself, in league with the doctor, as king of the castle in the quarter, managing the elections – town council, municipal guard, Chamber of Deputies! Long streets seem short when one speeds along with ambition astride imagination!

*

On returning to Pons's bedroom, Schmucke told him that Cibot was dying and that Rémonencq had gone for the notary, Monsieur Trognon. This name made an impression on Pons, for La Cibot had so often thrown it out in the course of her interminable harangues, and had so often recommended this notary as being the soul of honesty. Thereupon, the sick man, whose suspicions had hardened since that morning, hit upon a luminous idea which completed the plan he had formed to dupe La Cibot and unmask her entirely in the eyes of the credulous Schmucke.

'Schmucke,' he said, taking the hand of the poor German, whose mind was in a daze through all he had learnt and seen. 'The house must be in a state of great upheaval. If the porter is dying we can enjoy a few moments of freedom, that is to say free of spies, for you may be sure we *are* being spied upon. Leave the house, take a cab, go to the theatre and tell Mademoiselle Héloïse, our leading dancer, that I wish to see her before I die. Let her come at ten-thirty, after her act is over. Go from there to your two friends Schwab and Brunner, and beg them to come here tomorrow at nine asking for news of me and pretending to be coming to see me on their way elsewhere.'

This was the plan Pons had conceived, feeling that death was near. He intended to enrich Schmucke by leaving him everything, and in order to spare him any possible chicanery, he was proposing to dictate his testament to a notary in the presence of witnesses, so that no one could suppose he was *non compos mentis*, thus depriving the Camusots of any pretext for contesting his last dispositions. The name of Trognon had made him suspect some machination: he foresaw some deliberate flaw in drafting, some premeditated treachery on La Cibot's part, and he decided to get Trognon to dictate to him a holograph will which he could seal and lock up in the drawer of his commode. He counted on hiding Schmucke in a closet behind his bed and letting him catch La Cibot in the act of removing this will, unsealing it, reading it and sealing it up again. Then, at nine o'clock the following morning, he intended to cancel this will by making another before a notary, in due form and hence unchangeable. When La Cibot had called him a madman subject to delusions he had detected behind it the Présidente's hatred, vengefulness and avidity. In fact the poor man, during his two months in bed, his bouts of insomnia, his long hours of solitude, had been looking closely into all the events of his life.

Sculptors both ancient and modern have often set guardian spirits holding burning torches on each side of a funeral monument. The gleam from these torches enables the dying to read the scroll of their misdeeds and errors, and lights up the path of death. Such sculpture expresses significant ideas and is a register of human experience. The throes of death bring their own special insight. Often a simple-minded girl, dying at a very tender age, has shown the wisdom of a centenarian, foretold the future, passed judgement on her family and seen through all make-believe. This poetic gift of prophecy and clear vision, whether it looks backwards or forwards, is found only in those people whose malady is purely physical, whose death is due to the destruction of the organs sustaining the life of the flesh. Thus for instance, people attacked by gangrene like Louis XIV, or by consumption, or those who, like Pons, succumb to a liver disease or, like Madame de Mortsauf, to a stomach disease, or, like soldiers, to wounds inflicted in sound health – they alone enjoy that sublime enlightenment which arouses surprise and wonderment on their deathbeds; whereas those who die of what one may call diseases of the intelligence – the seat of which is in the brain and in the nervous apparatus which serves as intermediary between brain and body, supplying

material for cerebral activity – die in their whole being: with
them mind and body collapse together. The former are dis-
carnate souls and recall the spectres in the Bible; the latter are
mere corpses. Pons, this *virgo intacta*, this blend of Cato and
Lucullus, this innocuous and almost blameless soul, succeeded
– belatedly – in plumbing the depths of spite in the Présidente's
heart. He took the measure of the world he was about to leave.
And so, a few hours before, he had cheerfully accepted his lot
like a gay variety artist who finds all around him occasion for
caricature and mockery. That morning the last bonds which
had kept him tethered to life, the fetters of admiration, the
stout thongs which still attached him as a connoisseur to
masterpieces of art, had snapped. Knowing that La Cibot had
robbed him, Pons had bidden farewell as a Christian to the
pomps and vanities of art, to his collection itself, to his love
for the creators of so many beautiful things. He wanted to bend
his thoughts solely on death, like our forefathers, who counted
death as a high-day in the Christian pilgrimage. But, so tender
were his feelings for Schmucke, he wanted to watch over him
even from his coffin. This fatherly concern had determined his
choice of the leading dancer as a recourse against the perfidies
of the people around Schmucke, who would certainly not forgive him for being Pons's sole legatee.

Héloïse Brisetout was one of those who, by nature, however
false their position, can never cease to be genuine, though they
are capable of playing any sort of trick on the admirers who
pay for their favours. She was a light woman of the Jenny
Cadine and Josépha type, but a friendly soul who feared no
power on earth, since she was used to gauging human weakness
and well able to hold her own with interfering policemen at
the Carnival and Mabille's so-called rustic balls.

'If it was she who had my post given to her protégé Garangeot,' thought Pons, 'she will feel all the more obliged to help
me.'

Schmucke slipped out unnoticed thanks to the confusion
which reigned in the lodge; he returned with the greatest
celerity in order not to leave Pons too long by himself.

Monsieur Trognon arrived for the will-making at the same
time as Schmucke. Even though Cibot was at the point of

death, his wife went up with the notary, showed him into the bedroom and withdrew automatically, leaving Schmucke, Trognon and Pons together. But she equipped herself with a small hand-glass of ingenious design and posted herself behind the door, which she had left ajar. In this way she would be able to hear everything that was said and see everything that happened at a moment which was so supremely important for her.

'Monsieur,' said Pons, 'I am of sound mind – unfortunately, for I feel that I am on the point of death, and it is no doubt the will of God that no preliminary sufferings should be spared me! ... This is Monsieur Schmucke ...'

The notary bowed to him.

'He is my only friend on earth,' said Pons, 'and I want to make him my residuary legatee. Tell me what form the will should take so that my friend, a German, knowing nothing of our French law, may inherit my estate without the will being in any way contested.'

'Contestation is always possible, Monsieur,' said the notary. 'That is one of the drawbacks of human justice. But, as regards wills, certain kinds cannot be challenged.'

'What kinds?'

'A will made before a notary in the presence of witnesses who can certify that the testator is of sound mind, and provided the testator has neither wife, children, father nor brother.'

'I have nothing like that. All my affections are centred on my dear friend Schmucke, whom you see here.'

Schmucke was weeping.

'If then you have only distant collaterals, since the law allows you to dispose freely of your real and personal estate, provided that you do not bequeath them on terms of which public morality disapproves – you must have seen cases of wills disputed because of their eccentricity – a will signed in a notary's presence is unassailable. In fact, the person's identity cannot be called in question, the notary has taken note of his state of mind, and the signing of it can give rise to no discussion ... All the same, a holograph will, if it is clearly and properly drawn up, is also fairly unexceptionable!'

'I have decided, for reasons of my own, to write a holograph will at your dictation, and to entrust it to the keeping of my friend here. Is that possible?'

'It is,' said the notary. 'Do you wish to write it down? I will dictate it.'

'Schmucke, bring me my little Buhl escritoire . . . Do your dictating in a low voice, Monsieur,' he added, 'for we may be overheard.'

'Tell me then, first of all, what provisions you wish to make,' said the notary.

Ten minutes later, La Cibot, whom Pons had glimpsed in a mirror, saw the will being sealed, the notary having looked it through while Schmucke was lighting a candle. Then Pons handed it to Schmucke and told him to lock it away in a concealed drawer in the secretaire. The testator asked for the key of the secretaire, tied it in a corner of his handkerchief, and put the latter under his pillow. The notary, who out of courtesy had been appointed executor, and to whom Pons bequeathed a valuable picture, one of those objects which the law allows a notary to accept, left the room and found Madame Cibot in the salon.

'Well, sir, did Monsieur Pons think of me?'

'My dear woman, you surely do not expect a notary to divulge the secrets confided to him?' answered Monsieur Trognon. 'All I can say is that many greedy people will be thwarted and many hopes disappointed. Monsieur Pons has made a fine will, full of good sense; a public-spirited testament of which I strongly approve.'

One can scarcely imagine to what pitch La Cibot's curiosity was raised by these words. She went downstairs and spent the night at Cibot's bedside, intending to get Mademoiselle Rémonencq to take her place, and to go up and read the will between two and three in the morning.

25. The spurious will

MADEMOISELLE HÉLOÏSE BRISETOUT's visit at ten-thirty in the evening seemed natural enough to La Cibot. But she was so concerned lest the dancer should mention the thousand francs which Gaudissart had given her that, while she was showing the dancer upstairs, she lavished compliments ,and flattery upon her as on a royal lady.

'My dear,' said Héloïse on the way up, 'you're so much more at home here than in the theatre that I advise you to stick to your job.'

Héloïse, whom Bixiou, her latest lover, had brought along in a carriage, was gorgeously dressed, for she was on her way to a party given by Mariette, one of the most renowned dancers at the Opera.

The first-floor tenant, Monsieur Chapoulot, a retired lace-maker in the rue Saint-Denis, who was just coming back from the Ambigu-Comique with his wife and daughter, was dazzled – so, even, was his wife – at meeting such a pretty creature, so beautifully dressed, on his staircase.

'Who is she, Madame Cibot,' asked Madame Chapoulot. 'Just a nobody,' the concierge whispered to the lace-maker's wife. 'A dancing-doll you can see half-naked any evening for a couple of francs.'

'Victorine,' said Madame Chapoulot to her daughter, 'my dear, let Madame pass on ahead.'

Héloïse well understood this cry of maternal alarm and she turned round.

'Your daughter, Madame, must be more inflammable than matchwood if you're afraid she'll catch fire at the touch of me.' But she gave Monsieur Chapoulot a pleasant look and a smile.

'My word, she's very fetching off stage,' exclaimed Monsieur Chapoulot, lingering on the landing.

Madame Chapoulot gave her husband a pinch which almost made him yelp, and pushed him into their flat.

'This second floor,' said Héloïse, 'seems as far to climb to as a fourth floor.'

'And yet,' said La Cibot as she opened the door of the flat 'Mademoiselle must be used to climbing staircases.'

'Well, old friend,' said Héloïse as she entered the bedroom and saw the poor musician lying there with pale, drawn features. 'Things aren't too good, then? We're all anxious about you in the theatre. Our hearts are in the right place, but we're driven off our feet, and there's not much time to squeeze in a visit to one's friends. Every day Gaudissart talks of coming along, but every morning he's up to his eyes in theatre business. Still, we're all very fond of you . . .'

'Madame Cibot,' said Pons, 'have the kindness to leave me with Mademoiselle. We have theatre business to talk about, and my post as conductor of the orchestra. Schmucke will show Madame out.'

At a sign from Pons, Schmucke took La Cibot to the door and bolted it behind her.

'Oh, that rascally German! He's getting out of hand too!' La Cibot said to herself as she heard the significant click of the bolts. 'It's Pons that's teaching him such horrible tricks. I'll pay you out for it, my fine friends,' she muttered as she went downstairs. 'Well, if that dancing hussy tells him about the thousand francs, I'll say it was just a bit of theatre clowning.' And she sat down at Cibot's bedside. He was complaining of burning pains in the stomach, for Rémonencq had just given him a drink while his wife was away.

'My dear child,' said Pons to the dancer as Schmucke was seeing La Cibot out. 'I rely upon you to find me an honest notary to come here tomorrow morning at exactly half-past nine to take down my last will and testament. I'm going to leave all I have to my friend Schmucke, and if the poor man finds himself faced with legal proceedings, I rely upon this notary to advise and defend him. That is why I want a notary of high standing, well-to-do, one who will not stoop to the sharp practice to which lawyers are prone. As my heir, the poor man must be able to lean on him. I distrust Berthier, Cardot's successor; and you know so many people that . . .'

'Why yes! I know just the person!' said the dancer. 'Florine's notary, the Comtesse de Breuil's notary; Léopold Hannequin, an upright person who's never even heard of women of the streets. He's like a long-lost father, a decent sort who won't let you play the fool with the money you've earned. I call him the ballet-girl's papa, for he's given lessons in economy to all my friends. To begin with, my dear, he has sixty thousand francs a year, besides what his practice brings in. Secondly, he's a notary in the good old style! He walks like a notary and sleeps like a notary. He must have begotten little notaries and notaresses. The fact is, he's a tiresome old bore . . . But he wouldn't budge an inch even with the King in person once he's on the job. He's never had any little minx to fleece him. He's a family man and a fossil at that! His wife worships him and she's never deceived him – that's something for a notary's wife! . . . What more do you want? You won't find a better one in Paris, as notaries go. He came straight out of the Ark. Nobody's going to get much fun out of him as Malaga did out of Cardot; but he'll never slope off like little What's-his-name who lived with Antonia. I'll send him along at eight o'clock. You can sleep in peace. In any case I'm hoping you'll get better and write some nice music for us. But you know, after all, life's not much fun, what with producers haggling, kings niggling, ministers fiddling and rich folk tightening their belts . . . This is all artistes have left to them,' she said, tapping her heart. 'Life isn't worth living. Good-bye, old dear!'

'What I ask of you above all, Héloïse, is the greatest discretion.'

'This not being a theatre matter,' she replied, 'it's a secret no artiste would divulge.'

'What is the name of your present benefactor, dear child?'

'He's the Mayor of your district. Monsieur Beaudoyer: as stupid a man as the late Célestin Crevel, the cosmetics dealer, one of Gaudissart's sleeping partners. He died a few days ago, and he didn't leave me a thing, not even a jar of face-cream! That's what I mean when I say it's a disgusting time we live in!'

'What did he die of?'

'His wife . . . If he'd stayed with me he'd still be alive. Good-bye, dear old thing! Don't mind me talking about kicking the bucket. I can see you a fortnight from now, hopping along the boulevard sniffing out pretty little curios. You're not ill – your eyes are brighter than I've ever seen them . . .'

So the dancer went off, quite sure that Garangeot, her first cousin and protégé, was wielding his conductor's baton for good and all.

Every door in the house was ajar, and every household was on the watch to see the leading dancer go by. It was a great event for them.

Fraisier, like one of those bulldogs who never let go once they have their teeth in a morsel, was stationed in the lodge with La Cibot when the dancer arrived at the street door and asked to be let out. Fraisier knew that the will had been drawn up and had come to find out what provision had been made for the concierge, for Maître Trognon had refused to say one word about the will, either to Fraisier or Madame Cibot. Naturally, the lawyer took a good look at the dancer and made up his mind to profit by this visit *in extremis*.

'My dear Madame Cibot,' he said, 'this is a critical moment for you.'

'For sure,' she said. 'Oh my poor Cibot! To think that he won't enjoy anything I might get!'

'But we must know if Monsieur Pons left you anything – in short, whether he mentioned you or left you out of his will,' continued Fraisier. 'I am representing the natural heirs, and in any case you'll get nothing except through them . . . It's a holograph will, and so it's wide open to challenge . . . Do you know where our friend put it?'

'In the secretaire drawer, and he took the key. He tied it in his handkerchief, and stuffed the handkerchief under his pillow . . . I saw everything.'

'Is the will sealed?'

'I'm afraid so.'

'It's a crime to abstract a will and destroy it, but it's only a misdemeanour to read it . . . In any case, that would only be a trifling misdeed which no one would see. Does the man sleep soundly?'

'Yes, but when you were going through his stuff and valuing it, he should have been sleeping like a log; yet he woke up. Never mind, I'll see to it. Tomorrow morning I'll go and relieve Monsieur Schmucke about four o'clock, and if you care to come along, you can see the will for ten minutes . . .'

'Right. It's agreed. I'll get up about four and knock very quietly.'

'I'll warn Mademoiselle Rémonencq, who'll be taking my place by Cibot's bed. She'll open the door. But tap on the window so as not to wake anybody up.'

'Agreed,' said Fraisier. 'There'll be a light, won't there? A candle will do.'

At midnight, the poor heart-broken German was watching Pons [from his chair. The latter's features were contorted and his cheeks had fallen in like those of a dying man; after so much mental perturbation, he looked as if he were about to expire.

'I think I have just enough strength to keep going till tomorrow evening,' said Pons philosophically. 'No doubt, my dear Schmucke, I shall be in my death-throes tomorrow night. As soon as the notary and your two friends have gone, fetch our good Father Duplanty, the curate of Saint-François. That worthy man doesn't know I am ill and I should like to receive the Holy Sacraments tomorrow at noon.'

A long pause ensued.

'It was not God's will that I should have the life I dreamed of,' Pons continued. 'How I should have loved to have a wife, children, a family! That was my only ambition: to be cherished by one or two people, in some quiet spot. Life is bitter for everyone – I have seen people possessed of all these things which I have longed for in vain, and yet they were not happy . . . Then when my career was almost ended, God granted me unhoped-for consolation by giving me such a friend as you are! . . . So I need not blame myself for not having appreciated you at your true value, my dear Schmucke. I have loved you with all my heart and all my strength . . . Don't cry, Schmucke, or I shall say no more. And I find it sweet to talk about you and me . . . If I had listened to you, I should have lived on. I should have given up society and my accustomed ways, and I should not have suffered these mortal injuries. Anyway, you are now my sole concern! . . .'

'You shoult not sink of zet!'

'Don't gainsay me; listen to me, my dear friend. You are as guileless and simple as a six-year-old child who has never left his mother's side, and I respect you for it. It seems to me that God Himself must take care of people like you. But men are so wicked that I must warn you against them. Try then to shed your noble trustfulness, your saintly credulity, God's gracious gift to immaculate souls which is only found in men of genius or hearts like yours . . . You will soon be seeing Madame Cibot, who kept a close watch on us through a chink in the door. She will be coming to get hold of the spurious will – I expect the villainous woman will perform this operation in the small hours, when she believes you're asleep. Listen carefully, and do exactly what I say. Do you understand?'

*

Overwhelmed with grief, and seized with alarming palpitations, Schmucke had let his head droop on to the back of his armchair and looked as if he were in a faint.

'Yes. I unterstant, put tchust as if you vere two huntret yarts avay. I feel as if I vere sinkink into ze grafe viz you,' said the German, weighed down with his sorrow.

He then came close to Pons, took one of his hands in his, and in this posture, made a fervent mental prayer.

'What's that you are muttering in German?'

'I haf peen askink Gott to take us poss togezzer,' he answered simply, after finishing his prayer.

Pons doubled up in pain, for his liver was causing him intolerable suffering. He managed to lean towards Schmucke and kissed him on the brow, pouring out his whole soul in blessings on this being so like the lamb resting at the foot of God's throne.

'Come, listen to me, dear Schmucke. Dying people must be obeyed!'

'I am listenink.'

'Your bedroom leads into mine through the little door in your alcove, which opens into one of the closets in mine.'

'Yes. Put it iss schtoppt up viz picturess.'

'Get the doorway free immediately – and quietly! . . .'

'I vill.'

'Clear the passage on both sides, yours and mine. Then leave your door half open. When La Cibot comes to relieve you – she may well arrive earlier than usual – you will go off to bed as usual and pretend you're very tired. Try to look half asleep. As soon as she settles down in her chair, come through your door and stay there on the alert, drawing aside a little bit of the muslin curtain on this glazed door, and keep a good eye on what happens . . . Do you understand?'

'I unterstant. I sink ze vicket voman vill purn ze vill.'

'I don't know what she'll do, but I'm sure you won't take her for an angel after this . . . And now, play me some music. Cheer me up with some of your improvisations . . . It will keep you occupied, you'll get rid of your dismal thoughts, and you will fill this sad night for me with the poetry of your music.'

Schmucke sat down at the piano. After a minute or two at this, his chosen instrument, musical inspiration, incited by the tremors of sorrow and the agitation it had caused, carried the good German out of this world. Wonderful themes came to him, and on them he embroidered capriccios, now rendered with the pathos and the Raphaelesque perfection of Chopin, now with the fiery, Dantesque grandeur of Liszt – those two musical techniques which come closest to those of Paganini. Such a performance, reaching such a peak of perfection, seems to put the performer on a level with the poet. He is to the composer what the actor is to the author, one who divinely translates what is divinely conceived. But on this night, as he gave Pons a foretaste of heavenly harmonies, such delicious music as might make Saint Cecilia let her instruments fall from her hands, Schmucke was at once Beethoven and Paganini, creator and interpreter! Unwearying as the nightingale, lofty as the heavens under which it sings, rich in variations like the leafy forest it floods with its warblings, he played as never before and plunged the listening musician into such ecstasy as Raphael depicts in the Saint Cecilia painting at Bologna.

This poetry in sound was interrupted by a fearful clanging of the doorbell. The housemaid of the first-floor tenants had been sent by her employers to ask Schmucke to stop this witches' sabbath; it had awakened Madame, Monsieur and Mademoiselle Chapoulot, she said, and they could not get to sleep again. The maid pointed out that the day was long enough for rehearsing theatre music and that people ought not to 'bang on the piano' at night in dwellings within the Marais!

This happened about three in the morning. At half-past three, as exactly foreseen by Pons as if he had overheard the conference between Fraisier and La Cibot, the concierge appeared. The sick man threw a glance at his fellow-conspirator as if to say 'I told you so,' and settled into the posture of deep sleep.

La Cibot had such complete faith in Schmucke's guileless-ness – such apparent innocence is a major weapon and the cause of success in all the stratagems which children devise – that she could not suspect him of lying when he came forward to her, and said with an air that was at once plaintive and cheerful:

'He hass hat a terriple night! He hass peen tossink apout like a temon! I vass oplitchet to play music to qvieten him town, unt ze people from ze first floor came up to schtop me . . . It is a shameful sink. I vass tryink to keep my frient alife. I am so tiret after playink all ze night zet I am vorn-out zis mornink.'

'My poor Cibot's in a bad state too. One more day like yesterday and there'll be no hope . . . But what's the good of fretting? It's the Lord's will!'

'You haf so goot, so honest a heart, you are such a goot soul, zet if Papa Cibot shoult tie, ve vill lif togezzer!' said the wily Schmucke.

When simple, straightforward people take to deception, they are terribly thorough – exactly like children who set their little snares with a skill worthy of savages.

'Oh well, get some sleep, dearie,' said La Cibot. 'Your eyes are so tired they're as big as my fists. There then! The one thing that would help me to get over losing Cibot would be to think of ending my days with a good man like you! Don't worry, I'll give Monsieur Chapoulot something to think about! . . . Fancy a retired haberdasher making such a fuss! . . .'

Schmucke installed himself in the observation post he had prepared.

La Cibot had left the door of the flat ajar. Fraisier came in and shut it quietly once Schmucke had closed his own door behind him. The advocate was equipped with a lighted candle and an extremely fine brass wire for unsealing the will. It was all the easier for La Cibot to remove from under Pons's pillow the handkerchief in which the key of the secretaire was tied, since the sick man had purposely let it slide out from under his bolster and was facilitating La Cibot's manoeuvre by lying with his face to the wall in such a posture as to make it child's play to abstract the handkerchief. She went straight to the secretaire, opened it as quietly as she could, felt for the spring of the secret drawer and slipped out into the salon with the will in her hand. Pons was highly intrigued by these manoeuvres. As for Schmucke, he was trembling from head to foot as if he had himself committed a crime.

'Return to your post,' said Fraisier as he took the will. 'If he wakes up he must find you still there.'

After unsealing the envelope with an adroitness which proved that this was not a first attempt, Fraisier was plunged into deep astonishment as he read this curious screed:

This is my Last Will and Testament

On this day, the fifteenth day of April in the year of Our Lord eighteen hundred and forty-five, being of sound mind, as this testament, drawn up in concert with Monsieur Trognon, notary, will demonstrate, knowing that I must shortly die of the disease from which I have been suffering since the beginning of February last, and wishing to dispose of my goods and chattels, I have seen fit to set forth my last dispositions as follows:

I have always been impressed by the damage done by certain inconvenient circumstances to the masterpieces of painting, often resulting in their destruction. I have been pained to see beautiful pictures condemned to be for ever moving from country to country and never being housed in one place to which admirers of these masterpieces might travel to see them. I have always thought that the truly immortal productions of the great masters should be national property, perpetually accessible to visitors from every country, just as God's own masterpiece, the light of day, is accessible to all His children.

Now since I have spent my life choosing and assembling certain pictures, the glorious handicraft of the greatest masters; and since these pictures are unspoilt, having been neither touched up nor repainted, it has caused me some distress to think that these paintings, which have brought me so much happiness, might be sold at auction, that they might again be dispersed as they were before I bought them, and be taken to England or Russia. I have, therefore, resolved to preserve them from such misfortune, and with them the magnificent frames which enclose them, all of them the work of skilled craftsmen.

And therefore, with this intent, I give and bequeath to His Majesty the King, as an accession to the Louvre Museum, the pictures composing my collection, with this charge, that if the bequest be accepted, a life annuity of two thousand four hundred francs be paid to my friend Wilhelm Schmucke.

If His Majesty, as usufructuary of the Museum, do not accept this bequest subject to the above charge, the aforesaid pictures shall then form part of the bequest I hereby make to my friend Wilhelm Schmucke of all the assets of which I die possessed: with the following charges that *The Monkey's Head*, by Goya, shall be delivered to my cousin Président Camusot; the picture entitled *Flowers* by Abraham Mignon, representing tulips, to Monsieur Trognon, notary, whom I hereby appoint as my executor; also that an annual income of two hundred francs shall be paid to Madame Cibot, who has been my housekeeper for ten years.

Finally, my friend Wilhelm Schmucke shall give *The Descent from the Cross* by Rubens, the sketch for the famous painting now at Antwerp, to my parish for the decoration of a Chapel, as the expression of my gratitude for the kindness shown to me by the curate of that parish, the Abbé Duplanty, to whom I owe it that I die a Christian and a Catholic.

'This spells ruin!' said Fraisier, 'the ruin of all my hopes! Ah, I am beginning to believe everything the Présidente told me about the old musician's malevolence!...'

'Well, what's the position?' La Cibot came forward to ask.

'Your gentleman is a monster. He's leaving everything to the Louvre. We can't go to law against the State!... The will is unassailable ... We are robbed, ruined, despoiled, done for!...'

'What has he left me?'

'An annuity of two hundred francs.'

'Much good that will do me! . . . Why, he's an out-and-out villain!'

'Go back and keep watch,' said Fraisier. 'I'm now going to put the old villain's will back into its envelope.'

26. Re-enter Madame Sauvage

As soon as Madame Cibot's back was turned, Fraisier briskly substituted a sheet of blank paper for the will, which he put in his pocket. Then he sealed up the envelope very neatly and showed it to Madame Cibot on her return, to ask her if she could perceive the slightest trace of the operation. La Cibot took the envelope, felt the paper inside it and gave a deep sigh. She had hoped that Fraisier himself would have burnt the fatal document.

'Well, what can we do, my dear Monsieur Fraisier?' she asked.

'Oh, that's your concern! I'm not one of the heirs, but if I had the slightest claim to that lot' – he pointed to the collection – 'I know what I should do! . . .'

'That's just what I'm asking you,' she said somewhat obtusely.

'There's a fire in the hearth . . .' he retorted as he stood up to go.

'Yes indeed. Nobody will know about it except you and me!'

'A will that can't be found can never be proved to have existed,' the man of law replied.

'In that case, what will *you* do?'

'I? . . . If Monsieur Pons dies intestate, I can guarantee you a hundred thousand francs.'

'Oh yes, all very fine! People promise you piles of gold, and when they've got what they want and it's time to pay up they start niggling like . . .'

She stopped just in time, for it had been on the tip of her tongue to tell Fraisier about Elias Magus.

'I must be off,' said Fraisier. 'It's in your interest that no one should see me in the flat. We'll meet again down below, in your lodge.'

After closing the door, La Cibot re-entered with the will in her hand, firmly intending to throw it in the fire. But the moment she entered the bedroom she felt both her arms being gripped! ... She found herself caught between Pons and Schmucke, each of whom was leaning against the partition on either side of the door.

'Oh!' cried La Cibot, and she fell flat on her face as if in terrible convulsions – whether they were real or feigned was never known. The sight of this had such an effect on Pons that a deadly feeling of faintness came over him, and Schmucke left La Cibot lying there, in order to put Pons back to bed. The two friends were shaking like people who, in carrying out a painful resolve, have overtaxed their strength. When Pons was in bed again and Schmucke had recovered his strength a little, he heard a sound of sobbing. La Cibot was on her knees, weeping copiously and stretching her hands out to the two friends in a very expressive pantomime of supplication.

'It was only curiosity!' she said as she saw their attention turned on her. 'Kind Monsieur Pons! It's a woman's failing, you know! But I didn't manage to read the will, and I was bringing it back!...'

'Go avay!' said Schmucke, standing up on tip-toe, the immensity of his wrath adding appreciably to his stature. 'You are a monster! You haf triet to kill my goot Pons. He vass right! You are more zen a monster, you are a lost soul!'

Seeing the horror painted on the naïve German's face, La Cibot stood up as haughtily as Tartuffe, cast a glance at Schmucke which made him tremble, and left the room, carrying off under her blouse a splendid little picture by Metsu which Elias Magus had much admired and which he had pronounced to be a 'gem'. In her lodge La Cibot found Fraisier waiting, in the hope that she would have burnt the envelope and the blank sheet inside it. He was much astonished to see that his client was terrified and crestfallen.

'What's happened?'

'What's happened, my dear Monsieur Fraisier? Just this: pretending to give me good advice and guidance, you've lost me my income and those gentlemen's trust for good and all...'

And she burst into one of those torrents of gabble at which she was such an expert.

'Stop wasting words,' Fraisier curtly broke in. 'Come to the facts, the facts, and look sharp about it!'

'Well, this is how it happened.' She recounted the scene exactly as it had taken place.

'I've lost you nothing at all,' he replied. 'These two gentlemen suspected your honesty or they would not have set that trap for you. They were waiting for you, watching you! ... You're not telling me everything,' the lawyer added with a tigerish glare at the concierge.

'Me hide anything from you? ... After all we've been doing together?' she exclaimed with a shudder.

'My dear woman, *I* have done nothing reprehensible!' said Fraisier, thus manifesting his intention of denying his nocturnal visit to Pons's flat.

La Cibot felt as if her head was on fire and the rest of her body cased in ice.

'What!' she cried, stupefied.

'There's the criminal case against you ready to hand! You can be accused of purloining a will,' was Fraisier's chilling reply.

La Cibot gave a start of horror.

'Calm down,' he continued. 'I am your legal adviser. I only wanted to show you how easy it would be, one way or another, for what I told you to happen. Come now! What did you do to make that German simpleton hide in the bedroom without your knowing it?'

'Nothing, except what happened the other day when I stuck to it that Monsieur Pons had been seeing things. Since then those two gentlemen have turned against me completely. So you're the one who's brought all this trouble on me. I might have lost my hold on Monsieur Pons, but I was sure of the German. Why, he was already talking of marrying me, or of me living with him – it's the same thing.'

This explanation seemed so plausible that Fraisier was obliged to accept it.

'Have no fear,' he resumed. 'I promised you an income. I'll keep my word. Up to now the whole business has been problematical: now it's worth a mint of money ... You'll have not less than twelve hundred francs a year ... But, my dear Madame

Cibot, you must obey my orders and carry them out intelligently.'

'I will, my dear Monsieur Fraisier,' said the concierge, with no fight left in her, and pliant to the point of servility.

'Very well, good-bye.' And Fraisier left the flat with the will in his pocket.

He returned home full of glee, for this will was a terrible weapon in his hands. 'I shall have,' he was thinking, 'a strong guarantee against any bad faith on the Présidente's part. If she took it into her head to break her word I could lose her the inheritance.'

*

Early in the morning after opening his shop and leaving his sister in charge, Rémonencq went, in accordance with a recently acquired habit, to inquire about his good friend Cibot. He found the portress gazing at the Metsu picture and wondering how a scrap of painted wood could be worth so much money.

'Aha!' he said, looking over her shoulder. 'That's the only item Monsieur Magus was sorry he couldn't buy. He said that little article would put the finishing touch to his happiness.'

'How much would he give for it?'

'Look, if you promise to marry me within a year of being a widow, I undertake to get twenty thousand francs for it from Elias Magus. If you won't marry me, you'll never get more than a thousand francs.'

'Why not?'

'Because you'd have to sign a receipt as the owner, and then you'd have the heirs going to law with you. If you're my wife, I'm the one who'll be selling it to Magus, and all a dealer has to do is to enter it in his ledger: I shall write down that Monsieur Schmucke sold it to me. Come now, let me take charge of this painting. If your husband died, you might have a good deal of trouble, but no one would think it strange for me to have a picture in my stock. You know you can trust me. Besides, if you like, I'll write you an acknowledgement.'

'That's the idea. Bring me a signed receipt,' she said, locking up the picture in her chest of drawers.

'Neighbour,' said the dealer in a low voice, dragging La Cibot to the door, 'it's easy to see we are going to lose our friend Cibot. The doctor gave up hope yesterday evening and said he wouldn't last the day out ... It's a real blow! But after all, this wasn't the right place for you ... Your place is in a fine curio shop on the Boulevard des Capucines ... Do you know that in the last ten years I've made nearly a hundred thousand francs, and if you come to have the same amount, I guarantee to make you a fine fortune ... as my wife ... You'd be quite a lady, with my sister to do the work and look after the house.'

The would-be seducer was interrupted by harrowing cries from the little tailor, whose death agony was beginning.

'Get away from here,' said La Cibot. 'It's heartless of you to talk of such things when my poor man's in such a terrible state.'

'It's because I'm so much in love with you that I'd stop at nothing to get you.'

'If you were so much in love with me, you'd say nothing at a time like this,' she replied.

Rémonencq went back to his shop quite sure of marrying La Cibot.

About ten o'clock there was quite a commotion around the *porte cochère*, for the Sacraments were about to be administered to Monsieur Cibot. All the Cibots' friends, caretakers and concierges in the rue de Normandie and round about, occupied the lodge, the carriage entrance and the street front. Thus no notice was taken either of Monsieur Léopold Hannequin, who arrived with a colleague, or of Schwab and Brunner, who were able to get into Pons's flat without Madame Cibot observing them. The notary asked the concierge from the house next door to tell him on which floor Pons lived, and she directed him to the flat. As for Brunner, who came along with Schwab, he had already visited the Pons Collection, and slipped upstairs without a word, showing his partner the way ... Pons formally cancelled the previous will and made Schmucke his sole heir. Once the formalities were over, Pons, after thanking Schwab and Brunner and earnestly enjoining Monsieur Léopold Hannequin to watch over Schmucke's interests, fell into such a state of exhaustion as a result of the energy he had expended, both during the nocturnal scene with La Cibot and in this his last public act, that Schmucke begged Schwab to go and inform the Abbé Duplanty: Pons was asking for the Last Sacraments, and Schmucke refused to leave his friend's bedside.

La Cibot was sitting at the foot of her husband's bed, and since she had been expelled by the two friends, she had not made breakfast for Schmucke; but the morning's events and the sight of Pons meeting his end with heroic resignation had so wrung Schmucke's heart that he did not want food.

Nevertheless, at about two o'clock, not having seen the old German about, and moved as much by curiosity as by self-interest, the concierge asked Rémonencq's sister to go and see if Schmucke needed anything. At that moment the Abbé Duplanty, after hearing the unfortunate musician's last confession, was administering extreme unction. And so Mademoiselle Rémonencq disturbed this ceremony by her repeated ringing. Now as Pons had made Schmucke swear not to admit anyone, so fearful was he of being robbed, Schmucke let her go on ringing, and she went back in much dismay to tell La Cibot that Schmucke would not open the door. Fraisier took note of this significant fact. Schmucke had never seen anyone die and was about to experience all the embarrassments which have to be faced in Paris when one has a corpse on one's hands, above all when there is no one to give aid and succour or to act in one's stead. Fraisier was aware that genuinely afflicted people lose their heads on such occasions. He had had his breakfast and had remained in the lodge since the morning, in continuous conference with Dr Poulain. The idea then came to him to check all Schmucke's movements himself.

And this is how the two friends, Poulain and Fraisier, set about achieving this important result.

The verger at the church of Saint-François, one Cantinet, who had formerly kept a glassware shop, lived in the rue d'Orléans, in the house next door to Poulain. Now Madame Cantinet, one of the chair-letting attendants in the church, had been treated by Dr Poulain free of charge, and naturally she was full of gratitude for this and had often told him of all her misfortunes. The two 'Nutcrackers' had attended mass at Saint-François on Sundays and Holy Days, and they were on good terms with the verger, the beadle, the distributors of holy water, in short with all the clerical militia, known in Paris as the 'lower clergy', whose perquisites are the tips they get from the faithful. Madame Cantinet and Schmucke were therefore well acquainted with each other. This good woman was burdened with two afflictions which would enable Fraisier to use her as a blind and unwitting tool. Her son, who had a passion for the theatre and had refused to make his way in the Church with a view to becoming a beadle, had been given walking-on parts at the Cirque-Olympique; he was leading an undisciplined life which grieved his mother, whose purse was often drained dry by the loans she had to make him. Then there was Cantinet himself, addicted to drink and sloth, two vices which had forced him to give up his business. His duties as verger, far from pulling him together, provided him with an opportunity for indulging these two passions: he did no work, and hobnobbed with coachmen at weddings, with mutes at funerals, and with paupers drawing parish aid, so that by noon every day his face was as red as a cardinal's robe.

Madame Cantinet saw herself doomed to a poverty-stricken old age, although, as she said, she had brought a dowry of twelve thousand francs to her husband. This tale of woe, recounted a hundred times to Dr Poulain, gave him the idea of using her to facilitate the installation of Madame Sauvage in the Pons flat, as cook and domestic factotum. To present Madame Sauvage in person was out of the question, for the two 'Nutcrackers' were now suspicious of everything, and Fraisier had been sufficiently enlightened on this score by their refusal to open the door to Mademoiselle Rémonencq. But it seemed evident to the two friends that the devout musicians would blindly accept anyone the Abbé Duplanty put forward. Their plan was that Madame Cantinet should take Madame Sauvage with her; once there, Fraisier's servant would be as useful as Fraisier himself.

*

When the Abbé Duplanty arrived at the *porte cochère*, he was halted a moment by the crowd of Cibot's friends who had come to pay their respects to the oldest and most esteemed concierge in the quarter.

Dr Poulain doffed his hat to the Abbé, drew him aside and said:

'I'm on my way to poor Monsieur Pons. He might pull through. It's a question of persuading him to undergo an operation for the removal of gall-stones which have formed in the bladder. They are palpable and are setting up an inflammation which will cause death. There might still be time for surgery. You would do well to use your influence on your penitent to prevail upon him to have this operation. I can answer for his life, so long as no awkward complication occurs while I am carrying it out.'

'As soon as I have taken the Ciborium back to the church I will return,' said the Abbé Duplanty. 'Monsieur Schmucke too is in a condition which calls for the aid of religion.'

'I have just learnt that that good German is all by himself,' said the doctor. 'He had an altercation this morning with Madame Cibot, their housekeeper of ten years' standing, and they have fallen out – no doubt temporarily. But he can't get along without help in the predicament he's going to be in. It would be a work of charity to do something for him.'

'Come here, Cantinet,' said the doctor, beckoning the verger forward. 'Go and ask your wife if she will nurse Monsieur Pons and look after Monsieur Schmucke for a few days in Madame Cibot's place. In any case, even if this misunderstanding hadn't arisen, she would still have had to get someone to replace her. . . . Madame Cantinet is a good woman,' said the doctor to the Abbé.

'There couldn't be a better choice,' the good priest replied. 'The churchwardens have found her completely reliable as a collector of seat-rents in church.'

A few minutes later, Dr Poulain was at Pons's pillow observing the stages of his agony. It was in vain that Schmucke begged Pons to undergo the operation. The old musician only replied to the despairing German's supplications by shakes of the head alternating with outbursts of petulance. In the end the dying man summoned up some strength, directed a heart-rending glance at Schmucke and exclaimed:

'For Heaven's sake let me die in peace!'

Schmucke himself was ready to die of grief; but he took

Pons's hand, gently kissed it and held it in both of his, in yet one more effort to instil his own vitality into him . . . At that moment Dr Poulain heard a ring and went and opened the door to the Abbé Duplanty.

'Our poor patient,' he said, 'will soon be at grips with death; all will be over in a few hours. No doubt you will send a priest to watch over him tonight. But it is time to bring Madame Cantinet and a charwoman to wait on Monsieur Schmucke. He's incapable of giving a thought to anything. I fear for his sanity, and there are valuables here which ought to be guarded by completely honest persons.'

The good and worthy priest, incapable of mistrust or malice, was struck by the truth of these observations. Moreover he believed in the integrity of the local doctor. So he beckoned Schmucke to come and talk to him as he stood on the threshold of the death-chamber. Schmucke could not bring himself to let go Pons's hand which was convulsively clutching at his own – as if he were rolling down a precipice and clinging to anything that could arrest his fall. But, as is well known, dying people are subject to hallucinations which impel them to grasp at everything, like householders anxious to carry off their most precious possessions when their home is on fire. Pons released Schmucke's hand, clasped his blankets, and pulled them around him in a desperate effort which was suggestive of impetuous avarice.

'What will become of you, alone here with your dead friend?' the good priest asked of the German, who had now joined him. 'You no longer have Madame Cibot!'

'She iss a monster; she hass kilt Pons!'

'But you must have someone with you,' said the doctor. 'A watch must be kept over the body tonight.'

'I vill keep vatch mine self. I vill pray to Gott,' said the guileless German.

'But you must eat! . . . Who's going to do your cooking now?'

'I haf too much grief to vant foot,' was his simple reply.

'But look,' said Poulain, 'you will have to go with witnesses to notify the death. The body has to be undressed, wrapped and sewn in a shroud. The funeral arrangements have to be made with the undertakers. The nurse who sits by the body and the priest keeping vigil will have to be fed: can you do all that by yourself? . . . People can't be allowed to die like dogs in Paris, the capital of the civilized world.'

Schmucke's eyes were wide open with consternation, and for a little while he was beside himself.

'Put Pons vill *not* tie! . . . I vill safe him!'

'You can't go on much longer without getting a bit of sleep, and who will take your place then? There must be someone to look after Monsieur Pons, to give him his draughts and doses.'

'Ah, zet iss true,' said the German.

'Well,' said the Abbé, 'I had thought of bringing in Madame Cantinet, a good honest woman.'

The enumeration of the official duties he would have to perform for his friend if he died so dumbfounded Schmucke that he was wishing he could die when Pons died.

'He's a child!' said the doctor to the priest.

'A tchilt,' Schmucke echoed mechanically.

'Come now,' said the Abbé, 'I'll speak to Madame Cantinet and fetch her here.'

'There's no need to take that trouble,' said the doctor. 'She's a neighbour of mine, and I'm going back home.'

Death is like an invisible assassin with whom the dying person has to contend. The death-throes are so many blows levelled against him; he fights back and tries to return them. Pons had come to this final stage and was giving forth groans and cries. Immediately Schmucke, the Abbé Duplanty and Poulain rushed to the dying man's bed. Suddenly, now that the life in him had been dealt the final stroke which severs body and soul, Pons lapsed for a few moments into the perfect quietude which follows the death-agony. He came to himself and, with the serenity of death on his features, looked around him almost smilingly.

'Ah, doctor, how I have suffered! But you were right. I feel better . . . Thank you, my kind Abbé. I was wondering where Schmucke was! . . .'

'Schmucke hasn't eaten since yesterday morning, and it is four o'clock. There is no longer anyone to tend you, and it would be dangerous to bring Madame Cibot back . . .'

'She's capable of anything!' said Pons, manifesting all the horror that name aroused in him. 'It's true, Schmucke needs someone absolutely honest.'

'The Abbé Duplanty and I,' said Poulain, 'have been thinking about the two of you . . .'

'You are very kind,' said Pons. 'It hadn't occurred to me.'

'. . . and the Abbé suggests Madame Cantinet.'

'Ah, the chair-attendant in church!' cried Pons. 'Yes, an excellent creature!'

'She dislikes Madame Cibot,' continued the doctor, 'and she'll take good care of Monsieur Schmucke . . .'

'Send her to me, my good Abbé, both her and her husband, and I shall be easy in mind. There will be no more stealing . . .'

Schmucke had taken Pons's hand again and was holding it joyfully, believing that Pons was on the way to recovery.

'Let us be off, Monsieur l'Abbé,' said the doctor. 'I'll send Madame Cantinet along without delay. I am used to these situations. But she probably won't find Monsieur Pons alive when she gets here.'

27. Death's gloomy portals

WHILE the Abbé Duplanty was prevailing upon Pons to accept Madame Cantinet as a nurse, Fraisier had summoned her and had set to work on her, using all the corruptive persuasiveness, all the artful and well-nigh irresistible sophistry at his command. And so Madame Cantinet, a sallow, dried-up woman with prominent teeth and cold lips, her wits dulled by misfortune like so many working-class wives, being in such straits that she was glad to make a little extra money at daily work, readily agreed that Madame Sauvage should go with her as domestic help. Fraisier's servant had already received her marching-orders. She had promised to spin a web of steel round the two musicians and to watch them as a spider watches a fly caught in its web. The reward for her labours was to be a licence for a tobacconist's shop. Fraisier was thus killing two birds with one stone – getting rid of his alleged foster-mother and planting a spy, a police-officer as it were, in the Pons household as an adjunct to Madame Cantinet. Since a maid's bedroom and a small kitchen formed part of the two friends' flat, La Sauvage could sleep on a trestle-bed and do the cooking for Schmucke.

Just as the two women turned up, under Dr Poulain's escort, Pons had breathed his last without Schmucke being aware of it. The latter was still holding his friend's hand, which was becoming colder and colder. He motioned to Madame Cantinet to keep quiet. But Madame Sauvage's soldierly mien took him so much by surprise that he gave a start of apprehension – such as people usually gave on seeing that amazon for the first time.

'This lady,' whispered Madame Cantinet, 'is recommended by the Abbé Duplanty. She's been a cook in a bishop's palace and is honesty itself. She'll do the cooking.'

'Oh, you can talk out loud!' cried the stalwart – and also asthmatic – Madame Sauvage. 'The poor gentleman is dead . . . He's just passed away.'

Schmucke gave a piercing cry, felt Pons's hand which was already growing stiff, and remained there, staring hard into Pons's eyes. The expression he saw in them would have driven him mad but for Madame Sauvage. She was no doubt used to this sort of scene; she came over to the bed with a looking-glass, held it to Pons's mouth, and since it remained unclouded, abruptly pulled Schmucke's hand away from the dead man's hand.

'Let go, Monsieur, or you won't get your hand free. You've no idea how hard the bones set. Dead people soon stiffen up. If a dead man isn't got ready while he's still warm you have to break his limbs later on.'

And so it was this terrible woman who closed the eyes of the poor dead musician. Then, using her ten years' experience as a nurse, she undressed Pons, stretched him out, laid his arms along his sides, and pulled the blanket up to his head, for all the world like a shop-assistant wrapping up a parcel.

'We need a winding-sheet to put him in. Where can we get one?' she asked Schmucke, who had watched this operation in terror. After witnessing the profound respect with which religious ceremonial ministers to a child of God to whom heavenly bliss is promised, the grief he felt at seeing his friend packed up like a bale of goods was enough to deprive him of all capacity to think.

'Take vat you vant,' he replied like an automaton.

Poor innocent creature, he had seen a man die for the first time in his life, and this man was Pons, his only friend, the only person who had understood him and loved him.

'I'll ask Madame Cibot where the sheets are,' said La Sauvage.

'A camp-bed will be needed for this lady to sleep on,' said Madame Cantinet. Schmucke gave a nod and burst into tears. Madame Cantinet left the unhappy man to himself; but an hour later she returned and said:

'Monsieur, can you give us some money for what we have to buy?'

Schmucke turned to Madame Cantinet with a look which would have melted a heart full of the fiercest hate. He pointed to the white, drawn, angular face of the dead man in justification.

'Take anyssink zet you vant, unt leaf me to my tears unt prayers,' he said, sinking to his knees.

Madame Sauvage had gone to tell Fraisier that Pons was dead. He hurriedly took a cab to the Présidente's house, to ask her for power to act on behalf of the natural heirs.

'Monsieur,' said Madame Cantinet to Schmucke, an hour after putting her previous question. 'I went to Madame Cibot, since she knows all about your household concerns, to ask her where everything was. But she has just lost Monsieur Cibot, and she nearly drove me crazy with her wild talk . . . Monsieur Schmucke, will you listen to what I am saying! . . .'

Schmucke looked at the woman, who had no idea of the cruelty she was inflicting, for working-class people are accustomed to passive acceptance of the greatest spiritual suffering.

'Monsieur, we must have linen for a winding-sheet. We must have money for a camp-bed for this lady to sleep on. We must have pots and pans, dishes, plates, glasses, for a priest will be coming to keep watch and this lady can't find a thing in the kitchen.'

'That's not all, Monsieur,' La Sauvage added, 'I need wood and coal to get dinner ready, and I can't find anything! I'm not surprised anyhow, seeing that Madame Cibot kept you supplied with everything . . .'

'Look, my dear,' said Madame Cantinet, pointing to Schmucke, who was lying at the dead man's feet and not taking the slightest notice. 'Perhaps you'll believe me now – you can't get a word out of him.'

'All right, love,' said La Sauvage. 'I'll show you what to do in cases like this.'

She looked round the room with the practised eye of a burglar searching for likely spots where money might be hidden. Then she went straight to Pons's chest-of-drawers, pulled out the top drawer, found the bag in which Schmucke had put what money remained from the sale of the pictures and brought it over to Schmucke, who gave an automatic gesture of consent.

'Here's some money, love,' said La Sauvage to Madame Cantinet. 'I'll count it and take enough to buy what we need. Wine, eatables, candles, pretty nearly everything in fact – they haven't got a scrap of anything ... Look in the chest-of-drawers for a sheet to wrap the body in. It's right enough what they told me about the gentleman being a simpleton, but that's putting it mildly. He's like a new-born child. I expect we'll have to spoon-feed him.'

Schmucke was watching the two women and their activities with an idiot stare. Broken down with grief, having sunk into an almost cataleptic condition, he could not take his spellbound gaze from Pons's face, which now was softening into purer lines in the absolute repose of death. He himself longed to die; nothing else mattered now. He would not have stirred an inch if the room had been enveloped in flames.

'Twelve hundred and fifty-six francs,' La Sauvage told him.

He shrugged his shoulders. When La Sauvage tried to proceed with the laying-out and measured the sheet along the body in order to cut out and sew the shroud, a terrible struggle ensued between her and the afflicted German. He was exactly like a dog trying to bite anybody who ventures near to his master's corpse. La Sauvage lost patience, seized hold of the German, set him down on a chair and held him there with herculean strength.

'Come on, love, sew the dead man into his shroud,' she said to Madame Cantinet.

Once this operation was finished, La Sauvage put Schmucke back in his place at the foot of the bed, and said:

'Don't you understand? We *had* to make the poor man nice and comfortable.'

Schmucke was weeping again. The two women left him and took possession of the kitchen. Only a short time was needed for them to stock it with all the necessities of life.

After making out a provisional account for three hundred and sixty francs, La Sauvage began to prepare dinner for four – and what a dinner! The main dish was a fatted goose, the poor man's pheasant; there was a jam omelette, a vegetable salad and the inevitable *pot-au-feu*, whose ingredients were in such generous quantity that it was more like meat jelly than broth. At nine o'clock the priest whom the curate had sent to keep vigil over Pons arrived with Cantinet, who was equipped with

284

four tapers and some tall church candles. The priest found Schmucke lying alongside his friend on the bed and holding him in a tight embrace. The authority of religion was needed to separate Schmucke from the corpse. He knelt down and the priest ensconced himself comfortably in the armchair. While the latter was reading his office and Schmucke, on his knees in front of the body, was beseeching God to work a miracle and reunite him with Pons so that he might be buried in the same grave, Madame Cantinet had gone to a shop in the rue du Temple to buy a camp-bed for Madame Sauvage, for great inroads were being made on the twelve hundred and fifty-six francs. At eleven that evening, Madame Cantinet came to see if Schmucke would like a morsel of food. The German made a sign to be left in peace.

'Supper is ready, Monsieur Pastelot,' the chair-attendant then said to the priest.

Left alone, Schmucke gave a grin like a lunatic finding himself free to indulge a desire, as imperious as that of a pregnant woman. He threw himself on Pons's body and once more clasped it in a tight embrace. At midnight the priest returned and, at his scoldings, Schmucke let go of the corpse, and resumed his prayers. At dawn the priest departed, and at seven o'clock Dr Poulain came to pay Schmucke a friendly visit. He tried to persuade him to eat, but Schmucke refused.

'If you don't eat now, you'll feel very hungry on your way home,' said the doctor. 'You have to go to the council offices with a witness to notify Monsieur Pons's decease and get the death certificate completed.'

'Haf *I* to to it?' asked Schmucke in alarm.

'Who else? . . . You can't get out of it, since you alone witnessed the death.'

'My leks vill not carry me zere . . .' answered Schmucke, thus imploring the doctor to go with him.

'Take a carriage,' the doctor gently replied, with some show of sympathy. 'I have already given notice of the decease. Ask someone in the house to go with you. These two ladies will look after the flat while you're away.'

It is hard to imagine how much pestering genuine grief has to endure from legal formalities. It makes civilization hateful

and the customs of savages preferable. At nine o'clock Madame
Sauvage helped Schmucke downstairs, and when he got into
the cab he was obliged to ask Rémonencq to go with him to
notify the decease at the council offices. Moreover, in this as in
all other respects, class inequality leaps to the eye, in our
country which is so intoxicated with the principle of equality.
This dead weight of formalism becomes patent even in the
proceedings connected with death. In well-to-do families a
relative, a friend, or an appointed agent can relieve the bereaved
of these heart-breaking duties. But in this matter, as in matters
of tax-assessment, the lower orders, the helpless proletariat,
have to bear the whole burden.

'Yes indeed, you have every reason to mourn for him,' said
Rémonencq to the poor martyr when he gave vent to a moan
of sorrow. 'He was a very good man, a real gentleman, and he
leaves a very fine collection behind him. But mark this, Monsieur, you're a foreign gentleman, and you're going to find
yourself in a pretty fix, for everybody's saying you're Monsieur
Pons's heir.'

Schmucke was not listening. He was plunged in the kind of
grief which borders on insanity. The disease of tetanus can be
spiritual as well as physical.

'And you'd do well to get a counsel, a legal adviser to act in
your place.'

'A lekal atvisser!' Schmucke repeated mechanically.

'You'll find out you'll need somebody to act for you. If I
were you I'd get an experienced man, somebody well-known
in the quarter, a reliable man . . . Now in all my little business
affairs I call in Tabareau, the bailiff . . . If you give power of
attorney to his clerk you'll have no more trouble.'

This suggestion, prompted by Fraisier in concert with
Rémonencq and La Cibot, stuck in Schmucke's memory; for at
those times when sorrow congeals, so to speak, the thinking
part of us and suspends all conscious activity, the memory
records all the impressions that chance brings along. Schmucke
was now listening to Rémonencq, but the look on his eyes was
so completely devoid of understanding that the dealer did not
pursue the matter.

'If he stays as soft-headed as that,' thought Rémonencq, 'I

might well get the whole bag of tricks up there for a hundred thousand francs – if it comes to him . . . Here we are, Monsieur, at the registry office.'

Rémonencq had to help Schmucke out of the cab and lead him by the arm to the registry office, where they stumbled upon a wedding. Schmucke was obliged to wait his turn, for, thanks to one of those coincidences frequent enough in Paris, the clerk had five or six death certificates to complete. Waiting thus in this office, the poor German must have felt like Jesus in the Garden of Gethsemane.

'You are Monsieur Schmucke?' a man dressed in black asked the German, who was bewildered at hearing his name pronounced. He looked at the man with the same stupefied air as when he had been replying to Rémonencq.

'Here now,' said the dealer to the stranger. 'What do *you* want? Kindly leave this gentleman alone. You can see he's grieving.'

'This gentleman has just lost his friend, and without doubt, being his heir, he intends to show proper respect to his memory. He will certainly spare no expense. He will buy a burial plot in fee simple. Monsieur Pons was such a lover of the arts! It would be a great pity not to put three full-length weeping figures on his monument, representing Music, Painting and Sculpture . . .'

In an effort to drive this man away, Rémonencq made a gesture typical of a native of Auvergne. But the man replied with another gesture – one of commercial significance, as if to say: 'Don't be a dog-in-the-manger!' The dealer took the hint.

'I represent the firm of Sonet and Company, contractors for funeral monuments,' said the agent, whom Walter Scott might well have dubbed 'Young Mortality'. 'If this gentleman would care to entrust the order to us, we would save him the trouble of going to the Paris authorities to purchase the site needed for the interment of his friend, now, alas, lost to the arts.'

Rémonencq gave a nod of agreement and a nudge to Schmucke.

'Every day we take upon ourselves the burden of carrying out all the formalities on behalf of bereaved families,' the sales-

man went on, encouraged by the Auvergnat's latest gesture.
'In the first moments of grief it is most difficult for an inheritor
to take all this upon himself, and we are in the habit of performing these little services for our clients. Our monuments, sir,
are priced at so much a metre, in freestone or marble. We dig
the graves for family tombs . . . We take charge of everything
at a most reasonable figure. Our firm built a magnificent monument for the beautiful Esther Gobseck and Lucien de Rubempré – one of the finest monuments in Père-Lachaise. We employ
the best craftsmen, and I advise this gentleman to beware of
small contractors. They only do shoddy work,' he added as he
saw another man approaching, also dressed in black and preparing to speak for another firm of stonemasons.

Death, it is often said, is the end of a journey, but few people
know how apt this simile is in Paris. A dead man, especially one
of standing, is welcomed on the 'sombre shores' like a traveller
reaching harbour, pestered with recommendations from all
the hotel couriers. No one – except a few philosophers and some
families sure of survival who build themselves tombs as readily
as they buy themselves big houses – gives a thought to death or
its sordid implications. Death always comes too soon. Besides,
a very understandable scruple prevents prospective heirs from
looking upon it as a likely contingency. And so almost all those
who lose their fathers, mothers, wives or children are immediately pounced upon by funeral touts who batten upon their
distress by bullying them into giving an order. In former times
all the contractors for funeral monuments clustered around
the famous cemetery of Père-Lachaise, where they occupied a
whole street which would well merit the name of 'Tombstone
Street' and rushed at inheritors as they were standing round
the grave or leaving the churchyard. But little by little the spirit
of competition and speculation has enabled them to gain
ground, and today they have swarmed down into residential
areas and even installed themselves next door to the registry
offices. Moreover, their representatives often worm their way
into the homes of the bereaved with a design for a monument
in their hands.

'I am engaged in business with this gentleman,' said the
agent of the Sonet firm to his intruding rival.

'The Pons decease . . . Where are the witnesses ?' the registry clerk called out.

'Come, Monsieur,' said the agent, addressing Rémonencq.

Rémonencq asked the agent's help in lifting up Schmucke, who was sitting inert on his bench. They led him to the grille behind which the registrar of death screens himself from public sorrow. Rémonencq, momentarily Schmucke's good angel, was supported by Dr Poulain, who furnished the necessary details about Pons's age and birthplace. The German knew only one thing: Pons had been his friend. The signing over, Rémonencq and the doctor, followed by the salesman, put the German into a cab, into which the zealous agent slipped too, intent upon getting his order. La Sauvage, on sentry duty at the *porte cochère*, helped the almost fainting German upstairs with the aid of Rémonencq and the representative of Sonet and Company.

'He's going to be ill! . . .' cried the latter, anxious to conclude the piece of business on which he had claimed to be embarked.

'I should think so!' replied Madame Sauvage. 'He's been in tears for twenty-four hours, and taken not a scrap of food. There's nothing like grief for making you feel hollow inside.'

'My dear client,' said the salesman to Schmucke. 'Do take a bowl of soup. You have so much to do. You have to go to the town hall to buy the plot for the monument you wish to erect as a memorial to this lover of the arts – one which must be an adequate token of the gratitude you owe him.'

'There's no sense in all this,' said Madame Cantinet as she brought in some broth and some bread.

'Just think, my dear sir,' interpolated Rémonencq, 'if you're as ailing as all that, you *must* think of getting someone to act for you. You've so many things on your hands. You have to arrange for the funeral. You don't want your friend to be buried like a pauper, do you?'

'Come on, dear Monsieur Schmucke!' said La Sauvage. Seizing an opportunity when Schmucke's head was sunk against the back of his chair, she poured a spoonful of broth into his mouth and in spite of his resistance began to feed him like a baby.

'Now if you had any sense, Monsieur Schmucke, as you only

ask to be left alone to mourn for your friend, you'd get somebody to act for you . . .'

'Since this gentleman,' said the agent, 'intends to raise a magnificent monument to his friend's memory, he has only to leave all the arrangements to me. I will see to everything.'

'Why now, if you please, what's all this about?' asked La Sauvage. 'Has Monsieur Schmucke given you an order? Who might you be, anyway?'

'A representative of Sonet and Company, my dear lady. The most important monumental masons in Paris,' he said, pulling out a card and presenting it to the stalwart Sauvage.

'All right, that'll do, that's enough . . . we'll see about that at the proper time. But don't you take advantage of the state the gentleman's in. You can see he's half out of his mind.'

The representative of Sonet and Company drew Madame Sauvage out on to the landing and whispered in her ear:

'If you can manage to get the order for us I am authorized to offer you forty francs.'

'Very well, what's your address?' said Madame Sauvage, becoming more affable.

Finding himself alone and feeling better after this intake of bread and broth, Schmucke promptly returned to Pons's room and took to his prayers again. He was deep in his sorrow when he was aroused from his abyss of dejection by the voice of a young man in black crying 'Monsieur!' to him for the eleventh time. This was accompanied by such tugs at his coat-sleeve that the poor martyr could no longer turn a deaf ear.

'Vat iss it now?'

'Monsieur, we are indebted to Dr Gannal for a wonderful discovery. We do not dispute his title to fame: he has renewed the miracles performed in ancient Egypt. But improvements have been made and we have obtained astonishing results. And so, if you wish to see your friend once more as he was in life . . .'

'See him vonce more!' cried Schmucke. 'Vill he speak to me?'

'Not quite that! . . . the power of speech alone will be lacking,' replied the individual, an agent for an embalming firm. 'But he will remain for eternity as you see him after the embalming process. It only takes a few seconds. Merely an incision and an injection into the carotid artery . . . But we must waste no time. If you waited one quarter of an hour more, you could no longer enjoy the sweet consolation of having preserved the body . . .'

'Go to ze Tefil! It iss Pons's soul zet matters, unt hiss soul iss in Heafen.'

'The man's utterly ungrateful,' said the agent for the famous Dr Gannal's competitors, as he passed through the *porte cochère*. 'He refuses to have his friend embalmed.'

'What can you expect, Monsieur?' said La Cibot, who had just had her dear departed embalmed. 'He's coming into money. He's an heir. Once they've made their bit, death doesn't mean a thing to him and his like.'

28. Schmucke's Via Dolorosa

ONE hour later, Schmucke saw Madame Sauvage come into his room, followed by a man in black, apparently a workman.

'Monsieur,' she said. 'Cantinet has been so kind as to send you this gentleman. He makes the coffins for people of the parish.'

The maker of coffins gave a bow of commiseration and condolence – but as one sure of himself, knowing himself to be indispensable. He cast an appraising glance at the corpse.

'How would you like it, Monsieur? Deal, oak, or oak with lead lining? Oak with lead lining is what most people think proper. He's not outsize.'

He felt at the feet in order to measure the corpse.

'Five foot seven inches,' he added. 'I suppose you'll have a requiem mass, Monsieur?'

Schmucke gave the man the sort of look a madman gives before he launches an attack.

'Monsieur Schmucke,' said La Sauvage. 'You ought to take somebody on to go into all these little things for you.'

'Yes,' said the victim at long length.

'Shall I go and fetch Monsieur Tabareau, since you're going to have so much on your hands? Monsieur Tabareau, you know. The nicest gentleman in the quarter.'

'Yess, Monsieur Tapareau. I haf heart off him,' replied Schmucke, giving in at last.

'Well, if you do that, you'll have some peace and be alone with your grief, once you've had a talk with the man who'll act for you.'

About two o'clock, Monsieur Tabareau's senior clerk, a young man who aimed at being a bailiff, modestly presented himself. Youth is privileged: it does not allow itself to be taken aback. This young man, one Villemot, sat down beside

292

Schmucke and waited until he was ready to talk. Schmucke was touched by this forbearance.

'Monsieur,' he said. 'I am Monsieur Tabareau's senior clerk, and he has entrusted me with the task of looking after your interests and dealing with all the details of your friend's burial ... Will you consent to this?'

'You vill not be aple to safe my life, pecause I haf not lonk to lif. Put vill you leaf me in peace?'

'Oh, you'll have no disturbance whatsoever.'

'Fery vell. Vat muss I to zen?'

'Sign this paper appointing Monsieur Tabareau your representative in all matters pertaining to the inheritance.'

'Goot! Gif it me,' said the German, ready to sign straight away.

'Oh no, I must read out the terms to you.'

'Reat zem!'

Schmucke paid not the slightest attention to the reading of this general authorization; he merely signed it. The young man took Schmucke's order for the funeral, for the purchase of the plot, where the German too wished to be buried, and the requiem mass. He was told that he would be worried no more and not be asked for money.

'I voult gif all I haf to pe left alone,' said the unhappy man; and he knelt down once more in front of his friend's body.

Fraisier had won. The legatee could not make one movement outside the circle in which La Sauvage and Villemot had him confined.

There is no grief that slumber cannot conquer. And so, towards the end of the day, La Sauvage found Schmucke lying asleep at the foot of Pons's bed. She picked him up, put him to bed and tucked him up like a baby. He slept on till the following morning. When he awoke – that is to say when the truce was over and he became conscious once more of his sorrow – Pons's body was lying in state under the *porte cochère*, in the kind of improvised mortuary chapel to which third-class funerals are entitled. And so Schmucke looked in vain for his friend through the whole flat, and it seemed very large: he only found it full of heart-rending memories. La Sauvage, imposing on

Schmucke the discipline a nurse imposes on a child in her charge, made him take breakfast before going to church. While the poor victim was forcing food down his throat, La Sauvage reminded him, with lamentations worthy of a Jeremiah, that he had no black clothes. Cibot had looked after his wardrobe, and, even before Pons fell ill, it had been reduced, like his diet, to the simplest needs: two pairs of trousers and two frock-coats!

'You're not going like that to Monsieur Pons's funeral. It's a crying disgrace. Everybody in the quarter will look down on us!'

'How voult you vant me to go zere?'

'Why, in mourning of course!'

'In mournink?'

'It's only right and proper . . .'

'Right unt proper! Vat to I care for such stupit sinks?' said poor Schmucke. He had reached the highest pitch of exasperation to which grief can bring a man with the soul of a child.

'Why, he's ingratitude itself,' said La Sauvage, turning to an individual who suddenly appeared in the flat; one who sent a shiver through Schmucke.

This functionary, magnificently attired in black cloth, black breeches, black silk stockings and white cuffs, adorned with a silver chain to which a medallion was attached, wearing a cravat – such a correct cravat! – of white muslin and white gloves; this incarnation of officialdom, stamped with the very hallmark of public lamentation, was holding an ebony wand, his emblem of office, and, under his left arm, a three-cornered hat, with a tricolour cockade.

'I am the master of ceremonies,' said this important person in a soft voice.

This man, whose daily function was to conduct funerals and move among a whole succession of families plunged into one and the same affliction, real or feigned, spoke in low and unctuous tones, like all members of his confraternity. It was his profession to be decorous, polite, seemly, like a statue representing the angel of death. His announcement sent a nervous tremor through Schmucke, as the sight of the hangman might do.

'Monsieur, are you the son, the brother or the father of the deceased?'

'I am all zat unt more, I am hiss frient,' said Schmucke in a flood of tears.

'Are you the heir?' asked the master of ceremonies.

'Ze heir?' repeated Schmucke. 'Nossink in ze vorlt matters for me,' and he resumed his posture of gloom and sorrow.

'Where are the relatives and friends?' asked the master of ceremonies.

'Zere zey are, all of zem!' cried Schmucke, pointing to the pictures and objects of art. 'Nefer haf zey prought sorrow to my goot Pons. Zey are all he lofet except me.'

'He's off his head, Monsieur,' said La Sauvage to the master of ceremonies. 'Let him be, there's no sense in listening to him!'

Schmucke had sat down again; vacancy of mind was once more written on his countenance; mechanically, he wiped away his tears. At this moment Villemot, Tabareau's senior clerk, reappeared, and the master of ceremonies, recognizing the man who had come to him to order the funeral, addressed him thus:

'Well, Monsieur, it is time to go. The hearse has arrived. But I have seldom seen such a funeral gathering. Are there no relations, no friends ...?'

'We have not had much time,' replied Monsieur Villemot. 'Monsieur Schmucke has been plunged in such grief that he has been able to think of nothing. In any case there is only one relative ...'

The master of ceremonies regarded Schmucke with genuine pity: as a connoisseur in grief he was well able to distinguish the true from the false. He approached Schmucke.

'Come, my dear sir, keep your heart up! ... Think of the respect you must pay to your friend's memory.'

'We forgot to send out invitations,' continued Villemot, 'but I took care to send an express letter to Monsieur le Président de Marville, the sole relative whom I mentioned to you ... There are no friends ... I don't expect the people at the theatre at which the deceased was conductor of the orchestra will come ... but this gentleman is, I believe, the sole legatee.'

'Then he must be chief mourner,' said the master of ceremonies.

He cast a glance at Schmucke's clothes, and asked him; 'Have you no black suit?'

'All my plack I vear insite!' said the poor German in lamentable tones. 'So plack it iss, I haf deass in my soul. Gott vill pe goot to me and tchoin me viz my frient in ze grafe. I vill gif Him sanks for zat!' He folded his hands in prayer.

The master of ceremonies turned to Villemot.

'I have already told our management,' he said, 'which has already introduced so many improvements, that it ought to have a wardrobe department and hire mourning to next-of-kin. It is daily becoming more and more necessary. But since this gentleman is the heir, he must wear a mourner's cloak; and the one I have brought with me will cover him from head to foot, so that no one will notice how unsuitably he is dressed.'

'Will you be so good as to stand up?' he said to Schmucke.

Schmucke stood up, but he was unsteady on his feet.

'Hold him up,' said the master of ceremonies to the senior clerk. 'After all, you are his agent.'

Villemot supported Schmucke by putting his arm round him, and then the master of ceremonies grasped the horrible voluminous black mantle which next-of-kin wear as they walk behind the hearse from the house of death to the church, and fastened it on him by tying the cords of black silk under his chin.

So it was that Schmucke donned the accoutrements which an inheritor must wear.

*

'Now a great difficulty arises,' said the master of ceremonies. 'We have to allot the four tassels of the pall . . . With no relatives here, who will hold them? . . . It is now half-past ten,' he said consulting his watch. 'They are waiting at the church.'

'Ah, there's Fraisier!' Villemot cried out very imprudently – but no one was there to take note of this avowal of complicity.

'Who is this gentleman?' asked the master of ceremonies.

'He represents the family.'

'What family?'

'The disinherited family . . . He is acting for Monsieur le Président Camusot.'

'Good,' said the master of ceremonies, with a satisfied air. 'That settles two tassels: one for him, one for you.'

The master of ceremonies, glad to have two tassels allotted, went out and fetched two splendid pairs of white doeskin gloves and politely offered one to Fraisier and one to Villemot. 'Will you two gentlemen be so good,' he asked, 'as to take each of you a corner of the pall?'

The sight of Fraisier, all in black, pretentiously arrayed, with his white tie and official bearing, gave one the shudders: he looked like a prosecuting counsel with a hundred briefs in his case.

'Willingly, Monsieur,' he said.

'If only two other persons were to come,' said the master of ceremonies, 'all four tassels would be allotted.'

Just then there arrived the indefatigable salesman of the Sonet firm, followed by the only man who had remembered Pons and could bother to pay him his last respects. He was a hired assistant at the theatre, an underling whose task it was to lay out the parts on the orchestra music-stands. Pons, knowing that he had a family to keep, had given him a five francs' tip every month.

'Ah! It iss Topinard!' exclaimed Schmucke, recognizing the odd-job man from the theatre. 'You at any rate lof Pons.'

'Yes, Monsieur. I came every morning to inquire about Monsieur Pons.'

'Efery mornink! My tear Topinard!' cried Schmucke, shaking him warmly by the hand.

'But no doubt they took me for a relation. They gave me a cold welcome! It was no use my telling them I came from the theatre to ask after Monsieur Pons; they said they'd heard that tale before. I asked to see the poor dear sick man, but they wouldn't even let me go up to him.'

'Zat vicket Cipot!' said Schmucke, pressing Topinard's horny hand to his heart.

'He was the best of men, dear Monsieur Pons. He gave me

five francs every month. He knew I had a wife and three children . . . My wife is waiting at the church.'

'I vill share my last crust viz you!' cried Schmucke, joyful at having beside him a man who had loved Pons.

'Will this gentleman please take one of the tassels?' asked the master of ceremonies. 'Then all four will be settled.'

The master of ceremonies had had no difficulty in persuading the Sonet salesman to take one of the tassels, particularly as he showed him the fine pair of gloves which, according to custom, would be his to keep.

'A quarter to eleven! We simply *must* go downstairs . . . The clergy are waiting,' said the master of ceremonies.

And the six persons began to descend the staircase.

'Shut the flat up and stay in it,' said the odious Fraisier to the two women standing on the landing. 'Particularly you, Madame Cantinet, if you want to be caretaker. Ha! Ha! It's two francs a day!'

By a coincidence not at all unusual in Paris, there were two catafalques at the *porte cochère*, in fact two groups of mourners – one for Cibot, the defunct concierge, and one for Pons. No one had come to pay a tribute of affection to the impressive catafalque of the 'friend of the arts', but all the porters in the neighbourhood had come in a crowd to sprinkle holy water on the concierge's mortal remains. The contrast between the throng gathered for Cibot's procession and the sparse group around Pons's bier was maintained not only at the street-door but also along the street itself. Pons's coffin was followed by Schmucke alone – leaning on one of the mutes, for Pons's heir faltered at every step he took. From the rue de Normandie to the rue d'Orléans, where the church was, the two processions passed between a double line of sightseers, for, as we have remarked before, everything happening in that quarter arouses curiosity. And so everyone commented on the splendour of the white hearse, to which was appended a shield embroidered with a large 'P', but which had only one mourner behind it, whereas the plain hearse, of the kind used only for the cheapest funerals, was followed by a large crowd. Fortunately, Schmucke, bewildered by the onlookers at the windows and the double row of gapers, heard nothing of all this and could only glimpse the concourse of people through a haze of tears.

'Why, it's the "Nutcracker",' said one. 'You know, the band-leader.'

'Who are the people holding the tassels?'

'Pooh! They're only actors!'

'Look! Here comes poor old Cibot! That's one real worker the less! You couldn't keep him off the job!'

'He never went out, that man!'

'He never took Mondays off!'

'And wasn't he fond of his wife!'

'The poor woman!'

Rémonencq was walking behind his victim's hearse, acknowledging the tributes of condolence paid to him upon the loss of his neighbour,

*

The two funeral *cortèges* arrived at the church, and there Cantinet, with the beadle's assistance, took care that no mendicants should get near Schmucke. Villemot had promised Pons's heir that he would not be pestered: he was paying all the expenses and keeping an eye on his client. Cibot's modest hearse was accompanied to the cemetery by a crowd numbering between sixty and eighty persons. Pons's *cortège*, when it left the church, consisted of four mourners' carriages: one for the clergy, three for the relations. In actual fact only one of the three was needed, as the Sonet firm well knew, for its representative had left the church during the requiem mass in order to go and inform Monsieur Sonet that the procession was on its way, so that he might present the residuary legatee with the design and estimate for the monument as he came away from the cemetery. Fraisier, Villemot, Schmucke and Topinard were accommodated in a single carriage. The other two vehicles, instead of returning to the undertaker's headquarters, went on to the cemetery quite empty. Such an unnecessary journey of empty carriages often occurs. When the departed are little known and attract no concourse of people, there are always too many carriages. In Paris, where everyone would be happy to add an extra hour to the twenty-four-hour day, a dead person has to have been much loved in his lifetime for relatives or friends to follow his hearse right to the graveyard. But the coachmen would lose their gratuity if they did not complete their task. And therefore, full or empty, carriages go to the church and thence to the cemetery, and return to the house of the bereaved, where the drivers hold out their hands for a tip. One can scarcely imagine how many people look upon death as a sort of drinking-fountain. The 'lower clergy' from the church, the beggars at the church-door, the mutes, the carriage-drivers and the grave-diggers are as absorbent as sponges and come from a funeral dripping with gratuities.

In his transit from the church, where poor Schmucke was assailed by a swarm of beggars whom the beadle kept at bay, to Père-Lachaise, Schmucke looked like a condemned criminal on his way from the dock to the place of execution. He might well have been taken for chief mourner at his own funeral as he rode along, hand in hand with Topinard, the only other person in whose heart there was real regret for Pons's death. Topinard was extremely moved by the honour of being entrusted with one of the tassels of the pall, he was glad to have a ride in a carriage and to be the owner of a pair of gloves; and he was already beginning to look upon Pons's funeral as a great day in his life. Schmucke, submerged in sorrow, although he drew comfort from the contact of Topinard's hand and the sympathy which went with it, rolled along in his carriage just as passively as a cartload of terrified calves on the way to the slaughter-house. Fraisier and Villemot were sitting in front. Now those people who have had the misfortune to accompany many of their loved ones to their last resting-place are aware that all show of mourning is dropped as the carriage proceeds on its way – often quite a long way – from the church to the eastern cemetery of Paris, the one which is so rich in sumptuous monuments and in which all vanity and luxury hold rendezvous. Conversation is started by those who care least, and even the saddest mourners end up by listening, for mere distraction's sake.

'Monsieur le Président had already gone off to the courts,' Fraisier was saying to Villemot. 'I didn't consider it necessary to go to the Palais de Justice to tear him away from his work.

In any case he would have arrived too late. He is the natural and legal heir, but since he has been disinherited in favour of Monsieur Schmucke, I thought it enough that I should be here as his proxy.'

Topinard began to take notice.

'Who's the fellow who was given the fourth tassel to hold?' Fraisier asked Villemot.

'The representative of a firm of monumental masons who is hoping to extract an order for a tombstone on which he proposes to carve three figures in marble – Music, Painting and Sculpture shedding tears over the late lamented!'

'That's an idea!' said Fraisier. 'The old chap deserves that at any rate. But a monument like that will cost all of seven or eight thousand francs.'

'It certainly will.'

'If Monsieur Schmucke orders it, it can't come out of the inheritance. Expenditure like that would soon soak up any inheritance.'

'It would mean a law-suit, but we should win it.'

'Well then,' Fraisier continued, 'that will be his concern! It would be quite a pretty little joke to play on these contractors,' he whispered to Villemot. 'If the will is declared null and void – and I will see that it is – or if by any chance there were no will, who would settle their account?'

Villemot gave a toadying snigger. Then Tabareau's senior clerk and the man of law began a low, whispered conversation; but, despite the clatter the carriage made as it rolled along, and despite all other impediments, the theatre employee was so used to catching the drift of remarks made in the pandemonium of the theatre wings that he guessed the two lawyers were hatching a plot against Schmucke, and in the end the significant name of the debtors' prison – Clichy – came to his ears. Whereupon the good and worthy theatre assistant resolved to keep an eye on Schmucke's interests.

At the cemetery – where, through the agency of the Sonet firm's representative, Villemot had bought a three-metre plot from the City of Paris with the announcement that a magnificent monument was to be erected on it – the master of ceremonies conducted Schmucke through a crowd of sightseers to the grave into which Pons's body was to be lowered. But at the sight of this rectangular cavity over which four men were supporting the coffin with ropes, and while the priest was reciting a final prayer, the German had such a heart seizure that he fell down in a faint.

29. When wills are opened all doors are sealed

WITH the help of the Sonet salesman and Sonet himself, Topinard carried the poor German into the monumental mason's establishment where the most zealous and generous attentions were lavished on Schmucke by Madame Sonet and Madame Vitelot, the wife of Monsieur Sonet's partner. Topinard stayed on, for he had noticed Fraisier, whose face looked sinister to him, talking to the Sonet salesman.

An hour elapsed, and at about two-thirty the simple-minded German recovered consciousness. The last two days had been like a nightmare from which he hoped to awaken and find Pons alive again. After the application of many wet towels to his forehead, smelling-salts and vinegar to his nostrils, his eyes opened at last. Madame Sonet made him drink a bowl of good rich broth, for the stock-pot had been put on in the stone-mason's house.

'We don't often have to give such treatment to customers, and they don't usually take things as hard as he does; not more than once in two years, I should say.'

Finally Schmucke proposed to return to the rue de Normandie. Thereupon Sonet spoke up.: 'Here, Monsieur, is the design Vitelot has drawn expressly for you – a real inspiration! It will be very beautiful.'

'. . . The most beautiful in Père-Lachaise!' said little Madame Sonet. 'You *must* do honour to the memory of a friend who has left you all he has.'

This design, allegedly made to order for Schmucke, had first been prepared for a Minister's grave – that of the famous Marsay; but his widow had decided to commission Stidmann for the monument, and so the Sonet sketch was rejected, for the idea of such a vulgar memorial filled her with horror. Originally the three figures were to stand for the three 'Glorious Days' of the July Revolution in which that great statesman had come to the fore. After that, Sonet and Vitelot had made some alterations and transformed them into symbols of the Army, Finance and the Family as a memorial to Charles Keller the banker – again the commission was given to Stidmann. During the last eleven years the design had been modified to meet all sorts of family circumstances. And now, while doing the tracings, Vitelot had metamorphosed each figure into a genius of art – Music, Sculpture and Painting respectively.

'There's still a great deal to do if we consider the details and the installation of the monument,' said Vitelot, 'but we can finish it within six months. Here, Monsieur, is the estimate and the contract – seven thousand francs, not including the rough-ing-out.'

'If, Monsieur, you would like to have it in marble,' added Sonet, who specialized in marble, 'it will be twelve thousand francs, and you and your friend will go down to posterity . . .'

'I have just learnt that the will is going to be contested,' whispered Topinard to Vitelot, 'and that the natural heirs are likely to recover the inheritance. You had better try Monsieur le Président Camusot, for this poor innocent man won't get a farthing.'

'That's the sort of customer you always spring on us!' said Madame Vitelot to the salesman, warming up for an altercation.

Topinard took Schmucke back to the rue de Normandie – on foot because the funeral carriages had already made their way there.

'To not leaf me!' implored Schmucke, for Topinard had wanted to take his departure after leaving the poor musician in La Sauvage's care.

'It's four o'clock, my dear Monsieur Schmucke, and I must go home to dinner . . . My wife is a box-attendant, and she would wonder what had become of me. As you know, the theatre opens at a quarter to six.'

'Yes, I know zat . . . but tchust sink, I am all alone in ze vorlt, vizout von frient. You haf vept for Pons: explain zese sinks to me. I am altogezzer in ze tark, and Pons sait I hat scountrelss all arount me.'

'I saw that only too clearly. I have just saved you from spend-ing the night in Clichy!'

'Clichy?' asked Schmucke. 'I to not unterstant.'

'Poor dear gentleman! Well, don't worry. I'll come and see you. Good-bye!'

'Goot-pye for ze pressent,' said Schmucke, sinking back into his chair, tired out.

'Good-bye, my fine gentleman!' said La Sauvage to Topinard with a look which the theatre hand thought peculiar.

'What's the matter with you, my good woman?' he asked in a mocking tone of voice. 'You're standing there like a villain in a melodrama.'

'Villain yourself! What's your business here? I bet you think you're going to take over Monsieur Schmucke's affairs and get some pickings for yourself.'

'Pickings!' retorted Topinard in high disdain. 'Stick to your pots and pans, woman. Look, I'm only a poor theatre hand, but I stand by our artistes, and let me tell you this: I've never asked anything of anybody! Am I asking *you* for anything? Do I owe *you* anything? Just tell me that, grandma.'

'So you're a theatre hand. What's your name?' asked the virago.

'Topinard, to oblige you.'

'That's all I wanted to know,' said La Sauvage. 'My compliments to you and yours! Give my respects to *milady*, if *milord* has a wife.'

'What's wrong, love?' asked Madame Cantinet as she came in.

'What's wrong? You just stay here and look after the dinner. I'm trotting along to see Monsieur Fraisier.'

'He's downstairs chatting with poor Madame Cibot, and she's crying her eyes out,' replied La Cantinet.

La Sauvage rushed down the stairs in such haste that they shook under her feet.

'Look, Monsieur!' she said to Fraisier as she drew him away a few yards from Madame Cibot. And she pointed to Topinard just as he passed by them, proud of having paid his debt to his benefactor by using a stratagem inspired by life behind the stage, where everybody is more or less resourceful, and thus saving Pons's friend from falling into a trap. Furthermore, he promised himself that he would protect the unsuspecting musician from any other traps which might be set for him.

'You see that little beggar? He's a sort of righteous busybody who proposes to poke his nose into Monsieur Schmucke's affairs.'

'Who is he?'

'Oh, just a nobody.'

'There's no such thing as a nobody when it comes to legal matters.'

'Well, he's a handy man at the theatre and goes by the name of Topinard.'

'Thank you, Madame Sauvage! Carry on with the good work and you'll get your tobacconist's shop.'

Thereupon Fraisier resumed his conversation with Madame Cibot:

'I maintain, my dear client, that you have not played fair with us, and we recognize no obligations to a partner who deceives us!'

'How have I deceived you?' asked Madame Cibot, with arms akimbo. 'Do you think you'll give me the shakes with your vinegary stares and your wintry airs? ... You're looking for excuses so as to break your promises, and you say you're a decent man! I'll tell you what you are: you're a dirty swine! Go on, scratch your arms. But just put that in your pipe and smoke it!'

'Stop shouting and try to keep your temper, my love,' said Fraisier. 'Listen to me. You've been feathering your own nest ... This morning, while the funeral procession was being arranged, I found this catalogue, in duplicate, all in Monsieur Pons's handwriting, and my eye happened to fall on this.'

He opened the manuscript catalogue and started reading:

No. 7. A magnificent portrait painted on marble by Sebastiano del Piombo in 1546; sold by a family who had it abstracted from the Cathedral of Terni. This picture was one of a pair, the other being the portrait of a bishop, bought by an Englishman. This one presents a Maltese Knight at prayer, and used to hang over the tomb of the Rossi family. But for the date, this work might be attributed to Raphael. In my view it is superior to the portrait of Baccio Bandinelli, in the Louvre, which is a little faded, whereas this Knight of Malta owes its continued freshness to the fact that the painting was done on *lavagna* (slate).

'I looked,' Fraisier continued, 'at the place where No. 7 should be, and found a *Portrait of a Lady*, signed by Chardin, without a number on it! . . . While the master of ceremonies was making up the requisite number of pall-bearers, I checked all the pictures and found that eight commonplace oils, unnumbered, had been substituted for works which Monsieur Pons catalogued as first-rate, and which have disappeared . . . Lastly, a little painting on wood, by Metsu, also classed as a masterpiece, is missing.'

'Was it my job to look after pictures?'

'No, but you were a trusted servant, keeping house for Monsieur Pons and looking after his belongings. This is a case of *theft*.'

'Theft indeed! Look here, Monsieur Fraisier, those pictures were *sold*, by Monsieur Schmucke, on Monsieur Pons's instructions, to meet his needs . . .'

'Sold to whom?'

'To Monsieur Elias Magus and Monsieur Rémonencq.'

'For how much?'

'I really don't remember.'

'Listen, my dear Madame Cibot, you've made yourself a nest-egg, a big round one! I shall keep my eye on you. I have a hold on you, but if you serve my ends I will keep quiet. In any case, understand that you can expect nothing from Monsieur le Président Camusot now that you have seen fit to despoil him.'

'I knew perfectly well, my dear Monsieur Fraisier, that I shouldn't get even a sniff of that particular roast . . .'

The words 'I will keep quiet' had mollified her.

*

Rémonencq came up. 'Here,' he said, 'you're picking a quarrel with Madame. That's not right! The pictures were sold with Monsieur Pons's consent, and it took Monsieur Magus and me three days to bring him to the point, he was so crazy about his pictures. We've got proper receipts and if – as is always done – we slipped a few coins, say forty francs or so, across to Madame Cibot, she got no more than we'd give the servants in any respectable house where we do a deal. Oh no, my dear sir! If you're thinking of fleecing a defenceless woman you're making a big mistake! . . . You know what I mean, you meddlesome pettifogger? Monsieur Magus holds the trump cards, and if you don't play fair with Madame Cibot and give her what you promised, you'll find me in your way at the auction, and you'll lose a pretty penny if you get me and Monsieur Magus against you. We can easily stir up the dealers . . . You won't get seven or eight hundred thousand francs; you won't even get two hundred thousand!'

'Is that so? We shall see! We'll refuse to sell – or sell the things in London.'

'We know our way about London,' said Rémonencq. 'Monsieur Magus can pull as many strings there as he can in Paris.'

'Good-day to you, Madame. I'm going to look closely into your activities,' said Fraisier – 'unless,' he added, 'you are willing to do what I tell you.'

'Mean little pickpocket!'

'Mind what you say,' said Fraisier. 'I shall soon be a justice of the peace!'

So they parted, with threats whose purport was well appreciated on both sides.

'Thanks, Rémonencq,' said La Cibot. 'It's very nice for a poor widow to have somebody to stand up for her.'

That evening, at about ten o'clock, Gaudissart summoned the theatre employee to his office. He took up his stance in front of the fireplace, striking the Napoleonic attitude which had become habitual to him since he had begun reigning over a host of actors, dancers, supernumeraries and scene-shifters, and dealing with authors . . . He had acquired the trick of slipping his right forearm inside his waistcoat and holding on to the left-hand strap of his braces. He poised his head in semi-profile and gazed out into the void.

'Oh, it's you, Topinard. Have you any private means?'

'No, Monsieur.'

'Well then, are you looking for a better job?'

'No, Monsieur.'

The theatre handyman turned pale.

'Damn it all, your wife is a stage-box attendant here . . . I kept her on here out of respect for my predecessor when he went bankrupt. I gave you a day-time job, cleaning the lamps in the wings, and now you're in charge of the music-scores. And that's not all. You make a franc a day extra for working the monsters and organizing the demons when we put on a scene from Hell. A position all handymen in a theatre aspire to. There are jealous people in this theatre, my friend, and you have made enemies.'

'Enemies?'

'And you have three children. Your eldest takes children's parts at fifty centimes for each performance!'

'Monsieur . . .'

'Don't interrupt!' said Gaudissart in a thunderous voice. 'And yet, with a job like that, you want to quit the theatre!'

'Monsieur . . .'

'You want to meddle in legal affairs and get a finger in an inheritance! . . . Why, you poor fool, you'd be squashed like a beetle! One of my patrons is His Excellency the Comte Popinot, a man of unrivalled intelligence and character, a man whom the King, in his wisdom, has recalled to the Cabinet . . . This statesman, this political genius – I refer to the Comte Popinot – has married his son to the daughter of the Président de Marville, one of the most respectable and respected members of the higher judiciary, a luminary of the Palais de Justice – you know what that signifies. Well, he is the heir of his cousin, Sylvain Pons, our former conductor, whose obsequies you attended this morning. Be it far from me to blame you for going to pay your last respects to that unfortunate man . . . But you would certainly lose your post here if you meddled in the concerns of the worthy Monsieur Schmucke, to whom I am very well disposed, but who is about to find himself in a ticklish situation with regards to Pons's heirs . . . And since this German means very little to me, while the Président and the Comte Popinot mean a great deal to me, I urge you to leave this worthy German to muddle along by himself. Germans have their own special deity, and you would cut a poor figure as a deputy-deity. So just stick to your own job! . . . That's the best you can do!'

'I understand, Monsieur le Directeur,' said the woe-begone Topinard.

Thus it came about that Schmucke, who was expecting a visit from this humble odd-job man, the one person who had mourned for Pons, lost the protector that chance had sent him. When he awoke the next morning the unfortunate man, finding the flat completely empty, realized the tremendous loss he had sustained. On the two previous days the activities and worries which death entails had surrounded him with enough commotion and bustle to provide some distraction. But the silence which follows the departure of a friend, a father, a son, or a beloved wife to the tomb, the cold grey silence of the morrow is terrible and strikes a chill to the heart. He was irresistibly drawn to Pons's bedroom, but he could not bear to look at it. He retreated and regained the dining-room, where Madame Sauvage served him breakfast. He sat down in front of it but was unable to eat.

*

Suddenly there was a loud ring of the bell, and three men in black appeared, to whom Madame Cantinet and Madame Sauvage allowed free passage. The first was Monsieur Vitel, the justice of the peace; the second was his clerk of the court; the third was Fraisier, more rasping, more harsh than ever because he was smarting from the disappointing discovery that there existed a properly drawn-up will, cancelling the previous one, which he had so audaciously stolen to use as a powerful weapon.

'We have come, Monsieur,' said the justice of the peace, in a kindly voice to Schmucke, 'to affix the seals in this habitation.'

Such words had no meaning for Schmucke, and he gazed at the three men with a startled air.

'We have come, at the request of Monsieur Fraisier, barrister-at-law, attorney for Monsieur Camusot de Marville, heir of his cousin the late Sieur Pons . . .' added the clerk of the court.

'The collections are there, in that spacious *salon*, and in the bedroom of the deceased,' said Fraisier.

'Very well, let us proceed . . . Excuse us, sir, pray continue your breakfast,' said the justice of the peace.

The irruption of these three men in black had struck terror into the poor German's heart.

'This gentleman,' said Fraisier, casting at Schmucke the sort of venomous glare which hypnotizes its recipient as a spider hypnotizes a fly, 'this gentleman has caused a will advantageous to himself to be drawn up before a notary, and he must certainly have expected some opposition on the part of the family. No family allows itself to be despoiled by an outsider without offering some resistance, and we shall see, Monsieur, whether fraud and corrupt dealing or family claims will prevail! . . . We have the right, as natural heirs, to ask for seals to be affixed. They *will* be affixed, and I intend to see that these precautionary measures are applied with the utmost rigour. So it shall be!'

'Mein Gott! Mein Gott! Vat sin haf I committet?' said the naïve German.

'There's a lot of chatter going on about you in the building,' said La Sauvage. 'While you were asleep a young chap all in black, a little dandy who said he was Monsieur Hannequin's senior clerk, came up and was bent on talking to you. But you were asleep and so done up after the funeral yesterday, I told him you had given power of proxy to Monsieur Villemot, Tabareau's head clerk. I told him if he had come on business he should go and see him. Don't you worry, Monsieur Schmucke, you'll have people to defend you. Nobody's going to strip the shirt off your back. You're going to have somebody to fight for you tooth and nail. Monsieur Villemot's going to show them what's what. Speaking for myself, I've already had a row with that dirty slut Madame Cibot. Fancy a concierge taking it on herself to criticize her tenants and make out you're twisting the heirs out of a fortune, that you made Monsieur Pons's life a misery and got him in such a stew that he went stark staring mad! I tell you, I made mincemeat of her, the wicked baggage. "You're a thief and a bit of dirt," I told her. "You'll find yourself up before the beaks for all you've pinched from these gentlemen." And she shut her trap.'

The clerk of the court came to fetch Schmucke.

'Perhaps, Monsieur, you would like to be present at the affixing of seals in the mortuary chamber.'

'Get on viz it!' said Schmucke. 'Vy vill you not leaf me to tie in peace?'

'The right to die is indefeasible,' replied the clerk with a laugh. 'Death and inheritances are our main business. But I have seldom seen sole legatees follow their benefactors into the grave!'

'Zat iss vat I vill to!' said Schmucke. After suffering so many shocks, his heart was racked with intolerable pain.

'Look, here comes Monsieur Villemot!' cried La Sauvage.

'Monsieur Fillemot,' said the unhappy German. 'Vill you act for me?'

'At your service, Monsieur,' said the senior clerk. 'I have come to assure you that the will is perfectly in order, that probate will certainly be granted by the court, and that it will give you a writ of possession. A fine fortune will be yours.'

'Vat shoult I to viz a fine fortune?' exclaimed Schmucke, in despair at being suspected of covetousness.

'All the same,' said La Sauvage, 'what's the magistrate up to with his candles and little strips of tape?'

'He is applying the seals . . . Come, Monsieur Schmucke, you have the right to be present.'

'No, you go zere . . .'

'But why are they putting tapes on, if Monsieur Schmucke is in his own house and everything in it belongs to him?' asked La Sauvage, expounding the law as all women do, by applying the Code in the light of their own whims.

'This gentleman is not in his own house, Madame. He is in Monsieur Pons's house. No doubt it will all come to him, but when one is a legatee one can only take possession of the goods and chattels composing the inheritance after obtaining what we call "livery of seisin". The writ for this is issued by the court. Now if the natural heirs dispossessed by the will of the testator enter an objection to the livery of seisin, a law-suit ensures. And then, since it is uncertain to whom the inheritance will accrue, every article is put under seal, and the notaries appointed by the natural heirs and the legatee proceed to an inventory within a period prescribed by the law . . . That is the position.'

Hearing such jargon for the first time in his life, Schmucke was completely flustered. He let his head fall on to the back of his chair, and it was so heavy that he was unable to hold it up. Villemot went off to chat with the clerk of the court and the justice of the peace and, with the composure usual among legal practitioners, he witnessed the affixing of the seals. When no heir is present, this is not unaccompanied by pleasantries and comments on the articles thus preserved intact until the time comes for apportionment.

Finally the four lawyers locked up the *salon*; the clerk of the court repaired to the dining-room, followed by the others. Automatically Schmucke watched this operation, which consists either of affixing the magistrate's seal on a cotton tape applied to each leaf of folding doors, or of closing up wardrobes and single doors by running the tapes along both sides.

'This room next,' said Fraisier, pointing to Schmucke's bedroom, the door of which opened into the dining-room.

'But that's Monsieur Schmucke's bedroom!' said La Sauvage, rushing forward and standing between the door and the legal officials.

'Here is the contract of lease,' said the remorseless Fraisier. 'We found it among the papers. It is not under the joint name of Messieurs Pons and Schmucke, but under the sole name of Monsieur Pons. The whole flat forms part of the inheritance. And besides,' he added, opening Schmucke's bedroom door and addressing the magistrate, 'look, Monsieur, it is full of pictures.'

'That is so,' said the magistrate, immediately conceding Fraisier's point.

30. The Fraisier bears fruit *

'ONE moment, gentlemen,' said Villemot. 'Are you thinking of evicting the sole heir, whose right to succeed has not so far been contested?'

'Indeed it has!' said Fraisier. 'We are opposing the application for possession.'

'On what grounds?'

'That you will soon discover, dear colleague,' said Fraisier mockingly. 'At present we do not object to the legatee withdrawing what he claims to be his in this room. But the seals will be affixed to it, and this gentleman will find lodging where he pleases.'

'Not at all,' replied Villemot. 'This gentleman will remain in occupation of his bedroom.'

'How so?'

'I shall take out an injunction against you,' continued Villemot, 'claiming that we are joint tenants of this flat; and you will not be able to evict us. Take out the pictures, put a mark on whatever belonged to the deceased, and my client's chattels will remain here . . . *dear colleague*!'

'No. I vill leaf ze house,' said the musician, regaining energy as he listened to this appalling debate.

'That's the best thing to do,' said Fraisier. 'Such a decision will save you a lot of expense, for the law is against you on this point. The lease expressly states . . .'

'The lease! The lease!' said Villemot. 'It's a question of good faith.'

'Good faith cannot be proved, as in criminal cases, by witnesses . . . Are you going to get yourself involved in valuations, verifications, interlocutory judgements and full-scale litigation?'

'No! No!' cried the terrified Schmucke. 'I vill mofe house. I vill go avay.'

*See note to Chapter 21, p. 215.

Schmucke's way of life had been that of a philosopher, an unwitting Diogenes, so reduced was it to the bare necessities. He only possessed two pairs of shoes, a pair of boots, two suits of clothes, a dozen shirts, a dozen mufflers, a dozen handkerchiefs, four waistcoats and a superb pipe that Pons had given him together with an embroidered tobacco-pouch. He went into the bedroom shaking and seething with indignation, gathered up all his wearing apparel and put it on a chair.

'Zis iss all mine,' he said with a simplicity worthy of Cincinnatus. 'So iss ze piano.'

'Madame,' said Fraisier to La Sauvage, 'get some help, move this piano and put it out into the street.'

'You are much too hard,' said Villemot to Fraisier. 'His Honour the justice of the peace is entitled to state his orders. He is the sole authority in such matters.'

'But there are articles of value in there,' said the clerk, pointing to the bedroom.

'In any case,' observed the magistrate, 'Monsieur Schmucke is leaving of his own free will.'

'Did anyone ever see such a client!' said Villemot indignantly, now turning once more against Schmucke. 'You're as limp as a rag!' he said to him.

'Vot toess it matter vere von tiess?' said Schmucke as he went out. 'Zese men haf ze facess of tigerss . . . I vill sent for my poor pelonkinks,' he added.

'Where will you go, Monsieur?'

'Verefer Gott sents me,' replied the sole heir, with a sublime gesture of indifference.

'Please let me know,' said Villemot.

'Follow him,' Fraisier whispered to the clerk.

'So far so good,' said Fraisier to Monsieur Vitel when Schmucke had gone. 'If you intend to send in your resignation in my favour, go and see Madame la Présidente de Marville. You'll get on together all right.'

'That man is as soft as butter!' said the justice of the peace, pointing to Schmucke, who was taking a last look from the courtyard at the windows of the flat.

'Yes, the whole affair is nicely wrapped up!' replied Fraisier. 'You can marry your grand-daughter to Poulain without misgivings: he will be chief medical officer in the Hospital for the Blind.'

'We'll see about it! . . . Good-bye, Monsieur Fraisier,' said the justice of the peace with a friendly air.

'He knows his way about,' said the clerk. 'He'll get on, that shyster.'

Eleven o'clock struck. The old German mechanically trudged along the road he used to take with Pons. He was thinking of Pons; he could see him all the time; he believed he was walking along at his side. He arrived in front of the theatre, from which his friend Topinard was just emerging; the latter had been cleaning the standard lamps and musing over his employer's tyranny.

'Ah! tchust ze sink!' cried Schmucke, and he stopped the poor-odd-job-man. 'Topinard, you haf somevere to lif, haf you not?'

'Yes, Monsieur Schmucke.'

'You haf a house unt family?'

'Yes, Monsieur Schmucke.'

'Vill you take me in ass a lotcher? Oh, I vill pay you vell, I haf nine hundret francs a year . . . Unt I haf not lonk to lif . . . All I neet is to smoke my pipe . . . Unt ass you are ze only person who mournet for Pons, I lof you.'

'Monsieur Schmucke, I should be very pleased; but to begin with, I've just had a good wigging from Monsieur Gaudissart.'

'Vikkink?'

'That's to say he gave me a rare dressing-down.'

'Tressink-town?'

'He gave me a scolding for taking an interest in you . . . so we should have to be very careful if you came to live with us. But I doubt whether you'd stay long; you don't know what sort of home a poor wretch like me has to live in.'

'I like pesser ze simple home of a goot-heartet man who mournet for Pons zan I shoult ze Kink's palace viz men who haf ze facess of tigerss. I haf tchust come from Pons's flat vere zere are tigerss who vill defour eferysink!'

'Come along, Monsieur,' said the stagehand, 'and you'll see what it's like; but all the same . . . Anyway, there's an attic . . . Let's go and ask my wife.'

Schmucke followed Topinard like a sheep, and was led into one of those frightful slums which might be called the plague-spots of Paris. It is known as the Cité Bordin and consists of a narrow passage lined with the sort of houses that speculators build. It runs into that part of the rue de Bondy which is over-shadowed by the immense block in which the Porte-Saint-Martin theatre is situated, and this too is one of the eye-sores of Paris. This passage is on a lower level than the rue de Bondy and dips down steeply towards the rue des Mathurins-du-Temple. The Cité Bordin merges into an inner street running across it and forming a 'T'. Such is the layout of these two alleys which are enclosed between some thirty houses rising to six or seven storeys. The inner courts and all the buildings around them contain warehouses, workshops and factories of all kinds. It is like a miniature Faubourg Saint-Antoine where cabinet-makers, workers in brass, theatre costumiers, glass-blowers and painters of porcelain ply their trades. There in fact the whole variety of fancy goods known as *l'article Paris* is produced. Dirty but productive like industry itself, always thronged with people coming and going, with barrows and handcarts, this passage is a revolting sight, and its teeming population matches the locality and the objects within it: here dwells the factory population, intelligent in the use of its hands, but with no intelligence to spare for other things. Topinard lived in this flourishing industrial area because the rents were low. He had a flat in the second tenement on the left as one enters. It was a sixth-floor flat and looked on to the belt of gardens which have survived because they belong to the three or four large mansions situated in the rue de Bondy.

Topinard's abode comprised a kitchen and two bedrooms. The children slept in the first of these, which contained two small deal beds and a swing-cot, and the Topinards had the second as their marital chamber. The family took its meals in the kitchen. Overhead was a false attic, six feet high, with a zinc roof and a hinged skylight for a window. Access to it was provided by a flight of deal steps, of the sort known in builders' parlance as a 'miller's ladder'. This garret, designated as a servant's bedroom, enabled Topinard's lodging to count as a self-contained flat at a rental of four hundred francs a year. At the entrance, masking the kitchen, was an arched lobby, lighted by a bull's-eye window looking through into the kitchen – a space enclosed between three doors, those of the kitchen, the first bedroom and the landing. These three rooms had brick floors, hideous wallpaper which had cost six sous a roll; and, for additional adornment, the fireplaces were topped with ogee-moulding and covered with a coat of cheap, drab paint. They accommodated a family of five, three of them children. And any visitor could discern the deep scratches on the walls, made by the children as high up as their arms could reach.

*

No rich people would believe it possible to manage with so simple an array of kitchen utensils: a cooking-stove, a cauldron, a gridiron, a stew-pan, two or three jugs and a frying-pan. The brown and white earthenware dishes and plates were worth about twelve francs. One table served both as kitchen and dining-table. The furniture consisted of two chairs and two stools. Under the hooded stove was a supply of charcoal and wood. In one corner was the tub in which the family linen was washed, often at night. The children's bedroom, across which clothes-lines were stretched, was gaudy with theatre-posters and prints cut out of newspapers or illustrated prospectuses. Evidently the elder Topinard boy, whose school-books were piled in a corner, took charge of the house from six o'clock onwards, when his parents were on duty in the theatre. In many working-class families, as soon as a child reaches the age of six or seven, he acts as mother to his brothers and sisters.

This rapid sketch will indicate that the Topinards were, to use the stock phrase, 'poor but honest'. Topinard was almost forty; his wife, once a leading chorus-girl and the mistress, it was said, of the bankrupt director whom Gaudissart had succeeded, was probably about thirty. Lolotte had been quite a beauty, but the woes of the previous management had affected her so badly that she had found it necessary to contract a stage marriage with Topinard. She did not doubt that, as soon as the family had a hundred and fifty francs to its credit, Topinard would regularize their union, if only to legitimize the children whom he adored. In free moments during the mornings, Madame Topinard did sewing for the theatre wardrobe. By dint of tremendous effort these courageous theatre hands were able to make about nine hundred francs a year.

'Only one more flight!' Topinard kept saying, once they had reached the third floor, but Schmucke was so steeped in his grief that he was not even aware whether he was going up or down.

As Topinard, dressed in the white linen coat which all stage-hands wear to work, opened the kitchen door, Madame Topinard's voice could be heard crying:

'Less noise, children! Here's papa!'

And, since the children clearly did what they liked with papa, the eldest continued to head a cavalry charge – a reminiscence of the Olympic Circus – riding on a broomstick, while the second went on blowing her tin trumpet, and the third toddled behind the main body of the army as best he could! Their mother was stitching a theatre costume.

'Quiet now!' shouted Topinard in a fearsome voice, 'or you'll get a good beating! . . . Always have to tell them that,' he added under his breath to Schmucke. 'Look, my love,' he said to his wife, 'this is Monsieur Schmucke, the friend of our poor Monsieur Pons. He has nowhere to go and would like to come and stay with us. It's no use telling him we're not very smart, we live on the sixth floor, and we've only an attic to offer him. He's bent on it . . .'

Schmucke was sitting on a chair which Lolotte had brought forward. The children, abashed by the arrival of a stranger, had huddled together in order to carry out that close, mute and short-lived scrutiny characteristic of children – like dogs who trust more to their olfactory sense than to their judgement. Schmucke began to study this attractive group, which included a little girl of five with beautiful fair hair – the one who had been blowing the trumpet.

'She iss tchust like a little Tcherman girl!' said Schmucke, beckoning her forward.

'Monsieur Schmucke would be very uncomfortable in the attic,' said the box-attendant. 'If I didn't have to be near the children I'd be glad to offer him our room.'

She opened her bedroom door and showed him in. All the

luxury of the flat was contained in this room. The mahogany bed was adorned with blue calico hangings with white fringes. Similar blue calico, draped into curtains, decorated the window. The chest-of-drawers, the writing desk, the chairs, all in mahogany, were clean and tidy. On the mantelpiece stood a clock and candelabra, evidently presented in former days by the bankrupt manager, whose portrait, a frightful daub by Pierre Grassou, hung over the chest-of-drawers. The children, who were forbidden to enter this sanctuary, tried to peer inside to satisfy their curiosity.

'Monsieur would be comfortable in here,' said Madame Topinard.

'No! No!' replied Schmucke. 'Vy, I shall not lif lonk. I vant nossink more zen a corner to tie in.'

They closed the bedroom door and climbed up to the garret. The moment Schmucke entered, he exclaimed:

'Tchust vat I vantet! ... Pefore I lift viz Pons, I hat no pesser lotchink zen zis.'

'Well then, all we need is to buy a camp bed, a couple of mattresses, a bolster, a pillow, a couple of chairs and a table. It's not going to break our backs, that ... It might cost fifty crowns, with the wash-basin, water-jug and a little bedside rug.'

All was settled. But where were the fifty crowns to come from? Realizing he was only within a stone's-throw of the theatre, Schmucke naturally thought of going and asking the director for his salary, since he perceived how needy his friends were ...

He went straight to the theatre and found Gaudissart there. The director welcomed him with the somewhat strained courtesy he reserved for his artistes, and was astonished when Schmucke asked him for a month's salary. Nevertheless, he looked into this claim, and found it was a just one.

'Devil take it, old chap!' said the director. 'Germans are always good at reckoning up, even with their eyes full of tears ... I thought you might have appreciated my little gift to you of a thousand francs – your salary for one final year – and that would have made us quits!'

'Ve haf nossink receift,' said the good German. 'Unt if I

haf come to you it iss pecausse I haf been srown out on to ze street vizout a farzink . . . To whom haf you gifen ze money?'

'To your concierge.'

'Matame Cipot!' cried the musician. 'Zat voman hass killt Pons. She hass ropt him. She solt his pictures. She iss a vicket monster!'

'But, my dear man, how does it come about that you are penniless, thrown out, with no roof to your head, when you are Pons's sole heir? Surely that doesn't make sense?'

'I haf peen put out off ze flat . . . I am a Tcherman . . . I to not unterstant ze lawss.'

'Poor old devil!' thought Gaudissart, foreseeing the probable outcome of so unequal a contest. 'Listen, do you know what you ought to do?'

'I haf a lekal atchent.'

'Very well, make an immediate settlement with the Camusots. You'll get a capital sum and an annuity, and you can live in peace.'

'Zet iss all I vant!' said Schmucke.

'Very good. Let me arrange that for you,' said Gaudissart, whom Fraisier had told of his scheme the previous evening.

*

Gaudissart hoped to gain favour with the young Vicomtesse Popinot and her mother by helping this shady piece of business to go through. Thus, he thought, he would be at least a Councillor of State one day.

'I leaf it all in your hants . . .'

'Right! That's the spirit! Now, first of all,' said the Napoleon of the boulevard theatres, 'here are a hundred crowns.'

He took three hundred francs from his purse and offered them to the musician.

'These are yours: six months' salary. Later on you can repay me if you leave the theatre. Now let's work things out. How much do you spend a year? How much do you need to be comfortable? Come now, you don't live like Sardanapalus!'

'All I neet iss von set of cloze for ze vinter unt von for ze sommer.'

'Three hundred francs!' said Gaudissart.

'Unt shoes – four pairs.'

'Sixty francs.'

'Stockinks.'

'A dozen pairs – thirty-six francs.'

'Six shirts.'

'Six calico shirts, twenty-four francs. Six linen shirts, forty-eight. That's seventy-two francs. We've got to four hundred and sixty-eight francs. Let's say five hundred with ties and handkerchiefs. Laundry a hundred francs . . . six hundred francs in all. And now, what about living costs ? Three francs a day ?'

'No. It iss too moch.'

'And then you need hats too . . . That makes fifteen hundred francs plus five hundred for your rent. Would you like me to get you two thousand francs' income for life – absolutely guaranteed ?'

'Unt my topacco ?'

'Two thousand four hundred francs ! Oh, Papa Schmucke, is it really tobacco you mean ? . . . All right, we'll throw in the tobacco . . . And so, two thousand four hundred francs for life.'

'Zet iss not all. I vant some reaty money.'

'Pocket-money too ! Well, well ! And these Germans are supposed to be so simple ! The old bandit !' thought Gaudissart. Then, out loud, he asked:

'How much do you want ? And mind you, that's the lot.'

'It iss so zet I can pay a sacret tet.'

'A debt !' thought Gaudissart. 'The old swindler ! He's worse than a prodigal son ! He'll soon be inventing bills of exchange which have to be met. I must put a stop to this. That fellow Fraisier doesn't do things on a lavish scale . . . Well, old chap, what debt ? Tell me . . .'

'Zere iss only von man who hass vept viz me for Pons. He hass a lofely little girl viz vonterful hair. Ven I lookt at her I sought I vass lookink on the tchenius of my Vaterlant. I shoult nefer haf left it . . . Paris is not kint to Tchermans . . . Zey make fon of us.' As he said this he gave the wise little nod of a man who has got to the heart of things in this sad world.

'He's quite mad !' thought Gaudissart; but, out of pity for this simpleton, his eyes moistened.

'Ah: I see you unterstant me, Monsieur le Tirecteur. Vell, zis man viz ze little girl iss Topinard who serfs ze orchestra unt lights ze lamps. Pons loft him unt helpt him, unt he alone followet my poor frient's coffin to the church unt the cemetery ... Vell, I vant sree sousant francs for him unt sree sousant francs for ze little girl.'

'The poor man!' thought Gaudissart.

This unrelenting self-seeker was moved at the sight of such nobility, such gratitude for what the world would regard as a trifle; but it was something which, in the estimation of the tender-souled Schmucke, like Bossuet's glass of water, weighed more than the victories of military conquerors. Gaudissart, despite all his worldliness, despite his ruthless determination to climb and lift himself to the social level of his friend Popinot, had, at bottom, a good nature and a kind heart. And so he cast aside the rash judgements he had passed on Schmucke and decided to help him.

'All that you shall have! But I'll go even further, my dear Schmucke. Topinard is an honest man.'

'Yes. I haf tchust seen him in his wretchet hofel, unt he iss happy viz his chiltren.'

'I'll give him the post of theatre cashier, since old Baudrand is leaving.'

'Ah! May Gott gif you hiss plessink!' cried Schmucke.

'Very well, my good, worthy friend. Come this afternoon, at four, to the office of Monsieur Berthier the notary. Everything will be ready, and you'll be free from care for the rest of your life ... You'll get your six thousand francs, and you will carry on, with Garangeot, at the same salary, the work you did with Pons.'

'No, sank you,' said Schmucke. 'I shall not lif lonk enough ... I haf no heart now for anysink ... All my shtrengts hass gone.'

'As innocent as a lamb!' thought Gaudissart, as he showed Schmucke out and said good-bye to him. 'But after all, we live on lamb cutlets ... And, as that great poet Béranger wrote,

Alas! poor sheep! You always will be sheared!'

And he set to humming this tendentious ditty, the better to get over his emotion. Then:

'Bring up my carriage,' he said to his office messenger, and, going down to the street, he told the driver:

'Rue de Hanovre.'

He was all ambition once more, and clearly saw himself already as a member of the Council of State.

*

At this moment Schmucke was buying flowers. Feeling almost cheerful, he took them back with him, and also some cakes, for the Topinard children.

'I am gifing pressents!' he said with a smile: the first smile which had appeared on his face for three months – but anyone who had seen it would have trembled for him.

'I gif zese sinks on von contition!'

'You're very kind, Monsieur Schmucke,' said the mother.

'Ze little girl vill gif me a kiss unt put ze flowers in her hair, unt make a garlent off zem like a little Tcherman girl!'

'Olga, my girl, do what the gentleman tells you,' said Lolotte sternly.

'To not scolt my little Tcherman maiten!' cried Schmucke, for whom this child was a personification of his beloved country.

Topinard came in.

'We three commissionaires,' he grumbled, 'have to keep the whole theatre going!'

'Ah!' said the German. 'My frient, here are two hundret francs to pay for eferysink . . . Put you haf such a goot little voman, you vill marry her, von't you? I shall gif you sree sousant francs. Your little girl vill also haf sree sousant francs for her dowry unt you vill make an infestment for her. Unt you vill no more pe a seatre hant: you vill pe ze seatre cashier!'

'What, me? In old Baudrand's place?'

'Yes.'

'Who told you that!'

'Monsieur Gaudissart!'

'Oh! Do you want me to go wild with joy? – Rosalie, did you hear that? This will turn the other stagehands green with envy! . . . But the gentleman who has been so kind to us can't sleep in an attic! It can't be done.'

'Yes inteet! It iss goot enoff for the few tays I haf to lif!' said Schmucke. 'Goot-pye. I go to ze cemetery . . . to see vat zey haf tone viz Pons . . . and orter some flowers to put on hiss grafe.'

Madame Camusot de Marville was a prey to the liveliest alarm. Fraisier was holding council with Godeschal and Berthier. Berthier the notary and Godeschal the solicitor regarded the will drawn up by two notaries in the presence of two witnesses as incontestable, thanks to the clear terms in which Hannequin had couched it. The honest Godeschal's view was that even if Schmucke's present counsel succeeded in hoodwinking him he would be enlightened in the end, if only by one of those advocates who seek to draw attention to themselves by their disinterestedness and scrupulosity. And so the two legal officials left the Présidente, urging her to be wary of Fraisier, whose past history they had naturally looked into. At this moment Fraisier, after attending the affixing of the seals, was drafting the terms of a subpoena in the Président's office where Madame de Marville had installed him at the suggestion of the two legal officials – the latter had realized that the affair was too shady for a senior magistrate to soil his hands with it, as they expressed it, and they had wanted to voice their opinion to Madame de Marville in Fraisier's absence.

'Well, Madame, where are those two gentlemen?' asked the former advocate of Mantes.

'They have gone . . . and they advise me to drop this business!' replied Madame de Marville.

'Drop it?' said Fraisier, scarcely able to contain his fury. 'Listen, Madame . . .'

And he read out the following document:

BY THE PETITION OF, et cetera et cetera . . . [I leave out the preliminary verbiage.]

WHEREAS before His Worship the Chairman of the Court of First Instance has been laid a Will drawn by Maîtres Léopold Hannequin and Alexandre Crottat notaries in Paris in the presence of two witnesses namely the Sieurs Friedrich Brunner and Wilhelm

Schwab aliens domiciled in Paris whereby the Sieur Sylvain Pons deceased has bequeathed his estate to a Sieur Wilhelm Schmucke of German nationality to the prejudice of the Petitioner his natural and lawful heir

AND whereas the Petitioner engages to offer proof that the said Will was obtained by the exercise of undue influence and practices reprobated by the law in support of which he will call eminent persons to witness that the Testator's true intention was to bequeath his estate to Mademoiselle Cécile daughter of the aforesaid Sieur de Marville and that the Testament which the Petitioner requests the Court to declare void and of none effect was solicited from the Testator when he was failing in body and of wholly unsound mind

AND whereas the aforesaid Sieur Schmucke for the purpose of inducing the Testator to will his estate to him kept him in durance and denied the family of the Deceased all access to his deathbed and having attained this end committed such notorious acts of ingratitude as caused scandal to other residents of the house and quarter who by chance coming to pay their last respects to the concierge of the house in which the Testator died were witnesses of the said acts

AND whereas still graver facts evidence of which the Petitioner is at the present time collating will be set forth in detail before the Justices of the Court

THEREFORE I the undersigned Registrar of the Court et cetera et cetera in the name of the said Petitioner have cited the said Sieur Schmucke to appear as Defendant before the Justices constituting the First Chamber of the Court to show cause why the Will recorded by the notaries Hannequin and Crottat having clearly been obtained by the use of undue influence should not be declared null and void I have likewise in the name of the aforesaid Petitioner denied any claim on the part of the Sieur Schmucke to assume the quality and capacity of sole heir it being the intention of the Petitioner to oppose as he hereby opposes by this his Petition of today's date presented to the Chairman of the Court the request of the said Wilhelm Schmucke for a writ of possession and I have delivered him copy of these presents whereof the cost is . . . Et cetera . . .

'I know this man, Madame la Présidente. When he reads this little *billet doux* he will come to a compromise. He will consult Tabareau. Tabareau will advise him to accept our terms. Are you willing to give him the three thousand francs' annuity?'

'Certainly. I only wish we had come to the point of paying the first instalment.'

'It will be done before three days are out. This subpoena will reach him before he has got over the first shock of bereavement – he really is heart-broken over Pons, the poor man. He has taken this loss very hard.'

'Once the subpoena has been issued, can it be withdrawn?'

'Certainly, Madame. One can always desist from an action.'

'Very well, Monsieur, proceed with it! . . . Continue! Yes, the sum you are contriving to secure for me is well worth the trouble. Moreover, I have arranged the matter of Vitel's resignation; but the sixty thousand francs he is to have will have to be paid out of the proceeds of the Pons succession. So you see, we *must* succeed.'

'You have his letter of resignation?'

'Yes, Monsieur. Monsieur Vitel has full confidence in Monsieur de Marville.'

'Well, Madame, I have saved you the sixty thousand francs that I thought we ought to give to that despicable concierge, Madame Cibot. But I still hold to the tobacconist's licence for the woman Sauvage; also to my friend Poulain's appointment to the vacant post of senior medical officer at the Hospital for the Blind.'

'That is understood, and everything is arranged.'

'Thank you. There is no more to say. Everyone is with you in this matter, including the theatre director Gaudissart, whom I called on yesterday and who promised to deflate the theatre worker who might upset out plans.'

'Oh, I know Monsieur Gaudissart is entirely devoted to the Popinots!'

Fraisier left. Unfortunately he did not run into Gaudissart and the fatal subpoena was forthwith dispatched.

All covetous people will understand and all honest people will feel abhorrence for the Présidente's joy when, twenty minutes after Fraisier's departure, Gaudissart arrived to tell her of his conversation with poor Schmucke. The Présidente approved of everything, and was infinitely grateful to the theatre director for removing all her scruples by the observations which he made, and which she found very pertinent.

'Madame la Présidente,' he said on arriving. 'My idea was that this poor fellow would not know what to do with his inheritance. He has the simplicity of patriarchal times. He's ingenuous, he's Teutonic, he ought to be stuffed, or put in a glass case like a wax image of the Infant Jesus. In a word, I think he's already puzzled to know what to do with his two thousand five hundred francs' annuity. Really you're encouraging him to go in for loose living!'

'It is very noble-hearted of us,' said the Présidente, 'to enrich this fellow merely for lamenting over our cousin's death. But for my part I do deplore the little *misunderstanding* which estranged us, Monsieur Pons and myself. Had he returned, we would have forgiven him everything. If you knew how my husband missed him! Monsieur de Marville was very disturbed at not receiving notice of his death. He regards family ties as sacred. He would have gone to the church, followed the hearse, attended the burial. I myself would have gone to the requiem mass . . .'

'Well, gracious lady,' said Gaudissart, 'be so good as to get the agreement ready. At four o'clock I will bring the German to you. Commend me, Madame, to the goodwill of your charming daughter, the Vicomtesse Popinot. I hope she will tell my illustrious friend, her kind and excellent father-in-law, that eminent statesman, how devoted I am to all he holds dear; and may he continue his valuable benevolence towards me! I owe my life to his uncle the judge; I owe all my fortune to Monsieur le Comte. I could wish that I might be indebted to you and your daughter for the high esteem attached to people of influence and position. I hope to leave the theatre and become a man of consequence.'

'You are that already, Monsieur!' said the Présidente.

'You are most gracious!' Gaudissart replied, and he kissed Madame de Marville's scrawny hand.

Conclusion

By four o'clock several persons were assembled in the office of Monsieur Berthier the notary: first of all Fraisier, who had drawn up the instrument of settlement, Tabareau acting for Schmucke, and Schmucke himself, whom Gaudissart had brought with him. Fraisier had taken care to place the bank-notes for the six thousand francs stipulated, with six hundred francs as first instalment of the annuity, on the notary's desk, where the German could see them. The latter, in stupefaction at the sight of so much money, paid not the slightest attention to the reading of the deed. He had been picked up by Gaudissart on his way back from the cemetery, where he had communed with Pons and promised to rejoin him. He was still not in possession of all his faculties, so disturbed were they by the shocks he had received. That is why he did not listen to the preamble of the document, in which Maître Tabareau, bailiff, was cited as his proxy and counsel, and in which the motives for the proceedings initiated by the Président in his daughter's interests were recapitulated. The German was playing a sorry role, for by putting his signature to the deed he was pleading guilty to Fraisier's accusations. But he was so glad to set eyes on the money for the Topinard family, so happy to be confer-ring wealth – for such it seemed to his modest way of thinking – on the only man who had loved Pons, that he did not take in a word of this settlement out of court.

Half-way through the reading of the deed, a clerk entered the office.

'Monsieur,' he said to his chief, 'there's a man who wishes to speak to Monsieur Schmucke.'

At a gesture from Fraisier, the notary gave a significant shrug.

'You should never disturb us when we are signing docu-ments! Ask the name of this . . . what is he, an ordinary man or a gentleman? Is he a creditor?'

329

When the clerk returned, he said:

'He insists on speaking to Monsieur Schmucke.'

'His name?'

'Topinard.'

'I will go out to him,' said Gaudissart. 'Don't worry,' he added, turning to Schmucke. 'Just get on with the signing. I will find out what he wants.'

Gaudissart had understood Fraisier's gesture; each of them scented danger.

'What brings you here?' Gaudissart asked his employee. 'Do you want to be cashier or not? A cashier's first qualification is tact . . .'

'Monsieur . . .'

'You'd better mind your own business. You'll get nowhere if you meddle with other people's.'

'Monsieur, I will not eat bread every mouthful of which would stick in my throat! . . . Monsieur Schmucke!' he called out.

Schmucke had signed and had the money in his hand. He came out at Topinard's call.

'Look vat I haf for ze little Tcherman girl unt yourself!'

'Oh, my dear Monsieur Schmucke. You've given your money away to monstrous creatures, people who want to rob you of your good name. I took this document to an honest solicitor, a man who knows this Fraisier, and he says you should bring these scoundrels to book by fighting the case. He says they will withdraw . . . Read it!'

And this imprudent friend handed over the subpoena addressed to Schmucke at the Cité Bordin. Schmucke took the document, read it, saw what abuse was being heaped upon him and, since he understood nothing of the gracious terminology of legal procedure, received a mortal blow. His heart felt as if it were choked with gravel. Topinard put an arm round him to support him, and stumbled along with him to the notary's street door. He helped the poor German into a passing cab. By now the latter was suffering the agony that accompanies a serous congestion of the brain. His vision was blurred, though he still had strength enough to hand over the money to Topinard.

He did not succumb to this first attack, but he never re-covered his reason. He was unable to make any conscious movement and he ate nothing. He died ten days later without uttering a single complaint, for he had lost the power of speech. He had been tended by Madame Topinard, and he was given a quiet burial beside Pons, through the offices of Topinard; he alone walked behind the hearse of this son of Germany.

Fraisier, now a justice of the peace, is a frequent visitor to the Président's house and is very much appreciated by the Présidente, who did not approve of his marrying 'that Tabareau girl'. She has promised a much better match to the artful lawyer to whom she owes, so she avows, not only the acquisition of the Marville grasslands and the 'cottage', but also the Président's election to the Chamber of Deputies, which came about in the General Election of 1846.

No doubt everyone will want to know what became of the heroine of this story – a story which, alas, is only too close to the truth in every detail; a story which is complementary to its predecessor and counterpart *Cousin Bette*, since it shows that character is the main driving force in human society. You, amateurs, connoisseurs and dealers in the arts, have already guessed that by 'heroine' I mean the Pons collection! You only need to listen to a conversation which took place in the *salon* of the Comte Popinot a few days ago as he was displaying his own magnificent collection to a handful of foreign guests.

'Monsieur le Comte,' a distinguished Englishman exclaimed, 'you have a wonderful collection!'

'Oh, my lord,' was the Comte Popinot's modest reply, 'in the matter of pictures no one, not merely in Paris, but in the whole of Europe, can hope to vie with an obscure Jew named Elias Magus, a real old maniac, the prince of maniacs in so far as pictures are concerned. He has assembled a hundred or so, fine enough to discourage any amateur from starting a collection. The French government ought to devote seven or eight millions to the purchase of his gallery when that old Croesus dies ... As for *objets d'art*, my collection is fair enough to deserve passing mention ...'

'But how could a man so occupied as you are, one whose basic fortune was so scrupulously earned in the manufacture of . . .'

'Of cosmetics,' Popinot interposed. 'You mean how could he continue in the cosmetics business . . . ?'

'I don't mean that,' said the Englishman. 'I mean: how do you find time for collecting? *Objets d'art* don't come knocking at one's door . . .'

The Vicomtesse Popinot broke in. 'My father-in-law already had the beginnings of a collection. He loved art and fine pieces of workmanship. But it was I who brought him the most valuable part of his collection.'

'You, Madame? Young as you are, you cultivated a vice of that sort?' asked a Russian prince.

Russians are so addicted to imitating others that all the diseases of civilization have spread to their country. *Bricabracomania* is all the rage in St Petersburg, and thanks to their ingrained spirit of enterprise the Russians are responsible, in this 'line of goods', as Rémonencq would call it, for an increase in prices which is likely to render collecting impracticable. This particular prince was now in Paris for the sole purpose of collecting.

'Prince,' said the Vicomtesse, 'these treasures came to me by way of inheritance from a cousin who was very fond of me, one who had spent forty years or more, from 1805 onwards, ransacking every country, and especially Italy, in search of all these masterpieces . . .'

'And what was his name?' the English lord asked.

'Sylvain Pons,' replied Président Camusot.

'He was a charming man,' said the Présidente, taking up the tale in her soft, fluting tone of voice, 'full of wit, eccentric, but a man of great feeling. You are admiring, my lord, a fan which belonged to Madame de Pompadour: he brought it to me one morning with a charming *bon mot* which you will permit me not to repeat . . .'

And she threw a glance at her daughter.

'Do tell it to us, Madame la Vicomtesse,' begged the Russian prince.

'The *bon mot* is worthy of the fan . . .' replied the Vicomtesse, who was in the habit of repeating it on all occasions. 'He told my mother that it was high time that the plaything of Vice should become an adornment for Virtue.'

At the word 'virtue', the English lord eyed Madame Camusot de Marville with an air of polite incredulity which to so desiccated a woman was extremely flattering.

'He used to dine at my house three or four times a week,' she continued. 'He was so fond of us! We valued him highly, and artists are happy to be with those who appreciate their wit. My husband, moreover, was his only relative. And when this inheritance came – quite unexpectedly – to Monsieur de Marville, Monsieur le Comte preferred to buy the whole collection rather than let it go to auction. We too thought it better to dispose of it in this way: it would have been frightful to break up a treasure which had given such joy to our dear cousin! So Elias Magus valued it. And that, my lord, is how I was able to buy the cottage your uncle built – and I hope you will do us the honour of visiting us there.'

Monsieur Topinard is still cashier in the theatre whose licence Gaudissart passed on to other hands a year ago. But Monsieur Topinard has become sombre, misanthropic and laconic. Rumour has it that he committed some crime; malicious wits at the theatre claim that his moroseness is due to his having married Lolotte. This honest man gives a start whenever he hears the name of Fraisier. Incidentally, is it not strange that the only soul worthy of Pons should be thus relegated to below-stage activities in a boulevard theatre?

Madame Rémonencq is still so impressed by Madame Fontaine's predictions that she refuses to retire into the country. She lives over her splendid shop in the Boulevard de la Madeleine, and is once more a widow. In fact the Auvergnat, after devising a marriage contract by which all the property was to pass to the surviving partner, had left a liqueur glass full of vitriol within reach of his wife: he was counting on a mishap. His wife, with the best intentions in the world, moved it to another spot, and Rémonencq drank it. Such an end, fit for such a scoundrel, marks a point in favour of Providence, whose intervention in human affairs – so it is said – is overlooked by historians of manners. Perhaps they do this because such intervention is exaggerated in the finales of our present-day dramatists.

Pray excuse the copyist's errors.

Paris,
July 1846 – May 1847